NIGHT MOVES

By Jonathan Kellerman

The Butcher's Theatre
The Conspiracy Club
True Detectives
The Murderer's Daughter

Alex Delaware Novels

When the Bough Breaks	Therapy
Blood Test	Rage
Over the Edge	Gone
Silent Partner	Obsession
Time Bomb	Compulsion
Private Eyes	Bones
Devil's Waltz	Evidence
Bad Love	Deception
Self-Defence	Mystery
The Web	Victims
The Clinic	Guilt
Survival of the Fittest	Killer
Monster	Motive
Doctor Death	Breakdown
Flesh and Blood	Heartbreak Hotel
The Murder Book	Night Moves
A Cold Heart	

Novels featuring Petra Connor
Billy Straight
Twisted

With Faye Kellerman
Double Homicide
Capital Crimes

With Jesse Kellerman
The Golem of Hollywood
The Golem of Paris
Crime Scene

JONATHAN KELLERMAN

NIGHT MOVES

HEADLINE

First published in the United States by Ballantine Books,
an imprint of Random House, a division of Random House LLC,
a Penguin Random House Company, New York.

First published in Great Britain in 2018 by
HEADLINE PUBLISHING GROUP

1

Cataloguing in Publication Data is available from the British Library

ISBN 978 1 4722 0653 4 (Hardback)
ISBN 978 1 4722 0655 8 (Trade paperback)

Typeset in 11.75/16.5 pt Adobe Garamond Pro by Jouve (UK), Milton Keynes

Printed in Great Britain by Clays Ltd, St Ives plc

Headline's policy is to use papers that are natural, renewable and recyclable
products and made from wood grown in sustainable forests. The logging
and manufacturing processes are expected to conform to the environmental
regulations of the country of origin.

HEADLINE PUBLISHING GROUP
An Hachette UK Company
Carmelite House
50 Victoria Embankment
London EC4Y 0DZ

www.headline.co.uk
www.hachette.co.uk

To Zoe

CHAPTER

1

Nice house. If you put aside reality.

Sunset Boulevard, Sunday at ten thirty p.m., was an easy ride, cool April air sweetening the Seville's interior. To get here from my place in Beverly Glen, I'd driven through Bel Air and Brentwood, turned south a quarter mile into Pacific Palisades, continued through tree-lined stretches of architectural revivals: Colonial, Spanish, Mediterranean, Greek, Unidentifiable.

Not a Through Street warnings at most corners; a planned community discouraging casual visitors. GPS-tutored turns led me to a street named Evada Lane, three blocks terminating at a cul-de-sac.

Built-in-the-seventies tract, the Palisades but no palisades in sight. This was flat land, geographically undistinguished, too far from the ocean for someone to smell the brine.

In the Midwest, respectably middle-class real estate. In L.A., not a single structure worth less than a million.

The house garnering all the attention sat at the tip of the dead end like a cherry on a sundae. One of the aspiring Colonials, heralded by white columns, its brick façade strobed red and blue by LAPD cruisers. The same light show played upon a black Range Rover and a gray Lexus sedan in the driveway.

All that wattage courtesy of half a dozen cop cars, circled around a white crypt van waiting to transport. The crime lab van sat nearby, lights off, unoccupied. No sign of the coroner's investigators; come and gone.

Uniformed officers stood around doing nothing. Radios barked police calls, dispatchers' voices impersonal as they chronicled the evening's malice and misfortune.

Soft, spring breeze; the yellow tape billowed.

Just outside the tape, a mud-colored Impala I knew to be Detective Moses Reed's current ride sat next to a white Porsche 928 in which I'd been a passenger more than once. The off-duty drive shared by Lieutenant Milo Sturgis and his partner, a trauma surgeon named Richard Silverman.

Reed had arrived just over two hours ago, taken one look, and called the boss. Milo, suffering through a charity dinner for Rick's employer, the Cedars-Sinai E.R., sped over from the Beverly Hilton and called me.

"What's up?" I said.

"Complicated, see for yourself. Please."

He met me just outside the front door, wearing a hooded paper suit, booties, and gloves.

"Yeah, I know, I look like a giant sperm. You don't have to abase yourself, tech's nearly finished." He peeled off the suit, revealing a saggy black suit with lapels dating to the house's construction, a white shirt, and a silver tie that had to be Rick's.

"Very *GQ*."

"The almost-tux?" he said. "Damn banquet, I had to take the pants out three inches, four woulda been better—enough of my problems, let's go see a real one."

The paper garb had led me to expect horror and chaos. Milo opened the door on surprising calm.

A two-story entry floored in waxed walnut was centered by a mahogany table hosting a vase of silk roses. A bronze chandelier cast reassuring light. To the left, blandly pleasant landscape paintings filled a white wall; to the right a blue-carpeted staircase traced the ascent to a small landing.

Milo continued straight ahead, toward another wall decorated by sconces and broken by an open doorway.

A form moved into the gap. Moe Reed, young, ruddy, still wearing his paper suit but not the hood. Pink skin showed through his blond buzz cut. The suit was tight in places, power-lifter arms testing the tensile strength of wood pulp.

"L.T., Doc." Stepping aside.

I followed Milo into a modestly proportioned, nicely set-up living room that ended at a bank of French doors. Through the glass were glimpses of patio furniture, grass, trees. To the left, a dining room and, beyond that, another open doorway that led to a white kitchen.

When people are murdered in their homes, it's almost always in the bedroom or the kitchen. Milo kept going, crossing the living room and hooking right, toward a closed door.

He knocked.

A female voice said, "Hold on."

"It's me again."

"Just a sec, Lieutenant."

The door opened on a paper-suited lab tech name-tagged *I. Jonas*. The mask was pulled down, revealing a young female face the color of cocoa. Tweezers in one hand, vial in the other, something black and wormy in the vial.

She said, "Just a few secs and I'll be gone, sir, but you can come in."

"Thanks," said Milo. "I want Dr. Delaware to take a look."

I. Jonas looked at me. "Pathologist actually came to the scene?"

Milo said, "Different ologist. Psych."

The tech gave me a longer once-over. "Inez Jonas, Doctor. I'd shake your hand but obviously." She shifted to the right, gave me a fuller view.

The room was cozy and pine-paneled. What looked to be a library/den/office combo, with a book-filled repro-Victorian case and a matching desk. The desk's tooled-leather top was bare but for a green-shaded lamp and a glass jar filled with hard candies wrapped in multicolored foil. To the left of the desk was an open area. A plaid sofa and ottoman faced a sixty-inch TV.

That left plenty of floor space for the man lying on hardwood, between the couch and the screen.

Positioned faceup if he'd had a face.

The devastation visited on everything above his neck suggested a shotgun attack, and I asked if that was the case.

Inez Jonas said, "You bet, Doctor, tons of pellets in there." She frowned as her eyes trailed to where the man's hands should've been. I'd already gotten there.

Dual amputation at the wrists, clean and straight-edged. Stiffness in the limbs.

I said, "Still in rigor."

Milo nodded. "C.I. says depending on temperature, he was probably killed within twenty-hour hours, probably less. She's also sure the hands were cut off postmortem because there wasn't much bleeding at the stumps."

"Not much blood, period."

Inez Jonas said, "No kidding. I found a few little drops on the wood just under him, no spatter either high- or low-velocity, just a teeny bit of runoff from here." Pointing to the neck, which canted to the right. A wispy streak the color of rosé wine trailed down gray flesh.

She held the vial up to Milo. "The other thing I found was this, just before you came back. On the floor, under his butt."

He squinted. "Plastic?"

"Yes, sir," said Jonas. "Maybe it's just random dirt that was already here and his pants picked it up. But I'm thinking it looks like it's from a garbage bag and that could explain how they got him here, no? 'Cause he sure wasn't killed here. Or cut up here."

Milo said, "Done somewhere else, cleaned up meticulously, and bagged. Once he's here, bad guy does some fine-tuning and takes the bag. Yeah, I like it, good thinking."

Jonas beamed. "Psycho-crazy thinking but logical if you're in that orbit."

Looking at the corpse had made my eyes and teeth hurt so I shifted to a visual scan of the room. But for the corpse, as impeccable as the rest of the house.

I looked down at the poor faceless soul again, trying to ignore the gore and concentrating on the mundane details that sometimes tell you plenty.

Not tonight.

Medium height, medium build, age impossible to discern but thinning sandy hair and a bald spot suggested middle age. So did the clothing: a pale-blue button-collar shirt, tan windbreaker, pleated blue jeans pretending to be slacks, white socks, white Nike walking shoes. The pockets of the jeans had been turned inside out.

I said, "Was he left that way?"

Jonas said, "No, Doctor. C.I. went looking for the I.D. and turned them out. They were empty. Same for the jacket pockets."

Milo said, "No face, no hands, no I.D., pretty obvious what the goal was. Now the big question: How the hell did he end up here when the homeowners say they have no idea who he is?"

I said, "Where are the owners?"

"Nearby." He stared at the body, scowled, and played with an earlobe. His big, pale, acne-pitted face tightened as he brushed black hair off a lumpy forehead. A speck of some kind of foodstuff from the interrupted dinner sat just above his upper lip, left of center. Off-white, maybe rubber chicken. Or cheese. Another time, I'd have pointed it out.

Inez Jonas looked at me again. "It's a weird one, Lieutenant."

"Ergo, a psychologist. Any first-impression insights, Alex?"

I said, "Who are the owners?"

My non-answer made Milo frown. "A family, the Corvins. They left for a family dinner at six fifteen, Sunday thing, they do it once, twice a month. Usually they stay local. This time, they took a drive all the way to La Cienega, Lawry's, Restaurant Row. They get back just before nine, everyone goes upstairs except Dad who comes in here to record a show on his big-screen and finds this. Moments later, Mom comes down to ask him what's taking so long and screams and *that* brings the kids down and now it's a family affair."

Inez Jonas said, "Talk about a welcome home."

I said, "How many kids and what age?"

Milo said, "Coupla teenagers, or the young one's a tweener. They did the smart thing and ran the hell out and knocked on the neighbor's door. He's the one who 911'd. If you've seen enough here, I'd like you to meet them."

I said, "Let's do it."

Inez Jonas said, "Good luck, Lieutenant." Her expression said, *You're going to need it.*

Moe Reed was still posted in the doorway, working his phone. "Anything, L.T.?"

"Nah, go home, patrol can guard the scene."

"You're sure? I've got time."

"Positive, Moses." He told Reed about the scrap of plastic. "Could mean something or nothing."

Reed said, "Too bad those bags are pretty much generic."

"A bloody one isn't, Moses. On your way out, have a bunch of those uniforms do a six-block search for the bag—for anything bloody. It's unlikely someone who took the time to cut off hands and take I.D.

would be careless enough to toss evidence out in the open, but we can't assume."

"I'll canvass with them," said Reed. "Didn't notice any alleys or dumpsters on my way in, but there is that shopping area a few blocks west, got to be plenty of potential dump spots near there."

"Excellent idea."

Reed stripped off his paper suit. His on-call civilian threads were a gray *Gold's Gym* T-shirt and white sweatpants. Bouncing on his heels a couple of times, he jogged out of the house.

"Ah, youth," said Milo.

As we left the house, I said, "How many points of access?"

"If you don't count windows, the front door, a service door from a laundry room off the kitchen, and those French doors. Everything was locked when the Corvins got home, but the laundry door looks pretty dinky."

"Any security system?"

"An alarm, they're pretty sure they didn't set it."

"Casual approach to personal safety," I said.

"Nice neighborhood," he said. "People get lulled. The system came with the house, sensors on the ground floor but not the second. Like bad guys can't bring ladders. We looked for evidence of a ladder, any sort of disruption, couldn't find any, and the second-story windows were all closed. I'm leaning toward the utility door as point of entry."

"Someone familiar with the place? Knowing the lock was dinky?"

"That would explain it," he said. "Yet another reason to play Meet the Family." He scowled.

I said, "These people bother you."

"So far, nothing says they're dirty. But something about them, Alex—I'll let you be the judge."

2

"That one," he said, pointing to the house right of the Corvins'. Just south of the cul-de-sac's apex, an aspiring hacienda, fronted by a small walled courtyard.

A silver Ford Taurus was parked as far up the drive as possible, nosing a wrought-iron garden gate. The gate was padlocked, unlit, just black space between the curlicues.

That made me detour to take a look at the Corvins' fence. White wood pickets, three feet high.

I said, "No lock. Symbolic."

Milo went over to inspect, came back shaking his head. "Just reach over and unhook the latch. Can't remember ever being around here for anything nasty, so I guess I can't blame 'em."

We entered the courtyard. Paved with river rock; charming. But up close the economy that had been taken with the house's construction was obvious: flaking sprayed-stucco finish, cheap metal-framed windows, a molded door of some wood-like material trying to pass as carved.

The uniform standing sentry opened the door for Milo and stud-

ied me. She'd have to remain curious. As I had with the death house,
I followed my friend inside.

This entry was floored with Mexican pavers cracked and chipped at
the grout seams. Two steps dipped to a living room furnished with
off-white seating and mismatched end tables. A wreath of dry flowers
was the only thing on the wall. Sliding glass patio doors were ebony
rectangles.

A large, florid man with gray hair slicked and combed straight
back filled an armchair that faced the front door. Midfifties, navy polo
shirt, khakis, brown deck shoes.

The sofa perpendicular to his chair contained a thin, strawberry-
blond woman of the same vintage, pretty, freckled, with down-slanted,
pouchy eyes that looked accustomed to stress. Her clothes narrowed
her further: black cashmere crewneck and tailored slacks, black patent
flats, black purse.

A foot to her left a boy around thirteen or fourteen hunched and
picked a cuticle. Long-limbed and freckled with a rusty faux-hawk.
His out-for-the-evening duds were a blue-and-white perforated
Dodgers shirt, white board shorts, high-tops the color of canned green
beans.

Positioned at the farthest end of the sofa was an older girl, maybe
a high school senior, maybe a college freshman. Soft and chubby with
a doughy face from which dark eyes popped like raisins in an unbaked
muffin, she wore a curiously fusty floral blouse with puffed sleeves,
skinny jeans, and hiking boots. Her hair was brown, shoulder-length,
lank. Pudgy hands resting in her lap twitched every few seconds.

The big man bounded up, flashed a nanosecond grin, and said,
"Hey, Lieutenant," in a radio-announcer voice. "Anything yet on the
situation? You'll be cleaning up soon and letting us back in, right?"

Milo and I kept approaching.

"Soon?" said the man. "We need to get back."

The women frowned and said, "Chet."

"What?" The man turned to her, smile vanished. "They don't mind questions. Right, Lieutenant? Informed citizens are an asset to law enforcement." A glance at me. "New guy beefing up the team? Great idea, more the merrier, let's clear up this insanity A-sap."

He held out a hand. "Chet Corvin."

"Alex Delaware."

"Great to meet you, Alex." His grip was fierce as he pumped my arm.

He said, "Might as well do the intros for Detective Alex here, right, Lieutenant? I'm Chet Corvin, the guy who pays the mortgage next door. The vision in black is my bride, Felice, next to her is Brett, our star first baseman."

Wink at the boy; no response.

Chet Corvin glanced at the girl, as if in afterthought. "At the Siberia edge of the couch is daughter Chelsea."

Felice Corvin shot her daughter a quick look. As Brett had done with her father, Chelsea ignored her. Both kids looked as if they were orbiting in a distant galaxy. Their father's failure to notice was stunning.

A fifth person entered the room from the left—the dining room and kitchen area if this layout matched the Corvins' house.

Short, sparely built man in his late forties, wearing rimless eyeglasses and weekend stubble. Bald but for feathers of brown at the sides of a narrow face. Dressed for stay-at-home comfort in a white T-shirt, cargo shorts, rubber beach thongs.

"Paul Weyland," he said, wearily.

Milo said, "Thanks for doing this, sir."

"Of course." Weyland sat in a corner chair.

Milo turned to Chet Corvin. "I wish I could give you better news but I'm afraid your house is going to remain a crime scene for at least one more day, possibly longer."

"Longer? Why?"

"We need to be thorough, sir."

"Huh," said Corvin. "Can't see why it needs to—fine, you've got your job. But afterward you will do a thorough cleanup."

Milo said, "There are private companies specializing in—"

Corvin's hands slapped his hips. He canted forward. "You *don't* handle that?"

"We don't, sir, but I can give you some referrals and funds can be obtained through victim assistance. So can compensation for temporary housing, but I'm afraid the amount won't cover anything luxurious."

"Forget that, we're not public assistance people," said Chet Corvin. "We've got a place in Arrowhead so save the money for—people in Compton, wherever."

Milo motioned toward the recliner. "You might want to sit, sir."

Corvin remained on his feet. "I still don't see why—let's keep our heads clear, Lieutenant. Something crazy happened that has nothing to do with the Corvin family."

Milo said, "As I said, sir—"

"If you need to be thorough, why don't you accumulate sufficient personnel to do that in a timely manner?"

Felice Corvin stared straight ahead. Paul Weyland took out his phone and scrolled. The kids remained lost in space.

Milo nodded at the recliner. Chet Corvin sat. "Well, I suppose you know what you're doing."

Brett Corvin, still playing with his fingernails, said, "It was like murder, Dad. They can't just mess around."

Chet stared at his son. His eyes hardened. "Of course, slugger."

Felice Corvin said, "We can't go to Arrowhead, they've got school." To Milo: "How much does this victims' group pay, Lieutenant?"

Milo said, "I'm not sure, ma'am, but I'll see to it that you get the right contact information."

"Thank you very much."

Chet Corvin said, "What? Some cheesy motel in a crap part of town? I think not. In terms of school, the kids can get their homework and take it with them."

Felice Corvin said, "We'll discuss it."

Brett Corvin said, "Arrowhead would be cool, we never go, I can do my homework there."

His mother said, "Nice try."

Chet humphed and cracked his knuckles.

Through the exchange, no comment from Chelsea. The hands in her lap were twitching faster. Paul Weyland looked at her with what seemed to be pity, but neither parent paid her any mind.

Chet Corvin said, "Back to basics. Who's the poor devil in my den?"

"No idea, sir."

"What kind of lunatic would do that to a *house*?" To me: "We come back home, great dinner, prime rib, I could still taste the pie. Everything looks normal, we might never have found it until tomorrow morning but I left my reading glasses in the library and went down there and did find it."

To his wife: "And then *you* come down and scream."

Felice Corvin said, "You were down there so long, I got concerned."

"It wasn't exactly a dead mouse," said her husband. "I needed time to take it in, who wouldn't? Something like that, right off our damn *living* room?"

"Dying room," said Chelsea Corvin.

Everyone looked at the girl. She mumbled.

Brett gave a knowing smirk: Weird sister behaving predictably.

Chet and Felice shook their heads. Unified in bafflement, their odd child.

The girl bent over and began crying.

Paul Weyland looked ill at ease. A host whose guests had overstayed their welcome.

Felice Corvin went over to Chelsea and touched the girl's shoulder. Chelsea recoiled. "It'll be okay, honey."

"Easy to say, hard to accomplish," said Chet Corvin, looking at his daughter and wife with curious detachment. "But we'll get through this, the Corvins are made of tough stuff, right, gang?"

"Totally gross," said Brett Corvin, with little passion. He sniffled, gulped. Smiling as he mocked his sister.

His mother said, "Bretty—"

The boy made a hacking motion. "I saw it, no hands. Bleh. Messed *up*." To Milo: "Maybe they got thrown in the garbage."

Felice said, "Brett Corvin!"

Chelsea whimpered. Brett said, "Crybaby."

"Son," said Chet, "that really is a bit out of line."

The boy untied a sneaker, twirled a lace. "His face was like that stuff you ate last week, the Italian food. Tar-*tare. Bleh.*"

Chelsea Corvin made a gagging noise, clamped a hand over her mouth, and tottered upright. Panicked black eyes settled on Paul Weyland. "Ba-ru?"

Her father said, "What?"

Weyland stepped closer to her and pointed. "There's a bathroom right over there." Right-hand door on the way to his den. Maybe there was a matching room in the Corvin house. I'd been looking at other things.

The hand Chelsea used to cover her mouth was white and tight. She faltered, gagged again.

Chet Corvin said, "Go! Same place as our powder—go, g'won, don't mess up Paul and Donna's carpet."

The girl ran off, swung a door open, slammed it shut. Retching and vomiting followed immediately. A toilet flush. More gastric noise. Another flush.

Brett Corvin said, "Gross. This is like a whole gross *night*."

Milo said, "Mr. and Mrs. Corvin, in terms of where you want to stay tonight—"

Paul Weyland said, "If it helps, they can stay here." Tentative offer but far from a commitment. "My wife's visiting her mother, I've got three bedrooms. A couple have beds, for the other I've got futons in the garage."

Felice Corvin said, "That's so incredibly kind of you, Paul, but we couldn't impose."

Chet Corvin said, "Big of you, neighbor, deeply appreciated. But seeing as Arrowhead's off the table, I've got a better idea. My corporate card from the company will get us lodging in a decent hotel." To Milo: "At least for the *day* it takes to get our homestead back."

"We'll do our best but no promises, sir."

"You're making it sound as if you own the place."

"With a crime scene, Mr. Corvin, we do become custodians."

Chet turned to Weyland. "Thanks but no thanks, Paul. We'll take it from here."

"Sure," said Weyland, sounding relieved.

Brett said, "A hotel, cool. Let's do the one near Magic Mountain?"

Felice said, "What are we going to do about clothes, toothpaste, pajamas. Your snore-guard, Chet?"

Mention of the appliance tightened her husband's face. "There's such a thing as luggage, dearest. Lieutenant, I'm sure you can find a way to accompany us next door so we can take a few necessities without screwing up your procedures."

"I'm afraid not, sir. We need to preserve the crime scene strictly. If you need to purchase anything, the victims' fund will also—"

"We're *not* victims." To his wife: "Fine. We'll buy whatever we need and I promise not to saw wood."

"Yeah, right," said Brett, letting his mouth drop open and snuffling wetly.

His mother took hold of his arm. "Stop it."

"What?" he said.

The powder room door opened and Chelsea staggered out, face damp, strands of hair plastered to her cheeks.

"That do the trick for you?" said her father. "We don't want an accident."

The girl hung her head.

Silence from her mother.

Chelsea sat back down, rotated her body away from everyone else.

Chet Corvin said, "Can we at least take our cars?"

"They've been gone over, so sure, Mr. Corvin."

"Ooooh, *CSI*," said Brett. "Hey, Dad, are you like a serial killer?" Drawing a finger across his throat and bugging his eyes.

"Son, you might want to cool it."

"Why?"

"I appreciate the humor, champ, but—"

"It's gross," said the boy, jutting his mandible. "You can't make it *not*-gross."

"Son—"

"Stop it!" said Felice. "Everyone just stop it. Here we are gabbing as if nothing happened and all we care about is toothpaste. This is a *tragedy*. That poor *man*." To Milo: "I do hope you find out who he is. For his family's sake."

Paul Weyland nodded.

Felice smiled at him.

Chet Corvin watched the exchange. "Fine, we've got a consensus on sympathy. So may we go, now?"

Milo said, "We'd like to talk to each of you individually."

"Really," said Chet.

"Not for long, sir, just enough to get some basic statements."

"How much is 'not for long,' Lieutenant?"

"A few minutes each."

"Well," said Chet, "I don't mind personally, not that I have anything to add. But the kids, they need to be accompanied by an adult, right?"

"I'm not a *pussy*," said Brett.

"*Bretty,*" said Felice.

Out came the lower jaw. "What? I can *do* it by myself. I *wanna* do it."

She looked at her husband. He shrugged.

She said, "I suppose, if it's brief and you promise to be sensitive, Lieutenant."

"Scout's honor," said Milo.

"You were a scout?" said Chet. "I made Eagle, youngest ever in my troop, record number of badges. All right, go for it, kids. Strong stuff, the Corvins, all the way back to King Richard."

No one had asked Chelsea how she felt. Milo walked over to her. "Are you okay with talking to us alone?"

His voice was soft, gentle. The girl looked up.

"I don't need *them*," she said. "I can even go first."

3

Chelsea's offer was challenged by Brett and bickering ensued, the boy mouthing off as he dared to use obscenities, his sister sneering silently.

Felice Corvin said, "Obviously, they're in no state. I change my mind, Lieutenant."

Milo said, "Sure." He assigned the female cop out front to wait with both kids and Felice as we talked to Chet.

The venue was a few steps away, Paul Weyland's kitchen, a nineties concoction of generic white cabinets and black granite. The counters were cluttered with take-out pizza boxes, KFC buckets, empty soda cans.

Chet Corvin said, "Batching it, Paul?"

Weyland smiled weakly. "Gonna clean up before Donna gets back."

"Donna get on your case, does she?"

Weyland frowned, pointed to a round kitchen table set up with four chairs. "This work for you, Lieutenant?"

Milo said, "Perfect, we really appreciate it."

"No prob." Weyland stifled a yawn. "'Scuse me. Anything else I can do? Something to drink?"

Chet Corvin said, "You have Macallan Twenty-Four?"

Weyland smiled weakly. "Above my pay grade, Chet."

"School board getting miserly—"

Milo said, "No, thanks, Mr. Weyland. Feel free to go anywhere in your house or outside."

Chet said, "He's a free agent and we're . . . what a system."

Weyland said, "I'll go in my office and clear some paper."

Chet said, "Donna—"

Milo cut him off with a hand slash. "Thanks again, sir."

Chet Corvin said, "Lucky you, Paul. Your house isn't a *crime scene*."

Weyland left, lips pursed, exhaling.

Milo took out his pad and pen.

Chet arched an eyebrow. "You guys haven't advanced to a hand-held?"

Milo smiled. "Let's go over tonight, Mr. Corvin."

"Nothing to go over. We were out of the house at six fifteen, family dinner, like I told you."

"You do that regularly."

"You bet, family that dines together . . ." Corvin searched for a punch line, failed, frowned. "We try for two Sundays a month, sometimes we miss when I'm traveling but we make the effort."

"What business are you in?"

"Senior vice president and western regional supervisor at Connecticut Surety, Auto, Home and Transport."

"Insurance."

"Reinsurance. Not life, not medical, nothing iffy. I do casualty only, excluding homeowner auto. The big stuff, shipping, rail transport, interstate trucking. I'm in charge of California, Oregon, and

Washington, Alaska when our Canadian rep can't make it. Crazy place, Alaska, transport planes going down in blizzards."

"Sounds like a lot of travel."

Chet sat back and crossed his legs, warming to the topic. "Yeah, I'm troubleshooting all over. A little less now, some stuff can be done with face-timing." Conspiratorial grin. "More time for golf, this year I worked my handicap two points lower. Still, yeah, I'm on the road plenty. In addition to direct business there's ancillary business— conventions, meetings at the home office in Hartford. I handle a huge catchment area. Trucks alone is three-quarters of a million cumulative miles per year."

I said, "Lots of responsibilities."

"You got that, Alan. Big shoulders."

Milo said, "So you went to family dinner tonight."

"Like I told you the first time, usually we go somewhere close, the bride likes to eat light, you know women. The kids go for pizza, Italian fits that bill 'cause she can get a salad, lots of Italian places close by. This time I said time for a change, it was going to be meat, prime, no holds barred, the redder the better. I needed fuel, right? Had to be Lawry's, right? If the bride didn't like it, she could order a salad. In the end she had the lobster tails and everyone else did the meat thing, iron in the blood."

He chuckled. "Cholesterol-erama."

Milo said, "Bit of a drive to La Cienega."

"You bet," said Corvin. "Sunday, no telling what you can run into. So we left early. Turned out we had smooth sailing until West Hollywood, then some sort of construction, blocked-off lanes. But we made it right on the dot, my timing was perfect."

"And you returned . . ."

"What I told you the *first* time," said Corvin.

Milo smiled.

"Fine. What did I say—around nine, right? Still saying that, can't be more specific than that 'cause I didn't check, why would I? ETD I *can* tell you because I established the timetable so obviously I needed to check the old Roller."

Flashing a steel Rolex, he extended his head forward. His neck was meaty, taurine. "That work for you, Lieutenant? Definite ETD, approximate ETA back to base? Not that I see why any of this is relevant."

Milo scrawled. "So you got home around nine and went to your den—"

"Pure chance," said Corvin. "The original plan was catch up on DVR'd TV, one thing the bride and I can agree on is *Downtown Abbey*, I like the history, she's into the clothes and whatnot. We had two episodes taped."

"You went to look for your reading glasses."

"I didn't have them in the restaurant but because I knew what I wanted beforehand, the menu was irrelevant. Except for paying the check, for that I borrowed the bride's glasses." He laughed. "Pink girlie glasses, Brett thought it was a crack-up, thankfully the place was dark—"

"So you went downstairs—"

"Went downstairs, saw it, and boom," said Chet Corvin, punching a palm. "There was no smell, nothing to warn me, it was just there. I was a little thrown off, who the hell wouldn't be? You're in your own *house* and you find *that*? I mean it's *insane*. It's absolutely *insane*."

It. That. Not *him.*

Depersonalizing the body for a reason? Or just Chet being Chet?

Milo said, "You were there long enough for your wife to come down."

"That," said Corvin, "was my *bad*, Lieutenant. I should've kept her out but to be honest, I was still a little thrown. So she saw and started screaming her head off and that brought the kids down and now they're seeing it. She pushes them away, runs toward the front door, I'm saying where you going and she doesn't answer. So I follow and she looks around and heads here to Paul and Donna's. We ring the bell, he comes to the door, Felice is totally freaked, she's jabbering, I take charge and explain clearly, am ready to call you guys. Then I realize I hadn't taken my phone. So Paul calls you guys."

Shifting his weight. "And here we are, team."

Milo said, "Mr. Corvin, some of the questions we ask you may sound foolish but we still need to go through them. Starting with can you think of anyone who could be behind this?"

"Negative."

"Is there someone who'd want to target your home specifically?"

"Same answer," said Corvin. "What kind of target would we be? Dumping a body? It's not like it directly hurt us."

Milo said, "It could be a psychological assault—"

"Yeah, well, this has nothing to do with us, we'll get past it and move on. None of that PTSD crap I'm always getting from teamsters."

"Okay . . . any idea how whoever did it got in?"

"If I had to guess, Lieutenant, I'd say the utility door. Always remind the bride to lock, she gets careless. Same with the alarm, she's a smart gal but absentminded, like the professor she used to be."

"Professor of what?"

"Elementary education. Before that she was a teacher. Then a vice principal. Now she works for L.A. Unified, setting up curriculum. Important job, all kinds of responsibilities. You can see how she'd lose track."

"Is she in the district's main office, downtown?"

"Nope, satellite, the Valley, Van Nuys. Paul's at the downtown office, that's how he and Donna found out about the house—they rent, don't own. Felice told them."

"What does Mr. Weyland do at the district?"

"Search me," said Corvin. "They're not teachers, some sort of paper-pushers—he and Donna, both. Couple years ago, they met the bride at a symposium or something, she told them next door was coming vacant."

"Who's the owner?" I said.

"No idea. It's been rented out since we moved in."

"How long ago is that?"

"Six years." Corvin touched his chest. "Bought mine when I got transferred from the Bay Area, had to downsize property-wise from this great place in Mill Valley but lucky for us, the recession hit, we stole the place."

"So," said Milo, "your rear door could've been unlocked and the alarm off."

"I'm sure the alarm was off or the company would've texted me. In terms of the door, I'm sure she left it open." Wink and a smile. "Don't tell her I said that or you'll be aiding and abetting husband abuse."

Milo smiled back, checked his notes. "Your wife told me she locked it."

Corvin shrugged. "You know how it is, guys. Choose your battles."

Milo flipped a page. "Any strange events recently, sir?"

"Like what?"

"Hang-up phone calls, unusual vehicles parked on the street or driving around."

"Nope."

"Anyone who didn't look like they belonged?"

"Nothing," said Corvin. "Absolutely nothing."

I said, "Have there been any neighborhood conflicts?"

"Like what?"

"Disputes over anything."

"Nah, it's quiet here—okay, here you go, I just thought of something." He held up a finger. "There's an oddball, neighbor on the other side of us. Not that I'm saying he did anything but man, he's different."

Milo picked up his pen. "Who's that?"

Corvin glanced to the side. "Maybe I shouldn't have said anything. I don't want it getting back to him."

"It won't, sir," said Milo. "We're going to be canvassing all your neighbors, so talking to anyone will be routine."

"Yeah, but I need to—like I said, he's weird."

"You've had problems with him?"

"Not per se."

"But . . ."

"Nothing," said Corvin. "He's just weird, so keep me out of it." Half smile. "Scout's honor?"

Milo crossed his heart.

"Fine. His name is Trevor Bitt, writes comic books or something."

"How's he strange?"

"Lives by himself, keeps to himself, no visitors I've ever seen. He never comes out except to bring his cans to the curb or when he drives away in a noisy pickup—a Dodge. If you happen to be there and say hello, he makes like he doesn't hear."

I said, "Not a social guy."

"In his own world, Alan," said Corvin. "You'll meet him, you'll see. But we've never given him a reason to hassle us. One time we got his mail and I brought it over. He took it, even said thank you. But I could tell he didn't mean it. Next time, on can day, he ignored me. Weird."

"Comic books," said Milo.

Corvin said, "That's what they say, I read nonfiction."

"Who says?"

"I don't know, I just heard it—go Google him. Maybe I heard wrong and he's the head of Finland or something."

"How long has Mr. Bitt been living here?"

"You're interested in him? Listen, I didn't want to open some worm can."

"You haven't," said Milo, "but at this point we need to look into everything. How long's Mr. Bitt been your neighbor?"

Corvin frowned. "He moved in, I want to say, two years after we did. So four years, give or take? I brought him a bottle of wine. No answer at the door so I left it on his doorstep. Next day it was gone but not a single thank-you. The second time we got his mail, the bride brought it over. I warned her he'd snub her. She's sensitive, bruises like a peach. I used to call her that. My Georgia peach, she spent some time in Atlanta as a kid, father taught at Emory."

I said, "Did Bitt snub her."

"She didn't say, it's not like he's a topic. That's all I can tell you about him."

"Anyone else in the neighborhood we should be looking at? Even if it seems unlikely."

"Not a one, Al. This whole thing is unlikely. That it would happen to us."

Milo did the usual repetition of questions that often pulls up info. With Corvin it didn't and we walked him out of the kitchen. Brett was seated closer to his mother, fooling with his phone. Chelsea stood at the rear of the room, staring at black glass.

Milo said, "I know it's late, so how about we talk to the kids now, Mrs. Corvin. Let's start with Chelsea."

Felice shook her head. "You heard what I said before, Lieutenant. And actually, the kids and I have been discussing it and they have absolutely nothing to offer. Sorry, but that's the way it is."

Milo said, "How old are you, Brett?"

"Fourteen."

"Chelsea?"

No reply.

Felice said, "She's seventeen. They're both minors, so I'm taking responsibility here. They know nothing and I don't want their ordeal to be exacerbated."

Milo said, "Fair enough, ma'am. But kids, if you do think of something, tell your parents—"

Chelsea mumbled, "Bullshit." Turning, she faced us, focused on her mother, glaring. "I can talk, I don't care what anyone says."

Chet Corvin said, "Watch your tone, young lady."

"Bullshit."

Felice Corvin said, "Cheltz—"

"Bullshit, I can talk." A lower-lip tremor robbed the statement of potency.

"Cheltz, you said you had nothing to tell them."

"But if I did I could."

"'But if I did I could,'" said Brett in a baby voice. "Ooooh."

His sister wheeled on him. "Fuck off you little ass-wipe—"

Brett bobbled his head and waved jazz hands. "Ooooooh—"

Chelsea spat on the floor. "*Ant*-dick. I've seen it and you are."

Her turn to smirk. Brett turned crimson and began to rise. His mother restrained him with a hand on his arm. He squirmed. Jabbed the air with a one-finger salute.

"*Midget*-balls," said Chelsea.

The boy struggled to peel Felice's hand off.

She restrained him with both of hers. "Don't you dare, Brett Corvin."

Brett flopped back against the back of the sofa, growling. Flashes of red and blue as he bared his teeth. Designer orthodontics.

Chelsea said, "No-go gonad."

Chet Corvin, stunned, had done nothing during the exchange, eyes moving between his offspring.

Felice pushed Brett back and wagged her finger at Chelsea. Shooting to her feet, she extruded words through clenched lips. *"Both. Of. You. Shut. Up!"*

Instant compliance.

"Bar*bar*ians!" She turned to us, flashed a frosty smile. "Obviously, I've proved my point. Here's what's going to happen: I'll talk to you now, and then we'll be finished." To her husband: "Watch them properly and find a decent hotel. Make sure it's got good Wi-Fi."

Facing us, her back to him.

"Honey," he said, glancing at Chelsea, then Brett.

The girl trembled. The boy seethed.

Felice Corvin said, "*You* handle them. For a *change*."

Felice Corvin walked ahead of us to the Weylands' kitchen. We sat but she remained on her feet. "I'm at a desk all day. My chiropractor tells me to get off my butt whenever I have a chance. What do you want to know?"

Milo said, "Let's go over tonight. Your husband said you left for dinner at six fifteen."

"If he said it, it must be true."

We waited.

"Sorry," she said. "I'm on edge. For obvious reasons. Yes, that sounds right."

"You arrived at Lawry's at . . ."

"Whenever Chet says. I'm not a clock-watcher."

"Out for a normal Sunday dinner."

"Normal. Interesting word." She tossed her hair. "Sorry, again. Yes, it was just another meal, no special occasion. We try to go out with the two of them." She laughed. "Civilization and all that. Honestly, I'm appalled by what you just had to witness."

I said, "They're under a lot of stress."

"Of course they are but I won't kid you, this goes way back, the two of them have never gotten along. Nothing in common, not that that explains it." She shrugged. "Brett's a great athlete, he handles school basically okay. Chelsea . . ." She sighed. "She's seventeen but still in tenth grade. There are motor issues as well as cognitive and perceptual problems, so sports are out and learning's a challenge. That makes her an obvious target and Brett can be unkind—I don't know why I'm telling you this." She threw up her hands. "Probably just what you said, stress."

Milo said, "We appreciate your taking the time—"

"Sure. Can we get on with it?"

"Of course, ma'am . . . so you had dinner and got back around nine. Take us through what happened then."

"We all went upstairs then Chet went downstairs for his glasses and I heard this crazy noise. It took a second for me to realize he was screaming. Like he was in pain, last time I heard that was when he had prostatitis."

A fact Chet had chosen to omit, emphasizing his wife's emotionality.

"My first thought was, *He's had a heart attack.* What with his weight and all the garbage he puts in his system. So I ran down, saw him standing there staring at something. Then I saw what it was."

She shook her head. "That poor, poor man. It's still sinking in. Our house? How insane is that?"

We gave her time. She filled it with nothing.

Milo looked at me.

I said, "After you saw—"

"Oh, God," she said, shutting her eyes, then opening them. "I really don't want to think about it. Don't know if I'll ever get the image out of my head."

Her lids fluttered. Pretty hazel irises settled on me. "How do you people do it, day after day?"

"Time tends to—"

"So they say, I hope it's true." She tapped her forehead. "Because right now it's just sitting in here like a . . . a . . . I don't even want to fall asleep tonight, afraid of what I'm going to dream."

She sat down, exhaled, pushed hair behind her left ear. Spotting a Kleenex box, she grabbed a tissue, wadded it, passed it from hand to hand. "Everything's *jangling*."

I said, "It's a terrible thing to go through."

"I think I'd like some water."

Milo found a glass, rinsed and filled.

"Thank you." Tentative sips, then a deep swallow. She blinked. "Sorry."

"Nothing to be sorry for," I said. "Can we go on?"

"Sure."

"So you and Mr. Corvin were standing there—"

"Both of us freaking out. Chet's color looks nasty to me, purplish, he's got blood pressure issues. I'm thinking, *Oh shit, there'll be two dead bodies, what the hell am I going to do?*"

She drank more water, dabbed sweat from the sides of her nose. "If both of us had the foresight to be quiet . . . but we didn't and that brought the kids down and once I saw them, I snapped into mommy mode, not wanting them to see it. But I wasn't fast enough. At that point, it became utter chaos, Brett's whooping and yelling how gross it is, Chelsea's just standing there. Meanwhile, Chet's his usual inert self—what you just saw. Rooted in place and I'm trying to push the kids out of the room and now Brett's had an eyeful and he's white as a ghost. They both are, Chelsea was stunned from the get-go. As you saw, Brett recovered, he's not one for . . . lingering. Chelsea, on the other hand . . . this is the *last* thing she needs."

I said, "We can give you referrals for therapy."

"Could you?" she said. "That's kind, maybe at some point. But not now, Chelsea hates therapists, we tried a couple, they failed miserably. What can I say? I choose my battles."

Same thing her husband had said about debating her.

A family that saw life as a war zone?

I said, "So you have no idea who the victim might be?"

"Of course not! Why would I?"

"We need to ask."

"Proper procedure?" said Felice Corvin. "I get it, I work for L.A. Unified, it's all about procedure, a lot of it downright stupid. No, I don't have a clue. Nor can I tell you why they dumped him in our house."

She bit her lip. "What they did to his hands—was that to hide his fingerprints?"

"Could be."

"I hope that's what it is. 'Cause if it's some crazy satanic thing, that would scare me *completely* to death."

I said, "Hiding evidence *is* the most likely reason."

"But nothing's guaranteed." Strange smile. "Given tonight, that's pretty obvious."

I looked at Milo and he took over, covering the same ground he had with Chet. Hang-up calls, strange vehicles, anything out of the ordinary.

Identical denials from Felice. The first sign of accord between them. They'd never know.

Milo closed his pad. "So it's pretty much a quiet neighborhood, Mrs. Corvin."

"I'm not sure I'd call it a neighborhood. That would imply neighborliness."

"Not a friendly place."

"Not friendly or unfriendly, Lieutenant. Just a bunch of houses that abut each other. I grew up in Indiana and Georgia, we had block parties, no fences between the yards. Even later, up north—we used to live in Mill Valley before we came here—we knew the people around us, rode our horses together—we had equestrian zoning, it was lovely."

"Not here," said Milo.

"Hardly," said Felice Corvin. "Here, you rarely see people, period.

Weekends are dead." She colored around her freckles. "Sorry, that was . . . what I've heard is that a lot of the owners have second homes. And some are renters."

I said, "Like the Weylands."

Felice Corvin squinted at me.

I said, "It came up in conversation with your husband. Your helping them find the place."

"Did he call me a busybody like when it happened?"

"He said you were helpful." Ever the therapist.

"Well," said Felice Corvin, "I did tell them about the vacancy. I knew Donna because she's in accounting downtown, came to our office to deliver papers, we chatted, she told me she was looking for a place. Paul I only met after they moved in. Nice people but we don't see them much, they have no kids, do a lot of traveling."

Milo said, "Another neighbor came up in conversation with your husband. Mr. Bitt, on the other side."

Felice Corvin's head drew back. "What about him?"

"Your husband said he was a bit odd."

She drummed a granite counter. "Can't argue with that. Was there a reason Chet brought it up? As in something he knows but has chosen not to tell me about?"

"No, ma'am," said Milo. "We probed for anything out of the ordinary just as we did with you and Mr. Corvin said Mr. Bitt was a bit different."

"Okay. I'd hate to think Chet was keeping something important from me. Yes, Trevor's a bit of an odd duck. Keeps to himself, we rarely see him, though for all I know he emerges when we're at work. I did bring him his mail once and he thanked me but that's been the extent of it. As I said, no one around here is exactly gregarious. Except Chet, of course, *he's* never met a stranger."

Her smile was lopsided, unrelated to happiness.

"Never met a stranger, Chet," she repeated. "I guess now he has."

◆

We escorted her back to the Weylands' living room. Three people working their phones. The kids didn't look up but Chet did.

"Got us set up at the Circle Plaza, nice and close to the 405, make your commute a cinch."

"It'll do," said Felice. "We won't be staying long, anyway." To Milo: "Can you give me at least an educated guess as to when we can return home?"

"As I said, ma'am, it's likely to be a crime scene through tomorrow, possibly the day after."

"Okay, if I know, I can plan," she said. "In terms of that cleanup company, no need, we'll have our housekeeper do it. Get her some heavy-duty gloves."

Chet said, "I don't know, that's pretty intense—"

"*I* know. There wasn't much blood that I could see. Right, Lieutenant? It's something we can handle."

"Probably."

"No guarantees, huh?" She laughed. To her husband: "We'll be fine. It's only one room."

"My room."

"The *dy-ing* room," said Brett, not bothering to look up from his tiny screen. One hand finger-waved. "Ooooh, scary!"

Chelsea texted and ignored him.

Felice said, "We'll pick up what we need from the twenty-four-hour Ralph's in Brentwood, seeing as it's close to—oh, one thing, Lieutenant. May my children get their backpacks so they have their schoolbooks?"

"Sure," he said. "An officer will accompany one of you to get them."

"*I'll* be that one," she said. "Thank you."

Brett said, "Books for one day? I don't need 'em."

His mother said, "Enough out of you." But she smiled and her son returned the courtesy.

Chelsea had returned to staring at nocturnal nothingness.

◆

Milo radioed Moe Reed, who came to escort Felice as the rest of us waited outside.

Both family vehicles had been processed and released. No sign of blood, the only irregular find a silver flask of whiskey in the glove compartment of the black Range Rover.

Chet Corvin said, "I take it to the clubhouse, share some Oban with the guys."

Milo said, "I'd keep it somewhere else, sir." He returned the bottle, snipped the tape blocking the driveway.

"Duly noted, Lieutenant," said Corvin. Not a trace of sincerity.

Milo said, "Soon as your wife returns, you're good to go, sir."

Chet Corvin said, "I'm good *now.* You guys wait for Mom." Climbing into the Rover, he backed out too fast, bucked the vehicle as he shifted to Drive, and sped away. Brett and Chelsea, entranced by their phones, didn't seem to notice his departure.

Neither did their mother, toting two backpacks. Shouting, "Turn those things off, our bars are getting low and our bill's insane," she headed for the gray Lexus.

When the sedan was gone, Milo studied the Tudor Revival to the left. Clumsily built, with exaggerated slope to the mock-slate roof, too much half timber crisscrossing stucco and brick.

The landscaping didn't fit medieval England: cactus, aloe, and other sharp, spiky things bordering a C-shaped cobbled drive and fringing the bottom of the house. Drought-friendly but also human-unfriendly. A black Ram pickup, maybe twenty years old, was positioned so it blocked a view of the front door.

He said, "Too late to deal with neighbors, let alone the resident loner. Let's see what's going on, tech-wise."

A voice behind us said, "May I lock up?"

Paul Weyland had come out of his house. He'd put on a bathrobe. His front door remained open.

Milo said, "Go ahead, sir. Thanks for your hospitality."

Weyland rubbed his bald head. "I can't exactly say it was my pleasure. But they needed somewhere to go—what a terrible situation. Are they okay?"

"Good as can be expected."

Weyland yawned, raised a hand to cover his mouth. "'Scuse me. Guess I'll try to grab some shut-eye."

Milo said, "Long as we have you, could we ask a few questions?"

Weyland righted his eyeglasses. "Sure."

Milo repeated the pop quiz he'd given the Corvins. Same answers.

He pointed to the Tudor. "How well do you know your neighbor over there, Mr. Bitt?"

Weyland frowned. "Not well . . . he's not what you'd call friendly."

"A loner."

Nod. Weyland chewed his lip. "Are you saying you've got evidence of a problem with him?"

"Not at all, sir," said Milo. "The Corvins described him as a loner. We'll be talking to him along with everyone else on the block."

"Well, good luck talking to him," said Weyland. "He really is kind of antisocial. Shortly after we moved in, my wife happened to catch him going to his truck. Donna's friendly, she said hi. Bitt just ignored her and drove away. She said he made her feel like she didn't exist. She was kind of upset."

"I can imagine."

Weyland's lips folded inward. "If you do suspect him, I'd sure like to know. Look how close he is to us. To them, also. I guess bringing a body from his side would be possible—not that you suspect that. Of course . . ." Weyland shook his head. "I don't want to get involved in something I know nothing about . . . but isn't that how it sometimes happens? The quiet ones?"

I said, "Sounds like he's more than quiet."

"Well, yes—I'm sure it means nothing. Please don't quote me on anything."

"Of course not," said Milo.

Weyland removed his glasses. "I didn't actually see what happened. To that man. But Chet described it. Not that I wanted him to but Chet's kind of . . ."

"He does things his way," I said.

"Exactly. Anyway . . . good luck, guys."

Milo said, "Thanks for your time, sir. Try to get some sleep."

Weyland smiled and drew his bathrobe sash tighter. "Emphasis on try."

Inez Jonas exited the house and two coroners drivers rolled a gurney inside, wrapped, bagged, and removed the body. They were technicians in their own right, transporting with impressive speed and grace.

Jonas said, "Nice meeting you, Doctor, hope you find something psychological. 'Cause this sure is crazy."

I said, "Do my best. Have a good night."

"My night's just starting, got called to Pico-Union, normally not my area but there's no one else."

Milo said, "Gang thing?"

"They don't tell me but yeah, probably. Walk-by shooting, sounds like a simple one. Relatively speaking."

We met up with Moe Reed on the upstairs landing.

He said, "Second floor is three bedrooms, two bathrooms. Nothing interesting apart from some porn in one of Mister's dresser drawers and under Junior's mattress. Similar stuff, looks like Junior borrowed. Missus has nothing heavier than a romance novel on her nightstand."

"Paper-and-ink porn?" said Milo.

"You got it, L.T. Old-school. Well-used magazines that look old, nothing bloody or sadistic or freaky. Junior can access whatever he wants online but maybe he found Dad's stash quaint. Dad sees something missing, he's not exactly gonna complain."

Milo laughed. "Speaking of online, how many computers are we talking about?"

"Laptops for Mom, Dad, and the boy."

"Nothing for the girl?"

"Nope. Mom wanted to take them, I had no grounds to say no. I didn't pick up anything hinky from her, just someone who wanted to get back to normal."

Milo turned to me. "A kid without a computer, what's the diagnosis?"

I said, "She's not much of a student, her phone's enough."

Reed said, "Did I screw up by letting her take everything? I really couldn't see grounds."

"That's 'cause there aren't any, Moses. At this point, they're peripheral victims, not suspects. I'm assuming no weapons up here."

"Nope. Missus said none and she was righteous."

"Check downstairs."

Reed descended and Milo entered the master suite. Corn-yellow walls, matching en-suite bathroom redolent of lavender potpourri. The Corvins shared a clumsy rendition of an Edwardian sleigh bed, pale-blue bedding a bit threadbare at the corners, not even a close match to the rest of the furniture: almost-deco from the nineties.

I stood by as Milo deftly searched drawers and closets, making sure everything was replaced exactly as he'd found it. It's not that he doesn't trust Reed. Staying active elevates his mood.

We moved on to Brett's and Chelsea's rooms. Both were small and simply furnished, the boy's space reduced further by navy-blue walls, jumbles of sports equipment, and heaps of balled-up clothing.

Chelsea's white chamber was neat. The exception was the top of her desk, covered with pencil drawings.

Page after page filled with crude, repetitive geometric shapes.

Overlapping circles evoked a bubble-pipe gone mad. Parallel lines were so densely rendered they made the paper look like linen. Five-pointed stars and jags that might've been lightning bolts evoked an imploding universe.

Milo said, "What is she, autistic—the spectrum, whatever?"

"At this point, no diagnoses."

He flipped through the artwork. "No gory stuff. Okay, she's just an oddball."

Moe Reed came up the stairs. "No weapons or ammo, not in here or the garage. Nothing back there that could've been used on those hands, either, like a band saw. The only tools they keep are the basics: screwdriver, hammer, socket wrench, set of Allen wrenches. The rest of the garage was piled high with boxes. Like two-thirds of the space is boxes. I checked a few. The ones marked *clothes* have clothes, same for *kitchenware* and *books*. Looks like they moved and never bothered to deal with it."

"Books turn out to be books," said Milo. "Don't you just hate honesty?"

"Worst thing in the world," said Reed.

We walked him to his unmarked. "What time tomorrow, L.T.?"

"Can you do seven a.m.?"

"I can do six."

"But I can't, kiddo. Meet you back here at seven, we'll canvass with Sean and whatever uniforms I can commandeer. Before we talk to anyone, let's look for CC cameras. We've got a pretty good fix on the time frame and there won't be much traffic on the street, so fingers crossed. What shift is Sean on?"

"Not sure," said Reed. "I do know he just closed an assault."

"Then let's reward him with more honest labor, Moses. He's got kids, should be up early, anyway. Captain Brazil's on tonight, she can be okay. I'll make a strong case for six uniforms. She gives me a hard time, we'll make do. But I don't think she will. Know why?"

Reed looked at the death house. "Upscale neighborhood."

Milo patted his shoulder. "You are socioeconomically acute, Moses."

The young detective smiled and drove off.

I said, "I'd like to see the utility door."

Milo said, "That can be arranged."

We gloved up and walked the empty driveway to the Corvins' token gate. Milo arched his hand over the rim, undid the latch, switched on his flashlight.

The backyard was a rectangular pool surrounded by a wooden deck and little else. The water was black as oil when grazed by the flashlight beam, invisible otherwise. Serious hazard if you were unfamiliar with the place.

I said so.

Milo grunted, kept walking. I followed, straining for details in the dark. Three walls of ficus hedge blocked out neighbors on all sides. A pool net and vacuum sat on the far left-hand corner of the deck. Nothing else but a couple of folding chairs and a plastic owl for scaring away pigeons, perched near the shallow end of the pool.

The wood planking fed to the French doors I'd seen at the rear of the house. Easy access. Milo tried each door. Shut solid.

"Decent latches, be a challenge without breaking the glass." He continued to the side of the house, where concrete steps led to a plain white door.

No shreds of black plastic on the paved ground, no drag marks or footprints. He flashlit the two flanking windows. "Nailed shut, looks like for a long time. Fire department would love that."

I got close to the door. No pry scars.

Milo tapped the wood. Hollow. "Flimsy piece of crap, ol' Chet figured this would be the way. He may be a buffoon but a man knows his own house."

Pulling out his wallet, he removed a credit card, bent and fiddled.

No instantaneous success; this wasn't the movies. He worked the card into the space between door and jamb, jiggled, angled. Finally, a click sounded and the door swung open. The process had taken around a minute.

"A bit of work," he said, "but no Houdini-deal. And with the family gone, there was plenty of time and privacy."

He nudged the door. It creaked and swung a couple of inches. "Thing's a joke and they don't set the alarm."

I said, "Didn't you hear Chet? It's all her fault."

He laughed. "Yeah, he's a prince. I wish I could say carelessness is a big clue, Alex, but back when I worked burglaries, this was business as usual and we're talking the high-crime era. What I said before about not bothering with second-floor windows. People paying good money for a system then not using it. Even when citizens think they are being careful, there's inconsistency, points of vulnerability, like alarm screens gone bad."

I tapped the left-hand window. "Those boxes in the garage say they're fine with the status quo. These were probably nailed shut before they moved in."

"Overconfidence," he said. "My job depends on it."

He pushed the door wide open and we entered a beige-painted service porch. Washer, dryer, laundry basket, cheap prefab cabinets, most of which hung askew.

The floor was vinyl. Clean and shiny, no hint anything nasty had been dragged through.

I said, "Begging the question as to why the body was dumped anywhere in the house, why not just leave it here in the first place instead of dragging it clear across the house to Chet's den?"

"He's the target?"

"The crime feels personal, and like you said, charm isn't his thing."

"That's one helluva grudge, Alex. And if someone hates him that much, why not do *him*? Why take it out on some other poor devil?"

"Could be a warning," I said. "Or the poor devil had a relationship with Chet."

"Chet was pretty convincing about not knowing the guy. He's that good of an actor?"

"If concealing his involvement was at stake, he'd be motivated," I said. "Maybe all that bloviating was a cover."

"Hmm. Okay, let's assume Chet pissed someone off big-time. His business is transportation insurance. So, what, someone lost a train-load of whatever, didn't get paid in a timely manner? I don't see that leading to blowing off a face and hacking off hands."

"Maybe it was personal, not business."

He looked at me. "As in?"

I said, "Could be lots of things."

"Shoot 'em at me."

"A scam with an enraged victim. An affair—or even a sexual assault. Chet's on the road all the time, maybe a business trip went really bad. Or it's something to do with Felice's private life and the killer's throwing it in Chet's face. Or both of them are involved. I can keep going, Big Guy, but the point is, why was this house chosen? And again, why bother to schlep the body?"

"Questions," he said. "I'm getting a headache. But thanks." Grinning. "I mean that, you stimulate the gray cells."

We walked across the house, reached the den. Cleared of its morbid contents, curiously clean and serene.

Back outside, I said, "What bothered you about the family?"

"Couldn't put my finger on it," he said, cramming his hands into his jacket pockets. "Still can't. They're not exactly a happy bunch but who is? They just seemed . . ." He shook his head. "From where I was sitting, she can't stand him. And wanna bet he calls her something other than 'the bride' when talking to his pals? Or himself. Then there's the kids, couple of jackals tearing at each other. What's the theme, here?"

"They're disconnected," I said. "Less a functioning unit than four people operating independently."

His hands came out of his pockets. One held a panatela and a book of matches. The other rubbed the side of his face. "I knew there was a reason I called you. Exactly, they're strangers to each other. If this is the family of the future, we're fucked."

A finger rose to his temple. More massaging. "Not that it's necessarily relevant."

"It could be," I said. "Isolation is the perfect breeding ground for secrets."

"So I do more digging into their background?"

"I would. Start with Chet because it *is* his room. If nothing shows up, move on to Felice."

"What about the kids?"

"Brett's too young to be involved. Chelsea's old enough to have nasty friends but if she or her peers were involved, the scene would be a lot bloodier and messier. This was a meticulous staging."

"What about an older boyfriend, Alex? One of those disgruntled scenarios?"

"Mom and Dad disapprove so Romeo goes ballistic? This *is* a girl whose father seems to ignore her so I can see her looking for a substitute and gravitating toward an older man. Every time we've seen disgruntled, it's the parents who are targeted, not some surrogate. But sure, can't hurt to check Chelsea out."

"Those drawings of hers," he said, unwrapping the cigar. "And that thing she said—the dying room. Maybe that's something she heard before. Maybe that's why she ran out and heaved, she knows something. I never got to talk to her, courtesy of Mommy's protectiveness. Maybe because *Mommy* knows something, too."

He looked at the black pool water. Lit up, blew smoke rings. "Anything else back here interest you?"

"Nope."

"Then let's get the hell out."

He walked me to the Seville. Crime scene tape remained up. A couple of uniforms lolled.

I got in the car and lowered the window.

"Thanks for coming out late, amigo."

"I wasn't doing much anyway."

Smooth lie. I'd just finished making love to a beautiful woman, had looked forward to a long bath and an early bedtime. As the water ran, Robin and I lay in bed, her head on my chest, her curls tickling my face. She'd answered the phone, said, "Oh, hi, Big Guy," and passed it over.

Knowing Milo and decoding his tone: Serious Business.

As I'd gotten dressed, I'd said, "Sorry, honey."

Robin laughed off the formality, kissed me, looped her arm in mine, and walked me to the door.

I wondered if she was still up. If she was, how much I'd tell her.

Milo said, "How's your schedule tomorrow?"

"Phone conference with some lawyers in the morning, afternoon's clear."

"If I get answers by then, I'll let you know. If I don't, I'll probably call you. Especially if I get to him." Indicating Trevor Bitt's Tudor. "From what everyone says, mental health backup's a good idea. Maybe he *is* the bad guy and this'll close nice and tight. On the other hand, when has optimism been a valid concept?"

5

T he moment I'd arrived at Evada Lane, I'd switched to work mode: hyperfocused, aiming for logic, suppressing emotion. As I drove home, the vile reality of what I'd just seen hit me.

This was more than murder. It was erasure. An outrage had begun with dispatch, shifted to butchery, ended up with clinical choreography on that blandest of stages, a suburban house.

L.A.'s vastness and varied geography offered a universe of dump sites. Why Evada Lane? Why the Corvins?

Maybe by tomorrow morning the truth *would* boil down to the odd duck on the block, a sadistic psychopath closeted in his own upscale lair.

A vicious hermit who spied? Had Trevor Bitt, parting his curtains a smidge, watched the family drive away for their Sunday dinner and embarked on a personal Grand Guignol?

That said nothing about motive but it did solve a whole lot of logistical problems.

A brief walk separated Bitt's property from the Corvins'. Once he'd made it to the end of their driveway with a plastic-bagged package, flipping the gate latch would've provided privacy, courtesy of three walls of impermeable hedge.

After that, trip the flimsy lock and defile thy neighbor.

Why the Corvins?

Maybe because there's nothing like years of proximity to breed resentment.

Rosy idealists like to think throwing people together breeds tolerance and goodwill, but often it accomplishes just the opposite. The Corvins hadn't cited any conflict with Bitt, just curt rebuffs. But who knew how he felt?

Hostility grew deep roots in a certain type of psyche. Sometimes it didn't take much to trigger action.

The TV next door playing too loudly.

The kids fighting noisily.

Or, if I was right about Chet being the target, it could simply boil down to too many obnoxious comments by a blowhard with the capacity to irritate a saint.

Chet ridicules, Bitt says nothing. Chet keeps going, Bitt stews. Imagines. Plots.

One of the *quiet* ones.

His landscaping, all that stay-away flora. What if he kept the world at bay because he had a lot to hide? Unhealthy appetites, a grotesquely violent fantasy life that had spilled over to murder?

On the other hand, Trevor Bitt might be an artist who craved isolation in order to ply his talents. Or just a guy who enjoyed his privacy.

I'd research him tomorrow. After I figured out what to tell Robin. Meanwhile, drive and try not to think about the horror in Chet Corvin's den.

I put the radio on, already tuned to KJazz. Lucked out and got the first few bars of Stan Getz playing "Samba Triste," one of the most beautiful pieces of music ever recorded.

That helped but only until the song ended. Then came a bunch of public-service announcements and I started to feel human again.

In the early-morning hours, crossing from the Palisades into Brentwood, not a pleasant sensation.

6

Robin had activated the alarm. I switched off, rearmed, took off my shoes, and padded to the bedroom.

She was curled up under the covers. I went into the kitchen, thought about a body without face or hands, and filled a glass with tap water.

A high-pitched peep issued from the utility room.

Blanche, our little blond French bulldog, greeting me from her crate.

We leave the door ajar but she never pushes it open. Well trained, we congratulate ourselves. But I've always suspected she likes the privilege of us tending to her in the morning, extending a formal invitation to greet the day.

She looked comfortable enough, now, a rotund sausage of honey-colored fur topped by an oversized, knobby head. One eye shut, the other cocked open. I reached in and petted her. She purred, let loose several glorious farts, did that smiling thing of hers, yawned, curled her tongue, and extended a paw. When I took it, she licked my hand and studied me with a single, soft brown eye.

"Need something, cutie?"

She cyclops-stared at me. *You're the one with needs, buster.*

I rubbed behind her ears. She stretched and fell back asleep.

Standing at the sink and drinking water, I couldn't shake the feeling that I'd been comforted.

When I slipped into bed, Robin drew the covers over her head and rubbed my foot with her size sixes.

Two hours later, she was still asleep and I was wide awake. At some point I must've slipped under, because I woke at eight, feeling as if I'd been tossed in a clothes dryer.

No one on the other side of the bed. The shower was running. Stripping naked, I stepped into the bathroom. Blanche lay on a mat, chewing a jerky stick. The shower stall was coated with fog, reducing Robin to shifting flits of bronze skin. She was singing, not loud enough for me to make out the words or the tune.

I drew a smiley face in the fog. She opened the door, drew me in. Soaping me up, she resumed her tune. "Whistle While You Work."

Garbed and clean, we sat at the kitchen table drinking coffee and eating toast while Blanche continued to erode her jerky.

Despite the shower, I'd decided to run and was dressed for it. Robin, ready to finish up an archtop guitar for a jazz great, wore her shop uniform: black tee, blue overalls, red Keds. Snips of auburn curls restrained by a bandanna had come loose, endowing her with a halo.

"When did you get in, hon?"

"Around one thirty."

"Didn't hear a thing." She nibbled crust, raised her mug with one hand, let the other land softly on the back of my neck.

I said, "You were out solid."

She tickled the spot where hair met nape. "Complicated case?"

"Complicated and nasty."

"Ah."

"How much do you want to know?"

"As much as you want to tell me."

Sounding like she meant it. Once upon a time how much I disclosed had been an issue. My protectiveness, her need to be taken seriously.

All that resolved, now. As far as I could see.

I decided to keep it sketchy. Ended up telling her everything.

She said, "Poor man. How do you go about identifying a victim like that?"

"Check the missing persons files, something unusual in the autopsy could help. If none of that works out, maybe the media. But even without an I.D., there's already a person of interest. Your basic hostile loner living next door."

"Scary guy?"

"All we've heard so far is surliness. He works at home, rarely emerges, doesn't answer when spoken to."

"Works at what?"

"Comic-book artist."

She fiddled with her toast. "What's his name?"

"Trevor Bitt."

"'Mr. Backwards.'"

"You know him?"

"I know his work," she said. "My misspent youth. San Luis was even more conservative back then. Retired military, people working at the prison, small ranchers, blue-collar guys like my dad."

I said, "You had a counterculture phase I never knew about?"

She grinned. "More like I tried to please everyone. I got decent grades, didn't talk back to my parents, spent hours in Dad's shop learning to work with wood, zipped my lip to avoid blowups with Mom. At the same time, I was part of an outsider group in school. We called ourselves the Creative Cult—no snickers, please."

"God forbid."

"God and *me,* darling. We were an artsy bunch of twits, did our share of weed, a few of the more daring souls got into heavier stuff— some of *them* ended up *in* the prison."

"Rebels with a minor cause."

"That's giving too much credit. We were pretentious nerds pretending to buck authority. So when it came to music and art, the deeper underground, the better, and a big part of that was alternative comix. Crumb, the Hernandez brothers, Peter Bagge, *and* Trevor Bitt. He used to self-publish these pulpy little books that the first head shop in town carried. Mr. Backwards was his main character. Big body, small head, lecherously popping eyes, hairy hands shaped like this."

She formed claws.

"Good-looking guy," I said.

"Real Adonis. The main gag was that his head faced the opposite direction from his body, like someone had stitched him together the wrong way. As a result, he was always bumping into things."

She rolled her eyes. "Bumping into people. Specifically their genitals."

I said, "Convenient disability."

"'Oops, apologies, ma-*damme.* Well, hmm, er, I *say,* ma-*damme,* as long as we've ahem united our tantric *forces,* why don't we *con*summate . . .'"

I laughed.

"Funny stuff," she said. "Except when Mr. B happened to bump into his daughter. Or his mother. Or his grandmother."

"Oh."

"Über-creepy, Alex, and Bitt being so skillful as an artist heightened whatever reaction he was after, be it laughter or nausea. The boys in the group thought it was hilarious and rolled around like insane monkeys. The girls thought it was sick and tried to get the boys to stop reading Bitt. It caused a split, one reason we fell apart. But mostly, we disbanded because of short attention spans."

She put down her toast. "Bitt lives in the Palisades, now? Who'da thunk."

"In a two-story Tudor."

"Next you're going to tell me he drives a minivan."

"Pickup truck." I described the house and the landscaping.

She said, "That does sound pretty hostile."

"Did his cartoons get violent as well as sexual?"

"They were always about violence. Mr. Backwards liked to explode things, bumping into detonators, nuclear switches, switches for power saws. Bitt constructed these meticulously detailed Rube Goldberg–type scenes. Oversized rats escaping from feral cats knocking over lamps that fell into vats of oil and set off huge fires. Exploding bodies, mushroom clouds—lots of mushroom clouds. The stories usually ended up with massive pools of blood, heaps of organs, detached limbs—"

She put down the toast. "Oh, my. Wouldn't that be something. All the time we thought Bitt was satirizing and he was sick?"

I'd just showered a second time and stepped into my office when Milo called.

"Get any sleep?"

"Plenty. How'd the canvass go?"

He said, "It didn't. No one knows anything about anything. Like Felice said, this is *not* a neighborhood where they throw block parties. Only four houses have CC systems and one's bogus, dummy cameras mounted as 'deterrents.' The other three are operative and the citizens were happy to let us view the feeds but two had cameras trained tight on front doors and no view of the street. Which is kind of counterproductive but I got a clear sense no one expected bad stuff to happen on Evada."

"How'd they take to the news?"

"Appropriately worried. Not that it led to any decent information, everyone just wants promises we'll up patrol. The one camera with a long view was an antique and poorly maintained, the images are black and white and grainy, all you can make out is a blur when something passes by. During the time the Corvins were gone, nothing that looks like a person appears but three vehicles do show up. The first travels away from the Corvins' house at six sixteen, so that's the family leaving. Another circles the cul-de-sac and leaves without stopping, got to be someone who was lost and entered the dead end. The interesting one arrives fifteen minutes after the Corvins depart and you don't see anything else until a blur in the opposite direction appears sixty-eight minutes later. So the timing's right but I've got no clue about make or model, can't even prove it's the same wheels coming and going, for all I know one person parked out of view and another left later. I was hoping for enhancement but our video techie says no dice, all he can do is estimate size. Larger than a compact, smaller than a big SUV. So much for technology."

"Did you get to Bitt?"

"Not yet. His truck's still there but he didn't answer my ring. I didn't question his neighbors about him specifically because I've got nothing on him and the last thing I need is the peasants converging with torches and pitchforks. I did inquire about neighbor disputes in general and got the usual petty stuff: dog poop in flower beds, garbage cans left out too long. But no festering feuds. I extended the canvass to adjacent streets, Sean's still working but so far nada."

I said, "I learned a few things about Bitt." I summed up Robin's description of the books.

"Blood and guts and incest," he said. "Okay, I definitely wanna meet this prince. Wouldn't mind having you here when I give him a second try."

"I should be free by one."

"Then one it'll be."

CHAPTER

7

My phone conference ended early; a couple of lawyers working a contentious custody case finally serious about "emotional resolution for the sake of the children."

I called the judge and told her.

She said, "They can say that but the real reason's both clients are running out of money."

"Whatever works."

"What works for me is getting idiots off my docket."

I hung up and called Milo. "I can come now."

He said, "A sliver of hope on a highly flawed day."

Daylight was kind to Evada Lane, flowers and grass jewel-toned, tree shadows prettily dappled. Despite the yellow tape, the Corvin house looked jarringly benign. No more cops guarding the property, just Milo, sitting in his unmarked.

He got out and we walked to Trevor Bitt's house. This garden gate was seven feet of black-painted metal.

Milo said, "Exactly."

We climbed three steps to an oak door that looked hand-hewn. Instead of a peephole, a small sliding door caged by a grid of wrought iron.

Milo rang the bell. Knocked. Rang a dozen more times. Knocked harder.

Just as we'd turned to leave, the little door slid open and a brown eye surrounded by pale skin filled the rectangle of space.

"Mr. Bitt?"

No answer.

Milo flashed his badge.

The eye stared, unblinking.

"Could you please open the door, sir. We'd like a few words."

Nothing.

"Sir—"

A deep voice said, "Words about what?"

"There's been a situation—a crime was committed at one of your neighbors'."

No response.

Milo said, "A serious crime, Mr. Bitt. We're talking to everyone on the block."

Silence.

"Mr. Bitt—"

"Not interested."

"It would be easier, sir, if you opened the door."

"For you."

"Sir, there's no reason for you to obstruct us."

"This isn't obstruction. It's privacy." The tiny door slid shut.

Milo rang the bell another dozen times. His face was flushed. "No curiosity about what kind of crime, which neighbor. Maybe because he already knows."

We returned to the sidewalk. He pulled out his phone. "This is gonna be a total waste of time, but."

He got Deputy D.A. John Nguyen on the other end, described

the situation, asked if there could be grounds for a warrant. I couldn't hear Nguyen's brief reply but Milo's expression said it all.

He turned and stared at Bitt's Tudor. Daylight wasn't kind to the spiky plants. More menacing in full color.

Milo said, "Guy's an idiot, all this is gonna do is make me dig deeper on him." He strode back to his car and got behind the wheel. Upgraded sedan, equipped with a nifty new touchscreen that he began working.

But just as with the CCTV, technology can only carry you so far. Nothing on Trevor Bitt in the LAPD database, NCIC, the state sex offender file, or a national database operated privately.

Sitting in the passenger seat, I'd pulled up an image gallery of Bitt's cartoons.

Dope, nudity, gore, taboos abandoned with a ferocity that some-times seemed forced.

Mr. Backwards was a hirsute grotesque pinhead, favoring floral shirts, beads, sandals, and baggy bell-bottoms whose roominess failed to conceal frequent erections of unlikely dimensions.

When he collided with people, one eye winked and popped and drool dribbled from his slack mouth, a secretion often followed by copious productions of other body fluids.

All in all, a creepy mixture of slapstick and threat. Like the uncle you hope doesn't show up at reunions.

Photos of Trevor Bitt showed him as anything but unconven-tional.

Tall, thin, and narrow-shouldered, the cartoonist wore his hair neatly trimmed and left-parted. The most recent shot was a decade old, Bitt looking like a white-haired executive as he signed books at Comic-Con International in San Diego. Sitting primly, reading glasses perched on his nose, surrounded by fans, some of whom wore hand-sewn Mr. Backwards costumes complete with crude, leering masks. A huge blowup of the character's slavering countenance hung on the wall.

In contrast with the ecstatic faces of fans who'd avoided masks, the object of their idolatry looked as if he'd just passed a kidney stone.

Painfully shy? Social contact as torture? That could explain Bitt's lifestyle, maybe even his refusal to cooperate with Milo. On the other hand, he had spent decades creating twisted images and dialogue and expressed no curiosity about a crime next door.

Because he already knows?

Milo logged off. "Not even a misdemeanor. Uncooperative bastard."

I showed him the pictures. He scrolled through quickly. "Depressed-looking mope. That fit with what happened over there?" Eyeing the Corvin house.

"You know what I'm going to say, Big Guy."

"Yeah, yeah, insufficient data to diagnose." He called Binchy, put the phone on speaker.

"Hey, Loot, wrapping up. Only thing I got is a lady two blocks away who saw a truck driving by around eight, eight thirty p.m. She was burgled last year, claims she has her eyes peeled now, but that's probably not true because she couldn't be pinned down on the time, the make, or the model. She did say it was moving 'suspiciously slow.' Like casing the neighborhood. She meant to call it in but forgot."

"Eyes peeled but it slips her mind?" said Milo.

"She's around ninety and wanted to know if the department keeps a file on paranormal phenomena and when I said not to my knowledge she gave me a look like I was hiding something. Then she said her street was a target for 'extraterrestials' because the closer to the ocean, the easier it is for their ships to land."

I said, "Pity the poor folk of Malibu."

Binchy said, "That the doc?"

"Hi, Sean."

Milo said, "Perfect witness, huh? Now you're gonna tell me she wears Coke-bottle glasses."

"Actually, Loot . . ."

"Great. Guess what, Sean, eight p.m. matches the one vehicle that looks interesting."

"Wow," said Binchy. "It also fits with her street not being a dead end like most of the others. Take it north four blocks and you're back on Sunset, so it would be a good entry and exit route."

Milo said, "If you're landing a spaceship, who cares? She's definite about seeing a truck?"

"So she says."

"The weird neighbor drives an old Ram and he just refused to open his door and talk to me. I'm gonna send you a picture and see if it jogs Ms. E.T.'s memory."

He phone-snapped Bitt's Ram, sent the image, and paced the sidewalk.

Binchy called back. "She says maybe. Honestly, Loot, I don't think she has any idea."

"Honesty is a cruel mistress, Sean."

CHAPTER

8

I drove home, walked out to Robin's studio, told her about Bitt's refusal to talk.

She said, "I'm not surprised. Wouldn't expect him to be social."

"Do you know anyone who had a personal relationship with him?"

"Sorry, no." She wiped sawdust from her hands. Unscrewing a jar of jerky, she gave Blanche a stick, filled two cups with coffee and handed me one.

Two sips and her brown eyes got huge. "Maybe I *do* know someone, baby. Remember when I made that Danelectro copy for Iggy Smirch? I think he might've used Bitt's art for at least one album cover."

I said, "Albums, there's a quaint concept."

She played with her iPad. "Here we go, *Karl Marx's Toilet*. This is pretty representative of Bitt's art when he wasn't doing Mr. Backwards."

Black-and-white cityscape. A solitary figure walking a dingy alley shaded by skyscrapers. Strange oily sheen on the buildings. A closer look revealed them to be monumental piles of viscera.

"Gross but he's talented, no? Let me try to reach Iggy." She crossed to her desk in the corner, rolled her pre-computer manual Rolodex, shook her head. "Sorry, hon, it's been eons. I'm not even sure he's alive."

She worked her phone. "Google says he is . . . seventy-four years old . . . hasn't recorded in years—let me make a few calls."

She tried musicians, agents, managers, creating a telephonic chain that finally led her to a possible home number for Isaac "Iggy Smirch" Birnbaum.

The last link was a retired A&R man living in Scottsdale. "Ig? He's right there by you, Sherman Oaks. Tell him he still owes me for lunch."

The former icon picked up.

"Iggy, this is Robin Castagna."

"Who?"

"You probably don't remember me, I built you a—"

"*Who* are you?"

"A luthier. I built you a Danelectro replica with four pickups—"

"Oh, yeah, sure, that one . . . oh, *yeah,* the cutie with the power tools. Yeah, yeah, that was a great ax . . . that's you? The little curvy one with the magic hands? You feel like building me something else?"

"Sure."

"Nope," said Iggy Smirch. "I don't play any axes anymore anywhere for anyone and I don't want anything built, too much shit's piled up. But I do remember *you* because you were a real . . . pretty lady."

"Thank you."

"You're welcome. So to what do I owe?"

She began explaining.

He broke in. "You hooked up with a cop-shrink—was he with you when we met?"

"He was."

"Oh, yeah, you had that place in the Glen. I remember wondering how you could afford it. So, what, you still there?"

"We are."

"You and a shrink," he said. "Happy situation?"

"It is."

"Robin . . ."

"Castagna."

"Robin Castagna, go now—listen, didn't mean to diss the Dano, my not playing it. I dug it, I gigged with it for years, then I gave it to one of my granddaughters, she's a shredder, thinks I suck and Steve Vai rules and those pickups you stuck on it can do some interesting things when they're stressed out . . . a shrink, huh? The Glen. Talk about karma, I happen to be in close proximity to you, just gave a lecture at the U. Art as Constructive Falsehood, some dingbat professor thinking she's cutting-edge, the students look like they're still in diapers. I told them to ignore any bullshit she slings, fuck art and music, go get normal jobs, be responsible citizens. Dingbat gets all pizza-eyed, the kids look like they suddenly *need* diapers."

Robin said, "Sage advice, Ig."

"So," he said. "You want to talk about Bitt. He's a human crap-hole. You're still into him, huh? Not the crap-hole, the shrink. It's for him you're asking."

"True love, Ig."

"That's the way I felt about the fifth wife but five wasn't the charm, either."

"Can I put Alex on the phone?"

"Alex. He's got a name—nah, stay put, I'll come over. It's on my way home and I'm already walking to the parking lot. Only reason I did the speech in the first place is they gave me free parking. Back when I was a student I couldn't catch a break."

"You went to the U.?"

"Don't sound so shocked. B.A. in chemistry, cum laude. That's how I started, working my way playing loud garbage to make tuition and rent, who knew it would turn into a longtime gig? Refresh me on your address."

Fourteen minutes later, a black Ferrari F430 coupe roared to a stop in front of the house. It took the driver a while to extricate himself from the low-slung speedster, and when he finally succeeded he was wincing.

Back in his icon days, Iggy Smirch's stage outfit had consisted of black leather pants, red platform shoes, and a bare chest, the better to showcase a no-fat torso.

The pants and shoes were still in place but his chest had pigeoned and was cloaked by a black V-necked sweater.

Small man, but for the thoracic bulge, still spare, with a full thatch of dyed-black hair crowning an oversized head. Fat's a great wrinkle filler and even in youth, Iggy's face had been bony and seamed. Now it was a crumpled paper bag, brown eyes reduced to a couple of grease stains on the sun-browned surface.

He moved with a slight limp, massaged his chest, hugged and kissed Robin. Both gestures lasted a smidge too long and when he pulled away one hand lingered near her ass.

She inched away gracefully and said, "Ig, this is Alex Delaware."

Frail fingers shook my hand. "Got the trophy chick the first time around, huh?" Back to Robin. "So, what, he gives you psychological input, that's why you stay with him?"

"Something like that, Ig. C'mon in." She began climbing the stairs to the terrace that leads to the entrance.

Iggy Smirch watched the sway of her rear, then followed slowly, gripping the handrail. "Psychology doctor gets and keeps the trophy. I should've stayed in school."

◆

Once inside, he encountered Blanche sitting by the door and froze. "What is that, a midget pit bull?"

"French bulldog."

"It bites?"

Robin said, "No, Ig. See, she's smiling at you."

"It's the smiling ones you need to watch out for, she should be an agent. Nice place. Let's see that studio of yours. I'm thinking I remember it, be nice to verify I'm not losing it totally. Also, I could use a drink of water."

Easy walk through the house but he began wheezing.

"COPD, smoking," he said, as if used to explaining. "You play you pay."

We made it to the rear door, stepped down to the garden.

"Hey, nice fish. Yeah, yeah, now I remember. Look at that, they got bigger."

Inspecting the work on Robin's bench, he lifted the archtop. "Nice, don't have the finger strength for acoustic . . . yeah, it's all coming back—listen, would you mind if the dog stays a distance? I'm phobic."

"Sure, Ig." Robin motioned Blanche to a far corner, petted her, whispered something. Blanche purred and settled.

"What'd you just tell her, the old guy's nuts? Not compared with Bitt, he was the poster boy for way-out-there."

I said, "How so?"

"Why you so interested in him, Dr. Alex? I Googled you on the way over. No cop stuff. No website or Facebook, either. Do you actually do any work or are we talking trust fund?"

Robin said, "Ig, he works *too* hard. He doesn't advertise because people figure out a way to find him."

"That so . . . the only thing I *did* find was you were once a kiddie shrink, worked at the children's hospital. I love that place, had a grandkid, they fixed his heart, I gave them money." His hands clenched. "Are you telling me Bitt did something to a kid?"

I said, "Nothing like that."

"Because his art's pretty twisted. Rape, incest, everything's a fucking joke."

"This has nothing to do with children."

"What, then? Why're you interested in him?"

"Sorry, can't say."

"You're the fucking CIA?"

"A crime took place last night," I said. "There's no evidence Bitt's done anything wrong, but his name came up in the investigation. I wish I could say more but I can't. Robin said you might be able to fill me in about him."

Iggy Smirch massaged his chest and exhibited a mouth full of too-big dentures. "Don't mean to give you grief, just naturally curious. An investigation, huh? Obviously we're talking *something* criminal. Fine, I'll tell you what I know about him, I'm a strict law-and-order guy."

Limping to the couch, he sat and eyed Blanche. She kept her back to him; finely honed intuition. "I did one album cover with him on the recommendation of my producer. I wasn't shown all his work—not the twisted stuff—and was blown away by his talent. First time I met him was at a restaurant—Duke's in West Hollywood. He doodled on a napkin, ended up making a copy of the *Mona Lisa,* total masterpiece. I wish I'd kept it but it had sauce on it. So no question about his talent, but working with him ended up being a serious case of No Fun."

"Unreliable?"

"Reliably a pain in the *ass,*" he said. "The album was a concept. Communism, capitalism, vegetarianism—any ism—is a load of crap. I explained it to Bitt. He listened, said nothing, told me he'd do it for the right amount of money paid in advance. I asked him if he had ideas. He said, 'That's all I have.' Meanwhile, he's doodling, not even looking at the napkin. The fee he asked for was more than twice as much as we'd paid other artists and the one hundred percent advance was out of line, we'd always done half up front, half on delivery. But when I saw that napkin, I said go for it. He's drawing the *Mona* fucking *Lisa* while he's eating. A genius, like Giger. I dug Giger, but we already used him a bunch, it was time for something new. I paid Bitt right then and there. Tried to call him a few days later with ideas of my own, he never picked up. We kept trying to contact him. Nothing. Meanwhile the deadline's approaching, everything else is in place and no fucking cover."

I said, "He held things up."

"No," said Smirch. "That's the thing, he stuck to the deadline. Showed up exactly on the due day, carrying a big portfolio. Inside is the drawing in a plastic jacket. He takes it out, drops it on the producer's desk, and starts to walk out."

He threw up his hands. "It was nothing like what we talked about. Producer says so, Bitt stops walking, stands there, doesn't make eye contact. Like a fucking robot. Producer says, 'We discussed it in detail.' Bitt says, 'You talked, I listened.' Then he leaves."

"You used the drawing."

"What choice did we have?" said Iggy Smirch. "Also, it was brilliant. The album sold great."

"You never worked with him again."

"I'm promiscuous by nature, Dr. Alex. Like to shake things up. Giger was the exception because he was a whole different universe." A glance at Robin. She was inspecting the back of a nineteenth-century Martin guitar sent for repair by a Taiwanese collector.

I said, "You'd have switched artists, anyway."

Iggy Smirch said, "That's the truth, Dr. A, even if Bitt was as harmless as cornflakes."

"You think he's dangerous."

"You don't?" He smiled. "Don't bother answering, I get it. Next you're going to ask me did I ever see him do anything scary. Not really, but there was something going on in that brain of his. Like he was pressure-cooking. You'd talk, he wouldn't answer. Quiet, but not in a Zen way, more like a latent volcano. Then again, I spent maybe two hours with him, total."

"The producer who referred you," I said. "Would he know more?"

"Lanny Joseph," he said. "He might, if he has a working brain. He's even older than me, walking fucking fossil. Last I heard, he retired to Arizona. Or Florida. Or . . . somewhere . . . hold on."

Out came a phone in a black glitter case printed with red skulls. "Gift of the shredder grandbaby. I prefer Gucci but don't want to hurt her feelings." He scrolled, speed-dialed, spoke to someone named Oswald.

"Looking for Lanny Joe, he still breathing? . . . well, that's good to hear. Do you know if he's compos mentis—that's Latin for has his shit together, Oz . . . ha, yeah, I know, man, yeah we were all a little distracted back then . . . ha . . . so where's Lanny's crib nowadays? . . . no, we're all square on money, Oz, I just want to talk to him about a mutual friend, got his number? Okay, thanks, man."

He hung up and read off seven digits from memory. "Florida, Fort Myers Beach."

I copied and thanked him.

He turned to Robin. "What is that, an old Lyon and Healy?"

"New York Martin."

"What year?"

"Eighteen thirty-five."

"Almost as old as me—that an ivory bridge?"

"It is, Ig."

"Good, fucking elephants step on people, who needs 'em—hey, want to build me another ax?"

"You're getting back into playing, Ig?"

"Not a chance, baby. Give me an excuse to see more of you."

She walked Smirch back to his car, guiding his now quivering elbow with her hand and giving him his biggest thrill of the day.

I went to my office and phoned Lanny Joseph in Florida. A woman with a thick Cuban accent asked who I was.

"A friend of Iggy Smirch."

"Okay," she said. "Abou' wha'?"

"Trevor Bitt."

"He also a musicia'?"

"An artist."

"Me, too," she said. "Hol' on, I see."

Dead air for several minutes before a low, congested voice said, "This is Lanny, who're you?"

I began to explain.

He said, "Iggy. My favorite fascist. He's finally seeing a shrink? Good idea, what does it have to do with me? I was in the middle of looking for dolphins, they jump around this time of day."

I repeated the recitation. Lanny Joseph broke in again. "LAPD? One Adam Twelve, got a call at Lexington and Fifth, heh heh. Bitt did something bad?"

"We're just trying to learn about him."

"Wouldn't surprise me, he's messed up. The art he used to make. Very sick stuff."

"Used to," I said. "He's retired?"

"Far as I know, he quit," said Lanny Joseph. "Easy for him, big-time family money."

"Where's his family from?"

"Couldn't tell you. Iggy tell you about *Karl Marx's Toilet*?"

"Bitt got paid more than anyone else."

"A lot more. Including Giger, who everybody wanted. He got more than when we shelled out big bucks to use a photo of a freakin' Hieronymus *Bosch* painting owned by some dude in Germany. That one we used for *Exit to Oblivion*, I'm talking serious money but Bitt got more. He freakin' robbed us, then he delivered something totally off the rails. We used it because we had a deadline. When I found out he quit, I said lucky for the rest of the world."

"How'd you find out?"

"Couldn't tell you, Doc . . . someone must've let me know . . . oh, yeah, guy I knew, produced Tommyrot, they wanted to use Bitt because *Karl* sold so good. He found out Bitt quit, called me complaining, like it was my fault. Wanted me to try to talk Bitt into it, like I'd have anything to do with that psychotic ass-wipe. Why're the cops after him? Why do they have a shrink on it, because he's nuts?"

"Sorry, can't get into details."

"Forget I asked, who cares," said Joseph. "Curiosity kills non-hip cats. So Iggy told you I found Bitt for him, huh? He's blaming me?"

"Not at all," I said. "I asked him how he knew Bitt and—"

"What's your connection to Iggy?"

"My girlfriend built him a guitar."

"Girlfriend," he said. "The little gorgeous one with the studio up in the hills?"

"That's her."

"That's your girlfriend." He whistled. "Iggy liked her."

"How'd you come to know Bitt?"

"Same old story," said Joseph. "A chick."

"Which chick?"

"Bitt's girlfriend, intellectual type, I met her at a benefit for something, couldn't tell you."

"Here in L.A.?"

"San Francisco, I was up there a lot, producing a bunch of bands, renting a houseboat in Sausalito, going to parties. Like this benefit. For something . . . the usual boring shit, I spot this hot chick, move in, drop a bunch of names, I'm thinking it's going good. Then all of a sudden this guy materializes, never saw him coming, all of a sudden he's just *there*. Like the fog. Standing between me and the chick, smoking a blunt but wearing a suit and tie. He gives the chick a death-ray look, she splits. Then he gives *me* the look. I say who are you? He says, 'The Rembrandt of this century,' and walks away. I ask someone who is that asshole, they tell me. I knew his name, had seen his stuff at this exhibit of comix guys in some fancy gallery, I didn't figure he'd look like a CEO. Few months later, the *Karl* cover comes up, Ig was in a dark place, I'm thinking Bitt could be perfect. I get Bitt's number from someone, couldn't tell you, don't ask. The rest is what Ig told you. It was a crazy time, once some guys used to be in Zappa's band show up at Gold Star Studios and . . ."

I listened to several minutes of free-form reminiscence until Lanny Joseph caught his breath and said, "End of story."

"Anything else you can tell me about Bitt?"

"Guy could draw like crazy but that was his only good point. Hey, there's the dolphins. Ciao."

Internet research on Trevor Bitt revealed a tendency to evoke strong opinions pro and con. It also confirmed Lanny Joseph's rich-boy tag.

The cartoonist's wealth had descended from a great-great-grandfather, a New York financier and Rockefeller associate named Silas Bitt. No mention of professional accomplishments by any other descendants. Maybe the rest of the family had coasted.

I keyworded *silas bitt.* Just the Rockefeller connection so I returned to his great-great-grandson.

Like everything else about the cartoonist, Bitt's wealth sparked polarized judgments: He was either a wastrel tool of the Capitalist Monster or a genius who'd used his good fortune to make ground-breaking art.

I moved on, surfing. Bitt hadn't been active for nearly two decades and all his books were long out of print. Secondhand prices suggested gone *and* forgotten.

Theories explaining his dropping out included drug addiction—heroin/crack/meth/take your pick—or a prolonged psychiatric hospitalization for schizophrenia/manic depression/Vincent van Gogh syndrome, whatever that was, or a debilitating physical disease (Huntington's chorea/mad cow), or simply "burnout."

All of that wisdom offered by the kind of people who spout off anonymously online.

Nothing in Bitt's history came close to suggesting criminality.

Calling Milo with bad news seemed inconsiderate.

Better a twenty-four-karat silence.

Three days later, Milo phoned.

"No I.D. yet on my John Doe, just heard from the pathologist. Poor guy's brain was full of bird shot and wadding and like we figured the amputations were postmortem, probably a motorized saw, best guess a band or a jig. His arteries weren't great but no impending heart attack. But he did have some bad luck years before being killed: spleen and left kidney gone, coupla old breaks in his left femur, same for his left collarbone and four ribs."

I said, "Car crash?"

"Coroner said it could be any sort of collision."

"Would the leg breaks have caused a limp?"

"Likely," he said.

"Any estimate when the injuries took place?"

"Probably within the last ten years. Age estimate on the guy is between fifty and sixty, so we're not talking college football."

I said, "Could be something work-related. A truck driver, heavy machinery."

"Or just an unlucky fellow who tumbled down some stairs."

"Fifty to sixty puts him in Trevor Bitt's age range."

"An old pal? Sure, why not, now let's prove it. Bottom line: No magic from the crypt but maybe the injury will be helpful if I go to the media."

"If, not when?"

"Yeah, it's probably gonna end up that way," he said. "But I'm spending today going over the missing persons files again, maybe something'll jump out and I can avoid a ton of bullshit tips."

I said, "John Doe didn't lead a charmed life but Bitt did. Inherited wealth that goes way back."

I filled him in on the input from Iggy Smirch and Lanny Joseph.

He said, "Trust-fund baby. That could explain the snotty attitude. Got it again this morning. He cracked his door and stared at me like I was pond scum. After I finished my spiel, he turned his back on me and closed the damn thing. Days like this, I wish I was living in a police state."

I said, "You and Kim Jong busting down doors."

He laughed. "Rich kid retires, moves to the Palisades, it fits. But I still can't find anything nasty in his background. No dirt on Chet Corvin, either, other than some eye-rolling when I brought him up."

"With who?"

"His secretary. I went over to his office, yesterday. Door sign says it's the company's West Coast ancillary site. That translates to two rooms in a so-so building on the south side of Beverly Hills. Just Corvin and the secretary, uptight lady in her seventies. Looked to me like a mail drop, maybe something that qualifies the company to operate in California. She verified what Chet told us, he's on the road a lot. Books his own trips. She wasn't surprised to see me, Chet had told her about the body. In graphic detail. That's when she rolled her eyes. She said it made her sick. I asked who his pals were, work or otherwise. More rolling. 'Wouldn't know, Lieutenant, but I'm sure Chet's popular with *everyone*.'"

"The boss's charm has worn thin."

"I figured great, she can't stand him, won't be protective of him. But when I asked her about anyone with a beef against him, she didn't know of any. Didn't know much period. My sense is she gets paid to warm a seat and take messages. And no, there hadn't been any strange messages or mail for Mr. Corvin during the year and a half she'd worked for him."

I said, "He books his own travel. Maybe to keep the details private."

"Women in every port, pissed-off husbands? I thought about that but why not target Corvin directly? Why a handless John Doe in the guy's den?"

"Anything on John Doe's clothes? They looked pretty generic to me."

"That's 'cause they are," he said. "The shoes are Nike, everything else is Chinese-made, carried by discount chains and outlets all over the country."

"So probably not a country-club golf buddy of Chet's," I said. "Or the descendant of a Rockefeller crony."

"Unless he's one of those eccentric moneybags who lives on the cheap—hey, maybe he *is* one of ol' *Trevor's* cousins and the Bitts have been inbreeding too long. Where do they hale from?"

"The original money got made in New York."

"Make it there, you can make it anywhere. Okay, I'll see what I can find about this clan. If I learn there's some big-time inheritance dispute at play and Cousin Itt with a limp hasn't been heard from, you're my new best friend."

"New?" I said.

"Fine, *re*-newed. We will reach a new level, like one of those relationship encounter weekends. Except instead of 'Kumbaya' and meditation, I'll buy dinner. You, Robin, the pooch. I'll even spring for fish food."

◆

I did my own search. Like a lot of old-wealth recipients, the Bitts appeared to live invisibly.

A handful of people with the surname showed up on the Internet but none were the cartoonist's kin. I was logging off when my service called, a longtime operator named Lenore.

"Dr. Delaware, I have a Mr. Corvin on the line. He wouldn't say about what. I asked him to leave his number, he got kind of pushy, said you'd know what it's about. I asked if it was an emergency, he said it was. But I don't think it was—not that I'm a psychologist."

"None of the usual anxiety," I said.

"Just the opposite, Doctor. Smooth. To tell the truth, he sounds like he wants to sell you something. I've got him on hold, if you want me to tell him you're unavailable . . ."

"No, I'll talk to him. Thanks for being cautious, Lenore."

"Always," she said.

Click.

"This is Dr. Delaware."

"Hey, Doc, Chet. How's everything going?"

"With the investigation?"

"That. In general. Figure of speech. Looked you up, your name's Alexander, I thought it was Alan. Anyway, I can use you. My daughter can."

"Chelsea's having problems."

"I'll tell you what's going on: We've been home since Wednesday, that went fine. But last night I heard her get up, looked at the clock, it was three a.m. Then I hear her go down the stairs, fine, she wants a drink of water. *Then* the front door shuts and I'm thinking what-the? I go outside and see her walking around. Not in her p.j.'s, dressed like she's going somewhere, except no shoes. When I told her to go back inside, she gave me one of those looks."

"What kind of look?"

"You know," he said.

I waited.

Chet Corvin said, "What you saw, Alex. Defiant. I said, 'This is ridiculous, come back inside.' She gave me the look and went back inside."

"Did she seem to be sleepwalking?"

"You're the expert, Doc. But I'd have to say no, her eyes were open and it wasn't like she was on a different planet. More like daring me. *Defiant.*"

"Daring you to do what?"

"Maybe punish her? I don't know, was hoping you could tell me. How many times have you seen this kind of thing?"

"Kids leaving the house?"

"With clothes but no shoes," he said. "Three in the morning. You think it's some kind of PTSD?"

"Did she have her purse with her?" I said. "Her phone?"

"Nope, just her walking."

"Walking where?"

"In the cul-de-sac, back and forth."

"How far?"

"Not far, like . . . twenty feet in one way, then she turns around, then she does the whole thing all over again."

"You watched her."

"Well, yeah, sure, Alex, I wanted to know what was going on. When can you see her? This is something I *will* bill to that victims' fund."

I said, "I can refer you but I can't treat Chelsea."

"What? Why?"

"I'm already consulting on the investigation and need to communicate with the police. So I can't offer confidentiality."

"We don't care about keeping secrets, Alex. You figure her out, tell her what's what so she can snap out of this nonsense. Tell us, also, so we know how to handle her in the future. We all set, then?"

"It won't work, Mr. Corvin. I'm happy to give you a referral."

"Hmm," he said. "You're a pretty willful guy. Thought the therapy game was all about compromise."

It's about lots of things. Including boundaries.

"Would you like a referral?"

"Nah," he said. "I don't want to get involved with someone else. And I really can't see why you won't help us. If it's money, forget the victims' fund, I'll pay you directly."

I said, "It's not money."

"I hear that all the time, Alex, and it usually turns out to be *exactly* about money."

I said nothing.

Chet Corvin said, "Listen, Alex, let's put our heads together and work out a solution. Talk to her once, see if there's anything to worry about. There is, we take it from there. There isn't, no harm, no foul."

I thought about that.

Chet Corvin said, "You still with me, Alex?"

I said, "If Lieutenant Sturgis okays it, I'll see her once."

"You need his permission?"

"I need to avoid conflict of interest."

"Huh. Fine. Where's your office? Your girl wouldn't tell me."

"I'll come to your house. Be easier for Chelsea if it's on her turf."

"Turf," he said. "Like golf. Or gangs." Chuckling. "She's . . . different, you saw it. When can you come over?"

"What's a good time for Chelsea?"

"Alex," he said, "it's not like she needs a personal secretary. Do it any day—today, if you want. After school—she's back around three, make it four to play safe. I won't be there, hitting the road, actually on my way to the airport. That won't matter, she never talks to me anyway."

A hint of sadness. The faintest glimmer that he might have some depth?

Then he said, "I'm glad we're doing this. Now I can put her out of my head."

10

Milo said, "Go for it, you might learn something I can use. But he may not pay you, ol' Chet has a tendency to fudge his financial obligations."

"You found some dirt."

"I convinced a guy at the bank that handles his mortgages to talk to me off the record. Same with the finance company that holds the title to his cars. He doesn't default, he just takes his sweet time, stretching it out until just before default. Notices get sent, calls get made, at the last minute he pays up but ignores the late fees and the penalties and the whole thing starts again. Finance people can't do anything because technically he's satisfied his obligation."

I said, "He plays everyone."

"Like a bad harmonica."

"Any indication of financial problems?"

"That's the thing, not apparently. He's well compensated and Felice's school district job is a nice second income. Between them they pull in close to four fifty K. Mortgage and car payments are a little over five grand a month, which isn't bathwater, but with that income it's not a hardship. Maybe he's got a bad, expensive habit but so far I can't find it."

"So it's a game. He manipulated me, too."

"Only as much as you let him, amigo."

"True," I said. "I figured another look at Chelsea wouldn't hurt. Revisiting the house, now that the initial shock's worn off."

"What do you think's going on with the kid?"

"Could be a sleep disorder, we'll see."

He laughed. "The old reserving-judgment routine. Corvin's right about one thing, she is different."

Evada Lane at four fifteen p.m. was just another dead end. Like most so-called Westside neighborhoods, no pedestrians, not even a stray dog. That left easy pickings for a flock of ravens. The birds had found something in the middle of the street and I had to swerve around them.

Felice Corvin's Lexus sat in the driveway. She answered the door wearing a blue blouse, gray slacks, gray shoes. Staring at me as she wiped her glasses with a square of microfiber.

"Dr. Delaware?"

"Hi. I'm here to see Chelsea."

"You're *what*?"

"Your husband asked me to evaluate her—"

"He *what*?"

I said, "Obviously, you didn't know."

"What exactly did he want you to evaluate?"

"He said last night Chelsea got up and left the house—"

"Unbelievable," said Felice Corvin. "Chelsea's a fitful sleeper, she always has been."

"Does she usually leave the house?"

"Let me tell you, Doctor, if Chet was here more, he'd know about her sleep patterns and wouldn't be wasting your time."

"Sorry for the misunderstanding."

"Sorry you made a trip for nothing." She began to close the door, stopped midway. "Next time speak to me first. Not that there'll be a next time. We're coping just fine."

"Good to hear."

"Maybe not to you," she snapped.

"Pardon?"

"Sorry, that was uncalled for. All I meant was mental health people expect problems. I apologize, Doctor."

"No problem."

I turned to leave.

"Dr. Delaware, if there's a bill for your time, I can write you a check right now."

"No charge."

"Well, that's kind of you and, again, sorry. Any news on the poor man?"

"Not yet."

"Too bad—Doctor, may I ask why you came here for an evaluation rather than make an office appointment?"

"I thought Chelsea might be more comfortable at her home base."

"Yes . . . I suppose I can see that." Icy smile. "Well, it's not necessary to see her here or anywhere else. We're doing fine."

The ravens had migrated to a nearby lawn and jeered as I passed. One of them held something rosy and organic in its beak. The largest member of the gang exerting privilege.

I drove away thinking about what had just happened. Rotten communication fit my view of the Corvins as a quartet of strangers living under the same roof. It also varied from what I usually saw when parents disagreed: mothers seeking help, fathers convinced there's no problem.

There are sensitive dads but Chet Corvin seemed anything but.

I'm putting her out of my head.

Did his call have nothing to do with helping Chelsea? Had he used her—and me—to humiliate his wife?

Chuckling as he drove to the airport?

Children with issues often become marital weapons. When I teach grad students, I call them "blame-guns." Had Chelsea long been her father's heavy artillery?

Chet Corvin would know which of his wife's buttons to push. How better to tag her as a deficient mother than by calling in a psychologist behind her back?

Felice's reaction suggested she'd gotten the message.

Speak to me first.

I supposed I could be selling Corvin short and in his own crude way he was concerned about his daughter. But then why not simply inform Felice? And why insist on me and not another psychologist?

Because another psychologist wasn't a police surrogate and this was all about Corvin thumbing his nose at law enforcement?

A control freak who booked his own travel and jerked creditors around just for the fun of it.

Or did this latest manipulation go beyond that? Was he somehow involved in the murder of the handless man?

Why would Corvin soil his own nest?

On the other hand, if he cared little for family life, why *not*?

As I left the Palisades and crossed into Brentwood, I thought of his other traits: a grandiose, attention-seeking braggart, callous enough to unload gory details on his secretary when they clearly sickened her.

Shallow and cruel enough to describe his daughter as a problem to be disposed of.

Put it all together and you had a tidy description of a high-functioning psychopath. And psychopaths, particularly sadists, often enjoy the aftermath of a crime more than the act.

It's why arsonists show up at four-alarm blazes. Why kidnappers join search parties and child-murderers place teddy bears at memorials.

Was Chet Corvin having a grand time reminiscing about a man with a ravaged head and no hands?

I'd viewed him as the likely target because his personal space had been violated. What if that's exactly what he'd wanted—*talk about a bluff, heh heh heh. Alan. Er, Alex.* Sure, there'd be gore on the hardwood but that could be remedied. A fact Corvin had emphasized early on: *I'm assuming you'll do a thorough cleanup.*

Add to that Felice's reaction at seeing the body—freaking the bitch *out*—and the temporary mess would be outweighed by the big thrill.

And if the brats got a little traumatized, all the better.

Corvin being involved in the murder solved the problem of access: All he needed to do was slip a house key to a sidekick. Ditto the security code, just in case stupid Felice did remember to set the alarm. Alternatively, he could've simply switched the system off after the rest of the family exited the house.

He'd made a point of letting us know that Sunday dinner had been his show. Moving the venue from the usual nearby pizza joint to a restaurant clear across town.

Another brag? Practical, too, because it allowed the confederate plenty of time to drag and position the corpse, tidy up, and leave.

Then, for good measure, divert attention to the asocial weirdo living next door.

Something about these people.

After three-hundred-plus homicides, Milo's instincts were well honed.

I called his office phone.

He said, "Nothing so far on any New York Bitts."

"You going to be there for a while?"

"Just had a snack, doing some paperwork."

"I'm coming over."

"Chelsea told you something juicy?"

"Never got to talk to her," I said.

"So what's up?"

"Don't want to drive distracted, see you in twenty."

11

Milo's closet-sized office sits midway along a coldly lit corridor on the second floor of West L.A. Division. The remainder of the hallway is given over to storage and a couple of interview rooms reeking of anxiety. My friend's meager allotment looks like nothing but punishment, but it's not that simple.

He operates in isolation from every other detective in the building, an arrangement foisted upon him years ago as part of a deal with a corrupt, retiring police chief. The chief had viewed the windowless cell as a final dig at the gay cop who'd forced his hand. Little did he know that Milo welcomed the setup.

Years later, he still dens like a grizzly in a cave, gladly avoiding the din and scrutiny of the big detective room.

His actual job—a lieutenant who gets away from his desk and works—is another oddity. Two subsequent police chiefs bristled at the break in procedure and decided to correct it. Both changed their minds when they learned about his solve rate.

I arrived just after five, got a nod from the civilian clerk in the reception area, bounded up the stairs, and headed for the lone open door. Milo was waiting for me, filling a swivel chair that faced the metal straight-back he'd set up for me. Three feet between our noses. A large greasy pizza box leaned against a wall. The air was warm, close, saturated with garlic. The box was empty. Snack time.

He breathed into his palm, took a stick of chewing gum out of his desk and began chomping. "It bothers you, we can go outside."

I said, "No prob. Got a bunch of theory for you. Can't promise you'll like *that* smell."

He listened, rubbed his eyes, studied the low, perforated ceiling.

"All that," he said, "from a screwed-up appointment."

"More than screwed up," I said. "The more I think about it, the more convinced I am Chet was out to humiliate Felice."

I went on to list the psychopathic symptoms. "Maybe I am over-reaching, but I thought you should know."

He rotated his neck. "You really think he'd be that arrogant? His own damn house."

"If his home life is something he despises, why not? Right from the beginning you felt something was off about the family."

"That was in terms of them being targets, not participants. Which you went along with."

I said nothing.

He said, "Okay, I'll be open to new possibilities. Does that mean you consider Bitt lower-priority?"

"Not necessarily," I said. "I just think Corvin should be looked into."

"Multitasking, yippee," he said. "Looked into how?"

"Cellphone records, his travel schedule."

"That means subpoenas. You know the problem."

"No grounds."

"Not even close." He picked up a pencil, twiddled, laid it back down.

I said, "There's another potential avenue. His wife hates him."

"Hostile spouses and exes, the policeman's boon. You see Felice as approachable?"

"Not yet."

"What, then?"

"Keep Chet in mind and concentrate on I.D.'ing John Doe."

He stood, managed a vertical stretch, hands nearly touching the ceiling. "Not much of a plan."

He walked out of the office.

I said, "Where to?"

"When in doubt, nourish thyself, time for dinner—eh, eh, don't wanna know if you're hungry. Just tag along and pretend."

CHAPTER

12

A week after the handless man's murder, Milo got the department to issue a press release. Middle-aged male found in a "Westside location," missing his spleen and a kidney, "other" evidence of an old injury.

Coverage was rejected by the network TV affiliates, granted twenty seconds on the eleven p.m. news broadcasts of two local stations. The *Times* offered a squib in the online homicide file. Once the story was picked up by a few other sites, the phone began ringing, tips coming from the usual mix of well-intended citizens, pranksters, and a squawking menagerie of conspiracy theorists and other dimwits.

Information in the cyber-age might as well be written with invisible ink. Within twenty-four hours, the tip line had gone dead. Then, on a Tuesday, a single after-spurt caused Milo to phone me.

"Maybe I made Santa's good-boy list, a woman who actually sounds sane described the physical stats and the broken bones down to a T. Her ex-husband, Hal Braun, fifty-four. The accident was a fall during a hike eleven years ago. I'm heading out to see her. You free?"

"You need to ask?"

"I should take you for granted?"

Mary Ellen Braun, fifty-one, lived in Encino and sold handbags at Saks in Beverly Hills. By the time Milo picked me up, he'd done the usual background. Her sole infraction was three years ago, a failure-to-stop traffic citation at the intersection of Gregory and Roxbury.

I said, "A few blocks from Saks, maybe rushing to the job."

"Good work ethic," he said. "I'll take that as a positive." As we walked to his unmarked: "God, I hope she's not a loon."

B.H. was south but he turned toward the Valley.

I said, "She's not working?"

"Home, taking a sick day. I'm guessing she doesn't want to be seen with the cops. There was stress in her voice. I'll take *that* as a positive."

We pulled up to a white, three-story condo building labeled *La Plaza* that spread across four lots on a quiet street west of Balboa and north of Ventura Boulevard. Security cameras, warning signs, and a gated sub-lot offered emotional support. The directory said that *Braun, M. E.* lived in unit twenty-four. A button-push was followed by a whispery "Hold on," a click, and a buzz.

We rode the elevator up two flights, stepped into a red-carpeted hallway, made our way to the sixteenth of at least twice as many black doors.

The woman who answered Milo's gentle-version knock was of medium height with a medium build and medium-brown eyes. Medium-brown hair was cut in an unfussy bob. Stress in her voice but a face rounded by middle age looked composed.

"Lieutenant? Mary Ellen."

"Thanks for seeing us, ma'am. This is Alex Delaware."

Mary Ellen Braun's smile at me lasted as long as the eyeblink that accompanied it. She offered cold fingertips. "Please come in, guys."

Her unit was compact, well kept, with coral-colored couches and a bronze-and-glass coffee table holding muffins and coffee. An open plan allowed a full kitchen view of white cabinets and stainless-steel appliances. Apothecary jars filled with lemons sat on black granite, along with smaller vials of what looked like herb-infused oil.

The three of us sat and Mary Ellen Braun pointed to the muffins. "Please help yourselves."

"Thanks," said Milo.

"Let me pour for you. You, too?"

I'd had my fill of caffeine but said, "Please."

As I sipped minimally, Milo got to work on a chocolate muffin. "Thanks for calling us, Ms. Braun."

"Like I told you, I wasn't sure but I figured I should. Did you bring a picture?"

Milo said, "We didn't, ma'am. A picture wouldn't help."

"Why—oh. You're saying he's . . . disfigured?"

"Afraid so."

"Oh, God," said Mary Ellen Braun. "I shouldn't be shocked. But I am."

"You shouldn't be shocked because . . ."

She sighed. "Hal could be a crazy risk-taker. That's how he got hurt. Hiking by himself in Angeles Crest. He wandered off the trail, like he always did, lost his footing, fell thirty feet and was stuck there, unable to move. He was lucky some hippie-types were looking for wild greens or whatever. They heard him moaning and called for help. He had to be taken out on a stretcher and then airlifted."

I said, "Hiking by himself."

"Always," she said. "I don't like it, period. I know it's uncool to admit it but how many trees can you walk past without going eh?"

I smiled. "Hal disagreed."

"We were different in so many ways. He did his thing and I did mine."

"Were you married at the time of the accident?"

"Just divorced but we were still in contact. Friendly, we stayed that way. We separated twelve years ago, right after our tenth anniversary."

Mary Ellen Braun crossed her legs. "It's a cliché, but we drifted apart. I wasn't adventurous enough for Hal. I knew it and he knew it right from the start. The first time we dated I told him I was a homebody. He said he was fine with that, seemed to be for a while. He made no demands on me and I didn't expect him to change. But eventually . . . you know."

"The differences grew."

Her shoulders rose and fell. "No fights, no drama—no kids, thank God. We weren't able to have any and in the end it simplified matters. So did our money situation. Neither of us had any so we were able to shake hands and walk away."

I said, "Did Hal have a risky job?"

She laughed. "If you call selling shoes risky. We met at Nordstrom, Westside Pavilion. I was junior fashions, he was ladies' footwear. I guess I can understand why he'd want to spice up his life a little."

"What other risks did he take?"

"Biking at night with no headlights. He'd swim in the ocean when there were offshore alerts. *Especially* when there were alerts."

"Courting danger," I said.

"He prided himself on having a method with the riptides. Swimming parallel with the shore and working his way through it. He *loved* to come back and tell me about it. What else . . . all kinds of crazy stuff. Bungee jumping, parasailing, when we could afford it. He even did a skydive but that was way too expensive . . . oh, yeah, that thing on the wire—zip-lining. He even tried rock climbing at one of those gyms with the fake mountains, but couldn't hack it. Too out of shape. Hal didn't exercise regularly or eat well. He was actually a couch potato except when he got it in his head to do one of his adventures. That's what he called them, 'my adventures.'"

She began reaching for a muffin, thought better of it. "I don't usually have these around, try to avoid flour and dairy. Hal could eat four, five at a sitting. He wasn't fat but he was soft. Climbing that wall with the little plastic thingies in it was way beyond him. Personality-wise, he was soft, too. Basically, a sweet guy."

She touched the edge of the coffee table. "Is there a good chance it's him?"

Milo said, "We don't know. So you two stayed friendly."

"Oh, yes. We'd see each other at work, being friendly made life easier," said Mary Ellen Braun. "Sometimes we'd have lunch. I enjoyed that, being friends, no pressure. Then I moved over to Saks and he stayed at Nordstrom."

"Is he still employed there?"

"Oh, no. He left six—make that seven years ago. Moved clear out of the city to Ventura. After he got married the third time."

Milo said, "You're wife number—"

"Two. The first was long before we met, Hal was just out of high school, some girl he knew in Stockton—that's where he's originally from but all his family's gone. Only thing I can tell you is her name was Barbara and she died. Some sort of cancer. Hal didn't like talking about it so I didn't bug him. He'd been single for a long time when we met."

"Who's the third wife?" said Milo.

"Also a Mary, isn't that a hoot?" Her lips turned down. "Mary *Jo*. She's who you should be talking to if it does turn out to be Hal."

"Because—"

"Between Hal and her, there *was* conflict. She was tough on him. He told me."

"Tough, how?"

"He didn't go into details, just told me I was the coolest wife he'd had, Mary Jo wasn't nice to him. This was three years ago, Christmas. I remember because that year I had a little holiday party here, a few work-friends, we did potluck. An hour into it, Hal phoned, which was a total surprise, I hadn't heard from him in a while. He said he was spending Christmas by himself in a bar. I asked him why he wasn't home and he said something along the lines of 'You know. Stuff happens.' Then he told me that I was the coolest wife he'd ever had. I could tell he wanted to get together but I'd moved on, was seeing someone—not anymore, but at the time . . . anyway, I told him if he could find some way to get over without driving under the influence, he was welcome to join the party. He said he might try. But he never showed up. That's the last I heard from him."

"Had he complained about Mary Jo before?"

"A few times," she said. "No details, just that she could be super-critical. When I asked him about what, he changed the subject. I'm not trying to get anyone in trouble but if it is Hal, shouldn't you talk to her?"

Milo said, "We'll definitely look into it, ma'am. Did Mr. Braun do similar work when he moved to Ventura?"

"As far as I know, he stayed in sales, but not in shoes. A store in Old Town, selling olive oil. He sent me a couple of samples."

I pointed to the vials on the counter. "Those?"

"Garlic-infused and jalapeño. I never opened them because I'm not into heavy seasonings. Hal should've known that but that's Hal. Once he's into something, he can't imagine anyone else not seeing the light."

"Can you think of anyone who'd want to hurt him?"

"No one. But I'm not the one to ask, we haven't been in touch for years. Still, when I heard the description on TV, the injuries. . . ." She shook her head. "I really hope it's *not* Hal. Maybe you'll find him right on his couch, snoring. Or off doing one of his adventures."

"Do you have a current number for him?"

"I have his cell from three years ago." She recited from memory. Not in touch but remembering.

"Thanks. Is there anything else you can think of, Ms. Braun?"

"I'm actually *Mrs.* Braun," she said. "Never got into the ms. thing. No, that's it."

"Do you have a photo of Mr. Braun? Also, anything that belonged to him—for DNA."

"I have old photos, somewhere," she said.

"If we could borrow a couple."

"Hold on."

She got up and walked into a short passageway left of the kitchen. Milo was finishing another muffin when she returned with two color snapshots.

"These were taken soon after we got married. Before the whole digital thing. You had to pay Fotomat, so you actually held on to them."

Milo gloved up and took the photos. Both captured the same scene. In one a younger, slimmer ash-blond Mary Ellen Braun stood holding hands with a sandy-haired, moon-faced man. Both wore sunglasses, matching green windbreakers, jeans, and sneakers. In the second, Hal Braun had his arm around his wife's shoulder and her fingertips clasped his waist. The background was pines and mountains so dark they verged on black. The sky was murky gray swirled with white, tipped at the corners with sooty clouds.

"Sequoia," she said. "We went for a weekend, stayed at some lodge, it rained almost the whole time. I did crosswords while Hal did his thing. He came back soaked because of course he wouldn't take an umbrella. He did get me outdoors for these right before we left. Do you need both of them?"

"One's fine, Mrs. Braun." Taking the hand-holding shot and returning the other to her.

"If you could get it back to me," she said.

"We'll make a copy and do that. In terms of a physical object Mr. Braun might have—"

"No, sorry, can't help you there."

I said, "How about the olive oil bottles?"

"Hmm," she said. "Hal did send them to me so I guess he touched them. Unless someone else at the store packed them. Can you get DNA from glass?"

"We can, ma'am," said Milo.

"Well, then sure, I'm never going to use them."

He retrieved the bottles. Brown paper label from *The Olive Branch, Main Street, Ventura, Ca.*

As we walked to the door, Mary Ellen Braun said, "Garlic-infused and jalapeño. Once you know, can you tell me? Either way."

"Absolutely. And if you think of anything else—"

"I won't," she said. "Before you came I tried to come up with anything I knew that could possibly help you. Maybe *she* can clear it up."

Outside, Milo said, "Battle of the Marys." He popped the unmarked's trunk, put the bottles in an evidence bag, and sealed it. Before doing the same with the photo, he studied it again.

"Size and age are right. So's the hair."

I said, "A risk-taker."

"With a mean wife." He laughed. "If we're lucky, Mary Two will be a real Medusa."

13

The car idled as Milo made calls.

Hargis Raymond Braun had an active California driver's license. A ten-year-old brown Jeep had been registered three years ago. Address on Barnett Street in Ventura.

Fifty-one, then, five-ten, one seventy-five, green eyes, the sandy hair self-described as blond. No active wants or warrants but Braun had been arrested for drunk driving eight years ago, no jail time.

Milo said, "Big deal."

I said, "Ain't that the truth. Robin was on jury duty last year. Seven of the twelve people on the panel had DUIs."

Milo said, "It's a miracle any of us are alive. Okay, let's find out if Not-as-Cool Mary's still living there."

The house was a seven-hundred-seventy-nine-square-foot bungalow on a tenth-acre lot on the west side of town. Deeded to Maria Josefina Braun seven years ago, appraised value of two hundred fifty-nine thousand dollars. GPS pinned the location far from the beach, the foothills, Old Town, the Mission of Santa Buenaventura, anywhere scenic. Google photos showed a gray box hemmed by a white picket fence.

Neither of us knew anyone at Ventura PD but a couple of years ago we'd worked a multiple murder case with cops from the neighboring town of Oxnard. Milo phoned the lead detective, a bright, jovial man named Francisco Gonzales.

Gonzales said, "That's the tough part of town but not by L.A. standards. Some gentrification, some gang problems, mostly just working class trying to get by."

Milo thanked him and called the number given by Mary Ellen. Inactive. The reverse directory offered no landline. The woman who answered at the Olive Branch had no idea who Hal Braun was.

Milo said, "Would there be anyone who'd remember?"

"I've been here for five years, we've never had a guy, just gals."

"The Olive Branch. Too peaceful for testosterone, huh?"

"Pardon?"

"Thanks." Click.

He sat back, checked his Timex. "One oh eight. If I drive all the way to the lab, drop off the bottles and the photo, by the time we head north, we're talking a three-hour nightmare coming back and nothing says Mary Two will be home. On the other hand . . ."

I said, "If we leave now and hop on the 101, it's an hour. And if she is there, she'll have Braun's clothing, a toothbrush, maybe medical records that'll match the corpse."

"The other thing," he said, "if she's not there, we can have a late lunch, I'm thinking seafood."

"Consolation prize."

"Tsk," he said. "More like meeting basic needs."

The trip took fifty-four minutes, spurred by Milo's lead foot and livened by his frequent indictment of other drivers. ("Seven out of twelve, huh? There's a drunken asshole for sure.")

Exiting the freeway took us through mixed retail, light industry that was mostly car-related, and plain-wrap apartment buildings. The occasional rash of graffiti but nothing ominous. Single-story houses appeared a couple of blocks later.

Like its neighbors, the home shared by Hargis and Maria Josefina Braun was small, prewar, simply built. No cameras or alarm signs on the block but plenty of security bars. Sidewalk trees were irregularly placed and sized. Many struggled in the drought.

The structure was still gray stucco, the fence still white paint, both showing wear. An empty driveway was cracked; the tar-paper porch roof struggled with gravity. A collapsible metal ramp stretched from the top of three stairs to brown dirt.

Milo toed the ramp. "Maybe our boy's injuries were worse than we thought."

We climbed, setting off a bongo duet on metal. One of two screws holding the bell-push in place was missing and Milo had to fiddle to produce a sound.

Harsh buzzer, intermittent. A female voice said, "Finally," and the door spread open slowly, pulled back by the crook of a blue aluminum cane. The fine-boned hand on the other end of the stick belonged to a luxuriantly coiffed, dark-haired woman in her forties sitting in a manual wheelchair.

Pretty but pallid face. Huge black eyes topped by widely arched tattooed eyebrows. The ink created a look of perpetual surprise. The body below the face was spare and swaddled by a pink sateen house-dress.

As Milo showed her his badge, she wheeled away from us. "I thought you were the meal service."

"Are you Mrs. Braun?"

"Ms.," she said. "Missus is for old ladies." She looked out at the street. "They're late. A lot of time they are."

"Meals on wheels?"

"Like that but from the church, even though I don't go. Not delicious but twice a week I don't have to cook. The stove went out last month, it's been hot outside, no big deal. But sometimes you don't want cold food." She glanced past us, again. "They said any minute. So what do the police want? Another break-in?"

Milo said, "If you're Maria Josefina Braun, we're here about your husband."

"I'm EmJay," she said. "What about Hal?"

"When's the last time you saw him?"

"Like . . . ten, eleven days ago? He packed out for one of his adventures. Why, what happened?"

"May we come in?"

"Hal got in trouble?" Resigned more than anxious.

Milo said, "It's best that we talk inside."

She remained in place, blocking our entry. A third distant look. "Sure, why not?" Patting the cane, she placed it in her lap and wheeled free of the doorway.

The front of the house was a twelve-by-twelve living room painted sea green and a kitchen half that size. The counters on the right side of the kitchen were conventional height; those on the left were low. So was the refrigerator. Afghans lay across two old tweed chairs and a black leather sofa. The floor was worn pine.

No tables. The center of the room was an open swath to an archway that led to a hallway. A second broad path led to the kitchen.

EmJay Braun stopped her chair. "Go sit," she said. Just as we began to comply, the door-buzzer sounded. From inside, an angry-bee rasp.

She said, "Finally." Then: "No, I'll get it," as I started for the front door.

She rolled, hooked the cane around a pull-handle. A young woman wearing a black baseball cap stood outside, smiling and holding a plastic shopping bag. A few words passed between her and

EmJay Braun before the bag was handed over. EmJay Braun pushed the door closed and raced to the kitchen where she unloaded on the low counter, placed a few things in the fridge.

"They like you to say something religious when they give you food, like thanks for the grub, God." She returned and faced us. "I know he didn't pay his fine but does it look like we're millionaires?"

Milo said, "What fine?"

"Ninety bucks for when he planted that tree near the harbor without permission, that's why you're here, right? They also wanted him to dig it up but when they saw his leg, they let that go."

"Ms. Braun, we're from L.A. There's no easy way to tell you but a body was found several days ago. We're not certain but indications are it might be your husband."

"Might be? What does that mean?" No shock, just indignation.

"There was some disfigurement so we can't make a definite I.D. A pattern of old injuries matches that of Mr. Braun."

"Who told you about his injuries?"

"His former wife."

"The lazy one," she said.

"You know her?"

"Hal told me about her, she never lifted her butt to do anything. Why'd *she* stick her nose into it?"

"We released information to the media and she phoned in. She felt the description might match Mr. Braun."

"Description of what?"

Milo told her.

Her mouth twitched. "So what? Lots of people get hurt."

"The injuries match your—"

"So what," she repeated.

Then she fell apart.

Gasping and bending nearly double, she dropped her head, grabbed at her abundant hair with both hands, chuffed a few times and continued to breathe rapidly. A hand trembled. The cane tumbled to the floor. I picked it up and held on to it.

She said, "No, no, no, no, *no,* stupid, stupid, *stupid*!" Her right hand flew from her hair and began pummeling a wheel of her chair. She'd pulled out some black strands and they frizzed her fingers. She kept hitting rubber and the heel of her hand turned gray.

It took a while for her to go silent. She kept her head down.

Milo said, "Ms. Braun, if it is Mr. Braun, we're so sorry for your loss. But we need to know for sure."

"Of course it's him. Why wouldn't it be him? He was supposed to call a week ago, didn't but so what, that's Hal, he does crazy crap like that."

She sobbed. I got her a tissue from the kitchen. She snatched it, ground soft paper into both eyes. "He's so *stupid*!"

Milo said, "Ma'am, I hate to ask this, but a DNA match will tell us definitely if it's—"

She looked up. "When he left he wouldn't tell me what, just that it was his grand adventure. I told him he was being stupid, going off on one of his—the dumb jackass *fool.*"

She let the tissue drop to her lap. "You're thinking I should've reported him missing when he didn't call. But that wasn't how it worked. The deal was, I shut up and waited and he'd come back with a story. Everything all CIA."

"He told you he was in the CIA?"

"No! That's not what I mean!" Deep breath. Balloon cheeks as she held on to air, finally let it out. "I said he *got* all CIA—like it was a secret mission. I knew it wasn't, just one of his stupid, stupid, stupid adventures. I figured he needed to get it out of his system. Like a steam pipe, you know? Blow it off. Sometimes he needed to do that."

I said, "He went on other adventures."

"He'd be okay for a while then he'd get restless and do stupid things," she said. "Like the tree. *He* decided the harbor needed a blue eucalyptus because the color brought out the ocean. So he bought one and snuck out there at night and planted it and harbor security drove by and caught him. Turns out eucalyptus have small roots, it could've fallen down in a big wind. What did Hal care? He was speaking for the trees. A few years before that, he did the same thing with flowers near a gas station. No one complained about that, what did they care, they got free flowers. But the owners laughed at him and the flowers were dead in a month because no one watered them. Hal goes in for gas, starts complaining they don't care about nature, they kick him out, say don't come back. So now we got to drive farther for gas."

"For his Jeep."

"Piece of junk—he's not a bad guy, just does stupid things—like walking at night in bad neighborhoods, where the gangs hang out. Like . . . a dare, you know? Except no one's daring him. He'd get in people's business, that almost got him beat up."

"By who?" said Milo.

"This was a few years ago, he drove by a McDonald's, a guy was yelling at a woman. Hal stops, goes up, says that's no way to treat a lady. Guy's twice his size, grabs him and lifts him off the ground and throws him away like he's a piece of dust."

"You saw this?"

"No, he told me. Like it was funny. Like he was proud of himself. I begged him to stop doing it, he'd give me this pat on the head, say EmJay, it's keeping the code. I'm like what code? He's like back when honor mattered—knights and dragons and all that. He used to read books about knights. Then he switched to CIA books, Tom Clancy, whatever. He'd talk about how great it would be, going co-*vert*, no one knowing who you really are."

Tears dribbled down her cheeks. "I should've known. When he packed that duffel, I should've asked questions. But he wouldn't have told me. He never told me anything until afterward."

Her mouth worked. "When he didn't call after a week, I won't lie, I was mad. Then I said maybe his burner phone ran out."

Milo said, "He used a pay-as-you-go?"

"We both do, cheaper," said EmJay Braun. "We ain't exactly Bill Gates." She wheeled the chair to the side, showed us her profile "Why can't he be recognized?"

Milo said, "No need to go into details."

"That bad?" she said. "No, tell me."

"A shotgun was used."

She grimaced. "Oh, God . . . I was hoping maybe another fall. That's how he got messed up the first time. Hiking. An adventure."

She looked at her hand, untangled strands of hair, stared at them. "I should be careful, it's the only thing I've got going anymore, the hair." Dreamy smile. "I used to model. Hair *and* hands, once in a while even whole-body. When I was like twenty. Nothing fancy, discount catalogs, but I was doing okay. I got something called A.S. Not M.S. You tell people A.S., they think M.S., it's nothing alike."

I said, "Ankylosing spondylitis."

She stared. "How do you know?"

Years ago, I'd consulted to Western Pediatric's Rheumatology Division, learned about arthritis of the spine.

I said, "I know someone."

"They doing okay?"

"They are."

"Well, good for them, I'm hanging in. Mine started when I was twenty-one, a stupid backache. Then it was okay, then it came back." Soft tap on a tire. "I'm not a cripple, I can walk a little when I absolutely have to, but it hurts bad. That's how I met Hal. Physical rehab, he was working on his leg strength, I was getting my spine looked at again."

I said, "His accident."

"That had happened years before, he had the limp. He'd been okay but then his muscles started to get weak and they said he'd better do something about it, so he went to rehab. I wasn't that severe, myself, we started dating. When I got worse, he stuck with me, I thought, what a guy."

Her face crumpled. "When you put aside the craziness, he's a sweetie."

She cried some more. When she stopped, I gave her another tissue.

"Those injuries. I guess it really is him, huh?"

Milo said, "DNA would—"

"Sure, fine, what do you need for that?"

"A toothbrush, a hairbrush, anything he'd have regular contact with."

"He took his comb and his toothbrush with him," said EmJay Braun. "Stuffed his duffel, threw it in the back of the Jeep, and drove away waving at me and blowing a kiss. I didn't blow back." Head shake.

I said, "He left in good spirits."

"That's why I didn't worry. I figured he just needed to go off on his own. This ain't exactly a mansion and mostly we're with each other twenty-four seven."

She smiled. "I won't lie, I didn't mind a little alone time. I was planning to do some travel of my own. Maybe over to the outlets in Camarillo, some shopping if it was cheap enough."

"You have a vehicle?" said Milo.

"Got a van, equipped and all, but broke down, still being worked on, they keep telling me in a few days. Meanwhile, I'm stuck. Like I said, I can walk if I need to, the church brings me the meals, I don't want more than two a week, I want to stay busy—could you use one of his shirts for the DNA? Even it it's been washed."

"That may not work."

"Hmm," she said. "I wash everything right away, nothing sits around dirty—how about a bottle? He's the only one drinks cognac, I hate it. He's not a big drinker, just a cognac once in a while. There's the bottle and this little brandy glass, he says it's shaped that way so you can smell the aroma. I don't think he washes it, says he likes it with . . . what do you call it, patina?"

"That could do it," said Milo.

EmJay wheeled and faced the kitchen. "I'll get it for you."

Milo said, "Better I do." He gloved up, removed and unfolded a paper evidence envelope from an inner jacket pocket.

EmJay Braun said, "It's on the normal side of the kitchen, where it's higher. Cabinet closest to the wall."

He returned with the bag full and sealed.

"Hey," she said, "isn't fingerprints faster than DNA?"

If you've got hands to work with. Milo said, "This'll be fine, ma'am. Can you think of anyone who'd want to harm Hal?"

"Just that guy at the McDonald's but I have no idea who he is and that was years ago."

I said, "How often did he go on adventures?"

"Two times, maybe, three times a year. Usually it was short, a day or two, he'd say he'd just camped out, being with nature—that was his thing, nature. Like the Chumash Indians, he liked the Chumash Indians, said he wished he had Indian blood but his family was originally from Austria."

"Where'd he grow up?"

"Stockton, he said his family was gone, he was an only child, there wasn't much to say about his parents, they didn't live long, that's why it was important to make every day count. He liked me to talk about my parents, they were great, I loved them. After they died, I got the house. Without that, I don't know what I'd do."

"Hal didn't work."

"Not since rehab, we're both on disability." She laced her hands and stretched her arms. Strained and made as if to stand, got her buttocks an inch off the chair and plopped back down.

"Let me tell you what he was like. Once he went hiking over in Deer Creek and came back with his duffel full of dirty laundry plus a big plastic garbage bag that smelled of pizza. I'm like you camped and ordered pizza? He's like no, I took it out of the trash. I'm like what for. He pokes the bag and it starts moving and I scream. He reaches in and pulls out a snake! I'm screaming my head off and he's like honey, sorry for scaring you but no worries, it's not poisonous. And ain't it pretty? He said he found it off a trail, all by itself, where it could be stepped on. A baby snake. Once he put it back in the bag, I had to admit it *was* kind of pretty, bright colors, red, black, yellow, all striped. But it still creeped me out, I'm like get that *out* of here *now*. He's like he already called Animal Control, they were coming over. I'm like I don't care put it *outside*. He said, Em, I promise you it's harmless and I'm worried it's sick, I don't want some cat attacking it. He calmed me down, he was always good at that. I let him keep it on condition he put it in *two* bags and tied off the top. He poked holes so it could breathe and some woman in a uniform came and told him he'd done a good deed, it was this rare kind of rare king snake, not supposed to be where he found it, really a cool discovery, the biologists were all excited to get it, they were going to make sure it was okay and find it a good home. There I was and she's thanking Hal. Like he's a hero. He was all about that. Doing good and *feeling* good about it."

I said, "What's the last adventure he went on before this one?"

"Hmm," she said. "Like three weeks before, he spent a couple of nights in Santa Barbara but I'm not sure it was an adventure. He said he was hanging out there, enjoying the beach, he slept on the beach under a pier. But maybe. He did come home with that look in his eyes. Hot eyes, you know? Like he was planning something."

Milo said, "That's what we're trying to find out. Any reason he'd be in L.A.?"

"I can't see any. He used to live in L.A. but said he hated it, too much city. He liked nature—what was your—the guy you found, what was he wearing?"

Milo described the clothing.

EmJay Braun sank low. "Those stupid *pants*. I used to call them his grandpa jeans, he got them at a thrift shop—two pairs, the other could still be here if he didn't pack it."

She wheeled toward the doorway. "Got a photo of Hal, too. Of us. In the bedroom. Don't hang anything out here, when stuff hangs crooked it drives me nuts, I don't want to have to stand up and straighten."

I said, "When Hal was around, did he straighten?"

"Ha. He couldn't care less." Smiling. "Maybe knights don't straighten. C'mon, this way."

The pseudo-jeans sat at the bottom of two drawers that held most of Hal Braun's wardrobe. Same brand; Milo took them, along with a pair of boxer shorts and a T-shirt. The only other garments in the closet were a navy peacoat and a corduroy jacket.

EmJay lifted a standing frame from a nightstand. Casually dressed couple on the steps of a beautiful, cathedral-like structure.

"Ventura City Hall, the day we got married."

Maria Josefina leaned against her new husband's arm, smiling, strikingly pretty, her hair in an updo.

Hargis Braun's grin livened the same moon-face in Mary Ellen's photos and his driver's license.

He wore the same clothes as the corpse in the Corvins' den.

EmJay Braun said, "I don't have to give this to you, do I?"

Milo said, "No, ma'am. Did Hal have a computer?"

"A laptop. He took it with him, he always did."

We returned to the living room. Milo handed her his card. "If you think of anything."

"And *you'll* call *me*? Once you know?"

"Absolutely."

She pinched her lower lip between index finger and thumb. Let go and revealed a crescent-shaped indentation just short of a wound. "You wouldn't come all the way from L.A. if you weren't pretty sure."

"Ms. Braun, we honestly can't say at this point."

"Okay. But when you do know. I need to arrange things. Haven't done that since my parents. They at least put away money for their funerals, I don't know how I'm going to handle it."

I said, "Is there anyone you'd like us to call for support?"

"The church folk are good, I'll ask them what they think."

We walked to the door.

She said, "Will I get into trouble if I cash Hal's check? I mean if you don't know for sure? I'll probably get something anyway. Widow's benefits. I think."

"You'd best check with social services on that, ma'am."

"I don't want to do anything illegal but I could sure use both checks."

"You won't get into trouble because of us, ma'am."

"That's good. I need what I can get, it's going to be different, now." She blinked back tears. "What am I going to *do* without him?"

14

Milo stashed the evidence bags in the trunk of the un-marked, got behind the wheel, and studied the little gray house.

"At the risk of venturing into your territory," he said, "Braun sounds a little nuts."

I said, "I'm feeling more literary: How about quixotic?"

"Tilting at windmills?"

"And someone tilted back."

"Idiot looks for trouble, there's an army of people he could've pissed off. And the crime scene's potentially anywhere he could drive. At least I've got a vehicle to BOLO, if it shows up maybe the location will say something."

He got on the radio, put in the alert, hung up. "Nothing we heard from either Mary explains how he ended up on ol' Chet's parquet."

"Mary Two said the adventures were infrequent. The Santa Barbara trip took place shortly before he ended up in L.A. Maybe it was part of the same adventure."

"What, saving the whales and Ahab got irate?"

I laughed. "That does raise a question: Why drive forty miles for sand and surf when he lived in a beach town?"

"Maybe he liked high-priced sand better." He turned the ignition key. "God, I hope you're wrong about that. How am I gonna get a handle on something that started a hundred miles away?"

"Be good to know if the Corvins have any Santa Barbara connections."

"Sure, I'll ask . . . saving snakes, wanting to be covert. Sir Lance-a-little."

A man stepped out of the beige cottage two doors south.

Tall, Hispanic, wearing a powder-blue golf shirt, white slacks, and polished brown loafers. A deeply seamed bronze face was topped by thick white hair. A snowy mustache sprouted from beneath a strong nose.

Older man, easily seventy but solidly built with ramrod posture.

Pretending he was examining a bed of geraniums rather than checking us out.

I said, "We interest the neighbor."

Milo swiveled. The movement caught the man's eyes. He folded his arms across his chest and stared, as if inviting confrontation. When none occurred, he plucked a dead flower from the bed and went back inside.

"Beggars, choosers," said Milo and got out of the car.

The beige cottage's paint was fresh; same for the semisweet chocolate trim. A fake-grass lawn gleamed emerald. *No Soliciting* sign. No bell. Before Milo's fist landed on the lacquered red door, it opened.

The white-haired man said, "Here I was thinking you were lazy. You're obviously on the job. What happened with Braun?"

Milo showed his badge.

The man squinted. "L.A.?" He eyed the unmarked. "Back when I was on the job we used wheels like that. You have A.C. in that thing? We didn't."

"Theoretically," said Milo. "If you can spare a minute, sir—"

"Prieto, Enrique, everyone calls me Henry. Worked Oxnard patrol fifteen years, then Robbery, when I reached mandatory I went private and rousted bums around the harbor."

"Know Frank Gonzales?"

"Francisco," said Henry Prieto. "Loved food, always needed to watch his weight."

"Yeah, he's a gourmet."

Prieto patted his own flat stomach, took a long look at Milo's convexity. "How do you know Frank?"

"Worked a homicide case with him."

"Homicide. You still that?"

"Still."

Henry Prieto glanced at the Braun house. "You're saying one of them got killed? Just saw her wheeling her chair up and down her driveway this morning so it has to be him."

"Could be."

"Could be?"

"We've got a body needs identifying."

"What's the holdup?" said Prieto.

"It's in bad shape."

"Decomp? Hated those. Once I saw a tarp at the harbor, inside was a drunk, the wharf rats had enjoyed him for breakfast, lunch, dinner, and another breakfast. You went to ask her questions, see if you could get an I.D.?"

"Yup. What can you tell us about the two of them?"

"Couple of waiters. Waiting around for the monthly check. Her I don't mind, she's been sick for a long time." The mustache angled down. "Him? A little limp stops you from getting a job? All he does is loaf around all day, come to think about it, haven't seen him in a while, must be . . . what, a week? Two? Where in L.A. did he show up? Watts, East L.A.?"

"Westside," said Milo.

"That's a switch."

"What else can you tell us about them, Mr. Prieto?"

"Don't count on her being a suspect. Don't want to mess with your business, always hated when people did that to me. But I don't see her as doing anything bad. She's not too bright but she's a sweet girl, always was. I knew her parents. Salt of the earth. Gustavo worked park maintenance for forty years, Dorothy cleaned offices. The older girl, Sophie, she had no looks but she was the smart one, went to college, works as a paralegal or something. Mary Jo was the looker but not much brain-wise. Maybe it was getting sick so young. Maybe that's why she settled for *him*."

"You don't like Mr. Braun."

"I don't like idlers and loafers," said Henry Prieto. "This country, it's going down the tubes, people who work subsidizing loafers. What's a limp? Nothing says you have to play defensive tackle. Do *something*, right?"

"You bet."

"On top of being a loafer, he's a weirdo. Always smiling, even when there's no call for it. Like he's buttering you up for something. My world, you earn your friendship, you don't step into it like a pair of slippers. What happened to him in West L.A.?"

"Someone shot him."

"Someone. You don't know who."

"We're just starting out, Mr. Prieto. Anything you can tell us would be helpful."

"Helpful . . . the only thing maybe out of the usual is a black Camaro that came by to see him a couple of weeks ago. Day or two before he took that duffel of his and loaded it up in his Jeep. One individual, the driver. Eighteen to twentyish, parked right where you are. Seven a.m., I'd just brought in the paper, was waiting for my coffee to perk, I hear an engine rev, look out and see it. Minute later, Braun comes out of his house and the driver gets out and they have a talk. The driver gets back into the Camaro and leaves. Couple of days later, Braun loads his duffel in his Jeep again and does the same. Made me wonder about a dope deal or something else shady."

"Braun ever give you reason to wonder about that?"

"Someone doesn't have a job, I wonder," said Henry Prieto. "So the Camaro made me wonder. I never saw Braun before with anyone except Mary Jo and some church do-gooders who deliver free food. The two of them just yakked but the kid was a hippie-type so I paid attention. Nothing got bought or sold or paid for." Disappointed.

Milo took out his pad. "Anything else you can say about the hippie?"

Henry Prieto looked at the ruled sheets. "Same pad we used . . . average height, skinny, long hair, dirty-blond, one of those fuzzy things here." Touching his chin. "Someone who can't grow a decent beard, shouldn't "

He smoothed his own ample lip hair. "You got that down?"

Milo's pen lifted. "Yes, sir."

"Next, clothing: black T-shirt, white writing on it, I couldn't read what. Blue jeans, white sneakers. No visible tattoos or distinguishing marks but they put them everywhere nowadays. Eyeglasses. Not a tough-looking type, maybe a student or some other kind of wastrel."

"With a Camaro—"

"If you know how to work the system, you can have a Mercedes," said Prieto. "The car was third generation—'82 to '92. I owned a '70 and one of my sons customized a '78 that he took to the track until the brakes boiled. Nothing custom on this one, regular wheels, no stripes or decals or bumper stickers."

Prieto clacked his dentures. "Too far to see the tags."

Milo said, "Did the conversation seem friendly?"

"Not friendly, not unfriendly. Lieutenant—why's a man of your rank doing real police work?"

"Lucky situation."

"Every lieutenant I knew was a desk-jockey. Anyway, not friendly, not unfriendly—neutral. A couple of minutes of neutral yakking. Maybe Braun has a wastrel son I didn't know about. Right age, no?"

Milo nodded.

Prieto said, "I don't need to teach you your business but that's a lead, right? Someone gets killed, look at the family."

"You bet. Anything else you can tell us about Braun?"

"No, it's not like I was interested in him. I just know what I see when I see it."

Milo headed back toward the freeway, on-ramped to the 101 South.

I said, "No lunch at the harbor?"

"All of a sudden you develop an appetite?"

"Just looking after your welfare."

"Touched," he said. "Nah, too much to think about. What do you think about Camaro Boy? Probably nothing but it's the only contact for Braun we know about. Too bad it's wasn't a Ferrari or something else on a short list."

I said, "Prieto's point about a son was interesting but eighteen to twenty would also make the driver right for Chelsea Corvin's boyfriend."

"She's got a secret lover?"

"Maybe not so secret that her folks aren't up in arms. And we know where that can lead."

"Romeo-and-Juliet situation," he said. "We talked about that and you said the crime was too organized for that."

"Facts come in, I'm willing to change my mind. We know Braun liked seeing himself as a rescuing hero. What if that led to working for one of those deprogramming outfits? The kind parents turn to when they're trying to save kids from drugs and cults and bad influences. Or he did it on his own, operating as a lone warrior. Either way it could explain adventures he didn't tell his wife about."

He tapped the steering wheel. "Limping Lancelot augments his welfare checks. You see Chet and Felice going for someone like that?"

"Desperation loosens standards."

"Hmm." A couple of miles later: "If Braun was hired to pry Romeo and Juliet apart, why wasn't the conversation Prieto saw hostile?"

"Maybe a deal was cut," I said. "The boyfriend got paid to stay away. But then something went wrong—a change of heart on Romeo's part. Or Chelsea found out and freaked out and Romeo decided to redeem himself by dispatching the enemy. If so, the Corvins know more than they're letting on and want to keep it that way for Chelsea's sake. Meanwhile, she sneaks out of the house in the middle of the night."

"Trysting with Romeo." He chewed his cheek. "Young love gone mega-bad. It's a theory."

I said, "It fits your first impression. Something about this family."

No reply until we neared the 405 turnoff. "You think Chet trying to get you involved with Chelsea was a backhanded way of dealing with the romance? Roping in someone with police connections?"

"Maybe. Meanwhile he's driving to the airport."

"Lighting a fuse and running from the scene," he said. "For now, keep your distance from all of them, okay? I'm gonna drop you off and head to the crime lab. If there's still time, I'll pay the Corvins a visit, mention Braun's name, see how they react."

"Sounds like a plan."

"Not much of one but better than a few hours ago," he said.

15

O ver take-out Indian, I recapped with Robin as Blanche
snored by our feet.

She said, "Poor Mr. Braun. He sounds kind of desperate—wanting
to make his mark or just hungry for attention. Someone like that
might have a website or some interesting social media."

"We checked, nothing."

"If he considers himself some kind of secret agent, maybe he uses
a pseudonym."

"You're a very smaaht lady."

"Who's that, Cagney?"

"I was thinking Bogie but Cagney will do."

She smiled. "Go look, I'll get dessert ready."

I ran a search on deprogrammers, found setups ranging from corporate slicksters charging big bucks for unkinking wayward rich kids to
nonprofit religious groups fueled by their view of morality. A few lone
wolves, mostly born-again sobers, none of them Braun.

Nothing covert about the identities of most of these "operatives."

Quite the opposite: names, addresses, email and sometimes actual. Lots of headshots falling into two categories: grimly tough and be-atifically smiling.

No one resembled the moon-faced man in pleated jeans who went off on self-described quests.

I returned to the kitchen.

Robin read my face. "Oh, well, have some orange slices. I goosed them up with whipped cream, no sense being too virtuous."

Milo phoned at seven the following morning. The coffeepot was bub-bling, Robin was bathing, Blanche curled in my lap gnawing a chew-stick.

"Early riser," I said.

"More like no-sleeper. By the time I got out of the office last night, the blood was back in my alimentary canal so I stopped for dinner at the Pantry. I won't go into details but I will tell you pork chops are an excellent side for T-bone."

I thought: *Same for Lipitor.* "Sounds like a repast."

"The mind doesn't function until the body's happy, amigo. Around ten, I get a call from Reed: Braun's Jeep turned up in Playa Del Rey—more like pieces of it, parked in an alley, taken apart by the local lo-custs then torched. I drive over there, pressure the techies for a quick print wipe, they find partials on the sill of the driver's door. No AFIS match, best guess is Braun's but I'd need his damn hands to verify. By now it's pushing one a.m. Here's where it gets interesting."

"You drove to the Corvins and got surprised by something."

Silence. "What the hell's the matter with you?"

"I'm wrong?"

"You buzzkilled my punch line. Where you hiding the damned tarot deck?"

"Dog ate it."

"Not *your* dog, she's a gour-*mette.* Yes, O Oracle of Delphi, I drove to the Corvins to bleed off some energy and on the off chance that I'd missed something the other buncha times. I parked around the block and walked, avoided the CC cameras. It's a ghost town at that hour, most of the houses are dark. As I get near the cul-de-sac, I see someone stepping out of the shadows and heading to the Corvins'. Thank God for rubber soles, I manage to catch a glimpse before they duck around the side of the house where that dinky gate is."

"Same path the killer took."

"But this was no intruder, amigo. This was Chelsea doing her night-moves thing. Not with Chin-Fuzz or anyone else. By herself, just like her daddy described. Normally I'd say big deal, the girl's odd, she has a sleep disorder, whatever. But just as she slipped out of view one of the house lights went off. Next door at Trevor Bitt's. Can I prove she was actually in there with him? A few seconds before, I might've. But it's provocative, no?"

"Extremely," I said. "Chelsea and a much older man would be way more problematic for her parents than a peer they don't approve of. If they haven't taken action, they don't know."

"Agreed, but maybe Chet suspects something and he called you hoping you'd tell me and I'd do some snooping." He laughed. "Which just happened. I know it doesn't explain Braun. And it leaves the deprogramming theory in the dirt, unless I can establish a link between Braun and Bitt. But still."

"Braun doesn't seem to be linked anywhere." I told him about the futile Web search. "But if he knows Bitt based on a shared sexual interest, he could be using deep cover."

"Coupla dirty old men with a thing for teenage girls," he said. "Oh, man."

"Vulnerable teenage girls."

"That's Chelsea, all right. So who's Chin-Fuzz? The prey is both boys and girls? Or like Prieto said, he's just Braun's kid stopping by to see Dad before he packs out on an adventure."

"Or he's irrelevant," I said. "Someone selling a car Braun was thinking of buying."

"Either way, I'm back to focusing on Bitt. His messing with Chelsea would explain why he won't give me the time of day. I called a couple of judges about grounds for a warrant, got the answers I expected. Any suggestions?"

"Sorry, no."

"Then I'll go with the original plan: drop Braun's name with Chet and Felice, see how they react. Say tonight, six-ish. You up for it?"

"Can I bring the tarot deck?"

"Nah, leave it at home with the crystal ball and the turban," he said. "We'll stick with the usual: I provide the official presence and the personal security, you handle the tact and sensitivity."

At six thirty p.m. I pulled up behind Milo's unmarked, parked at the mouth of Evada Lane. As we neared the Corvin house, he stopped and pointed. "That's where I saw her."

Narrow patch of grass and concrete fronting Trevor Bitt's keep-away gate.

I said, "In the dark, a nice niche. If she wasn't inside, she could have been sneaking a smoke or a drink."

He trotted over, returned. "No bottles or cans or butts, tobacco or otherwise. Also, I didn't spot anything in her hands and if she wasn't inside Bitt's place, why did his light go off right after she left?"

Without waiting for an answer, he swiveled toward the Corvins' driveway. "Both cars. Chet's back home."

I said, "Nothing like family time."

Felice Corvin came to the door wearing green velvet sweats, hair bunched up and clipped, face scrubbed of makeup, a can of Coke Zero in her left hand.

Well-shaped eyebrows rose. "Yes?"

Milo said, "Evening, Ms. Corvin. If you've got time, could we come in for some follow-up?"

She eyed me. "Does that mean police work or psychotherapy?"

"The former, ma'am."

A beat. "We just finished supper, okay if it's brief."

Fancy name for take-out KFC at the kitchen table. No sign of Brett or Chet. Chelsea stood at the sink with the water running, washing a drinking glass that looked clean.

The walk from the front door had taken us through neat, clean, perfectly composed space. No hint of the horror the family had been through ten days ago. Next to a toaster oven, a Sonos speaker streamed music. Indie folk-rock; electronically tweaked but still whiny vocals coping with two minor chords.

Felice cleared away the paper cartons and stashed the ketchup packets in a drawer.

Chelsea kept washing the same glass. She hadn't turned to look at us.

Milo sat at the table without being invited. When I did the same, Felice's eyebrows climbed again. "Would you like something to drink?"

Milo said, "No, thanks."

"I'm having tea. You're sure?"

"Okay, then, appreciate it."

She got busy with bags of Earl Grey and mugs silkscreened with national park scenes, turned to her daughter and spoke softly. "That won't get any cleaner, honey, and I need the instant-hot."

Chelsea didn't move. A gentle nudge inched her away from the spigot. Her hands dripped but she didn't dry them. Placing the glass on the counter, she backed away, bumping into a butcher-block table and turning abruptly.

Doughy face, raisin eyes, stringy hair. Expression hard to read but nothing happy about it.

Milo and I smiled at her. We might as well have been baring fangs. She hurried out.

Felice watched her for a second, then brought tea to the table, smiling tightly.

Milo said, "How's everything going?"

"Lieutenant, that does sound like therapy."

He smiled.

"Sorry," she said. "Hellish day at work, city bureaucracy, then crazy traffic. In answer to your I'll-assume-courteous question, everything's fine, thank you for asking."

"Chet upstairs?"

"Chet's out of town. Portland. I believe." The last two words and a half sneer said it all: *I don't ask, he doesn't tell, neither of us gives a damn.*

"His car—"

"A driver took him to the airport. Sometimes he does that when he's on a tight schedule and has to work in transit."

"Ah," said Milo.

"A busy man, Chet." Making it sound like an insult. "So how're things going in your world, Lieutenant? Yours, as well, Doctor."

Her vocal pitch had climbed, talking about her husband. Now she strained for buoyancy, sounded doubly tense.

Milo said, "We may have identified the victim."

"May have?" she said.

"I'm sure you remember the state of the body."

"Oh. Of course. Who is he?"

"A man named Hargis Braun."

No response.

Milo said, "He went by Hal."

Continued silence. Then the third eyebrow arch of the evening. "Oh, you're asking if I know him. I don't. Never heard of him. Who is he?"

Milo showed her Braun's DMV photo. She had the courtesy to actually study it. "Nope. Is he from around here?"

"Ventura County."

"Then what was he doing here?"

"Good question, ma'am. Does your family have any ties up there?"

"Not at all," she said. "I was in Goleta for a conference last year but I never met that man."

"What about Chet?"

"Chet handles the West Coast," she said. "So I can see him having business up there. You think this could be related to Chet's business?"

Milo said, "I wish we were at the point where I could think any-thing, Ms. Corvin."

"Would you like me to call Chet and ask him?"

"That would be great."

She took a cellphone out of a sweatpant pocket, speed-dialed, clicked off. "Straight to voicemail."

"No prob, I've got his number."

She stirred her tea, looked at the photo. "Sorry, wish I could help you." She smiled. "Actually, I probably *don't* want to be helpful if it means I have to keep thinking about what happened. But he is an absolute stranger to me. Could he be some kind of tradesman—a plumber, a handyman, who worked around the neighborhood and somehow got . . . sorry, that's silly. It explains nothing."

"He didn't do much, ma'am. On disability."

"And somehow he ended up in my house." She shook her head. "Crazy. It gets crazier as time passes. And your showing up with his name and his picture kind of brings me back to it."

"Sorry."

"It's okay, you're doing your job."

"Could we show the photo to Chelsea and Brett?"

"Absolutely not. They're children and why in the world would they know this person?"

"I'm sure you're right but like you said, doing the job."

Felice Corvin turned to me, frowning. "You think it's psychologi-cally okay to suck the kids back in?"

Rhetorical question but I answered. "Depends on how they're doing. Mood, appetite, sleep patterns, in school."

She blinked. "I figured you'd just give me the official line."

Milo said, "Dr. Delaware's an independent consultant. In every way."

"Apparently," said Felice Corvin. "How've they been doing? To my maternal eye, they're fine. Meaning, Brett's being Brett, emotionally he's made of titanium. Chelsea's . . . Chelsea. I won't hide anything, she's always had issues. What you just saw with the glass is typical. OCD. According to several *experts*. Along with all kinds of other labels and diagnoses. But has she changed since the . . . since it happened? Not that I can honestly say. Then again, Doctor, someone of *your* training might know better."

"My experience," I said, "is that no one knows kids better than their mothers."

She stared at me. "You actually sound as if you mean that."

"I do."

Felice Corvin took a sip of tea and looked at Hargis Braun's photo. "He looks harmless enough . . . no gore, not like what they saw when it happened . . . fine, what the heck."

She called for both kids at the foot of the stairs. Brett came bounding down, loud as a herd of buffalo. An oversized L.A. Kings jersey tented freckled legs. Hustling past his mother, he high-fived Milo and me. "Whuh? You got the perp?"

Milo suppressed laughter. "Your mouth to God's ears, Brett."

"Whuh?"

Felice said, "That means—never mind. They've got a picture to show you. The man who was—the person."

"The dead guy? *Cool.*"

Milo handed him the photo.

Brett said, "Fat dude."

"Brett!"

"Whuh? He *is*." Shaping a sphere with his hands.

Felice said, "You don't know him, right?"

"Yeah."

"Yeah, meaning no you *don't* know him."

"Yeah." The boy laughed and bounced and shadow-boxed. Felice reached for the photo but he feinted away from her and waved it. To Milo. "Who is he?"

"Don't know yet, Brett."

"*Fat* dude." Brett's lip began curling upward, prepping a supplementary wisecrack. But his eyes dulled and all he could come up with was, "Fat."

His mother said, "Go back and finish your homework, young man."

"Boooooring," said Brett, high-fiving air before running off.

Another ungulate stampede up the stairs. A bellowed *"Fat!"*

Felice Corvin looked at me. "Please tell me that will pass with maturity."

I said, "His sense of humor?"

"His lack of emotionality. I've tried to get him to talk about it but he just makes jokes."

I said, "Boys his age go through all kinds of stuff." Putting on my best therapeutic Sphinx-face as I thought of Brett's father.

Apples falling close to trees.

Felice said, "I hope it's just a stage," and called out Chelsea's name. The girl stepped out of her room, stared down at us, fidgeting, finally descended.

Felice explained as Milo handed Chelsea Braun's photo. Her appraisal was brief and mute: a quick head shake then a turn to her mother, as if for confirmation.

"Thank you, darling," said Felice. The girl trudged back up the stairs, clutching the banister.

Milo looked at me. I stayed neutral and that was enough for him.

"One more question, ma'am, and I hope it doesn't offend you, but I need to ask."

Felice Corvin folded her arms across her chest. "What now?"

"I'm sure you can understand that our experience tells us certain situations need to be looked into—"

"What, Lieutenant?"

"This has nothing to do specifically with your kids, ma'am, but we've seen cases where young people's relationships lead to violence."

"What in the world are you saying?"

"Kids dating people their parents don't approve of. Sometimes it gets—"

Felice cut him off with a horizontal air slash. Her laughter was harsh, a witchy cackle. "Neither of my children *dates*. I'm not sure anyone does, nowadays, kids just hang out. But apart from that, Brett's too young for a relationship." She breathed in. "And Chelsea's not into any level of emotional . . . entanglement. Never has been."

"No boyfriend."

"I wish." Felice's eyes filled with tears. "I wish so *many* things for her. Is that all? I have things to *do*."

She hurried us to the door. Milo said, "Sorry for bothering you."

"That poor man. Braun. You've told me nothing about him."

"That's 'cause we don't know much other than his name, ma'am. When we figure it out, I promise to let you know."

"When, not if," she said.

"We're always hopeful."

"Sorry," said Felice Corvin. "I don't know what's gotten into me— you've got a tough job, I don't envy you. Good luck."

Headlights washed across her face. A car pulling into the driveway of the Spanish house next door. Paul Weyland stepped out of his silver Taurus. Carrying a briefcase, moonlight doming his bald head. He didn't seem to notice us, braced himself on the roof of the car. Rocked on his feet.

Off kilter? A narrowly avoided DUI? He pushed away, stood in place for a moment, and slumped, a small man getting smaller.

Felice said, "Hi, Paul."

Weyland stopped, waved, saw us. "Oh, hi. Anything new?"

"Follow-up," said Milo.

"Oh," said Weyland. Weak voice. His shoulders heaved.

Felice said, "Are you okay?"

"No worries. No police worries, anyway." His voice caught.

She walked over to him. "Are you ill or something?"

"No, fine," said Weyland. He righted his glasses. "Oh, what the heck, can't hide it forever. You've noticed Donna hasn't been around."

"Visiting her mom."

"True," said Weyland. "But she's not coming back—we're breaking up, Felice."

"Paul, I'm so sorry."

"It happens." He shrugged. Poked a finger under a lens and wiped something from his left eye. To us: "Sorry, don't want to interrupt."

Felice walked over to him, arms spread.

As Milo and I left, the two of them were still embracing.

Halfway up the block, Milo looked over his shoulder. No one around. "Touching scene. Makes you wonder."

"About suburban intrigue?"

"About the future on Evada Lane." He rubbed his face. "She's tired of Chet, who's less Chet than ol' Paul?"

"Could happen," I said.

"Meanwhile, Chet's off doing who-knows-what on the road, Chelsea could be hanging with the creepy neighbor, and the boy's got the emotional range of a newt. Does anyone lead an uneventful life?"

I said, "Hope not."

"Why?"

"Neither of us is ready for retirement."

We drove back to the station where he phone-photo'd Braun's face and sent it to Chet Corvin's cell, then scanned his message slips.

Wastebasket, wastebasket, wastebasket. Then: "Crypt says Braun was A-negative, which isn't rare but also not that common. They got a decent match between blood from his body and a speck they found on the boxer shorts I got from EmJay, best guess, a popped zit. Some subtests—HLA—also match . . . basic DNA'll be back in a few days. Once it's confirmed I'll tell her what she already knows."

He pocketed his phone. "Mary Ellen, too, maybe one of them will remember something else about the Happy Warrior."

I said, "There was a first wife. Barbara in Stockton."

"Who died of cancer."

"So Braun said."

He looked at me. "Good point, I'll check on her tomorrow, enough for today, Rick's off call, we're aiming for some quality time."

"Have fun."

"Since you didn't probe for specifics, 'quality' means dinner at a new Argentinian place on Fairfax. I'll relax my standards and eat grass-fed steak. He'll do tilapia, sauce on the side, and shoot me the cholesterol glare."

16

Before I drove off, I checked my own messages. Lots of junk and a call forwarded by my service from "Mr. Joseph." That meant nothing until I looked up the 239 area code. Florida.

Lanny Joseph, the record producer who'd referred Iggy Smirch to Bitt.

I tried the number, no answer or voicemail. First thing the following morning I made my second attempt and got the woman with the Cuban accent.

"Hol' on."

Several minutes, then: "Doctor, *buena morninga.* Talking about that asshole Bitt got me thinking, thinking got me remembering, remembering popped a name into my head. I talked to her yesterday, she said she'd talk to you."

"She being . . ."

"Let's leave it at someone you'll want to talk to," said Lanny Joseph. "If you still want to learn about that asshole Bitt."

"We do."

"We?"

"As I told you, I work with the poli—"

"I got that, Doctor, but let me give you some wisdom: Go easy on that. She's not jazzed about talking to you, singular, I did you a big favor and convinced her. But no way will she get officially involved with the cops."

"Got it. Thanks for taking the time."

"Iggy said your girlfriend's beyond hot and you been with her forever. I like faithful people and also Bitt was a total asshole. Here's the name, she's right by you, in L.A."

Maillot Bernard.

I was pretty sure a maillot was some kind of bathing suit—one of those factoids you have no memory of actually learning.

The Internet confirmed that and added dancer's tights to the mix.

Artistic woman? I looked her up on the Web, found nothing, made the call.

A tentative voice trilled, "Yes?"

"Ms. Bernard, Dr. Alex Delaware."

"Yes?"

"Lanny Joseph gave me your number."

"Yes. I told him he could."

"This is about Trevor Bitt."

"Yes."

"Could we talk about him?"

"I guess," said Maillot Bernard. "Somewhere basically . . . out in the open."

"Whatever works best for you, Ms. Bernard."

"Best," she said, as if learning a new word. "There's a place on Melrose, Cuppa. Serves breakfast all day. I'm going to be there by ten."

"See you then."

"Wait a few minutes, come at ten after," she said. "So I have time to figure out what I want to eat."

"Ten ten it is."

"Yes." A beat. "Lanny said you're a police psychologist, like on TV."

"I don't actually work for the police, more of a freelance."

"How interesting," said Maillot Bernard, with scant conviction. "I used to freelance as a dancer. Then I taught dance to children. Free-lancing always has you wondering. When's the next check coming in. Now I do nothing."

"Ah."

"Make it ten fifteen," she said. "I'll be wearing orange."

Cuppa sat beneath two stories of undistinguished, brick office build-ing. Lampshade store on one side, Chinese laundry on the other. The restaurant's front was all glass.

Inside, a boomerang-shaped, gold-flecked Formica counter faced chartreuse vinyl booths. Bullfighting posters and a wall menu served as art. The young woman behind the counter, white-uniformed with Lucille Ball hair and crimson lipstick, had nothing to do. The pass-through to the kitchen offered a view of a white-capped man smoking an e-cig.

What had once been a coffee shop transformed to a place that sold eight-dollar mocha drinks, six-dollar Postum, and omelets/scrambles/frittatas offered with options like ramps, glassfish, Belgian wheat beer, and sweetbreads.

Cheap oatmeal, though. Three bucks and represented with pride as "*not* steel-cut."

A corner booth was occupied by a rabbinically bearded, brooding hipster genuflecting before a tiny cellular screen. Two other stations were taken up by white-haired throwbacks to the Kerouac era, reading newspapers and spooning oatmeal.

A woman in an orange dress sat in the farthest booth, watching me and ignoring a glass of red juice, a mug of something, and a bowl of what looked like lawn shavings sprinkled with fried onions.

Painfully thin would've been Maillot Bernard after a month of gorging.

She could've been anywhere between thirty-five and sixty; when emaciation sets in, distinctions blur. Her hair was long, white-blond, frizzy, her face a spray-tanned stiletto.

I waved and she smiled painfully. Enormous green eyes, contours that suggested genetic beauty long eroded. The dress looked flimsy, with glass beads studding a scoop neckline.

"Alex Delaware."

"Mai-la." The fingers she offered were flash-frozen shoestring potatoes. As I sat, she said, "Coffee? They do it great, here."

"Sure." I looked over at Lucy. She remained behind the counter and shouted, "What can I get you?"

"Coffee, any kind."

"Be careful, that includes Jamaican Blue Mountain. Twenty bucks."

"Thanks for the warning. What can I get for ten?"

Crimson-framed grin. "The world."

"You have African?"

"Do we," she said. "Kenyan's always great." To Maillot Bernard: "A smart one."

Bernard said, "He's a doctor."

"Whoa," said Lucy. To me: "I feel great, maybe I shouldn't." Grinning and giving her hips a rhumba shake.

One of the old men looked up. "Someone's son the doktuh? You take Medi-keah?" He laughed moistly. His female companion kept eating oatmeal.

Lucy brought the coffee, winked, and left.

I said, "Mai-la, I really appreciate your taking the time."

"Yes," she said. "Lanny said the cops were investigating Trevor. I suppose that makes sense."

"How so?"

She shook her head, toyed with her salad. "Confession, first: I used to like him. More than like. We were together for half a year."

She poked some more. Up close, mowed grass was alfalfa sprouts and some sort of stunted-looking lettuce. What I'd taken for onions were desiccated threads of a bacon-like substance, maybe from an animal.

"Trevor used to be a handsome man," she said. "Might still be."

"How long ago was this?"

"Ages. Eons, light-years . . . twenty real years. I was living in San Francisco, dancing ballet, jazz, and modern interpretive."

Her fork lowered. "That didn't pay the bills so I also danced in North Beach clubs."

The mecca of topless. I said, "Branching out."

"That's a nice way to put it," she said. "The money was good but the decision wasn't."

She placed a hand on a flat chest. "They convinced me to enhance. Not only did it ruin ballet, it messed me up physically. It was just loose silicone those days, not even bags. I leaked, got infected, spent four months in the hospital, and ended up like this."

"What an ordeal."

"It was a long time ago." She reached over and touched my hand. "Life's an ordeal, no?"

"It sure can be."

"Maybe not for you? You seem like a happy man."

"I work at it."

"Yes, it is work," said Maillot Bernard. "I gave up on happiness a long time ago, am aiming for content. I think that's a more mature emotion, no?"

"There's an adage," I said. "Who's rich? Someone content with what they have."

"That's brilliant, Doctor—I'm enjoying talking to you, wasn't sure how I felt about facing a therapist again. But I'm glad I agreed. So what's the story with Trevor?"

"That's not clear, yet. And even if it was, I'm sorry, I couldn't give details."

"One-way street, huh? No problem, I don't really care about him. Just making conversation."

She picked at her salad. I drank coffee. The hipster left with his cellphone. The old wag watched and said, "All that ink on him, a wawking hi-ro-glyphic." Lucy laughed. The old woman got oatmeal on her face and wiped it away.

I said, "So you and Trevor were—"

"An item, yes we were," said Maillot Bernard. "When I first met him, he ticked off some serious boxes. Handsome, super-talented. Rich, too, that never hurts. But it was mostly his acceptance. Of me. After I got out of the hospital I was feeling maimed and deformed and he didn't care, he really didn't."

Another pat of her chest.

"I was upfront with Trevor, after I got maimed, that was my approach, put it on the line right away, expect them to bail. Most men did. Trevor didn't. He said he liked me the way I was. I think he meant it, but who knows?"

"How'd you meet?"

"Where else? A party, don't ask where, who threw it, whatever, because I have no idea. I was in serious pain and taking serious painkillers, a lot back then is a blur. All I can tell you is one of those parties that seem to crop up, you get invited but can't figure out why. I do remember it being in some incredible house—maybe Pacific Heights?"

Shrugging. "Amazing mansion, amazing drugs for anyone who wanted them: coke, pills, heroin, of course weed, weed was like cocktails, they served doobies on silver trays. I arrived already grokked out, only did weed. It was good stuff and it totally downed me and I shrank off to a corner and just sat there. I must've fallen asleep because I woke up and found this tall good-looking guy in a blazer and of all things an *ascot,* standing over me, smiling. Like he cared."

She lifted another bacon filament with her fingers. Murmured,

"Bison, low fat, calories like halibut," nibbled half a thread, put the rest back atop the salad. "An ascot, when's the last time you saw one of those except in a British movie? I thought I was dreaming, some duke had appeared, was going to say something with an accent and take me off in his Rolls-Royce. He sat down next to me, asked if I was okay without an accent, and we started talking and I didn't wake up. So I realized I was already awake. Am I making sense?"

"Total sense."

"I hope you're right." She glanced over at Lucy. "Can you pack this up, Angela?"

"You bet." The waitress came over, picked up the bowl, shot me a conspiratorial glance. *This is what she always does.*

When she left, Maillot Bernard said, "Where was I?"

"You realized you were awake."

"Yes. He was very nice. Soft-spoken, offered to drive me home and I said sure. He didn't have a Rolls but he did have a nice Jaguar and he walked me to my door, didn't try anything. So of course I said yes when he asked for my number. I'm a yes-girl, in general, always had trouble with no. It's made life hard but I'd still rather be that way."

"Keeping it positive."

"Keeping it obedient, Doctor." She sighed. "Okay, full disclosure: I'm a submissive. I hope you don't find that psychiatric or anything."

"Different strokes," I said. "Long as you stay safe."

"I didn't always pay enough attention to safety but I do now. If you're thinking Trevor was a dominant and that's why we hooked up, he wasn't. He was a normal. In that regard, anyway. No control issues but I still liked him. Maybe it was because of the gold piano."

I sat there.

"Of course you'd have no idea," she said. "Okay, one of the clubs, there was this gold piano hooked up to pulleys. A girl would sit on it and they'd lower her to the stage while she stripped." Smiling. "We were the showpieces. Served up like a meal. Anyway, one of the bouncers used to have a thing for me and one time I stayed late with him and he wanted to . . . use the piano for you-know-what. I said sure but while we were doing it, Billy—that was his name—must've triggered a switch and the piano started climbing toward the ceiling. By the time we realized what was happening, it was pushing up close to the ceiling. Billy was a big guy, like a football player, and he got crushed between the piano and ceiling until I finally figured out where the switch was. He didn't die but he broke a lot of things inside and got crippled. Only reason I was okay is I was a lot skinnier than him so all the crushing was happening to him."

She pinged a bitten nail against her mug. "After that, I decided always to be skinny. The piano freaked me out, I didn't go back to the club, wanted a different environment so I started teaching little girls ballet for crap money. I lost my apartment, had to room with some . . . not-so-great people. It was around then that I met Trevor. No control issues with regard to you-know-what. In fact, he wasn't much into it, period."

"Asexual?"

"More like super-low-sexual. Which was fine with me. My body the way it was, the pain, feeling deformed, last thing I wanted was someone jumping my bones."

She smiled. "Top of that, he had an amazing house. Victorian that he restored, close enough to the wharf to walk. At the time I thought he was my savior."

"That changed."

She looked out the window, watched cars pass for a while. "It's the same old story, I'm sure you hear it all the time. Especially working for the police."

"Not sure what you mean."

"Relationships," she said. "They go bad. With Trevor it wasn't dramatic, it just crept in. He got more and more possessive. Not physically, just—okay, here's the thing: We never went anywhere, which was fine with me in the beginning. I was happy to have a refuge. And his house was big, beautiful, and quiet. Trevor drew all day, then he slept, then he drew some more, then he slept. At first, I didn't mind."

"What changed?"

"I got bored," she said. "Felt like getting out. Just once in a while, maybe start teaching kids again—'cause I'd quit that job. All I was doing was watching TV and videos of dance exercises. I ended up sleeping a lot, myself, and it made me tired. So I asked Trevor if I could go out for a while and he said don't do it, I was vulnerable. I wasn't ready to stress myself out, so I agreed. Then I started doing it— sneaking out when I knew Trevor would be locked up in his studio. Nothing weird, I took walks. It felt like I landed on another planet. I liked the feeling. But then I'd rush back, afraid he'd find out."

I said, "Sounds a little like prison."

"I guess it does," said Maillot Bernard. "I guess it was. One night, late at night, Trevor was doing one of his marathon drawing things. Even when he came out of the studio, he'd been super-quiet, ignoring me when I talked to him. So I went out and took a longer walk than ever and when I got back he was in the doorway, just standing there, no expression on his face. I thought, *He's not going to allow me back.* But then he stepped aside. And once I was inside, his face got different."

"Angry?"

"No, that's the thing, angry I could understand. I was raised with it." Lowering her eyes. "But that's another story . . . no, Trevor didn't show angry, he just got cold. Like I was there, in his house physically, but I didn't matter spiritually—humanly."

"Dismissing you."

"Exactly, Doctor. I knew I was being punished but figured it would end. Then, when I said I was ready to go to bed, he pointed to a chair and had me sit there while he left. Then he came back with a gun and stood over me."

"He pointed it at you?"

"No, he just held it at his side," she said. "But it was a gun."

"What kind?"

"How would I know?" she said. "I *hate* guns."

"Was it long like a rifle or small like a pistol?"

"Long," she said. "Made out of wood."

I pulled out my phone, called up an image of a 12-gauge Remington.

Maillot Bernard shuddered. "I hate them . . . maybe."

A photo of a deer rifle evoked a head shake. "They look the same to me."

I said, "Trevor just stood there holding it."

"For a long time," she said. "Not saying anything. Then he left, came back without the gun and said, 'Time for bed,' and we went to bed. And that night he—we—he didn't touch my chest. He used to make sure to do that, being super-gentle. It was like he looked at me different."

"Scary."

"I couldn't sleep, terrified he'd bring the gun back and shoot me. I got up twice in the middle of the night. One time, I went to the bathroom and threw up. Trevor slept through totally, he was always a deep sleeper. The next morning, he's not talking, he goes into the studio and I'm sitting there watching soaps. The day after that, he finally left to buy art supplies. I packed my stuff and got out of there. I didn't even want to stay in San Francisco so I went to the Greyhound station and bought a one-way to L.A. Because I used to dance here, too. The Seventh Veil, places like that, but I also made it to the Hollywood Bowl stage for their big Fourth of July celebration. I was a stand-in but that was *something*, we had these star-spangled costumes."

"Did you know people here?"

"I thought I did but the numbers I had for them weren't good anymore. The only money I had was in my purse, like fifteen bucks. I went to a shelter downtown. It was crazy, full of addicts and psychos. But you know, I felt safer there. A few days later, I remembered my checking account, Bank of America, I'd forgotten about it because

Trevor had been paying for everything. I managed to get funds wired and found a room in a motel on Hollywood. That was pretty sketchy, drug dealers out front, all night you could hear sirens. Finally, I located a girl who didn't dance anymore and worked for a lawyer who did disability. He couldn't believe I hadn't applied, got me a doctor appointment and that got me signed up, and that's where I've been since."

She smiled. "Stuff happens, right?"

"Did Trevor try to make contact?"

"I was scared he would, but no, never," she said. "Guess he's not a stalker, just had a moment."

"A gun," I said. "That's some moment."

"I never even knew he owned one, Doctor. That's what freaked me out, is he telling himself it's time to kick it up to a new level?"

She leaned forward. "You can't tell me? Did he do something really bad with a gun?"

"All I can say is his name came up."

"Wow. I don't wish him bad," she said. "But talking to you made me feel a lot better. The police actually suspect him of something. I wasn't crazy to worry, I was smart."

She pretended to object when I paid the check, said, "If you insist," and squeezed my hand when I got up.

"Thanks for your time, Mai-la."

"Maybe I should be the one thanking you," she said. "Maybe this was therapy."

17

I phoned Milo at his desk. He said, "You and your hunches, just talked to Braun's first wife, Barbara from Stockton. Not the sharpest in the drawer and she's not a legal wife, she and Braun lived together for three years."

"How'd you find her?"

"Masterful detection. I looked up Barbara Braun in Stockton."

"They weren't married but she uses Braun's name."

"It's her name, too, they're second cousins, he was an orphan, lived with her family for a while."

"So that part of his story was true."

"But the part about Barbara's illness was a mix of truth and bullshit. She had cancer but survived it. Chemo, radiation, she couldn't even tell me the diagnosis. Apparently, Hal stuck with her every step of the way, a real prince. In terms of why they split up, all she could say was they ended up different and that she was the one to initiate. She didn't say initiate, just 'I did it.' She came across as basic, Alex. Maybe even a little impaired."

"Hal was there for her but he claimed she was dead."

"I didn't tell her that, why burst her bubble? She had nothing bad to say about him. Broke down big-time when I informed her. Blamed herself, in fact."

"Why?"

"If she hadn't broken up with him, he never woulda left Stockton and gotten carried away by big-city sin. I asked her about their years together, the picture I got is a couple of poor kids barely scratching by. Rented trailer, Braun pumped gas part-time, both of them picked crops seasonally."

"From that to knight in armor," I said.

"Speaking of which, Braun had hero fantasies way back. Talked to Barbara about joining the FBI, the CIA, the Secret Service. Only place he actually applied was the Coast Guard but they turned him down. Something about allergies."

"Any attempts to be a cop?"

"Nothing she was aware of, though in high school he'd been a police cadet. She does recall him participating in a search party for a missing kid. Nothing obviously creepy about his motives, the whole town turned out and the kid was found safe."

"Maybe he wasn't drawn to the city by sin," I said. "More like expanding his altruistic horizons."

"Being a big-time hero but he ends up selling shoes and then messing up his leg? Sure, but it doesn't explain how he ended up on the Corvins' hardwood. I asked Barbara if Hal had spent any time in San Francisco, trying to connect him to Bitt. It's not far from Stockton but she said she never knew him to go there."

"Speaking of Bitt." I told him Maillot Bernard's story.

"A long gun. But he didn't threaten her with it?"

"Just held it and stared at her. She can't tell the difference between a rifle and a shotgun, but wouldn't it be interesting if what Bitt showed her was a 12-gauge that he still owns?"

"Easy enough to find out if I could get a warrant to cross his damn threshold."

I said, "If Chelsea could be documented actually going into Bitt's house, could you make a case for a welfare check?"

"On what grounds?"

"Mentally impaired minor sneaks into the home of a person of interest in a homicide."

"Elegantly devious, Alex. But if she just goes in and comes out, iffy . . . maybe a coupla nights' surveillance will help. I get lucky, see the two of them actually make inappropriate physical contact, I can go in there with no paper."

Night one, he parked a block from Evada and watched through binoculars from the far end of the block. Chelsea Corvin never left her house. Bitt's lights were out.

Night two, just after ten p.m., Bitt's front door opened and the artist, carrying something, got in his pickup and drove away. Too dark to make out details. By the time Milo made it back to his car, the truck was out of sight.

He enlisted Binchy and Reed for two more nights. Nothing on Binchy's Sunday watch. Two weeks had passed since the murder. The Corvins didn't go out for dinner.

On Monday night, when Reed arrived, Bitt's truck was already gone. No spotting of Chelsea.

Tuesday morning, both of the young D's were pulled from Milo's supervision, Reed handling a bar fight in Palms, Binchy catching an armed robbery in Pico-Robertson.

Milo said, "So much for that. Nguyen says it woulda been doubtful without an obvious felony."

I worked long days on two custody evals but found time to recheck social network sites for anything on Hargis Braun and the three women who'd lived with him.

Barbara Braun's Facebook page was a skimpy thing. A few relatives, no human friends. The only posted photographs were her and a massive black Newfoundland.

Wally was certified as a therapy dog and demonstrated his interpersonal skills by never leaving the side of a small, pinched-faced woman.

Barb Braun was dependent on a pair of forearm crutches. Add that to EmJay's arthritis and you didn't need to be Freud.

Mary Ellen Braun had seemed healthy. I Googled her anyway. Her LinkedIn listing reached out to retailers, said nothing about health problems. But her name showed up in a support group for women with chronic fatigue syndrome.

A man attracted to disability.

The impulse was to tag that as pathological. My training leads me to avoid dime-store diagnosis.

Joining search parties. Planting unsanctioned trees. Butting in during a domestic.

Saving a snake.

For all I knew, Hal Braun's taste in women spoke to a rare nobility. A man with ideals and goals, however absurdly romanticized.

A poster boy for No Good Deed.

Voicemail on all of Milo's lines. I left messages but he didn't call back. Maybe sixteen days of nothing on Braun had put him in a funk. Or his attention had shifted to a more manageable crime.

That night, Robin and I had a late dinner at the Grill on the Alley and were walking to the Seville when my cell chirped.

Ten ten p.m.

He said, "Sitting down, amigo?"

"Upright."

"Then maybe you should brace yourself. You're not gonna *believe* this."

18

At eight forty-nine p.m., Hollywood Division patrol officers finishing their dinner at Tio Taco had responded to
an anonymous report of a "415"—unspecified disturbance—and
driven to the Sahara Motor Inn on Franklin Avenue just east of Western.

Parking in the mostly empty lot, they knocked on the door of
room fourteen. After receiving no reply, Officer Eugene Stargill pretended to peer through a slit in the plastic vertical blinds and see
nothing out of order.

"Bogus," he pronounced. "Let's book."

His partner, a gung-ho kid fresh out of the academy named Brad-
ley Buttons, insisted on having the manager check.

As Stargill figured out ways of getting back at the pain-in-the-ass
rookie, the manager, Kiran "Keith" Singh, unlocked the door.

At eight fifty-four p.m., Stargill phoned in a dead body, making it
sound as if he'd been conscientious.

Hollywood detectives Petra Connor and Raul Biro arrived on the scene at nine eighteen. By nine forty, a coroner's investigator had gone through the DB's pockets and produced I.D.

During the brief drive from Wilcox Avenue, the victim's name had sparked Petra's memory but she couldn't get a handle on it. One of those tip-of-the-mind things.

Just as Biro turned off the ignition and she saw the motel, she figured it out. Scanning the homicide list and checking out the details of weird ones was a daily habit for her, though it rarely paid off.

This time it did.

She called Milo. He called me.

I arrived at ten forty-eight, spotted both of them just inside the yellow tape, bootied and gloved. The air smelled of cheap gasoline and fried food. The motel layout was basic: fifteen green doors arrayed to the right, a pitted but generous parking lot. The building was sad gray stucco with a matching warped roof. If the east end of Hollywood ever really got renewed, the value was the lot. The obvious replacement, yet another strip mall.

Milo was facing away and didn't notice me. His clothes were rumpled, his hair ragged. Petra stood next to him, slim, elegant, black wedge cut swept back from a finely molded ivory face. She looked like a socialite hanging with the uncle who'd blown his inheritance.

She waved. He turned and said, "As promised, insane."

By ten fifty, I was looking at the prone form of Chet Corvin, face-down on a pink, blood-soaked polyester carpet.

For a hot-sheet Hollywood motel, not a bad room. Management here utilized something minty-fresh to disinfect. The fragrance failed to compete with the copper of fresh blood and the sulfurous emissions from relaxed bowels.

Walls covered in flesh-colored vinyl were freckled with red halfway up and to the right of the corpse. A royal-blue velveteen spread that looked cheap but new lay smoothly, neatly atop the queen-sized bed. A pay-by-the-minute vibrating gizmo, complete with credit card reader, gave off a chromium glare.

The thirty-inch flat-screen facing the bed was tuned to a pay-per-view menu. Adult Entertainment. Men's clothing was draped over a chair, calfskin loafers lined up neatly, each stuffed with a precisely rolled argyle sock. Chet Corvin wore nothing but boxer shorts, now soiled, as were his thighs. His bare back was broad and hairless, bulky muscles padded with fat. One hand was concealed under his torso. The nails of the other were manicured and glossy.

Two ruby-black holes formed a neat colon on the back of his neck, visible in the thin strands just above the hairline. One wound placed precisely above the other.

I said, "Skillful shooting."

Milo nodded. "C.I. says the first woulda likely put him right down—straight to the brain stem. After that, the shooter could take time lining up the second."

"Maybe a statement," I said.

Petra said, "Such as?"

"I'm proud of my work."

Both of them frowned.

My gaze shifted to the wood-aping plastic nightstand bolted to the wall left of the bed. A man's alligator-skin wallet sat next to two water glasses and a bottle of Chardonnay. Sonoma Valley, Russian River, three years old. A label that looked high-end but I'm no expert.

I said, "Date night?"

Milo said, "Heavy smell of perfume in the lav says some kind of party. Petra informs me it's Armani, probably sprayed—aqua what?"

"Acqua di Gioia," she said. "I sometimes use it myself." Smiling. "When I need to wake Eric up."

I said, "Expensive?"

"I get mine at the outlets but even with that, not cheap."

Milo said, "Rounding out the picture, we've also got some longish brunette hairs that aren't Chet's on the bathroom counter. The kid at the front desk claims the room was cleaned a few hours before Corvin checked in at eight eleven, no one else used it in the interim, hopefully he's being straight and we're not talking leftover debris."

"I think he is, nice kid," said Petra. "Goes to college during the day, just started working here. We're not talking some street-smart compulsive liar." To me: "Anything else occur to you?"

I said, "Corvin drove a Range Rover. Didn't see it out front."

"Wasn't here. We'll check local CCTV, see if we can pick it up."

Milo said, "No video here except behind the desk, good shot of Corvin checking in. He looks relaxed. Used his real name, paid with a company credit card."

I said, "Someone else who was proud of himself."

"Fits with what we've seen of ol' Chet." To Petra: "Like I told you, guy was a blowhard."

I said, "Shot dead thirty-eight minutes after he got here. He check in alone?"

"No one else on the video," said Milo. "Whether his amusement for the evening was waiting in the car or she arrived separately is impossible to know at this point. The setup is everyone pulls up to their own door and for obvious reasons there are no cameras in the lot except for one at the far end with a view of the rear alley."

Petra said, "Monitoring the dumpsters, God forbid someone should hijack the trash."

I said, "His clothes are off and most of the wine is gone but the bed doesn't look as if it's been used."

Milo said, "We're figuring they were warming up and it never got to the next stage."

"Is that wallet full?"

Petra said, "Three hundred and some change, plus all his credit cards. Pictures of his kids, too. But not his wife."

"No surprise," said Milo. "Like I said, disharmony ruled his roost."

I said, "So not a robbery."

Petra said, "Unless the Rover was the target."

"Take the car and leave all this money? Line up those bullet holes and clean up the casings? Looks more like an execution."

She shrugged. "In view of the body in his den, you could be right. But the car *was* taken."

Milo said, "Maybe as a bonus—spot the keys, book."

"So how did the murderer get here?"

Silence.

I said, "Are you looking at the woman as a suspect?"

Petra said, "Could be. Or she and Corvin got invaded, he got shot, she escaped." Frowning. "Or she didn't. If I find out a female called it in, she gets lower priority as a suspect."

"No 911 tape?"

"No, it came to us on the non-emergency line as a nonspecified 415. We've got civilians working the desk, I'll talk to whoever took the call. The body was warm when patrol got here so whoever it was called pretty soon after."

I said, "Not using 911 could've theoretically slowed the process and given the caller time to gain some distance from the scene. That could fit with Corvin's companion escaping but not wanting to get involved."

Milo said, "That, long hair, perfume, this neighborhood, a lady of the night is a decent bet. Easy to see why she wouldn't wanna be involved."

I said, "A Hollywood hooker using Armani?"

Petra said, "You'd be surprised, Alex. I've seen girls come into the jail soaked in really good stuff."

"The wine doesn't look cheap, either."

"You know it?"

"Nope, but Russian River's a prime Chardonnay region."

Milo said, "See why he's so useful?" He peered at the label, ran a search on his phone, whistled. "That particular year, seventy-nine bucks a bottle."

I said, "So maybe it wasn't a commercial transaction."

Petra said, "A tryst with a girlfriend? He's got an expense account and platinum cards and brings her here?"

I pointed to the porn menu. "A little bit of sleaze to spice things up?"

Milo grinned. "There's a psychological insight . . . yeah, why not."

Petra's slim fingers drummed her forearm. "Slumming for fun? Okay, I can see that."

She looked at the body. "Talk about a party with an unhappy ending. We'll do a neighborhood canvass, try to find out if anyone remembers seeing him with a female."

Milo said, "We'll also be looking for Mr. Bitt, skulking around." To me: "I filled her in."

Petra said, "I'll also subpoena his credit cards and his phone."

"I can do that," said Milo. "If you don't mind."

"Why would I mind not dealing with the phone company? Be my guest, but how come you want to?"

"This is your turf, kid. I need your brains on the street."

"Sure," said Petra. "If we are dealing with the same offender as Braun, he's super-organized, no? I suppose Bitt could be like that. His art's extremely meticulous."

Familiar with the cartoonist? Then I remembered: Before entering the police academy on a lark, she'd worked as a graphic artist. "You know Bitt?"

"I know *of* him, Alex. One of the guys I went to school with loved his work and used to bring it in for the rest of us to admire. I could see the talent but I thought it was mega-sick."

She tapped her foot, took a step closer to the body, retreated. "Even so, that's not what I find interesting, art and personality aren't an obvious link. It's his stonewalling and the gun story. On the other hand, if Chet Corvin was targeted first by dumping Braun in his house, why would Bitt call attention to himself? And why would he go after Corvin, here? This scene and what Milo tells me about Corvin's life on the road, there could be a long list of angry husbands and boyfriends."

Milo said, "All true but I'm not ready to put Bitt aside. We surveilled him four nights and it came to zilch but Sean took it on himself to do a drive-by tonight at eight thirty, God bless the lad, and Bitt's truck was gone. So maybe he *was* stalking Corvin. We need to check every camera we can find, see if the truck shows up. That's what I mean about keeping it local."

Petra said, "Raul will love that. You know how he is, makes compulsive look sloppy. If there's something there, he'll find it. If we do get Bitt in proximity to the scene, I can't see you *not* getting your warrant."

"Fingers crossed."

Knock on the open door. A pair of crypt deliverymen with a collapsible gurney and a body bag stood outside.

One of them said, "We ready?"

We left as the clacking and sacking commenced. Cool night, thin traffic on Franklin. Some of the surrounding buildings were prewar and pretty, conceived when Hollywood was Hollywood. The Sahara motel and others looked like scars on an actress.

A dark-haired man in a cream-colored suit approached. Detective Raul Biro, compact, prone to striding confidently, had one of those faces that didn't age in real time. His hair was black with blue overtones, thick and glossed with something that subdued every loose strand, his skin as smooth as that of a toddler.

I'd seen him at the most brutal of murder scenes. He never looked anything but put-together and tonight was no exception: in addition to the impeccably tailored suit, a baby-blue shirt woven by agreeable silkworms and navy-blue suede loafers with gold buckles.

Something new, tonight: instead of the usual silk cravat, a braided leather string tie fastened by a polished oval of black onyx.

He saw me looking at it. "From Sedona, I think it's over the top but the wife's one-twelfth Navajo and she likes it. Usually, I take it off when I get to the office and put on a normal one. Tonight I forgot."

I said, "It's a good look, Raul."

"You think?"

"You bet. Texas Ranger comes to L.A."

He laughed. "There's a TV show for you. How's it going, Doc?"

"Great. You?"

"Better than great, new baby," he said. "Gregory Edwin. Blond, like the wife, can you imagine?"

"Congrats."

His smile was wide and bright. "First-class baby, meaning he sleeps, we finally got it right." He looked at unit fourteen. "This is a bizarre one, no?" To Petra: "I got us six uniforms for the canvass. What parameters do you think?"

She said, "Let's start with Franklin, go a mile east and west. Nothing shows up there, we can either expand it north–south, or just south and concentrate on the boulevard."

"Boulevard's going to have tons of cameras," said Biro. "We could be going through it until who knows when. And unlikely Corvin's going to be walking, at best we'll see his car passing, at super-best, leaving here."

"There's another target vehicle, Raul."

She told him about Trevor Bitt's black Ram pickup. Described Bitt and the fact that he'd stonewalled for over two weeks.

He said, "Guy sounds nuts." To me: "You've probably got a better word for it."

I said, "Not tonight."

He laughed again.

Petra said, "You want this to be our case, Milo? Or are we assisting on yours? I want to know in terms of organizing my own mind. As in who notifies the wife and kids."

Milo said, "I'll do it. Tomorrow morning, family's been through enough, no sense waking them up in the middle of the night."

Biro said, "You viewing the wife as a potential suspect? Seeing as he was messing with another woman?"

"Nothing points to that, Raul, but nothing says no."

"We get lucky, another domestic murder for hire. Not that it would account for your body in the den."

Milo said, "Alex has always said that pointed to Chet as the likely target."

Petra said, "Obviously, Alex was right. And if Braun was connected to Chet in some way that made her beaucoup mad, she could've hired a professional to do both of them."

Biro said, "Dump a corpse in hub's private space, there's a big middle finger for you."

Milo said, "You see that, Alex?"

I said, "I can't see Felice traumatizing the kids."

"Fair enough," said Petra. "But if she's got money separate from his, let's try to find out if she's spending it unusually, as in unspecified cash payments going out."

Milo said, "There is a decent chance of separate accounts. These people have been separate for a long time."

19

As we walked away from the motel, I noticed a young man standing near the office door picking a cuticle at warp speed. A boy, really, eighteen, nineteen. When our eyes met, he looked away.

"The clerk?" I said.

"That's him. Keith Singh."

"You mind?"

"Go for it."

As we approached Singh, he startled and turned to go back inside.

I said, "A second, Keith?"

He stopped, rotated. Kicked one ankle with the other. "Yes, sir." Lanky, Indian, with shoulder-length black hair, wearing a yellow Lion King T-shirt, jeans, and sneakers. If he was able to grow a beard it didn't show. But his eyes looked old, bottomed by dark crescents, managing to be weary and wary at the same time.

I said, "Tough night."

"Total disaster, sir. My parents didn't want me working here, now they'll insist. One of my dad's friends owns the place, but Dad says

Waris—Dr. Waris Singh, he's a dentist but he's mostly into real estate—isn't careful."

"About security?"

"In general," he said. "My parents are more religious than him. They think he could be a bad influence." His eyes dropped. "I'll have to quit. Which is crap, I still have tuition."

"Where do you go to school?"

"The U. I'm out of state so the tuition's crazy."

"Sure is."

"I was a late admission, all the work-study jobs were taken. I *have* to find another one but the only other sure thing is a restaurant Waris owns. But that place is all the way in Pasadena and it's crazy busy. Here I can get a lot of studying done."

The gurney was wheeled out of the motel. Keith Singh's eyes saucered.

I said, "What's your major?"

"Econ." His eyes drifted to the yellow tape, moving in the night breeze like a harp string lightly plucked. "It's crazy, sir, I didn't hear anything."

I said, "You probably wouldn't, too far away."

"Exactly."

"Have you remembered anything else about Mr. Corvin?"

"The guy?" he said. "Like what?"

"Did he say anything when he checked in?"

"He said a lot," said Keith Singh, clapping his index finger and his thumb together. "Talking talking talking."

"About what?"

"Random crap. How's it going, young man, nice night. I kind of blocked it out. He saw my econ book, told me he took micro and macro in college. Told me it was too theoretical, he majored in accounting and business management, not econ, I should do the same thing if I wanted to make serious money."

"He's there ten seconds and is giving you advice."

"I'm used to it," he said. "Dad."

"What else did Corvin have to say?"

"Nothing, sir—oh, yeah, he showed me the wine."

"He brought the wine into the office."

"Yeah," said Keith Singh. "In a bag, said he just got it, it was expensive. Said it was worth it." Keith Singh licked parched lips. "He winked when he said that. That it was worth it."

"What do you think he was telling you, Keith?"

The kid colored, chestnut skin turning to mahogany. "What do you mean?"

"Sounds like he was trying to impress you."

"Why would he do that, sir? More like bragging. Like he was used to that."

"Did you see the woman he was with?"

"I didn't see anyone, sir. I was here in the office, like I'm supposed to be, he gave his card and drove over. I didn't look at him much. Waris told me that at the beginning. Don't look at the customers, they want privacy."

"Lots of hot dates show up here, huh?"

He frowned. "I mean, people . . . you know . . . I mean Waris doesn't rent by the hour like some other places but his rates are cheap." He shrugged.

I said, "A lot of customers choose not to spend the night."

Keith Singh's Adam's apple rose and fell. "My parents thought it was a *real* bad idea. Waris convinced them but not really, you know?"

"They gave in."

Another ride of the gullet elevator.

"My dad owes Waris money. Waris kind of pressured him." A flap of black hair fell forward. He tucked it behind his ear. "I probably would've quit anyway."

"Not happy with the job."

"It's gross, you know?"

Milo said, "No-tell motel."

The boy blinked. He'd never heard the phrase. "All I want to do is study, it's hard enough. My parents wanted me to stay in Tucson, go to Arizona, live at home. I thought I'd have to but last minute I got into the U. from the waiting list and it's way higher-rated so I wanted to. I have a cousin, a CPA in Boston, he told them where you go makes a difference so they finally allowed me."

I said, "Good luck with your studies. Is there anything else you can tell us about Mr. Corvin?"

"Just what I said to you." Looking at Milo. "He used a platinum— not like some people, they're, you know . . . looking all over the place, embarrassed, using cash. He was just the opposite. Kind of full of himself, you know? Like he wasn't expecting anything bad to happen."

I said, "People usually don't."

"Oh, man," said Keith Singh. "I'm *probably* going to quit tomorrow. Maybe I'll *have* to go back to Tucson."

Milo and I continued to the Seville.

I said, "Chet bringing the wine in, still bagged, could mean he'd just bought it."

"I'll tell Petra and Raul to check out nearby liquor stores, maybe someone's memory will be jogged."

He loosened his tie. "I'm figuring to catch Felice and the kids before they leave for school, say seven a.m. You up for rise and shine? You're not, I understand."

I said, "I'll be there. If you want, I can tell the kids. To make sure it's done right and you'll have more time to gauge Felice's reaction."

"That would be great."

At the Seville, he said, "All these years I still hate death knocks. And kids? Thanks. See you bright and early. In my case, just early."

◆

I parked in front of the Corvin Colonial at six fifty-six a.m. Milo's unmarked sat in front of Trevor Bitt's Tudor. The black Ram was there.

A bit of activity on the street: a couple of gardener's trucks pulling up but waiting before unleashing mowers and air guns, neighbors leaving for work or taking in newspapers, a few of them looking at us, most pretending not to.

Felice Corvin came to the door dressed in a hip-length tweed jacket, a black blouse, and gray slacks. Hair combed, makeup impeccable, mug of coffee in her hand. No sign of the kids. She said, "This is a surprise."

Milo said, "Can we come in?"

No *Good morning, ma'am,* no friendly-cop smile.

"What's going on, Lieutenant?"

"Inside would be better."

She looked down the street. "I've got to get going soon."

Milo said, "Please," making it sound like a command.

She stepped back and we entered. Footsteps from upstairs pinpointed the kids' location. Breakfast smells—eggs, toast, coffee—drifted from the kitchen.

Milo said, "I'm sorry to tell you, Ms. Corvin. Your husband's body was found last night."

Long stare. Three blinks. "Body?"

"He's been murdered, Ms. Corvin."

"Body," she repeated. She stood there, not moving a muscle. Then she teetered and when Milo caught her elbow, she didn't resist.

Her hand pressed against her mouth and her breathing raced as he steered her into the living room. The kids' footsteps stopped and Felice Corvin looked at the staircase with panic. Then the noise resumed and she allowed Milo to sit her down on a sofa. He and I took facing chairs. He edged his closer to her.

"I'm sorry for your loss, ma'am."

"I don't understand," she said. Dry eyes, rigid posture. Every hair remained in place. "Body?"

Flat voice. Her complexion had lost color; makeup could only go so far.

"Last night, Mr. Corvin was found in a hotel shot to death."

"He's always in hotels."

"This one was in Hollywood."

"The Roosevelt?" she said. "That's the only hotel I know in Hollywood. It's supposed to be haunted. I went to a concert there a few years ago. The Da Camera Society. Baroque music. I loved it, Chet slept through the whole thing. Why would he go to the Roosevelt?"

Milo exhaled. "This was more like a *motel*."

Felice Corvin's face whipped toward him. "Why didn't you say that at the beginning? Why can't you be precise?"

We sat there.

She said, "You really need to be *precise*. Precision *matters*. If the educational system was more precise . . ." She shook her head. "Who killed him in a *motel*?"

"We don't know."

"A *motel*." Lips curling around the word. "Are you trying to tell me something icky about Chet?"

"We don't know much, yet, ma'am."

"That seems to be your pattern," she said. "Not knowing much."

"It's a tough job."

"So is mine. So is everyone's. Life's frigging *tough*. I wish my kids could learn that, they're growing up expecting everything to come their way. At least Brett is. He's spoiled, Chelsea . . . for her, everything's a challenge. I'm not sure she really understands what she's up against . . . a mo*tel*? What are you really *telling* me, Lieutenant?"

"Just that, ma'am."

"I know about motels. What they connote. Are you denying that?"

Milo said nothing.

Felice Corvin hugged herself and glanced at the stairs, again.

"Ma'am, would you like us to tell the children?"

"Us?" she said. "The two of you are a team? Or does that just mean you want Dr. Delaware to tell them? Psychological *sensitivity* and all that." To me: "You want to make them psychiatric patients? No, thanks, they're mine and I'll handle it."

A thump from above.

Felice Corvin said, "When I'm ready."

We sat there.

Her grip on her own shoulders tightened. "I am *so* angry. One friggin' damn thing after another—it just keeps—okay, let's stop beating around the bush. Was he with a *whore*?"

Milo said, "Did Chet make a habit of—"

"I have no *idea* about Chet's habits. Other than the ones he displayed *here*." She huffed. "He was gone all the time. *Business.* I'm not stupid. I know what men are like. I know what Chet was like. He didn't give a damn about anyone but himself."

"Is there a specific woman he was—"

She laughed, clawed air, yanked on her hair. "Why don't you just log onto whores.com or something and run your finger down the list."

"So you were aware—"

"I was aware that Chet had the sexual scruples of a wolverine in heat. And that when he returned from his 'business' "—she shaped quotation marks—"he paid even less attention to me than usual, which was pretty minimal to begin with. Are you *understanding*? His *needs* were being *tended* to. A while back I decided to confront him. So he wouldn't give me a disease. Of course he denied it but I told him if you ever infect me with something, I'll kil—"

She cut herself off. Literally, with a hand over her mouth. When her fingers dropped, her lips formed a crooked, icy smile. "That was a figure of speech. I certainly didn't leave my children last night, drive over to some disgusting motel I had no idea existed in the first place, and shoot my husband. I've never fired a gun in my life."

Milo nodded.

"You agree?" said Felice Corvin. "Don't tell me you're not considering it. Isn't the spouse the first person you look at? Am I one of your friggin *suspects*? Fine, do your thing, I have nothing to hide."

She charged to her feet, stomped to the entry hall, raised a fist. "I am *so, so* angry. It never *stops*."

Milo said, "What doesn't?"

The fist waved. "*Crap* doesn't. The endless flood of crap and . . . and . . . and . . . *issues*. Now I have to go tell my children something that's going to screw them up forever. How are they ever going to have faith in the future?"

She covered her face with both hands, fought tears and lost.

I guided her back to the living room. Her body stiffened when I touched her elbow but she returned with me and sat in the same place.

I fetched tissues from the powder room. She dabbed her eyes dry, sat with her hands in her lap, a chastened child.

Milo said, "Ma'am."

Felice Corvin said, "I apologize, Dr. Delaware. I'm not one of those people—afraid of therapists. I believe in therapy, used to be a teacher, wanted so many kids to get help who never did. Then I had my own and—I'm sorry. I've been rude to you, Dr. Delaware, and I want to explain."

"Not neces—"

"It is necessary! I need you to understand! It was nothing personal, I'm sure you're a good psychologist. But a bunch of your colleagues did nothing for my daughter and some of them made her feel much worse. So I lost faith . . . I'm sorry. For being so angry and for being such a pain in the butt and now it's really hit the fan and what the hell am I going to *do*?"

More tears, followed by a lopsided smile. "During challenging times one needs *especially* to be gracious. My mother always said that. Her mother, too. I told them I agreed. I do." Tears trickled down her cheeks. "I've obviously failed that challenge miserably."

Milo said, "It's a terrible thing to go through. Again, we're so sorry."

"I believe you, Lieutenant. I really do."

"There *are* questions we need to ask about Chet."

"Chet," said Felice Corvin. "Who knows anything about Chet?" She shrugged. "Maybe I'll miss him."

Milo managed to get the basics in. Could she think of any possible link between her husband and Hal Braun?

Not to my knowledge.

Did Chet have any business dealings in Ventura, Oxnard, or Santa Barbara?

I know nothing about his business.

Had he been involved in exceptionally bitter business conflicts— denied claims that led to personal attacks?

I have no idea.

I believed her and from the looks of it, Milo did, as well.

Separate lives.

What he didn't bring up were Chelsea's night moves, the possibility of contact with Trevor Bitt.

We'd discussed broaching the topic, agreed it was a bad idea, no sense overwhelming the widow and alienating her completely.

We got up to leave.

Felice stood, too, reaching out and grazing my fingertips. She moaned, "Oh, Dr. Delaware, I'm . . . *could* you tell my children?"

CHAPTER
20

Brett and Chelsea came down the stairs led by their mother. She said, "Sit, guys," in a voice working far too hard to be calm. Surprisingly, neither young Corvin seemed to be alarmed by that.

Chelsea plopped down and stared into space.

Brett scratched behind his ear and mumbled, "Whu?"

Felice said, "Tuck in your shirt in front, Bretty, it's half in, half out."

"Huh?"

"Your shirt, honey. Tuck it in."

Baffled, the boy complied.

"Thank you, sweetie. Okay. Here we go." Sick smile. "Okay . . . okay, there's something you need to hear and Dr. Delaware, you re-member Dr. Delaware, he's going to tell it to you."

Brett's mouth gaped as he squinted at me. Chelsea didn't react.

I edged my chair close enough to look at both of them simultane-ously. Brett's eyes bounced. Chelsea's were still but unfocused. "I'm sorry to be giving you really bad news. Your father passed away last night."

Brett's lips stretched, taking an eerie emotional journey from grin to something toothily grotesque and feral.

"What?" he shouted.

I said, "I'm sorry, Brett. Your dad—"

He shoved his fist toward me. "Fuckin' *bull*shit!"

"I wish it was, Brett."

"Fuckin' bullshit! Fuckin' fuckin' *bull*shit!"

Chelsea said, "It's not."

Everyone looked at her.

She looked at me. "You said it. So it's true."

Not a trace of emotion on her pale, soft face.

Her brother lunged at her. I got between them.

"You cunt fuckin' bullshit!" The boy let out a wordless roar. His body vibrated. Tears shot from his eyes; projectile grief. Stumbling out of the living room, he vaulted up the stairs, punching the banister, swearing, screaming.

Felice said, "My poor baby," and went after him.

Chelsea said, "Crybaby."

A couple of minutes later, Felice returned alone, trembling. "He needs some private time." To me: "That's okay, right?"

I said, "Of course."

During her mother's absence, Chelsea hadn't uttered a word, her only response a head shake when I asked her if she had any questions.

Felice said, "You okay, hon?"

"Uh-huh."

"It's a terrible thing, Cheltz."

The girl shrugged.

Din from above. Something colliding with plaster, over and over. The ceiling thrummed.

Felice said, "He's throwing his basketball. Normally, I wouldn't allow it." Her mouth twisted.

Milo said, "This isn't a normal situation."

Felice turned to Chelsea. "Honey, if you have any questions for these gentlemen, now's the time to ask."

"Uh-uh."

"You're sure."

"I have a question, Mom. For you."

"Of course, darling. What?"

"Am I still going to school today?"

Felice's head retracted. "No, Cheltz—why don't you go upstairs, too. But please, do not go into Brett's room, okay?"

"No way," said the girl. "It smells."

When she was gone, Felice said, "This is unreal."

Milo said, "Is there anything you can tell us that might help us figure it out?"

"I wish there was, Lieutenant. At least one thing I don't have to worry about is money. Chet had an excellent income, I'll grant him that. But the truth is, I brought most of the funds into the marriage."

She looked away. "My parents were professors but they invested extremely well and I'm an only child. So in case you feel like looking for life insurance policies, we don't have any. At least I never took any out on Chet. What he chose to do, who knows? I'm sure you noticed he did his own thing. A lot of men would kill—" Sick smile. "What I'm getting at is I have nothing to hide, anything you want in terms of paperwork is yours."

"Appreciate it, ma'am. We could use access to Chet's phone accounts and his credit cards, right now."

"Give me some time to get you the details—say by later today?"

"That would be great. Thanks for the cooperation."

"Why wouldn't I cooperate? I *want* you to find whoever did it. Chet and I had our differences but no one deserves . . ." She threw up her hands, letting one settle along the side of her face. "A motel. He'd *hate* ending up like that, with Chet it was five-star this, five-star that, getting upgraded to a suite. I grew up with a trust fund but couldn't care less."

She exhaled. "Who to call . . . Chet's parents are gone but he does have a brother in New Jersey. Harrison. He's an optometrist. They're not close but Harrison needs to know . . . I'm sure I'll think of other . . . issues."

She walked us to the door. Milo stepped outside but I said, "A minute, Lieutenant?" and remained in the entry with Felice.

He looked at me, said, "Sure," and kept going.

Felice Corvin said, "What is it, Doctor?"

"If at any point, you feel that I can help, please call."

"If I feel that I will, thank you, that's kind," she said. "Right now, I don't feel much of anything—kind of fuzzy in the head—like I'm in some sort of felt straitjacket—is that normal?"

"It is."

I turned to leave. She clawed my sleeve. "Dr. Delaware, what if I don't end up feeling anything? Does that make me horrible—or abnormal? Will it get in the way of helping my kids?"

I said, "No to all of that."

She stared at me.

I said, "Really. Just take it at your own pace."

"It's nice of you to say that, but I wonder. Maybe I *won't* feel. I sure don't now. Maybe that does say something about me."

"Felice, to feel loss there has to be something to miss."

She flinched. "Ouch. It's been that obvious, huh? Yes, of course it has, I haven't exactly been subtle about our relationship. That's the way I was brought up, say what's on your mind. Some people find me abrasive. I sometimes try to soft-pedal but you are what you are. And with Chet, all these years . . ."

Her hand tightened on my arm. "The crazy thing is, Doctor, I really *loved* him. In the beginning. It wasn't just some half-baked thing, there was *passion*. At that point in my life, I thought he was perfect. Exactly what I needed."

"A take-charge guy."

"Take-charge, self-confident, boisterous, sense of humor. All the things I wasn't, back then. He could talk to anyone about anything at any time. I thought that was amazing. It let me relax and sit back if I didn't feel like talking. I grew up listening to my parents and their professor friends, every topic picked over until the life had been squeezed out of it. Chet was different, he painted with a broad brush. He thought my parents and their friends were pretentious eggheads and told me so. At the beginning, I liked that. How he took charge of me in *every* way."

Spots of color lit up her cheeks.

"What I didn't realize was that he wouldn't wear well. It didn't take long."

"But you stayed together."

She smiled. "I could say it was for the sake of the kids. And that's partly true. But mostly you get to a point and it's inertia, why bother? I'm not a people person, Doctor. I find dealing with people exhausting, they weary me when they get too emotional. So after so many years together, I just didn't see the point of upsetting the apple cart."

She looked down, let go of my sleeve. "Oh, I've wrinkled your jacket, sorry."

I smiled. "I'm sure it'll recover."

She smoothed down the fabric, anyway. "My little speech must've sounded pathetic."

"No—"

"Whatever, Doctor. Thanks for your offer, hopefully I won't need to take you up on it. And I do want Lieutenant Sturgis to catch whoever murdered my husband. I'm going to think of him that way. My *husband*. I'm going to think about him like he was in the beginning. Maybe I'll *feel*."

21

True to her word, just after two p.m., Felice phoned Milo's office and left the details of Chet's cellphone and his credit card accounts. I was there and he put her on speaker.

"Thanks, Ms. Corvin."

"Whatever helps, Lieutenant."

"How're the kids?"

"Brett's taking it really hard. I haven't seen him cry since he was in diapers—he and Chet had this macho thing going. He stopped but now he wants to be by himself and I respect that. I did manage to get some food in him. I'm telling myself it's probably a healthy reaction. Getting in touch with his feelings—we'll work it out. Hope the information will be useful."

"Me, too, ma'am. How's Chelsea?"

"Chelsea's being Chelsea. The sad truth is, she and Chet were never close. Not that he—he was fine with her, he accepted her. She actually seems okay. At least as far as I can tell, she's okay, thanks for asking."

Milo clicked off. "Checked with Petra before we set out. Nothing from the canvass, Chet doesn't seem to have bought the wine near the motel. Raul did find an image of a Range Rover heading east on Franklin a few minutes before Chet checked into the Sahara. No view of the tags, too dark to see who was inside, it tells us what we already know but no harm having a time line. In terms of the woman with him, still nothing."

He looked at the credit info Felice had provided. "Already have one of these cards, Amex Platinum issued by Connecticut Surety for the business expenses of their West Coast regional manager. Got it from his secretary. She was appropriately shocked by the news, had no idea who the boss partied with or if he had a special place he bought wine. What else . . . no luck with GPS on the Rover. It's equipped with a system but it's non-operative. Corrosion, our car guys say it happens."

I said, "A guy who travels all the time with no electronic guide because he failed to fix it. Maybe he sticks to the familiar. Like a woman he saw regularly whose address he didn't want on record."

"Good point. Okay, let's learn more about our new victim."

He phoned in subpoena requests, got eventual cooperation from the credit companies, resistance from the phone provider demanding a written application on "proprietary" forms supplied by its own legal department.

A patient tone of voice as he kept requesting supervisors didn't help, nor did enough pleases and thank-yous to appease the Sycophant Gods. No hint he'd been giving the one-finger salute throughout most of the conversation.

He hung up, said, "Bastards. If Nguyen can't facilitate, I'll go over in person and fill out their damn forms. Enough info on Chet, something's gotta break—hey, aren't you proud of me? Still believing in happy endings?"

I said, "That's just realism."

"What do you mean?"

"Your solve rate. A whole lot more success than failure."

He put his hands over his ears. "Positive thinking? Irish heresy!"

Worming up from his desk chair, he put on his jacket, knotted his tie. "Time for nutrition, let's go dig po*day*-does out of the cold, hard sod."

"No corned beef sandwich?"

"Hmm," he said. "Triple decker, extra mayo, three greasy sides, and a nice frosty lager? You're right, much better: something to feel seriously guilty about."

22

Bert's Deli, a few blocks from the station, was the obvious destination. Aromas streaming from a new Italian place thirty feet closer snagged him first.

The interior was hard black leather and perforated metal. Milo ordered without looking at the menu. The waiter said, "Sure, Lieutenant Sturgis. You, sir?"

When he left, I said, "You two play boccie together?"

"Better game," he said. "I tip big, he pays his rent."

Mushroom and sausage pizza, salad, baked ziti, iced tea, all for two. When I'm with him, I usually don't eat much. This time I was hungry.

As I picked up my second slice of pizza, he said, "Look at you. Gastric juices stimulated by anything in particular?"

"No breakfast."

"Huh . . . let me ask you something: Chelsea being numb about Chet is one thing but the way she made fun of her brother was pretty damn cruel. Is she more than just a dull kid? Actively hated Daddy for a reason?"

I said, "Chet abused her? There's no evidence of it but I guess anything's possible."

"It's not fun to think about, Alex, but it could explain Braun. What if Mr. Do-Gooder was covering up nasty tendencies. What if he and Chet bonded over them."

"Chet pimped his own daughter out to Braun?" I pushed my food away.

He said, "Yeah, it's gross, sorry, but I have to think of everything. Maybe it wasn't that overt. Just photographs, covert videos. Those assholes love to share, right? What if Felice found out, went nuclear, and decided to take care of business. Phase One was luring hubby's sicko buddy somewhere with promises of more nasty. Instead of that, Braun got a hired pro who de-faced and de-handed him and dumped what was left in hubby's personal space. A message to Chet, just like you've been saying all along."

I said, "If so, it didn't get through to Chet. He didn't seem the least bit scared."

"That's because he was a narcissist, shallow, a psychopath, whatever, couldn't imagine anyone aggressing against him. Maybe he didn't even realize it was Braun. Now, if that's the case and I'm Felice, that would piss me off even more. So I set up Phase Two and take care of the problem once and for all. She's got the money for a coupla serious contracts. Just told us so."

"It's a theory," I said.

"But not much of one."

"If you find evidence—"

"Talk about role reversal—lost your appetite?"

"Full."

"Yeah, sure," he said. "Here's a diet idea: the paleo-stress method. Make a hell of an infomercial."

By five p.m., we were back in his office, checking our messages. Thin gruel for both of us.

He read and cursed and clicked off.

I said, "Waiting for something?"

"I asked Reed to check for life insurance. Nothing for Chet or Felice, though Chet's company took out a policy on him that pays them if he attempts to 'sever relations' prematurely. Wonder if they'll try to claim. That would be some court battle, huh? Casualty insurance company up against a life insurance company."

I said, "Godzilla versus Rodan."

"More like Hitler versus Stalin."

At four fifty-five, Raul Biro called to say no video of the Rover had shown up anywhere but he had located the liquor store that had sold Corvin the wine.

"Fancy place, Sunset and La Cienega, transaction was at six thirteen p.m. Owner's daughter was working the register, she didn't have to find the receipt to remember him. He asked for something romantic. Same wink-wink deal he gave the motel clerk. She thought he was quote unquote 'a little slimy.' He also bought a sandwich, roast beef on rye, they get 'em from a deli on the Strip. Coroner bothers to open him up, they can confirm."

Milo said, "Six thirteen is a couple of hours before he checks into the motel. How did he spend the time?"

"Good point," said Biro. "The liquor store's location says he was heading west from West Hollywood to real Hollywood. I'll check along Sunset—pharmacies for condoms, whatever else looks interesting, see if I can fill in some blanks."

"Thanks, Raul."

"Hey, I just thought of something. The Hustler store's not far from the liquor store. Guy's all hyped up and ready to party with a chick, maybe he did a stop-and-shop for a toy or something. Not that I'd know about stuff like that."

"Heaven forfend, Raul. You driving there or taking a jet?"

"Ha. Speaking of sex, none of the girls working the area around the motel know Corvin, so far. So it doesn't look like he picked the place 'cause he was a regular. I know they lie but it fits with what the motel owner told me yesterday. Dr. Waris call-me-Wally Singh runs a discount dental practice in Koreatown along with a whole lot of other businesses, keeps all his paperwork on the dental computer. Corvin's name doesn't show up prior to last night."

"Alex suggested a party with his honey, bit of naughty to spice it up. Notice the menu on the TV?"

"*Cock Hungry Housewives* as choice number three?" said Biro. "Nope, never saw it. Okay, I'm off. No luck at Hustler, there's always Naughty Lingerie and Frederick's. Speaking of Corvin's honey, I've got no feeling on whether she's taken alive or dead. Do you?"

"Who the hell knows, Raul."

"That's my daily affirmation, Milo."

Click.

I said, "There's a third possibility. She was allowed to leave because she was part of it. As in bait."

His phone rang. He pointed to the screen. *Dr. W. Macy*, at the county coroner.

The conversation was brief. No need to open Corvin up beyond cracking his skull and pulling out two severely deformed 9mm slugs. That happens a lot with nines because they bounce around, which is why the lab likes casings. With none, a match to any prior was unlikely.

What the pathologist did find interesting was an angle of entry suggesting the shooter was well above the victim.

"Tall victim," said Macy. "Carpet fiber on his knees, splatter four feet up the wall. I'm guessing kneeling and shot from behind."

Milo thanked him, asked him to email the prelim, hung up.

I said, "Kneeling, shot from behind. Toss in no forced entry and it's Execution 101, maybe carried out by someone he knew and trusted."

He said, "Ms. Armani, herself?"

"Bait *and* hook."

"Get down, snookums, I've got a surprise for you? That's cold."

"Someone with Corvin's self-esteem, it would've made things easy."

His phone again. Petra.

She said, "No roots on the hairs from the bathroom because they're synthetic."

"A wig."

"Afraid so. DNA's possible if they got handled enough but the lab says don't count on it. They did pull up prints. Four sets plus Chet Corvin's, all in the bathroom, we're talking a serious wipe-down in the bedroom. Locations were a glass shelf, the mirror, the rear of the sink near the wall, and the top of the toilet tank, guess they don't clean that thoroughly, ugh. Three belong to veteran Hollywood prostitutes. One died a few months ago of an overdose, one's in jail in Vegas, the third is a charmer named Ms. Piggy with an alibi."

"Ironclad?"

"Titanium-clad, I'm afraid. During the time of the shooting, one of our plainclothes guys on the boulevard spotted her escorting a john toward a dive that makes the Sahara look like the Beverly Wilshire. Officer Jefferson was there because we've got a new prevention thing going per the city council. Nip it in the bud rather than waste time with arrests. The customer was one of those hapless Scandinavian tourists, gave Jeff attitude—offended by American prudishness, an African American should know better than to oppress."

Milo said, "Life's better in the land of herring and darkness?"

"Ha. You're making me want to go out and buy a Volvo. Anyway the idiot got the STD lecture and Piggy got the speech we give the girls. Which is basically, next time you go to jail, which everyone knows is not true. Anyway, she was nowhere near the Sahara when Corvin got shot. The fourth set has yet to be identified, no match in AFIS. From the size, probably female. So either a rookie who hasn't earned an arrest record or a civilian girlfriend."

Milo said, "Fast turnaround. Thanks."

Petra said, "Thank yourself. I used your name on the request, rank has its privileges."

He said, "Speaking of girlfriends," and gave her the bait/hook theory.

She said, "I've been thinking about her—dead or taken alive. Didn't think of that. If the fourth print is hers, we're talking a female executioner with no criminal past."

"Maybe she's kept her nose clean because she's really good at what she does."

"Just what we need, a mastermind. That's a dismal thought, Milo. I guess anything's possible but the personal angle's sticking in my head: jealous spouse or boyfriend. The other thing is my captain wants Corvin to be an extension of Braun."

"Punting," said Milo. "No prob."

"I promise we'll work it like it's ours. Which, yes, it should be. But we've got a situation here. Computer conversion of our records, it's a total nightmare. Constant freezes, glitches, data loss, nerds skulking around the station wreaking havoc."

"Like I said with the phone-company calls, happy to do the paperwork."

"Appreciate it, Milo. One more thing: I found the person who took the 415 call. New civilian hire, pretty clueless. She *thinks* the caller was a female but she's not sure, it could've been a male with a high voice. I'm not sure she actually remembers anything, just eager to please. Anything else turns up, I'll let you know."

"What do you think about Raul's theory?"

"What theory?" she said. "Haven't talked to him all day, he's out in the field."

"He found the store where the wine was sold and time of purchase leaves a couple of hours to account for. Showing admirable initiative, your partner suggested the Hustler store as a possible stopover for the late Mr. Corvin."

"Inspired. Raul's over there, now?"

"Should be."

"Maybe that's why he's not answering his phone."

"Concentrating on one thing at a time, kid."

"I'll bet," said Petra. "Can't wait to see how you write it up."

23

Nothing more that day until Milo phoned me at home, just after nine p.m.

"Raul's hypothesis confirmed, the crafty devil. Corvin purchased a pair of crotchless leopard panties at Hustler just after seven. That gives him an hour and some minutes for a low-stress rush-hour Sunset cruise. He used the company credit card for the panties, too, talk about chutzpah."

I said, "With all the receipts he submitted, easy to bury a few items. And I'll bet the store didn't get specific on the invoice."

"Bingo on that, they use number codes, Raul had to bug 'em to get the specifics. But still, it's nervy, no? I've got Sean back on Evada tonight, doing four hours of surveillance. Miss Chelsea takes one of her nocturnal strolls and actually goes *into* Bitt's house, I will be able to enter to do a welfare check, per the usually obliging Judge Edgar McCarrey and John Nguyen's backup opinion. But if she just knocks on Bitt's door, stands outside, and has a conversation, it's a no-go. Got two more weeks, hopefully we'll close this mess before that."

I said, "What happens then?"

"Chelsea turns eighteen, she's a consenting adult, harder to make a case for anything. Meanwhile, I'm trying Bitt again. If his truck's there, I'm pounding his damn door until he gets a migraine."

I sat in my office and thought about Chet Corvin's final hours.

Dominant, narcissistic. Breezily confident, until he'd found himself kneeling on the floor of a cheap motel.

The perils of too much self-esteem.

The following day, just after noon, Milo dropped by looking sour but purposeful. He marched to the kitchen, flung the fridge open, took out eggs and whatever else he could find, and set about constructing a terrifying omelet.

I said, "No luck with Bitt."

"Truck wasn't there. I knocked anyway, got the expected silence." He waved a wooden spoon, used it to push a yellow mountain around the pan. A few flecks of egg landed on the floor. Blanche bounced over and gobbled them up.

He said, "There you go, symbiosis."

"More like exploitation," I said.

"Huh?"

"What does she give you in return?"

"Oh, pooch, you've got a *mean* dad." Blanche smiled up at him. "What does she give me? The restorative joys of visual beauty." He turned off the gas, petted her, plated the mountain, brought it to the table, and began consuming.

Blanche trotted to his feet.

"Can I give her some more?"

"Please don't. Eggs make her gassy."

"Daddy's mean *and* ecologically insensitive to the virtues of wind power." Bending low. "He wasn't such a fuddy-duddy, we could get a government subsidy."

Straightening, he shoveled food. Blanche settled, closed her eyes, began snoring lightly.

Milo said, "In terms of Bitt's movements, Sean logged him coming out once, around midnight, followed him to a twenty-four-hour pharmacy over in Pali village. He came out with a small paper bag. Sean said his nose appeared swollen and he didn't look happy. I'd like to think he's got a raging coke habit, but probably a cold and NyQuil. That coffee still hot?"

I poured him a mugful.

He said, "Gracias. Sean left at four a.m. Sometime between then and nine when I showed up, Bitt left again and stayed away. He seems to be moving around more but for all I know he went to the doctor to get his sinuses reamed. Moe'll try tonight, again. I have energy, I'll come by when he leaves. Meanwhile, no night moves from Ms. Chelsea."

His phone kicked in. New ringtone: a few bars of Puccini's "Babbino Caro." Gorgeous piece of music. Shame to abuse it that way.

He said, "Hey, Sean. When'd you get in . . . good for you . . . it did? One's better than nothing, I'm at Dr. D's place, email it to him, we'll print it from his computer."

Forkful of omelet. "I told him to check my computer every hour. The rest of Corvin's corporate credit card records just came through."

"You can't get downloads to your phone?"

"I can technically but it's iffy, regulation-wise," he said. "Department's still working out specifics on interfacing with personal devices."

"My computer's okay?"

He grinned. "Your screen's larger."

As he washed the fry pan, I printed. Five pages of fine print covering three billing periods that I brought to the kitchen.

Chet Corvin had traveled extensively up and down the coast,

charging business and first-class airline tickets, rental cars, meals, and hotels from San Diego to Seattle. No stops at or near Oxnard, Ventura, or Santa Barbara, which caused Milo to curse under his breath.

At the bottom of the fifth sheet: the Sahara Motor Inn, the wine, "merchandise" at Hustler, and something Raul had missed: a "delux. assort" purchased at "Haute Eu. Choco." Ninety-three dollars and some change.

I said, "High-priced dessert?"

Milo said, "Candy's dandy, liquor's quicker, when in doubt go for both."

Haute European Chocolatiers had one location: the north side of Sunset, 1.3 miles east of the Hustler store. Open three days a week, closed yesterday when Raul had searched.

The "elite confectionary" offered a pricey assortment of French macarons, Swiss sweets, and other "Continental temptations."

Milo said, "Ninety-three bucks. *Definitely* a party. But why there?"

I said, "Maybe his girlfriend lives nearby—Hollywood Hills, Los Feliz, Silverlake."

"Chet and Madame X," he said. "He thinks he's in for fun and she turns out to be Ms. Murderous. Or she got taken and ended up like he did. Let's learn about dessert. You drive."

The shop was a fifteen-foot storefront sandwiched between two clothing boutiques, both featuring gray, cachectic manikins and abbreviated dresses with S&M overtones, tight enough to highlight pores.

By contrast, the chocolate store looked old-school, with a yellow, umbrella-shaped awning doming the window and a glass door printed in gilt script. The display window featured boxes of assorted candies resting in beds of tinsel.

I said, "Refined sugar doesn't seem like a good fit for the size zero crowd."

"Or this place caters to the worst dregs of humanity."

I looked at him.

He said, "Zombies—the evil undead. They eat what they want and stay skinny."

He pushed the door open. A bell tinkled. Inside, the air was creamy and sweet and cloying. A display case held more high-end sucrose nestled in little brown paper cups. Joan Jett's "I Love Rock 'n' Roll" streamed. Performed by a string quartet.

The woman behind the case smiled. "Hi, guys. How can I tempt you today?"

Pretty, late forties to early fifties, with long hair, blond on top, black at the ends. A heart tattoo graced the left side of her neck topped by inked Asian lettering that might mean something. Ebony gauges the size of quarters stretched her earlobes.

The kids of tomorrow will have interesting grandparents.

Milo flashed his badge along with a smile.

The woman said, "We haven't had any problems recently. Should I be worried?"

"Recently?"

"The usual, you know. Drunks and homeless making a mess in the morning and a few months ago there was that burglary at Adrienne Ballou up the block. *Should* I be worried?"

"Not in the least, ma'am. We're wondering if you remember a specific customer."

"How far back?"

"Day before yesterday."

"I'm not senile, c'mon! Who?"

He began describing Chet Corvin.

"Yeah, yeah, yeah, Mr. CEO," she said. "He got the deluxe assortment. Why're you asking about him?"

"He's a person of interest."

"Well, he didn't interest me. Talk about inept."

"In terms of—"

"Flirting," she said. "Like it was expected of him, like it was his usual—what do you guys call it . . . a priori?"

"Modus operandi."

Perfect smile. "That's it! He was a tool! Winking and leering, and showing off his Range Rover fob, like that's supposed to impress me. My ex drove a Bentley and he was no catch. What'd he do?"

"Any idea who he bought the chocolate for?"

"He sure wanted *me* to know," she said. "Not the actual person, the fact that they were going to do you-know-what. Wink wink. I expected him to start drooling."

She rolled her eyes. "Like that's special. Women come in here because they appreciate fine confection. With guys, it's either they're like him, out for some play, or they're trying to get on a chick's good side after doing something gross or stupid—no offense to you guys. I'm sure you treat your women great."

Milo smiled. "You've got that right. He's a sensitive guy and I revere my mother. So what else can you tell us about Mr. CEO?"

"That's it. He's never been here before since I bought the place and that's four years ago."

"One-shot walk-in."

"We get them," she said. "Kind of like church or temple, you know? Atoning?"

Milo showed her Hargis Braun's photo. "Is he one of your customers, also?"

She studied the image. "No. Who's he?"

"Part of an investigation."

"What, there's some sort of middle-aged white-guy thing going on?"

"Nothing scary," he said. "Thanks for your time."

"Can I give you guys samples?"

"Appreciate it but we're on the job, Ms.—"

"Nola. Aw c'mon, I won't tell your mommies. Soft center or hard?" Eyelash aerobics.

Milo said, "I'm a sucker for caramel."

"Then you're in luck, ours is like nirvana, we use creamery butter from the Alps. You, sir?"

"Anything semisweet."

Nola tossed her hair. "*Très* sophisti*cah*-ted." Fishing two truffles out of the case, she dropped them in fluted paper cups. "Here you go, I picked the color specially for you guys."

The cups were a perfect match to the tan uniforms of West Hollywood sheriffs. LAPD's blue but Milo said, "Great, thanks, Nola."

"Enjoy! Try them right now so I can see your reaction. I *love* to make people happy!"

I bit off half of my truffle. A hard shell encased something liquid, alcoholic, and nicely bitter—maybe Campari.

I said, "Great," and finished with a second bite.

"There you go!"

Milo's caramel was sheathed in milk chocolate, shaped like a teardrop, and dotted with white chocolate. He popped the whole thing into his mouth, jaws working on the caramel as he thanked her again.

"I love it, Nola, it's amazing. Would you mind if I showed you another photo? I'm sure it's nothing but what the heck."

"Why would I mind? Anything for you guys, you keep us safe."

Out came Bitt's DMV shot.

Nola said, "That's Trevor the artist."

"You know him?"

"I know his name is Trevor and that he's an artist. He did me a drawing—I've got it in back, want to see?"

She returned with a five-by-seven pencil sketch in a thin black frame. A pair of fluffy white rabbits feminized by long lashes. One animal was half the size of the other. Baby bunny smiling sleepily as it nestled in the refuge of its mother's curling body.

Nola said, "I told him I had a daughter and he left for like a minute, came back with paper and a pencil, and drew it right here, on the
counter. See—he signed it to me."

The inscription was near the bottom, beautifully printed, slanting
forward. What a comic-book artist might use for emphasis.

To Nola and Cheyenne. May all your dreams be sweet. Best, Trevor.

She said, "He just stood here and *did* it while I watched, didn't
erase once. I figured to give it to Cheyenne but she thought it was
silly." Shrug. "She's sixteen. So I kept it for myself—you're not going
to tell me he's a bad person, are you?"

Pressing her palms together.

Milo said, "Not at all."

"Then, what?"

"I wish I could give you details, but like I said nothing for you to
worry about."

"I'm not worried but I am curious," said Nola. "You have his picture along with that other guy. And you asked about that CEO sleaze-
ball. Hmm, let's see how good I am at detecting. A gang of middle-aged
white guys, has to be a shady business deal. What, real estate? A Ponzi?
My ex was—but you don't want to hear about that."

Her expression said she hoped we did.

Milo said, "How often did Trevor come in?"

"Just twice. When he did the drawing was the second time, that
was right before last Christmas. The first was around a year ago. Look
at these super-smooth lines, that's pretty impressive. At least to me."

Milo said, "Any idea who he was buying chocolate for?"

"Someone super-lucky, he put out some bucks," said Nola.
"C'mon, what's up, some sort of Enron thing? My ex thought they
were a *great* company, invested some of our savings with them. That's
why I'm here. Though I do love it, turns out."

"No, Trevor's an artist, just like you said."

"Last name?"

"Bitt."

She phone-Googled. "Oh, with two *t*'s . . . he's got a Wikipedia bio . . . famous comic-book artist? Is this *worth* something? I bet it is, thanks guys, eBay here we come. How about some bonbons, got them in the freezer out back, milk chocolate for guava, dark for raspberry."

With obvious pain, Milo said, "No thanks," and headed for the exit. Before he got there, the door was pushed in hard, forcing him to sidestep.

No apologies from the man charging forward, head down, shoulders tight.

Thirties, as emaciated as the manikins next door, wearing blood-red skinny jeans, a scooped-neck orange tee, and electric-blue high-tops. His hair was buzzed at the sides, piled high on top, his beard a black chunk of topiary.

Milo muttered, "Undead."

The new arrival raced to the counter. "I need something, Nola." As if ordering a casket.

She said, "Oh, Richard. What did you do *now*?"

CHAPTER

24

Back in the Seville, Milo said, "Chocolate. A link between Corvin and Bitt?"

I said, "What made you show her Bitt's photo?"

"Wish I could say it was brilliant deducing but just grasping." He pulled a cigar out of his pocket, rolled it between his fingers. "Besides a sweet tooth, what the hell else did the two of them have in common?"

"Maybe nothing."

"Did we just inhabit parallel universes, amigo? A fancy candy store they both happen to patronize?"

"There's another way to look at it."

He sighed, put the cigar back. "Isn't there always. *What?*"

"Corvin's only been here once but Bitt bought gift boxes twice. The first time was around a year ago. 'Around' could mean a couple of weeks, give or take. What happens in two weeks?"

"What—oh, shit," he said. "Chelsea's birthday? Bitt bought her a present?"

"Maybe that and a box for Christmas. The connection to Chet

could be nothing more than him seeing the chocolates in Chelsea's room and asking her about it. If she shined him on, he'd likely drop it. But what if he filed the store's name away and noticed it on his way to the Sahara. It jogged his memory."

"You believe in that level of coincidence?"

"I believe there's a relationship between Bitt and Chelsea. Her after-dark expeditions and his being so squirrelly point that way. And those drawings we saw in Chelsea's room—all those pages of repetitive designs—might be her attempt to impress a real artist."

"She digs Bitt, he pretends to be impressed, nasty stuff ensues in the studio." He frowned. "You really think Corvin wouldn't push things with Chelsea if he saw high-end goodies in a shiny box? More to the point, Felice wouldn't?"

"From what we've seen, Chet and Chelsea didn't have much of a relationship. He called me in to see her without consulting Felice, used the girl to embarrass her mom and me. I don't think he told Felice much, period. Even if Felice did find out, she might prod a bit, but if Chelsea sank her heels in and refused to say, I think she'd have backed off. Assuming it was a gift from a boy. Finally."

The cigar reappeared. He bit off the tip, spat it out the window. "Anything's possible, but I'm still thinking the simple route. Like Nola just said, a gang of white dudes. Daddy plus the weirdo next door plus too-good-to-be-true guy named Hal."

I thought: *The simple route? All from a box of chocolate?* Said, "Sure," and started the car.

We were back in his office thirty-five minutes later. The rest of Chet Corvin's credit card history sat on his desk. Fewer charges on the remaining cards but the same pattern: cities up and down the coast, a few more stops south in San Bernardino, Riverside, and San Diego. Hotels, restaurants, occasional charges for groceries and men's clothing.

No alcohol, no chocolate, no lingerie. The last day of Corvin's life had been different and I said so. "Maybe because he was about to make a change. Preparing to leave his old life behind and venture out with a new love."

He poked the pile of charge records. "This is business stuff."

"But romance could easily be buried in here. Book a single-occupancy room, someone sleeps over, who's going to know? And with a double meal charge, who's to say he didn't take a client out? As long as he kept it reasonable, no one would take a close look."

He placed the forms in the murder book. "I need those phone records."

He checked with Binchy, Reed, the desk officer, the downstairs clerk. No messages from the phone company, the mail had come and gone, nothing.

Snatching up his desk phone, he punched numbers, shook his head. "This is Lieutenant Sturgis from LAPD West L.A. I seem to keep missing you. Wondering about those logs I requested on a homicide victim. Chet. Middle initial M. Corvin."

A voice you might interpret as friendly if you couldn't see the way his facial muscles strained the bones below.

He slammed the phone down. "At least I learned about a place for a good Christmas gift."

"Rick likes chocolate?"

"Allergic," he said. "I'm talking self-gratification."

At eight thirty the following morning, he called, sounding buoyed. "Phone logs got emailed just as I was about to leave last night. Can I bring them by?"

"When?"

"I'm parked outside."

I'd been playing guitar in my bathrobe out in the studio with Blanche. By the time I reached the front door, Milo was standing inches from the threshold, olive-drab vinyl attaché case in hand, his bulk blocking out most of the light.

He forged in like a gust of wind, sat down in the living room.

His hair was nearly tamed by some sort of product, his ravaged face razored as smooth as it was going to get. A brown sport coat woven from a nubby fabric that evoked a cheap couch went nicely with wheat-colored jeans and a yellow shirt new enough to sport box creases.

Planning to go somewhere, later.

I said, "Natty."

He humphed and popped the case and took out a sheaf of papers. Six months of phone calls on the personal cellular account of Chet M. Corvin.

Each had been checked off in blue ballpoint. A few were margined by notes in Milo's hand. *Hyatt, Portland; Embassy Suites, Tacoma; Firewood Café, Oakland airport.*

Two numbers were circled repeatedly in red. Twenty-eight calls to and from a 310 listing over the past two months. Eleven to the 909 area code were clustered during the last week of Corvin's life.

Milo tapped the twenty-eight-caller. "Local but disposable and expired, no way to trace. I was hoping Chet used the Burner app on his phone to create his own temporary but no such luck, just your basic by-the-month dope-dealer accessory."

I said, "Something to hide."

"That girlfriend scenario of yours is looking better. And maybe we can find her. The 909 is in San Bernardino, a landline. I tried, no answer, no machine. But it's active. Any guesses?"

"Lake Arrowhead's in San Bernardino County. First time we met Corvin, he mentioned a weekend home there."

He grinned. "Great minds. Yeah, I called Felice, she confirmed it. Said the family hadn't used the place since two winters ago. She wanted to know why I was asking. I said Chet seemed to be calling there, I had yet to find out why. But she got the point, became rather irate."

I said, "The call dates say the relationship began at least two months ago in L.A. For the past week or so, he moved her to the family getaway."

"In preparation for his new life." He stood, bowed, sat back down. "Felice's anger worked in my favor. She gave me permission to go there and take a look. There's a local guy, sees after the place twice a month, has a key. I left him a message, haven't heard back. But I don't need him, Felice said she'd leave one under the mat."

"New friend."

"Common enemy."

I began walking out.

"Where you going?"

"Shave, shower, et cetera."

"Getting yourself dapper?" he said. "Good. I have my standards."

25

A manila envelope leaned against the door of the Corvin house. Trevor Bitt's pickup was parked next door. Milo studied the cactus Tudor, scratched the side of his nose and contemplated, then returned to the unmarked he'd picked up this morning. A smooth-driving slate-blue Dodge Charger that still smelled of new car. Way above his usual ride. Hope leads you to all sorts of self-affirming places.

Once behind the wheel, he uncoiled a string on the flap of the envelope. Inside was a key chained to a fob and a folded piece of white paper. The fob was a plastic Disneyland souvenir. Snow White, chaste and unaware she was despised. The paper listed computer-typed directions to the Arrowhead house, the alarm code, and the number of Dave Brassing, the occasional caretaker.

Programming the car's GPS, Milo checked it against Felice Corvin's directions. "Perfect."

Big V-8, muscular and smooth.

I said, "How'd you score the hot wheels?"

"Got A's on my homework and begged Daddy for the keys." Big

grin. "Found out a mere sergeant in Burglary was planning to use it tomorrow and pulled rank."

"What's next, an Oscars after-party."

"Actually, I coulda gone to one last year. One of Rick's patients is the bimbo girlfriend of a noted producer. Drove into a pole while taking a selfie. Rick put her arm and her shoulder together. Well enough to service Daddy Filmbucks because he extended the invite."

"Why didn't you go?"

"More allergies. Both of us."

"To what?"

"Ego cancer and bullshit."

The route from the Palisades to the Inland Empire's resort areas was the 405 North, the 134 East, merge to the 210, State Route 18 up to the mountains.

Decades ago, European road architects figured out that curves keep drivers awake, hence the Autostrada, the Autobahn, and the like. Not so, Caltrans. The result is thousands of miles of hypnotic straightaway that scalpel through marginalized neighborhoods. It's a nonstop display of trailer parks, houses that might as well be trailers, discount malls, car lots the size of small towns, big-box retailers with the grace of an unshielded sneeze.

Intersections in freeway districts are built around gas stations, grease pits, and fast-food joints. The less fortunate citizens of California contend with toxic air, brain-scraping noise, and opportunistic criminals hopping off the freeway to felonize before on-ramping back in celebration.

When I'm not behind the wheel, I find it hard to stay awake on the freeway and I dozed off halfway through the ninety-mile drive.

I woke up on the outskirts of San Bernardino and checked my watch. What should've been a ninety-minute drive had stretched to two hours and thirteen minutes.

"Accident?"

Milo's jacket had taken on wrinkles. His hair spiked where he'd rubbed his scalp. "Coupla semis tangoed twenty miles back, ambulance injuries. Cleared by the time we got there but that didn't stop idiots from gawking, now it's even worse, with the cellphone photos. Explain that to me. What's the thrill?"

I said, "New-age slapstick. Enjoying the fact that the other guy slipped on a banana peel."

"Cruel world," he said. "Lucky for me."

A mile later: "You were snoozing away, amigo. How the hell do you sleep like that?"

I rarely do but how would he know? "Clear conscience."

"Damn," he said, slapping his forehead. "Too late for that."

The outskirts of San Bernardino were what you'd expect, made dreary by Beijing-level smog.

The airborne dirt vanished a few miles into Highway 18, the state route's primary access to the San Bernardino Mountains. Four lanes that shift gradually to a gear-challenging climb and top-of-the-world views.

Eighteen snakes up to a series of ski resorts before sloping east and descending to the Mojave Desert. The final stop is Adelanto, a town founded over a century ago as a citrus-growing community, switching to poultry farming when that didn't work out, continuing to struggle as the economic allure of two private prisons proved illusory.

I'd been there a few years ago, evaluating the custodial fitness of a father imprisoned for a massive insurance scam and about to be released. The kind of guy who could easily fool a polygraph. My report was thin on details but loaded with implication. The judge got the point.

Today's trip included only the first twenty or so miles of 18, as we entered Arrowhead Village. Along the way, signs proclaiming gated, guarded communities and admonishing trespassers had alternated with flecks of lake view that pierced the tree canopy randomly—loose sapphires in a green velvet box. On the water side of the commercial center's cottagey shops and restaurants, the forest had been cleared, exposing an expanse of blue peppered by white boats.

The lake itself is pure Southern California: theatrically gorgeous but artificial. Created as a reservoir left unfinished after being ruled illegal and subject to decades of shifting ownership, fraudulent land transfers, and inside deals, it had finally settled as a weekend escape where dockside mansions served as stopovers for movie stars and tycoons.

We continued west, turned onto Brewer Road, and entered a tract of modest residences widely spaced on generous lots. Weekend places for the financially comfortable. The attraction here was the much smaller Grass Valley Lake and a golf course. No gates, no warnings.

Our destination, marked by a rustic address sign on a tilting stake, was curtained by white pines, black oaks, and ponderosas and visible only as a smear of cedar siding.

Milo said, "Just Molly and me-ee, in our brown heaven," and hooked onto a long dirt driveway bordered by rocks the size of Galapagos tortoise shells. The house finally came into view seconds later, shoved off center by a clutch of monumental firs.

One-story A-frame, cedar planks oiled long ago and graying at the edges. No garage, no fencing. Two large plastic garbage cans stood to the left.

We got out of the car, greeted by chittering birds and rustling leaves. Milo checked the cans. Empty. His eyes shifted to the ground nearby. Three mousetraps, one hosting a rodent skeleton. Close by was a rogue patch of grass defying its host patch of gravel. Ruts and tracks ran through the blades and continued to the gravel: wildlife partying, most likely squirrels, chipmunks, and raccoons. The trashcan lids were held in place by metal clasps. Claw marks scored the tops. Coons or bears—juveniles lacking the skill and attention span to pull off a prolonged assault.

Milo returned to the Dodge, now dusted with pollen, popped the trunk, and removed his attaché case. Out came two sets of booties and gloves.

I said, "Expecting a crime scene?"

"Expecting anything." We covered our shoes and hands and I followed him to the front door.

Big lumbering shape in coarse brown.

Adult bear, ready to forage.

The alarm panel just inside the door whined. Milo punched buttons from the code he'd memorized, created silence, took in the layout.

A single high-peaked space was sectioned by furniture and appliances into a living room with a doorway to the left, a dining area, and a kitchen separated from a laundry room by a waist-high partition.

Open beamed ceiling. Cheap blue felt carpeted the entire floor. The rear wall was glass, a triangle composed of several window frames and interrupted by a rear door. Outside was a skimpy lawn, then a mass of black-green, the rear boundary unclear. A glass-shaded chandelier—unreasonable facsimile of Tiffany—dangled from a center beam. The furniture was bolted-together blond wood and plastic, contrasting with dark-stained wood walls and ceiling. Every upholstered surface was brown; if Milo sat down, he might disappear.

Still in the doorway, he called out, "Police. Anyone home?"

Nothing.

Placing his hand on his Glock but leaving it holstered he motioned me to wait and entered.

A minute later he was back. "All clear."

He picked up his case, sniffed, nostrils flaring.

I said, "Exactly."

Empty house but the air lacked the dirty-socks must of disuse. Instead, a pleasant scent washed through, aromatic, familiar.

Armani.

I pointed to a brown princess phone on the floor, next to a couch. Eighties vintage, the closest thing to an antique.

He took an evidence bag out of his case, uncoupled the phone from its cord, bagged it. "If there are prints anywhere, they'll be here. Not that we don't know who was answering Chet's calls. This clinches it, again, you're right. Girlfriend, not a pro, in that motel room."

I said nothing.

He said, "Stop bragging. Look what happened to Chet."

He walked around, opening and shutting drawers and cabinets. Cheap crockery, glassware, utensils, pots and pans. Stepping around the partition to the laundry room, he took his time with the washer-dryer.

Empty, spotless, dry. Same for a plastic utility sink and a cheap wicker hamper. Utility storage consisted of detergent, bug spray, a coiled garden hose, a toolbox whose stiff latch said it hadn't been opened for a while, four mousetraps in heat-sealed plastic packets.

We returned to the living room, continued through the left-hand doorway. Two identical nine-by-nine bedrooms were dimmed by pebbled windows set high in a tongue-and-groove wall and separated by a Jack-and-Jill bathroom. Nothing in the medicine cabinet.

The master bedroom at the end of the hall was larger but far from generous. The smell of perfume was stronger. Clear-glass windows provided the same green view as the living room triangle. The lav was en suite but drab. No sheets, pillows, or cases on the queen bed; one dresser, also unused. No clothes in the closet but lots of neatly folded percale and terry cloth.

I said, "Rarely used until now. And she cleaned up compulsively. Same as the motel. Same as Braun."

He stared. "She's more than a love interest?"

"Just throwing out ideas."

Noise from the front of the house whipsawed both our heads.

A door closing. Footsteps.

Milo unsnapped his gun and pulled it out, sidled toward the doorway.

He tensed for a second, slipped through, pointed the Glock. "Freeze!"

A male voice said, "Oh, Jesus God!"

The man's hands were up and they trembled. So did his legs. "Please, man." High-pitched nasal voice. "Take what you want and—"

Milo said, "Police. Continue to cooperate." Extricating his badge, he flashed it.

The man said, "Jesus Mary Mother of God." A meaty face that had gone pale began to take on color, achieved ruddiness within seconds. His posture loosened but he continued to shake.

"Can I?" he said, waving his fingers. "Got a sore rotator cuff."

Milo said, "Name."

"Dave Brassing."

"The caretaker."

"That's me, sir, I promise, there's I.D. in my pocket."

"Okay, at ease. Didn't mean to startle you but I called and you never answered so I wasn't expecting you."

"Sorry, sir, I was going to." Brassing waited until the Glock was reholstered before letting out a wheezy sigh and flopping his arms to his sides.

Late forties to early fifties, stocky, he had a broad face bristled by bushy sideburns and bottomed by eight inches of graying, spade-shaped goatee. A battered, broad-brimmed leather hat sat askew. A gray work shirt was splotched with fear-sweat. Baggy cargo shorts revealed callused knees. The soles of hiking boots were crusted with leaves.

"Oh, man," he said, placing a hand over his heart. "You scared the stuffing out of me." His cheeks fluttered as his head moved to the side.

Milo said, "So, Dave, what brings you here?"

"Checking around," said Brassing. "For you, actually. I was going to call after I saw that everything was okay."

Not getting the point of evidence preservation.

Brassing said, "Whew." His chest heaved.

"You want some water, Dave?"

"No, I'm okay . . . can I sit down?"

"Sure. Didn't mean to freak you out, Dave."

"My fault, should've answered you sooner," said Brassing. "I saw your car, figured it was police, but when you rushed out with that heater . . ." He exhaled, face glassy with sweat. "Guns are a thing with me. I used to hunt, nothing bothered me. Then I got held up a few years ago and when I see 'em, I get kind of queasy."

"Sorry 'bout that."

"Yeah," said Dave Brassing. "Armed robbery. It was hairy."

Milo said, "It happen around here?"

"Down in San Berdoo. I was working at a tire store, couple of hoodies came in and shoved iron in my face and had me clean out the register, I thought I was going to—thank God there was some cash in there."

I said, "What a thing to go through."

"Wouldn't wish it on my enemy," said Brassing. "I'm not saying I got rid of my weapons, fact is I'd have been better off packing when they showed up. But I look at guns different, now. The one they used was a .38 Smith-W. One of mine was one of those, I got rid of it."

He bit his lip. "I don't even want to watch movies with shooting. Anyway, I should've called out *Hello, it's Dave,* or something, I didn't figure. Phew. Okay, I'm breathing again."

Milo said, "You're sure you're okay? Don't want water?"

"I'm fine, thanks, no worries—actually, yeah, water sounds good, mind if I get it myself?"

"Go for it, Dave."

Brassing walked to the kitchen, filled a glass from the sink, held it up to window light.

"It was good last time I checked but winter there was runoff-silt. Nothing dangerous, just minerals, but it tasted bad."

He chugged the entire glass, filled another, repeated. "Took me a while to convince them to fix it, finally did. Deposits in the tank, not a small job."

I said, "They don't use the house, don't want to put out the money."

"You got it."

"How long have you been taking care of the place?"

Brassing put down the empty glass and sat back down. "I don't really take care, like a big, detailed deal. What it is, I come in once a month except winter, when it's two three times, got to make sure the pipes don't freeze, all that good stuff."

He pointed to the rear window. "Also that, in the winter. That much glass, you get constriction of the frames, the glue dries, you get leaks."

I said, "Then there's the mousetraps."

"Oh, yeah, that, too. Little buggers used to get inside, poop all over the place, that was gross. I sealed off holes and cracks, baited outside to keep them away from inside." Tensing. "You're not saying you saw some in here?"

"Just traps near the garbage cans."

"That's okay," said Brassing. "I also got them placed clear back to the end of the property."

"Where is that, Dave?"

"Right where the grass ends."

"Not the trees," I said.

"That's the neighbor, super-rich guy, computers or something, he's got fifteen acres, at least. Big stone house. Not that he uses it, either. That's the way it is here. They say it's an investment—he said that. Mr. Corvin. He wasn't a bad type. Still can't believe what happened to him."

"Mrs. Corvin told you."

"On her message. That was kind of . . . but I'm not judging."

I said, "Unemotional?"

"Yeah," said Brassing. "'Hi, Dave, need to let you know.' Then she lays *that* on me. Like please check the garbage cans and oh, yeah, Chet got killed."

"Is that her usual approach?"

"Couldn't tell you, maybe I seen her three times, I always dealt with him."

"Could we hear the message?"

Looking puzzled, Brassing produced his phone, scrolled, activated.

Felice Corvin's voice came on, cool, soft, articulate. "David Brassing, this is Mrs. Corvin. Not sure of your schedule but I'm calling to let you know the police will be examining the house in the near future. Mr. Corvin was shot and killed."

Click.

Dave Brassing said, "Wow, that's colder than I remembered."

Milo said, "You've met her three times."

"Maybe, could be two."

"What about the kids?"

Brassing shook his head. "They said they had kids but never seen any."

"And Mr. Corvin?"

"More," said Brassing. "But not a lot. They bought the place something like two and a half, three years ago. I worked for the people before them, the Liebers. That was real caretaking, they were older folk, retired, they used it all the time, were still skiing when they were like eighty. They recommended me to the Corvins."

I said, "How many contacts have you had with Mr. Corvin?"

"Oh . . . I'd say . . . eight, nine? Mostly on the phone. Don't know, really."

Milo said, "In three years."

"Yup. It's mostly copacetic, here."

"How about this year?"

"Hmm . . . twice, three? Last time was like . . . a month ago? The mice. I guess he was here and saw droppings. He called me up, said, 'What do I pay you for?'"

"Copping an attitude."

"Well," said Brassing, "can't say I blame him, who wants to see that? I finally figured out there was a small hole in the lint trap vent. Sealed it off, no more little Mickeys." He smiled. Lots of missing teeth and the dentition that remained was yellow and ragged.

"Problem solved," I said. "Was he grateful?"

"He never complained." Removing his hat, he scratched dense, gray hair.

Milo said, "When Mr. Corvin stayed here, who was he with?"

"Who?" said Brassing. "I'm assuming her."

"Mrs. Corvin."

Brassing's bushy eyebrows flickered. "You're saying not?"

"Not saying anything, Dave. When's the last time the master bedroom got used?"

"Hmm," said Brassing. "Not for a while. I haven't been here in a month but even before that—it's not like it was regular."

"How could you tell?"

"They always cleaned up real good," said Brassing. "New sheets, new pillowcase."

I said, "There's perfume in the air. Smell it?"

Brassing sniffed. "Can't smell so good—yeah, I'm catching a whiff."

"Familiar?"

"No, not really."

"Deviated septum?" said Milo.

Brassing tapped his right nostril. "Tumor. Back when I was in high school. Played football, got a monster headache, everyone figured it was a hard tackle but it was a tumor. Benign, they rooted around and got rid of it, I had headaches for years but now it's okay. But not much sense of smell. Some of my taste, too, my wife says it don't matter, anyway, I'm no gourmet."

Gap-toothed smile. "Guess I'm the lucky one."

Milo and I looked at him.

"The tumor, then getting held up and surviving?" said Brassing. "A few other things in between, God pulled me through."

"I admire your faith, Dave," said Milo.

"My pastor says it's easy to have faith when things work out good, the key is when it's rough—think I'll get myself more water."

He drank a third glass, came back.

Milo said, "So you have no idea who Mr. Corvin stayed with?"

"I'm getting a feeling it wasn't the wife, huh? You're thinking that's what got him killed?"

"Let's not get ahead of ourselves, Dave, we're just asking questions."

"Got it. Wish I had answers for you."

"No idea who might've stayed here with Mr. Corvin."

"Sorry, nope."

"What about something left in the garbage—a credit slip, anything with I.D.?"

"No garbage," said Brassing.

"What do you mean?"

"The cans were always empty. I guess they could've taken it to the dump. It's at Heap's Peak, a few miles down the mountain, on the way back to the freeway."

"They don't pay for trash collection?"

"They do," said Brassing. "When I throw stuff out—mousetraps, whatever—it gets picked up." He tugged at his beard. "Fifty bucks a month doesn't sound like much but I like to come up here, anyway, breathe some good air."

"Come up from where?"

"San Bernardino. I'm semi-retired, do flea markets on the weekend. Used to do other houses but now it's just this and another one closer to the village."

"When Mr. Corvin was here, which car did he drive?"

"The first time I met him he had a Jaguar—the big sedan. The only other times—maybe one, maybe two, he had a Range Rover."

Brassing slapped his forehead. "Shoot, I forgot, sorry. A week ago, after I checked my other house—the Palmers—I decided to drive by, just an overall look, nothing huge I needed to deal with. And this car drove toward me the opposite way, seemed to be coming from the property. I can't be sure but the houses are pretty far apart, it seemed to be coming from here. It was already up the road by the time I got here and nothing looked wrong so I figured it was just someone doing a three-point turn."

Milo said, "What kind of car?"

"*That* I can tell you," said Brassing, "Camaro, eighties. Cool color: black. It makes them look more racy, you know?"

I said, "A week ago. So last Friday."

"That's when I do the Palmers. Twice a month. They play golf, I go in and check around."

Milo said, "Catch a look at who was driving?"

"Nope, it was going pretty fast."

Milo handed Brassing his card. "You see it again, try to get the license plate, even if you don't, give me a ring, okay?"

"It's important? Sure," said Brassing.

The three of us stood.

Brassing said, "Uh, one thing, sir. I'm not sure if I still have the job. Thought I'd give Mrs. Corvin some time to settle down before I ask her."

"My advice," said Milo, "is let it ride. You don't hear from her, you've got the job."

Brassing winked. "Don't upset the apple cart, huh?"

"Exactly, Dave. When's your next visit scheduled?"

"Like in a couple weeks."

"You can drive by but don't go inside until I tell you it's okay."

"Why's that?"

"I need to keep the place as is."

"For CSI stuff?"

"That kind of thing."

"Got it." Brassing read the card. "Homicide. Can't believe that actually happened."

26

Milo and I stood outside as Brassing drove away in an old Ford van.

He said, "Braun, Bitt, Chet, Chet's girlfriend, and now the Camaro kid at Braun's house and here. So he's definitely involved and there's definitely a link between Chet and Braun. The whole chocolate thing . . . I was starting to think the case was coming together but it's feeling like a magician's gag. Poof, nothing materializes—are you seeing something I'm not?"

I said, "Wish I was."

"Brutal honesty," he said. "So what now?"

"I'd resume the surveillance on Bitt and call Henry Prieto to let him know he was onto something with the Camaro. He still thinks of himself as a cop, will eagle-eye. Who handles law enforcement here?"

"San Bernardino sheriff, Twin Peaks station."

"Would they do a forensic workup of the house?"

"With no obvious crime? Hard to say."

"Long as we're here," I said, "we could check the places where Corvin spent money. Could give us something on the girlfriend."

"He's got a love nest here, why would he use a hotel in San Berdoo?"

"Moving around to be less conspicuous, creature comforts, or just plain novelty. The company was paying for everything, so why not take advantage. On the way, we can stop in Arrowhead Village and ask around."

He shot a cuff and looked at his Timex. "It's pushing four, we'll be coming back late."

"Less traffic."

He slapped my back. "Unbridled optimism. Patent it and you'll own your own jet."

We sat in the Dodge and examined Chet Corvin's recent San Bernardino expenditures.

Six stays in three hotels, all tagged as "Inns." Three restaurant tabs at two Italian and one Mexican restaurant. Everything close to the freeway, in the inland city's business core.

A call to the Twin Peaks sheriff's station produced bafflement when Milo admitted the house wasn't a likely crime scene. He got shunted up the brass rod, ended with a captain named Bacerra who resisted but finally agreed to "limited cooperation": Once permission to enter was granted in writing by the current owner and non-intrusive access could be guaranteed, the A-frame would "eventually" be processed for prints, fibers, and "obvious" body fluids. Meaning a visual inspection but no dogs or alternative light source unless something "probative" came up.

Milo said, "Thanks," trying to mean it. "I can get you a key for access and there's also a caretaker. In terms of written consent, would a fax work?"

"Probably," said Bacerra. "It's going to take time, anyway. We're swamped with real stuff."

◆

In Arrowhead Village, forty or so trendy-leaning businesses were backdropped by the lake. Emphasis on clothing and personal appearance—beauty salons, a Pilates studio, a gym.

We walked from store to store, showing pictures of Chet Corvin, Hal Braun, and Trevor Bitt, eliciting head shakes. Several merchants said, "Some of the weekenders never come in."

The losing streak was broken at one of the last shops, Snowbird Jewelers. Just over a month ago, Chet Corvin had purchased a silver filigree necklace set with amethysts for $612.43, paying with cash. The proprietor, an older Iranian man in a white shirt and tie, remembered Corvin because he was "very enthusiastic."

Milo said, "About what, sir?"

The man adjusted his eyeglasses. "Buying it. Winking all the time." He demonstrated, the result more comical than lascivious.

"Did he come in alone?"

"He did," said the man. "It was a surprise. You're saying not for the wife, eh? I figured."

"Why's that?"

"The winking. Wives get presents, they don't get winking."

We got back in the car and began the descent of Highway 18. Covering the shopping center had taken time and the sky was fighting to stay lit, bashful lemon-colored sun hiding behind cotton-puff clouds. Below the firmament, the forest had turned black. As dusk set in, the road curves grew challenging.

Milo took a turn without braking. The Dodge squealed in protest. He slowed down.

Two mile markers later, he said, "Six-hundred-dollar necklace. So he was in love or lust or whatever guys like him are in. Let's check out the local hostelries."

CHAPTER

27

Nothing inn-like about the Hampton Inn by Hilton, just a four-story beige rectangle logo'd in tomato red.

The cheerful young woman at the desk lost her cheer when Milo showed her his badge along with Chet Corvin's photo.

Samantha.

"Um, I don't think I can talk about guests."

"This guest is deceased." He'd gentled his tone. That made it sound worse, which was probably his intention.

Samantha shrank back. "Dead?"

Milo said, "Murdered. So if you could help us, we'd really appreciate it."

"Um . . . hold on." Backing away, she opened a rear door and slipped through. Nothing happened for several minutes. The lobby was empty, no one checking in or out. Soft rock streamed from above.

A grave-looking woman in her midthirties emerged from the back. "How can I help you, Officers?"

Briana.

Milo repeated what he'd told Samantha.

She said, "I'd have to check with Legal Affairs to verify that we can divulge that and they're gone for the day."

Milo placed an arm on the counter and leaned in. "Appreciate your being careful, Briana, but we're not asking for state secrets, just checking to see if anyone around here remembers Mr. Corvin."

She looked away. Fiddled with her name tag. "Actually, I do. He's been here a few times."

"Three times, between five and eight weeks ago," said Milo. "We have his credit card history."

"Oh," said Briana. "Well, I can't tell you much more than that. I only remember him because he was kind of . . ." She sucked in breath. "I don't want to . . . put anyone down. Certainly not a deceased person."

"Of course not, Briana. But this was a particularly nasty *cold*-blooded murder, so anything you could tell us would be appreciated."

Her eyes flicked upward. "One of those times, I checked him in. It's not like I had a strong memory of it, but your picture reminded me."

"He stood out."

"Well," said Briana. "More like he was . . . too friendly? I didn't do anything special for him but he told me I was A-one, said he'd ask for me personally from now on."

"Flirtatious?"

"He didn't engage in inappropriate touch or use suggestive language and gestures."

Someone who'd attended the corporate seminar.

I said, "But . . ."

"He acted as if we already knew each other. And now that I think about it, I guess he did use a suggestive gesture. Winking."

"Did you find him creepy?"

"Not really, more like annoying. Too much of what my grandma calls being 'forward.' I feel kind of bad talking about him, now that he's been . . ."

Milo said, "Did he stay here alone?"

"It was a single-occupancy reservation. All three times." Her eyes shifted up again, then to the left.

Milo said, "That's not exactly what I asked, Briana."

"I'm sorry, Lieutenant. I can't divulge those kinds of things."

"Not even off the record?"

"I heard there really was no such thing in law enforcement."

"From who?"

"My grandpa, he was a sheriff in Fontana."

"Maybe in his day," said Milo. "There sure is off the record, now." He crossed his heart.

"Hmm. I should probably ask Grandpa to make sure." Sudden, icy smile. "Just kidding, I believe you. Okay. Off the record."

She looked around.

"The third time he was here, he checked in alone, also. But later that evening I did see him with someone and they were pretty friendly. She went up in the elevator with him. I *can't* tell you if she stayed over. Not because I don't want to, because I don't know. But she definitely went up with him and they were kind of . . . affectionate."

She blushed. Nice to see that was still possible.

I said, "Just that once."

"I wasn't on night shift for the other two, so I can't tell you what happened."

Milo said, "If you took a peek at the room-service charges, maybe we could figure it out."

"You said you had his credit charges."

"They don't specify." He opened his case, took out the records, showed her.

She said, "Oh. That makes sense, for guest privacy we don't itemize . . . I'm sorry, I *definitely* can't show you our paperwork without authorization from Legal." Sly smile. "But I guess I could see for myself."

She smiled. "Grandpa would tell me to stop *pussyfooting* and help you out. He's always griping about the ACLU. Hold on."

The lobby door swung open with an assisted whoosh, admitting a Doppler wave of traffic noise and a harried-looking couple in their fifties. Both wore baggy T-shirts, shorts, white socks and sneakers, pushed matching red roller bags toward the counter.

When they were ten feet away, the man announced, "Checking in."

Briana said, "Be right with you, sir," and walked through the door that had taken Samantha.

The woman said, "She disappears, that's some idea of service."

Samantha reappeared. "Hi! I can take care of you, here." She motioned the couple to the far end of the counter.

"Not so bad," muttered the man.

"We'll see," said the woman.

The check-in process commenced. One credit card declined, then a second. Incredulous looks from the couple. Card three was the charm. Lots of face-covering scowls as they race-wheeled toward the elevators.

Samantha typed on a computer, avoiding looking at us. Briana returned and told her to go back in the office and check "the month-lies."

When the office door closed, she said, "Okay. What I can tell you is the second and third times, your Mr. Corvin either had a huge appetite or someone was with him."

"Two steaks, et cetera," said Milo.

Briana recited from memory. "Dinner was one surf and turf, one chicken salad, two garden salads, two ice cream sundaes, a bottle of wine. Breakfast was two omelets, two orange juices, and toast for two. Plus they used two vodka minis from the self-serve fridge."

"Hearty breakfast plus screwdrivers," said Milo. "Was the wine Chardonnay?"

Her eyes rounded. "How did you know?"

"Lucky guess. So what did this woman look like?"

"Can't really say, sir. I barely had a look at her."

"What do you remember?"

"Honestly, not much."

"Age?"

"I guess like him but I couldn't swear to it. Maybe a little younger."

"Heavy, thin?"

"I'd have to say average."

"Tall, short?"

Briana shook her head. "Nothing stood out. Probably average, again. Sorry."

"You're doing fine. What about hair color?"

She smiled. "That I can tell you. Dark and kind of longish. The truth is, the two of them walked fast. Straight over there." Eyeing the elevators. "I mostly saw the back of her." Deeper blush. "His hand was on her . . . tush."

"Chummy," said Milo.

"Pardon?"

"Friendly."

"If that's what you call it," said Briana. "I just figured they were all heated up and raring to go."

"She didn't remove his hand."

"Oh, no," said Briana. "She kind of wiggled."

Her response to photos of Hal Braun and Trevor Bitt was quick and serene. The easy questions on the test.

Never seen him. Not him, either.

Milo thanked her again. The "Anything else?" that sometimes provides pleasant surprises produced a head shake.

As we walked away, she said, "Grandpa will be proud of me."

The Hilton Garden Inn wore the same beige-and-red livery as its cousin. Again, four stories. Nothing inn-like *or* garden-like.

Milo went through the same process with a cheerful young man named Cooke, eager to tell us he'd been on the job five days.

Enough time to know the drill: He punted to a supervisor, a woman who could've been Briana's sister. *Lara.*

Maybe there's a machine somewhere, extruding staff for the corporate hydra.

Lara had no memory of Chet Corvin but she was more forthcoming than Briana: checking her records without prodding and confirming that room-service charges from six weeks ago "sure looks like two people. But I can't tell you who he was with."

No recognition of Braun or Bitt.

She returned to her office.

Cooke fist-bumped air as we left. "Good luck, guys."

When we were out of earshot, Milo said, "Name like that, kid should work in the kitchen."

Stop three was a Residence Inn Marriott where Corvin had checked in just over a month ago. Beige stucco and a huge creative leap to white lettering. Except for the corporate logo in—big shock—red.

More pleasant young people, what had now become a routine of refusal, cadging, followed by a trickle of information.

Dinner for two, no specific memory of Corvin, blank stares in response to Bitt's and Braun's photos.

That left the restaurants.

28

Papa Giorgio was closed for renovation and had been since two days after Chet Corvin had charged dinner. San Remo and Mexicali Café were bustling, throngs of hungry weekend diners crowding the host stations. The people behind the stations looked harried and distracted and pretended not to notice us.

Milo made his way past the crowd, stepped in close to each of them, and announced, "This is about a homicide," loud enough to be heard over the din.

A few people near him recoiled.

Wilson R. at San Remo said, "Oh, man—just hold on for a sec."

Lourdes Briseno at Mexicali said, "Omigod, sure, sure, please just wait."

Two quick shuffles through computers produced Chet Corvin's receipts at both restaurants. Dinner for two, the unifying factor, red meat: at San Remo, spaghetti Bolognese and fettuccine with beef cheeks; the *Combo Grande* at Mexicali, a masterpiece for two built around carne asada.

Two bottles of high-priced Chardonnay.

Corvin's quirky taste in wine, or pleasing his companion?

Milo asked each of the hosts if they could recall the couple who'd eaten those meals.

Wilson R. said, "Not unless they're regulars . . ." Examining the receipt. "Nope." To the queue: "Bainbridge, party of four?"

Lourdes Briseno said, "I really wish I could help you guys but I really don't remember. Really. So sorry." She walked away with the next lucky eaters.

The Mexican place was our last stop. We'd arrived just after eight p.m., had been kept waiting as the population of salivating citizens swelled. Lots of families, lots of kids.

Milo said, "Post-hunger baby boom."

Cupping his mouth to be heard above human chatter, flatware clatter, and piped-in mariachi music.

Lourdes Briseno returned, looking surprised to see us.

Milo said, "You didn't hear my last question. Do you remember the party?"

"Oh. No, I don't, really sorry."

"No prob." He loomed a bit, gave the wolf-grin. "Been a long day. Any way you could squeeze us in for dinner?"

"I . . ." She looked past us. "Sure. Of course. We really appreciate what you do."

Picking up two menus, she guided us toward the rear of the restaurant, raising grumbles.

Milo mumbled, "Bring on the pitchforks and the lanterns."

Lourdes Briseno, sounding utterly unconvincing, called out, "One second, people. They have a reservation."

She hurried us to a table set into a corner. More of a drink stand, barely wide enough for two people if elbows were kept at bay.

I thought: *Just like his office.*

Milo rolled his shoulders and slid in.

Lourdes Briseno said, "I know it's really cramped, but it's really the best I can do, really sorry."

When she left, Milo said, "I really believe her."

He studied his menu like a monk assigned to an illuminated man-uscript. "Everything sounds pretty good—place *smells* good, finally something to block out that damn perfume."

He began to lay the menu down. That would've covered his half of the table, so he held on to it. "The combo—what Chet ordered—actually sounds pretty good."

"It's for two."

"You're back to being ascetic?"

"Go for it."

"Great," he said. "Once I get my share down here"—patting his gut—"maybe I'll have one of those new-age mystical experiences."

I said, "Cow-induced insight?"

"Ingest what the victim did and stimulate empathy."

"Better than ingesting the victim."

He laughed.

Lourdes Briseno returned with a handheld device. "We're really jammed so I'm taking care of you guys. Do you know what you want?"

Milo gave her the order.

She said, "Great choice, it's really popular. To drink?"

"The heart says cerveza, the job says iced tea."

She pouted. "Aw, poor guys. Okay, some chips and salsa will be coming up in a sec."

She bounced away. No mention that we'd ordered the same thing as Corvin. She probably hadn't noticed.

That's the way it is with most people: Details are an intrusion. Then there's the rest of us, lying in bed at three a.m., scrolling through volumes of mental small print.

I said, "Cow and Chardonnay."

Milo nodded. "Don't tell the gender police but I'm thinking lady's choice. That, the necklace, whoever she is, they had more going on than porn in a motel. And the fact they've been together two months points against a hit woman. So the question is what happened to her at the Sahara. And if she escaped and cared about Chet, why not come forward?"

"Fear," I said. "That fits with her being the one who called it in. Avoiding 911 to stay anonymous and keep her voice unrecorded."

A busboy brought a mini-trough of corn chips, a soup bowl full of salsa, beer steins filled with frosty tea. Using a comically dainty finger grasp, Milo extracted a chip, dipped, tasted, sipped, repeated, and let out a contented sigh. "Quality but not at the expense of quantity. The key to success in the Home of the Brave."

A dozen pulverized chips later: "Chet and Madame X tryst up at the lake and down here in the city. Maybe she's someone local. Now, what about the Camaro?"

I said, "Ventura to Arrowhead covers a lot of ground. Strong emotion can do that."

"Hatred as jet fuel of the soul. Didn't some psychologist say that?"

"Never heard it."

He grinned. "That's 'cause I just made it up. Yeah, you're making sense. The hippie had some kind of beef with Braun and Corvin. His age, that could slam us back to what you said before: Chelsea's forbidden boyfriend. He stalked both his victims, took care of Braun first, spotted Chet driving here and then back to Hollywood."

I said, "Maybe EmJay Braun's remembered something since we spoke to her."

He phoned Wife Number Three. She continued to know no one with a black Camaro.

Milo listened for a while, said, "Not to my knowledge . . . no, honestly, ma'am, we're just asking questions . . . exactly . . . okay, I will . . . I'll definitely put in the request. Take care."

He hung up. "She'll be looking at cars on her block all the time now and freaking out. On top of that she's having a painful arthritis attack. I'm definitely meant to feel guilty."

He demolished a few more chips. "My atonement is I call Ventura PD, ask for some drive-bys at her place."

He followed through, got referred up the chain, per usual, ended up with a tepid "We'll see," from someone of his own rank.

He said, "Long as we're in the Ventura groove," and called Henry Prieto. This time, he hung up laughing. "He's already got his eyes peeled, don't I think he'd let me know if he knew something?"

Twin mountains of marinated beef each ringed with slices of avocado and radishes arrived. Side bowls of refried beans, rice, and posole stew, supplemented by a coarse, black-stone bowl of guacamole and a platter of glazed, pepper-rubbed pork ribs.

"Whoa," said Milo.

"She says *mucho gusto*," said the server, pointing to Lourdes Briseno, holding an armful of menus as she shepherded a party of eight across the room. Grumpy octet, the squinty-eyed look of plane-wreck survivors assessing their friends' nutritional value.

Milo waved at her.

She returned the gesture wearily.

"At least someone likes me," he said. "Too bad she's *really* irrelevant."

I was hungry and adrenalized, put away more food than usual before hitting the satiation wall. I pushed my plate away. Milo's attention was fixed on his own dinner, his arms food-ingesting turbines. I was drinking tea when he came up for air.

A glance at my partially eaten alp. "*She* probably did that. Ms. Armani."

"Did what?"

"Sat there like you, self-righteous and slim, while ol' Chet packed it away."

I said, "You engaging in culinary snobbery?"

"Just pointing out the sin of moderation. It's a cross I bear. Not just you, Rick. The rest of the unreasonably reasonable world."

He hunched over his food and got back on task. Another avocado heard from.

His remark made me think about Chet Corvin and his mistress, rendezvousing, dining, partying at several locations. That sparked another thought.

I said, "This is far-fetched but what if Donna Weyland—the woman who just left her husband—is a brunette around Chet's age or younger?"

He put his utensils down. "What brought that on?"

"Mental meandering. I thought of that scene we saw a few nights ago, Paul Weyland, driving up, all hangdog, telling Felice his marriage was over. In all this time, we've never seen Donna. A new relationship would explain that, and where do people find lovers? At work and close to home."

"The old neighbor game," he said. His eyes sparked. "Hey, Felice was pretty touchy-feely with Weyland. Otherwise she's been an ice queen. What if the infidelity cut both ways?"

"Chet and Donna, Felice and Paul."

"Sounds like a movie, but why not, your basic steamy suburbia. Hell, the whole goddamn cul-de-sac could be a nest of sin—Bitt and Chelsea on one side, marital messes on the other."

He frowned. "Be great for prime time but how does Black Camaro fit in? Not to mention Braun . . . hell, there's *one* thing I can do."

He phone-Googled an image search, handed me the cell.

Five Donna Weylands, three of them in their twenties. A gorgeous black cheerleader at the University of Houston was caught in midair, an Alaska Air flight attendant from Vancouver, British Columbia, posed in a bikini on an unnamed beach, a game-show developer from Williamsburg, Brooklyn, sported more iron in her face than a high-power magnet, Donna Ethelina Weyland of Paterson, New Jersey, had passed away in 1937.

Donna A. Weyland, an employee of the L.A. Unified School District, appeared once, in a group shot of an educational task force convening in Reno.

Middle-aged, full-faced and zaftig, hair that could be gray or blond clipped in a no-nonsense page, oversized eyeglasses, a hesitant smile.

Milo said, "She mighta broken Paul's heart, but I'm not getting Armani, pricey chocolates, and vino from someone like Chet."

I handed the phone back. He swabbed at his mouth with a napkin, motioned the busboy over, and ordered coffee.

Milo drank two cupfuls, pried his bulk upward, and tossed cash on the table. No need to wait for the check, he always surpasses.

I said, "Let's split it."

"Like *that's* gonna happen."

Scooping more chips out of the bowl, he tilted his head toward the front door. "Pitchforks are gone, let's head back to alleged civilization."

29

Not a word from Milo the following day. Nothing on my Saturday calendar other than dinner with Robin. Meanwhile, she was working.

I drove to the Palisades, parked a quarter mile from the Corvins', and walked.

Using your legs in L.A. when you're not accompanied by a dog makes people nervous. When I was a block away I clipped my expired LAPD consultant badge to my belt. It entitles me to nothing but can mute anxiety.

At the mouth of Evada Lane, that was put to the test.

As I entered the cul-de-sac, an older, pale-blue BMW 6 drove past me, stopped for a moment, then rolled up the driveway of the second house on the north side of the block. Illinois plates, the paint salt-pocked and grimy.

A man got out carrying a macramé shopping bag. Forties, thick mop of gray hair, matching beard. He wore a tweed jacket, pressed jeans, a blue work shirt, brown-and-tan wingtips. Standing near his driver's door, he pressed a finger to his chin as if considering options.

I kept going, positioning myself so the badge was easy to spot.

"Police?" he said.

I stopped. He put his bag down. "If I'm correct, I've noticed another one of you guys, looked like a weight lifter? I was coming home after a weekend away, early morning, saw him around the corner. When he saw me, he started jogging, which seemed odd at that hour. I hope he's one of you and not some muscle-bound burglar."

I smiled.

He said, "Knew it! I'm pretty impressed with how you guys are sticking with it. How long's it been—weeks."

"Exactly."

"Kudos. Where I'm from, good luck getting follow-up."

"Where's that?"

"South Side of Chicago."

"Professor?"

"It's that obvious?"

"You don't look like a gangster."

He chuckled. "South Side's all thugs and academics? That's a little facile. Actually, you're right. Actually, there's considerable spillover between thugs and academics."

I laughed and walked over to him. The macramé bag was filled with groceries. Packaged steak on top; grass-fed, organic, Whole Foods.

I held out my hand. "Alex Delaware."

His grip was firm. "Bart Tabatchnik. I'm at the U. for a semester teaching economics. I hope I'm not about to oversell something I observed. I really didn't think it was important, still don't, but seeing you, I figured why not? Seeing as it's still unsolved."

I said, "Anything you can offer would be appreciated."

"This was a couple of weeks before it happened," said Bart Tabatchnik.

"Even so."

"Okay. I'm sure you know that the fellow who lives to the left is an artist named Bitt. After the murder, people were murmuring about him, apparently they think he's odd. I've had no contact with him but it made me curious so I looked him up and his work is pretty out there. Normally, I'd assume a clash of norms is at play—it's a pretty conservative neighborhood, I wouldn't want to get anyone in trouble. But then I saw his face and I realized I'd seen him before. Only once, but it might be substantive. Then again, it might not."

He stroked his beard. "Sorry, I tend to get prolix, occupational hazard, get paid to lecture, cut to the chase: Around a week after the murder I saw Bitt and another man having a confrontation. I wondered if that was Corvin—on the off chance, I don't know anyone here but it was his house—anyway, I looked him up and it was Corvin."

Pausing. "If he's already told you about it, I have nothing to add."

No idea Corvin was dead. It takes a village to breed gossip. The residents of Evada appeared to relate on the emotional level of cans on a pantry shelf.

I said, "What did you see?"

"I'd have to term it an encounter between Bitt and Corvin. I won't call it an exchange because Corvin was doing all the talking. Quite a bit of talking. His body language seemed somewhat assertive." He demonstrated by leaning forward.

I said, "How did Mr. Bitt react?"

"Not at all, he just stood there. I felt there might be tension brewing, though I had no overt indication of that. But living on the South Side, you develop a feel for that. I felt as though something might occur."

"Physical violence."

"It struck me as a possibility. I didn't want any part of that so I went inside, put my things away, returned to my front window. Whatever had begun was over. Corvin was walking back toward his house and Bitt had crossed the street and was headed in the opposite direction. I came out to smoke a cigar—my landlord won't allow it in the

house. And the woman who lives right there"—pointing to the left—
"came out and asked if I'd seen the 'fuss.' I said I had, she called them
a couple of stupid little boys, went on a rant about paying huge property taxes to live in a nice neighborhood and still having to deal with
stupidity."

He smiled. "She's a bit of a crank."

I said, "Name?"

"Don't know—if you're going to speak to her, please keep me out
of it."

"You bet. Bitt and Corvin live at the other end of the block but
they took their issues here."

"I did wonder about that," said Bart Tabatchnik. "Perhaps they
were out walking, encountered each other, and some sort of prior
issue rose. As to what that might be, sorry, no idea."

"Appreciate the input, Professor. Anything else you'd like to tell
me?"

"Nope and please keep my name out of everything. My interest is
in spotting micro-trends, I tend to be more observant than most. But
I really don't want anyone in my face."

"Of course."

Lifting his shopping bag, he trotted to his front door, turned
toward me, fist-bumped air, and went inside.

He hadn't taken a single look at my badge.

Nothing like the neighborhood crank when you wanted details.

The mat in front of the house adjoining Tabatchnik's said Not Buying What You're Selling. No answer to my knocks or the doorbell.

I returned to the Seville, called Milo's office phone, relayed Tabatchnik's account.

He said, "The guy made Moe last night. Damn. An encounter, huh?"

"It doesn't sound friendly," I said, "so the mutual interest in chocolate may not mean camaraderie."

"Okay, good to know. I was gonna call you, Moe spotted Chelsea doing one of her night moves at one a.m. She slipped through that joke of a gate, meaning she left through the rear door. She headed straight for Bitt's place, lit up a cigarette, looked up at Bitt's window, and went back home. Bitt's lights were out so maybe she didn't want to wake him. Or I'm dead wrong about something creepy going on, she just wants to sneak a smoke. The other bit of nothing is no prints or DNA on the phone I lifted at the A-frame, and the unidentified one from the motel is too incomplete to analyze."

A car drove past me. Older gun-metal gray Mercedes diesel, an intent, white-haired woman scowling and crawling forward, two hands clenching the wheel. She turned into the driveway bordering Tabatchnik's.

I said, "Call you back," and watched as the car lurched to a squeaking stop, bucked, and repeated that staccato performance several times.

The white-haired woman, tiny, thin, ponytailed, dressed in black knit pants and top and black flats, walked around to the passenger side. Opening the door with effort, she extricated a black purse, positioned the strap on a narrow shoulder. Next came a paper shopping bag—Gelson's—that she placed on the ground. It took two attempts to shut the Merc's heavy door. She manually locked the car on both sides, retrieved the bag, and held it in two hands as she approached the front door.

I was a Boy Scout as a kid, have that impulse to help, but the hostile doormat killed any idea of chivalry. I waited until she'd managed to bring her groceries inside and shut her front door. The dead bolt snicked. I gave her additional time to settle before ringing the bell.

A raspy voice said, "Who is it?"

"Police."

"Prove it."

I unclipped my badge and held it up to the peephole.

"Hmph," said the voice. Nothing happened for a few moments and I wondered if she was calling the station. Without Milo prenotified, that could complicate matters. But the door opened and she stared at me, then the badge.

"Let me see that."

One of the few. I handed it over. She squinted. Maybe farsightedness would save me.

"You're a good-looking guy, this does nothing for you . . . Ph.D.? What kind of police is that?"

"I'm a psychologist who works with the police."

"Have a niece who's a psychologist. She's also a tattooed lunatic." Giving me the once-over. "What can I do for you, I guess it's Doctor."

"We're doing some follow-up on the incident at the Corvin house."

"That's their name, huh?" She snorted. "The incident? Just come out and say it, a lunatic sliced someone up and left body parts in their house."

"That's another way to put it," I said, smiling. She didn't reciprocate.

"Don't soft-pedal for my sake, I was an emergency room nurse for thirty years. Before that, I was in the military." A bony hand shot out. "Edna San Felipe."

She squeezed hard, flung my hand away like a used tissue. "Know anything about hospitals?"

Strange question. "Used to work at Western Peds."

"The kids' hospital," said Edna San Felipe. "Even so. The name 'Horatio San Felipe' ring a bell?"

"Sorry, no."

"My brother was the greatest heart surgeon who ever lived. Pig-valve substitution for the pneumonic, he figured out how to repair with minimal invasion. Our father was U.S. ambassador to Honduras. Our grandfather and great-grandfather grew more bananas than Dole."

She shook her head. "No one learns history, anymore. So what can I do for you, *Doctor*?" Making my degree sound like a correspondence-course joke.

"If there's anything you want to tell me about the murder—"

"A stranger's corpse ends up in someone's house? That's not random. How'd it get there? Why them? It's still not solved, they have to be hiding something."

"Is there something about them—"

"No, I'm just being logical."

"Do you have any impressions of them?"

"So I'm right," she said.

"At this point—"

"No, I haven't any impressions," she said. "Never had dealings with them except once in a while I'd see him—the husband—and he'd try to chitchat. He's an oily type, pretending we know each other when we don't. Like a politician."

"Any contact with Mrs. Corvin?"

"She's a typical one," said Edna San Felipe. "The tinted hair, the clothes, the manicure." Displaying her own nails, blunt and unpolished. "The E.R., you're elbow-deep in someone's bowels, you don't fool around with talons."

"One of my friends is an E.R. surgeon."

"Where?"

"Cedars. Dr. Richard Silverman."

"What does he patch?"

"He's a trauma surgeon."

"Bet *his* nails are short." She began to close the door.

I said, "So there's nothing about the Corvins you can—"

"The wife works, I'll give her that. I know that because I see her load the kids in the morning and she doesn't come back until late afternoon when she brings them home—now, those are a couple of . . ." Finally, at a loss for words.

"The kids."

"The boy looks to me like a potential reprobate," said Edna San Felipe. "One day I heard my garbage cans clunk to the ground and when I went out to check, that one was skateboarding up the block."

"Did you complain?"

"What good would that do, there's no discipline anymore." She smiled crookedly. "What I did do was line the lid of my cans with habanero paste, that's a chile pepper able to blow a hole in your colon. If the brat tried it again and touched his face, he'd learn."

She held my gaze. "You think that's child abuse? I call it education. Same for someone's dog nosing around, habanero the grass, let the mutt learn by experience. And don't worry about risk to the garbagemen, they've got these automatic trucks, sit on their keisters and use a power hoist."

She folded her arms across a scrawny chest. Daring me to argue.

When I didn't she said, "Then there's the girl. There's obviously something wrong, there. Is she retarded or autistic? It's one or the other, that blank look in her eyes. She walks around at night. I've come home late from my place at the beach, seen her. At night. Late. Where's the parental supervision?"

The door swung a few inches wider. "The police have no idea so they called you in to psychoanalyze?"

"Something like that," I said. "I'd like to ask about another of your neighbors—"

"No one's a neighbor, here," said Edna San Felipe. "We co-reside but there's no socializing. It wasn't that way in Honduras. Our workers were happy as clams to be picking bananas, everyone socialized, from all levels of the social ladder. Who?"

I said, "Trevor Bitt."

"That one was my *first* thought when I heard about it."

"Why's that?"

"Basic logic. Something bizarre happens, look for a bizarre person."

"Have you had dealings with him?"

"None whatsoever. But he's also not normal, no question about it."

"A person on the block witnessed what might've been an argument between Mr. Bitt and Mr. Corvin."

She glanced at Tabatchnik's house. "He sent you to me?"

"No, ma'am."

"I happened to see it, I don't rubberneck. Unlike him, what do *those* people call snoopers—yentas. Like the Streisand movie. Love her voice but never bought her as a man."

"What can you tell me about the encounter between Bitt and Corvin?"

"I saw two grown men acting like children in a playground."

"Aggressive."

"Facing off," said Edna San Felipe. "Like brats."

"Any idea what the conflict was about?"

"Not a clue."

"Professor Tabatchnik said Mr. Corvin was doing all the talking."

"He was."

"And Mr. Bitt just stood there."

"Like the Sphinx," she said. "He wasn't happy, that was obvious from what you people call body language. I'd take a long, hard look at him. Like I said, not random and the man's clearly unhinged. Slouches around looking like a robot. Pretends not to hear when you say hello. Which I did just once, believe me."

I said, "At least he didn't kick your cans over."

She glared at me. If faces were tools, hers was a filleting knife. "That supposed to be a joke?"

The door closed.

A crank, but her instincts were good: nothing random about the body dump, focus on the unusual neighbor. Now that I knew about Bitt absorbing Chet Corvin's anger, he deserved further observation.

31

Evada Lane, one a.m. A starless sky sagged like a rain-soaked tarp, a malnourished moon cast anemic light.

The first time I'd been here after dark, LEDs on poles and flashing bars atop cruisers had turned the cul-de-sac into a miniature theater district. No show tonight; the silence was constricted—that of a gagged victim.

I parked a block farther than this afternoon, wanting to avoid some antsy resident's memory jog. My sneakers had the squeak long run out of them; my sweatpants and shirt were black. I could be taken for a burglar. If Moe Reed or Sean Binchy was on watch, he'd figure it out.

No sign of either detective as I made my way. Maybe because they were pros. Or the overtime budget had run out.

As my eyes adjusted, contours of rooftops suggested themselves. Where the street wasn't as inky as my clothing, specks of purple and lilac showed like pinprick wounds. Lights on in front of Bart Tabatchnik's house but his car was gone. If I *was* a burglar, I'd be interested.

Illumination appeared at only three other residences, one of them

Trevor Bitt's Tudor, where a single second-story window facing the street formed a flesh-colored rectangle.

Lights off at the Corvins'. I wondered how the kids were doing.

I covered a third of the block *feeling* like a prowler. Made my way halfway up with still no sign of either young D. The trunks of street trees were too thin to provide cover and I saw no obvious hiding spots unless you got uncomfortably close to houses.

Not on watch.

I kept going, planning to reach the end of the cul-de-sac, circle back, and repeat before returning home and hoping for sleep.

A sound from up the block froze me midstep.

Sound duo: a thump, then a click.

I shifted off the sidewalk onto someone's drought-scratchy lawn, squinted and focused on the origin of the noise. Purple specks helped me, strobing movement from the side of the Corvin house.

The barest suggestion of human form emerged before flicking out of sight.

I trotted closer.

The form headed toward Bitt's house, stopped below Bitt's street window.

Chelsea Corvin, slightly stooped, standing there.

She did something with her arms. A yellow tongue flicked, an orange dot appeared, and the flame turned into sprinkles of earth-bound stars plummeting to the ground.

A lit match flung to the ground. A cigarette end brightened under the force of a long inhalation.

Chelsea smoked it dead, tossed the butt away, let it burn itself out, and did nothing for a while. Then she moved, heading for the side of Bitt's house that bordered hers.

I race-walked, stopped two houses away.

The scrape of feet shuffling on cement.

She coughed. A signal? Or tobacco having its way with young lungs?

She'd done this before. For all any of us knew, Bitt had no idea she preferred his property for surreptitious teenage rebellion.

Most likely, she'd sneak back home.

Two more coughs that sounded intentional. Then: faint, drum-like rapping.

Shave and a haircut six bits.

A squeal as hinges rotated.

"You're here," said a man's voice. "Good."

Squeal, hiss, clap as the door closed.

I waited a few seconds before sneaking over. The cigarette butt had landed near a patch of agave, losing the battle of survival to night-dewed succulents.

Bitt's street window went dark. Another rectangle on the side of the house lit up, as if in compensation. A window that faced the Corvin house. Chelsea's bedroom.

I hung around for a while and when the girl didn't exit, I got out of there. Waiting until I'd passed Bart Tabatchnik's house before making the call.

Milo's semi-awake voice was a spit-clogged tuba. He recovered fast; all those years of late-night homicide calls. "Hold on, let me go to another room."

Moments later, he was back, a saliva-free trombone. "We surveil, get zilch, you show up once. Keeping your lottery ticket in a safe place?"

"Beginner's luck," I said. "I didn't spot Moe or Sean."

"Moe just picked up his own murder and Sean's started excavating a cold case. So she definitely went inside."

"No doubt."

"I *knew* we were right, he's a creep. Okay, what now . . ." Muffled yawn. "Raiding the place just because she's in there is a bad idea, by the time I make arrangements she'll probably be gone. And too many unpredictables. But this should be enough for a warrant, gotta be, I'll talk to Nguyen or go straight to find a damn judge. Only glitch I can see is your presence, you might need to be named as a police sub-agent or something along those lines." He laughed. "You'll get paid sooner."

I said, "I'm fine with that but there's another issue. As a psychologist I'm obligated to report suspected child abuse."

"Defined how?"

"That's the problem," I said. "There are no clear definitions of 'suspected,' the rules change all the time, and whenever I try to get clarification from the state board they give me gobbledygook. If you move quickly, I can make the call at the same time. And I think Felice should know right away. She'll get upset, might be able to open Chelsea up."

"Complications," he said, "but on balance, you've made my life simpler."

32

At ten the following morning, I phoned Felice Corvin's work number. Her voicemail message said she'd be back in the office in the afternoon. I asked her to call me.

She didn't, I tried again, same result. No answer at her personal cell or her landline. At five fifteen, she phoned my service and they patched me through.

"What is it, Doctor?"

"I'd like to come by to talk to you."

"What about?"

"It's better discussed in person."

"I don't understand."

"I'll clarify when we meet."

"This is—is it something about Chet?"

"Related to Chet."

"Related," she said. "I just got in, Brett's basketball practice. You can't tell me what this is about?"

"I'd rather not."

"Okay, come over within the next couple of hours. But I'll be cooking dinner."

She met me at the door, holding a dish towel, hair clipped loosely, wearing a green *Lake Tahoe* T-shirt, white yoga pants, and makeup that appeared fresh.

"That was quick," she said. "You're a motivated guy, Doctor."

I smiled. She stepped aside, eyes wary, led me to the kitchen.

An empty KFC bucket sat on the center island, along with an uneaten biscuit, a container of coleslaw, paper napkins, and plastic utensils.

No sign of the kids.

She said, "Coffee? It's decaf, after three I can't handle the real stuff." Bouncing on her feet, lilt in her voice, the kind of tension that came from forced casualness.

I said, "Sure, thanks."

Clearing the island, she poured two mugs, brought milk and sugar. Once I was settled she sat to my left, positioned so she could avoid eye contact if she chose.

Untying her hair, she let it swing and sipped. "You really do have me curious."

I said, "The investigation into Chet's death has included surveillance of your street."

Her eyebrows arched. "Even though it happened somewhere else?"

"The surveillance has produced some information that may or may not be related to either murder. Either way, I feel strongly that you need to know. My decision, not the police. As we both know, Chelsea leaves your house late at night. Last night she left shortly after one a.m. and entered Trevor Bitt's house. I'm required to report suspected child abuse."

I braced myself for shock, horror, anger.

Felice Corvin shook her head as if I'd said something foolish and let out a shrill laugh. "Oh, boy." She put her cup down, took a deep breath, faced away. "First off, it's not child abuse because she's not a child. She'll be eighteen soon. In a few days, as a matter of fact."

"Legally, she's still—"

"Oh, please. *Really?*"

"It doesn't bother you."

"You've obviously convinced yourself something ugly is going on."

"You disagree."

"Oh, Lord." She returned to the sink, yanked a drawer open, shut it. "I know you mean well. But this isn't going to help Chelsea."

I said nothing.

She returned to the island, this time facing me, but staying on her feet. "I have no doubt you're thinking, *She's a horrible mother.*"

Tears formed in her eyes.

I said, "If there's something I should know."

"Oh, there's something." Scanning the room like a hungry animal scrounging for scraps, she settled on her purse and got it. "There's a *whole* lot of something."

Removing her cellphone, she punched a one-digit pre-program. "Hi. We've got a situation . . ." Glancing at me. "Can't. Needs to be now . . . yes, please."

Sitting back down, she drank more coffee.

A doorbell rang. Not from the front; the utility door leading from the backyard to the laundry room.

Chelsea's exit route. The body-drag route.

Felice Corvin called out, "It's open!" A latch turned. Footsteps. A man trudged into the kitchen, shoes scuffing the floor.

Tall and rangy with a narrow, pallid face crisscrossed by wrinkles. White hair, precisely side-parted. His clothes bagged, his cheeks were twin hollows, wrinkles deepening toward the bottom, as if dragged down by tiny fishhooks.

Executive haircut, executive-at-leisure clothes straight out of a cruise-ship ad: gray cashmere V-neck sweater, white polo shirt, razor-pressed khakis, oxblood penny loafers each bearing a shiny copper image of Lincoln.

Washed-out aqua eyes flecked with brown nested in flesh-colored crepe. No interest in me. He looked at Felice and spoke her name.

His voice was a feeble croak. He looked ready to cry.

"This is the psychologist I told you about."

The man looked at me, blinking convulsively, lips quivering. She pulled out a chair. He sat. She placed a hand on his shoulder. He trembled.

"Dr. Delaware, Trevor Bitt."

No news there. Same face as on the Internet, older, wearier.

I said, "Alex Delaware."

Bitt said, "Psychologist. I've known a few." Flexing his fingers. Spidery, graceful, restless digits, the nails elongated and filed smooth. Ink stains on the right thumbnail and the meat of the right hand.

Felice had kept her hold on his shoulder. The ink-stained hand inched upward, was about to make contact with her fingers when footsteps from the left made the three of us turn.

Chelsea shuffled in, barefoot, holding a bowl in one hand, a spoon in the other. She wore a shapeless gray sweatshirt and jeans.

Her eyes raced to Bitt. "You're *here*." The bowl tumbled from her hands, hit the floor, shattered. The spoon followed an instant later, bouncing and pinging.

Trevor Bitt got up, retrieved the utensil. "Where's your broom?"

Felice Corvin said, "I'll handle it, Trev."

Chelsea Corvin said, "*I* will, Daddy!"

She ran to Bitt, threw both arms around his waist, rested her head on his chest.

"Let me do it," he said. "I don't want those pretty hands of yours cut."

"I can *do* it, Daddy."

Bitt reached down and took her right hand. "Save them. You've got art to make."

Still hugging him, she said, "Let me at least get the broom."

"Sure."

She let go, tottered, ran off, and returned with a Swiffer that she handed to Bitt like a ceremonial sword. In her other hand, a dustpan. The two of them set about cleaning up, working in obvious harmony.

Felice leaned close and whispered, "Now you know. So we can move on, okay—Trev, Cheltz, when you finish why don't you go work on a project."

Chelsea turned to her mother. Joy on her broad, pasty face. First time I'd seen that.

"Really?" she said. "When it's still light?"

"If Trevor's okay with it."

"More than okay," said Bitt. He straightened with what looked like pain, held out the dustpan. "Where do I toss this?"

CHAPTER

33

ather and daughter left in lockstep, a trudge duet.

When the utility door closed, I said, "This is the first time he's been inside your house."

Felice Corvin nodded. "It was going to happen, eventually. I wasn't sure how to do it." Wan smile. "Guess you took care of that . . . you didn't touch your coffee. I'm having more—what I'd really like is a double Martini."

"Go for it."

"And make myself vulnerable? Don't think so, Doctor."

She walked to the coffeemaker, took a long time to do a simple task, returned to the island. Positioned so she'd have to face me.

"Okay. Here goes." The flat of her hand landed on her left breast. "Okay. Nineteen years ago, I was living in the Bay Area, getting my master's at Cal, and I met Trevor at a party. I'd just ended a toxic relationship—a professor, don't ask."

The "intellectual girlfriend" Lanny Joseph had mentioned.

She played with her hair. "Trevor was an underground celebrity but I knew nothing about him or his art. I just thought he was a nice, quiet guy, which is exactly what I was looking for. Turned out he'd also ended a fling, some stripper with a subterranean IQ."

Bitt's uncharitable assessment of Maillot Bernard. No doubt he'd sidestepped the incident with the gun.

I waited.

Felice Corvin said, "That's it, basically. We started something, it lasted a year, it ended."

"Basically" is a favorite word of liars and evaders.

I said, "Go on."

"Oh, Jesus." She reclamped her hair. "It ended with Trevor because I met Chet and he swept me off my feet, okay? Trevor was handsome but so was Chet, in a different way. What I saw as super-masculine, back then. He had—was nothing like what you saw. Really. I've long thought of him as fruit that didn't ripen properly. I suppose we all change but Chet *really* changed. When I met him he was courtly, attentive. The proverbial sweep off the feet, nothing was good enough for me. I loved it."

"Trevor hadn't provided that."

"Trevor was quiet and inoffensive. He needed his alone time, lots of it. After the professor, who was a total sociopath with insane mood swings, I was attracted to peace and quiet. But then it became . . . I'm not proud to say this but I grew bored with Trevor and meeting Chet intensified that. He was stimulating, gregarious, we laughed all the time, always had something to talk about. When I was with Trevor, there was a lot of silence. At first I was content but then I realized I was never joyful. After a while I felt burdened—having to carry the ball socially."

"If you didn't talk, no one did."

She reached out, as if to touch my hand. Drew back. The downward eyes of a child caught in the act.

"With Chet," she said, "I was the audience, could just sit back and be *entertained*. I loved that. Loved *him* for quite some time. Then—

enough, okay? You don't need to know about all our relationship garbage."

I said, "Did you see Chet and Trevor simultaneously?"

She stiffened. "Wow. Someone's being brutally direct. Was I a
two-timing slut?"

"Not my question."

"I know, I know, you're being logical. Yes, there was overlap. And
during that overlap, something happened."

She touched her mug. "Do I need to spell it out?"

"Pregnancy."

"Which I didn't realize for a while. I'd never been regular and I
didn't gain a lot of weight until my sixth month. By that time, doing
something about it seemed . . . I just couldn't. I was terrified to tell
Chet, he said no problem, let's get married."

"Chelsea was Trevor's but Chet never knew. Did Trevor?"

Her cheeks flushed. The rest of her face followed, rosiness spreading beneath her neckline. "I was *with* Chet by then. To you it probably sounds cold-blooded but I didn't want to hurt him."

Answering one question, no sense pushing. "How did you learn
Chelsea was Trevor's?"

"I always suspected it," she said. "The timing. The blood typing
proved it. Chelsea's AB blood, the same as me. Trevor's A, so he could
be a contributor. I knew Trevor's type because we gave blood together.
Some benefit in Berkeley for Africa or somewhere that I pushed him
into."

Smile. "Once upon a time, I was quite the idealist. When they
typed me, I got treated like a big star, AB's rare. When the needle went
into Trevor's arm, he nearly passed out."

"Chet's type is . . ."

"O-positive. And no, he never had a clue. Medical details weren't
his thing. When the kids were sick, he always managed to disappear.
That was his approach to life in general. Anything that didn't fascinate
him personally, he ignored."

Her fingernails rapped her mug. "Like Chelsea. The moment it became clear she was different, he abandoned her emotionally. Brett, on the other hand, was his guy. Conventional, concrete, athletic. He was never mean to Chelsea, she was just a big zero to him. He'd talk a good case to outsiders, but there was nothing real emanating from him to her and she knew it."

"Did she talk about that?"

"Chelsea doesn't talk about anything but it affected her, a mother can tell. That's why I got so angry when Chet made that call to you. All of a sudden he's the concerned parent? Pu-*leeze*. Have you figured it out, now? His ulterior motive?"

"He suspected something inappropriate going on between Chelsea and Trevor, wanted to point me in that direction so I'd snoop around."

She nodded. "It made me mad but it also scared me."

"His learning the truth."

"At exactly the wrong time, Doctor. Eventually, we were going to get divorced—mutual decision. So far, the discussion had been civilized. But there are money issues, as I told you most of it's mine. I didn't want him using that against me."

"When did you start talking divorce?"

"A while back. A year, at least. We'd bring it up, agree, get busy and forget about it. Our talks were always friendly, splitting up was one of the few things Chet and I could cooperate on."

She burst into tears. No tissues in sight. I tore a paper towel from a roll on the counter and handed it to her.

"Thanks," she said. "Sorry for being mawkish but I just remembered something. The things you think you've forgotten."

She sniffed, dabbed the corners of her eyes. "Don't know if you noticed but one of the *many* obnoxious things Chet used to do was call me his bride."

I nodded.

"I couldn't stand it. But one day, when we were talking about the divorce, he got a look on his face. Troubled. What actually looked like a deep emotion, which for Chet was rare. He reached across the table and took my hand like he used to. Massaging my knuckles gently. I used to *love* that. When he wanted to, he could un-*wind* me. Then he said, 'Guess you won't be my bride anymore.' And his voice choked up."

More tears. "If he'd been like that all along . . ."

Footsteps cut her off. Brett bounced into the kitchen, miming jump shots.

Felice wiped away tear-tracks. Not necessary. The boy's eyes were on the fridge.

"Hungry, Bretty?"

Quiver in her voice. No evidence Brett noticed. He said, "Chelsea had Ben and Jerry's. I want some."

"Go for it, honey."

"Get it myself?"

"That would be nice, darling."

The boy grunted, flung the freezer door open, located a pint container and a soup spoon, and left.

"My sensitive soul," said Felice Corvin. "Maybe it's good to be like that. Maybe his life will be easier."

"How's he doing with his dad gone?"

"Lately he seems to be moping but for the most part, he's okay."

"Chelsea never reacted."

"Now you understand."

"When did she learn Trevor was her father?"

"Do we really need to get into that?"

"We do."

"It's a new thing for her, Doctor. I told her the day after you and the lieutenant came to inform us about Chet. I acted quickly because she's not a . . . typical girl. Yes, she's been going to Trevor's, but for art, a tutor-student thing. I didn't want to lose control of the situation, have her undergo some sort of breakdown."

"You're sure she didn't already know?"

"I wasn't sure, so before I had a sit-down with Chelsea, I asked Trevor and he swore to me he'd never said a thing. That was the deal we had. Pacing was up to me."

"Your eventual goal was formalizing their relationship."

"After the divorce," she said. "Not in the sense of adoption or anything legal, just so Chelsea could feel . . . a part of something. Being with Trevor has been terrific for her. They do art together, he tells her she's talented."

"How long has she been going over to his house?"

"Since last fall. And not often. And yes, at night, because we've needed to keep it under wraps. For another child, I'd worry about disrupting her school. But school's never been Chelsea's thing."

"Trevor's been living here for years. Why just recently?"

"My decision after I knew Chet and I would be breaking up. Chelsea's always been into drawing. I showed some of her work to Trevor and he brightened up like I've never seen. So I went to Chelsea and told her Mr. Bitt wanted to see more. She'd go over when Chet was out of town and we could be sure Brett wouldn't notice. He's a heavy sleeper, that helped. Trevor's just the opposite, total insomniac, so he was up late quite a bit."

"Chet eventually found out."

"A fluke," she said. "A few months ago, he had some sort of virus, the guy was never sick, used to talk about germs being terrified of invading the sacred temple that was his body."

She shook her head. "Anyway, he did catch something, got up in the middle of the night to take a pill, heard the side door close and went to check and saw her. She didn't knock on Trevor's door, but she went to the side of Trevor's house and smoked a cigarette and came back. Maybe she sensed she was being watched, or maybe she just wanted to smoke. And yes, I know it's a terrible habit and no, I have no idea how she started and yes, I've tried to talk to her. You choose your battles."

Her shoulders slumped.

I said, "Does Trevor smoke?"

"Are you asking if he's a bad influence? No, Doctor. He used to but he hasn't for years."

"So Chet spotted her."

"And got all worked up and I convinced him it was no big deal, kids do that. I thought I'd calmed him down but turns out when he was home he kept an eye out and he saw her go out again. Did he do the logical thing and tell me? No, he kept it to himself and did nothing. Which shows me he really didn't care—he never has cared about Chelsea. He just wanted to make trouble so he called you."

"A manipulation."

"More like sabotage. I'd thought we'd kept our breakup civil but it got me thinking. Maybe he was setting me up as a bad mom so he could get more money, I really don't know."

She'd just offered me plenty of motive for murder, seemed unaware.

I said, "Did Chet ever see Chelsea actually go into Trevor's house?"

"Thank God, no. It was the smoking he concentrated on. Even he likes a cigar now and then."

"When did Chelsea start calling Trevor 'Daddy'?"

"What you just saw was the first time. I was as surprised as you."

"Trevor didn't seem surprised."

"Trevor's different, Doctor. His reactions are different," she said. The blanket explanation for Chelsea extended to her father.

I said, "How did he come to live next door?"

"Oh, God," she said. "I feel like my whole life's being exposed—what the heck, that was my fault. Everything seems to be." She used the crumpled towel to dab the corners of her eyes.

"After we moved here, I was at a low ebb. Boring neighborhood, boring job, the marriage thing, I was pretty down. I don't know what possessed me, but a year or so later, out of the clear blue, I phoned Trevor. Still had his number. Still thought about him. He was happy to hear from me. Told me he'd missed me. That got to me, Doctor. I kind of lost it and blurted out the Chelsea situation. One of those things you do but you really don't understand."

"Sure," I said. "How'd Trevor react?"

"Different from what I expected. He said, 'Really? That's great.' I said, 'Trev, did you hear me?' He said, 'I'm a dad and I never had to change diapers. Sounds like a good deal.' I was stunned, he thanked me for letting him know, neither of us had more to say so I hung up. I immediately decided I'd just made a huge mistake that could come back to bite me. But it didn't. I never heard from him. A couple years later, the house next door went up for sale."

Another poke with the towel. "It was on the market for a long time, ugly pile of bricks, those crazy cactuses. Then one day there was a *Sold* sign, I see the real estate agent and she tells me who my new neighbor is. I thought I'd have a stroke."

She used the towel to wipe a clean corner of butcher block. "I kept waiting to see him. Dreading but also . . ." Shrug. "One day a truck was parked out front but no sign of him. Weeks went on. I used to take a two-mile run an hour after dinner, like clockwork till I hurt my meniscus. One night the kids were doing whatever and Chet was on the road, as usual. I was running back, had slowed for my wind-down, and saw him standing in front of his door. I nearly tripped and fell. My first reaction was anger. What the hell had he done, it felt so intrusive. And why hadn't he bothered to come over and talk about it? I asked him what the hell he was thinking. He said my call had changed his life. He was tired of San Francisco and hearing from me had helped him put things in perspective."

"About Chelsea."

"That's what I took it to mean and I made it clear he needed to keep his mouth shut. He swore he would. I could tell he was sincere. There's no duplicity in Trevor, what you see is what you get."

I said, "How'd he locate the house?"

"He looked up my address on the Internet and used real estate sites to find available properties nearby. When he found one right next door, he took it as a sign. A massive dose of karma, he called it. Seeing him unsettled me but what could I do? I reiterated that he was forbidden from saying anything to Chelsea or anyone else, he'd screw up her life and mine and I'd never forgive him. Again, he swore he wouldn't."

I said, "How long has he been ill?"

Her eyes slid to the right, caromed back to me, drifted again. "What do you mean?"

"He moves like a sick man."

"Does he, Doctor?"

She took a sip of coffee, muttered, "Cold," and pushed the mug away. "All right, no sense hiding reality. He's got a situation. No one in his family lives past sixty, it's a heart thing, they get congestive failure, fade away. Trevor's fifty-nine and he's doing okay, considering, but he's weakening. So he tries to take life easy. Money's not an issue for him, he's got plenty. Could've lived in a huge estate with an ocean view but he chose here and has enriched Chelsea's life. How could I not honor that?"

"And now he can beef up his karma," I said.

"Pardon?"

"With Chet gone, he's free to be Chelsea's father."

She stared at me. "Are you saying what I think you are?"

I kept silent.

She said, "You are *so* wrong, Dr. Delaware. Trevor would never do *anything* like that and I really don't want to continue this discussion. In fact, I'd like for you to leave right now."

"No problem," I said. "But Trevor's made himself a suspect and that won't go away."

"Ridiculous. What exactly has he done?"

"Lieutenant Sturgis has been trying to talk to him since Hargis Braun's body was dumped in your house and he's been stonewalling."

"Braun has nothing to do with Trevor. If it has to do with anyone, that would be Chet, it was *his* space that got invaded."

"Who do you suspect?"

"I don't suspect anyone! All I'm saying is it could have to do with business. Chet's outside life. Which I'm not privy to and neither is Trevor. All the years I spent with Chet and I'm a total ignoramus about what he did when he left home."

I said, "With a homicide, a neighborhood canvass is part of the routine. Everyone else on the block cooperated. Trevor didn't."

"I told you he's different. And he's sick, needs to conserve his energy."

I didn't respond.

She said, "You'd have to know Trevor to understand him."

"That's the point, Felice. To know him, we'd have to spend time with him. He's prevented that and the longer he holds out the worse it looks. Especially now, with Chet murdered. Neighbors have seen Chet and Trevor in a confrontation."

She seemed genuinely surprised. "About what?"

"We don't know yet but Chelsea's paternity supplies a motive. Maybe Chet knew more than you thought."

"I don't believe that—even so, it's not relevant, Trevor would never hurt anyone."

I said, "Maybe the confrontation was based on chocolate."

Her eyes rounded.

I said, "Two boxes, birthday and Christmas. Heart-shaped."

She gasped. Pressed her hands to the side of her face, compressing her features. Her eyes clamped shut. When she spoke, I could barely hear her.

"You know about that. Omigod."

"We're talking two murders, Felice. The cops don't just sit around."

"Okay," she said. "Yes, that happened, yes it . . . complicated things."

"What happened?"

"Trevor was stupid, giving her the candy was absolute idiocy on his part. I never knew about the first box, Chelsea ate everything and hid it. But the second one, soon after Braun, she left right out on her desk. Along with a drawing that he signed. A little deer, like Bambi."

"Was the signature his name or 'Dad'?"

"His name, the dad part *never* came out, I promise you Chet had no clue. He just thought Trevor was being . . . over-attentive. Even after I explained that I'd showed Chelsea's drawings to him and he thought she was talented. Was just trying to encourage her with the candy."

I said, "Not the whole story."

She gave a long dreary head shake.

"Chet was a glutton and a big treat-stealer. Any of us would be eating something yummy and he'd just come over and take some without asking. He thought it was hilarious, the kids hated it and I wasn't too fond of it, either. I told him over and over to respect their boundaries but he just laughed and said he paid the bills, everything was his. That's what happened with the chocolates. He walked past Chelsea's room, noticed the box, came over to steal, and saw the drawing."

Her right fist punched her left palm.

"Everything hit the fan. Chet told me I was a gullible idiot, Trevor was probably a pervert, you don't give expensive gifts to a kid without ulterior motives. He began interrogating Chelsea. She shut him out totally, wouldn't say a word. That made him mad and he began calling her names. Space cadet, moron, retarded. It was horrid, I'd never seen him that way. Brett came out in the hall, I shooed him away. Chet kept going on, Chelsea just sat there and continued to tune him out. I managed to drag Chet out of there, he had the box in his hands. I gave him my . . . limited explanation. He looked me in the eye, removed each of the chocolates, and crushed it between his fingers before tossing it back in the box. Except for the last one. He grinned and said, 'Chocolate mint, my favorite,' and popped it in his mouth. Then he tossed the box in the trash. That night, Chelsea cried like I'd never heard her. I felt like crap because I hadn't been able to protect her. Because nothing sick had happened but I couldn't tell Chet the truth. Meanwhile, he's threatening to call the cops on Trevor. Or better yet, to go next door and pound the crap out of Trevor. I begged him not to. Promised him Chelsea would cut off the relationship, I'd be more vigilant."

Another guilty eye drop. "That night, I even had sex with Chet. Anything to calm him down. I thought I'd succeeded but yesterday Trevor told me Chet had come over several times and pounded on his door. He was frightened and didn't answer. So you can see why when the cops—anyway, Chet dropped it. That was Chet, short attention span, and it's not like he actually cared about Chelsea, he just wanted to be outraged."

A beat. "What do the neighbors claim they saw?"

"Chet in Trevor's face, talking, Trevor listening."

"That's it? Thank God that ended it."

"Not from Trevor's end," I said. "Chelsea continued to visit him."

"What I told you, Doctor, only on days when Chet was out of town and not often—you know, I think your showing up was what sparked Chet's hostility. A psychologist he could use as a weapon against me. That's why he called you."

"I agree."

"You do? So you'll drop the whole thing? Tell the cops to forget about Trevor?"

"Unfortunately, I can't."

Her right hand curled into a fist. "You're not being reasonable. Hasn't this family been through enough?"

"If Trevor has nothing to hide, he can clear things up easily."

"Please," she said. "He's the only positive thing in Chelsea's life and Chelsea deserves to be happy."

I said, "I appreciate that and the solution is simple: When the cops ring the bell, he needs to come to the door, welcome them in, and be cooperative."

"Simple," she said. "I thought someone with your training could see life never is simple."

I got up. She stood in place.

I'd taken four steps when she said, "See yourself out."

34

I phoned Milo's cell from the Seville. He picked up after one chirp. "How'd it go with Felice? Get me anything for a warrant?"

I talked, he was silent but for occasional *no shit*s and *unbelievable*s and wordless growls.

When I finished, he said, "*Fucking* unbelievable. Bottom line is I'm that Greek guy, Tantalus, with the hanging fruit. No possible grounds for a child-molester warrant and Bitt's an even stronger murder suspect."

"I told Felice it was in his best interest to cooperate. She resisted but maybe she'll cool off and convince him."

"Hope springs infernal. The guy's Chelsea's baby-daddy, moves next door and lives there for two years with Felice keeping it secret from Chet? You believe her?"

"I do, but I'm not sure Chet didn't figure it out."

"The thing on the street wasn't just chocolate, huh? You pick up any strong chemistry between Felice and Bitt?"

"Not during the minute I saw them together," I said. "You're thinking just another domestic murder?"

"Why not, Alex? Maybe she's lying and they rekindled. Maybe they've been screwing since he moved in. She gives him a key, getting in would be no problem."

That didn't explain Braun. Or the Camaro. While I considered pointing that out, he said, "Or Chelsea gave him the key. She wanted her real dad—or her best friend, whatever Bitt was to her at that point—to protect her against Fake-Dad who never gave a damn about her. *And* stole her candy. We know Bitt wasn't home the night Chet got shot. He coulda followed Chet to the motel, done the deed, taken the Rover and the girlfriend, done her in some other spot, and put himself up in a hotel. Next morning he comes back and continues to ignore me. You know something, Alex, with the paternity thing and the confrontation, I'm feeling I *can* put together a warrant, gonna go judge-hunting."

"What about Braun and Mr. Camaro?"

"I'm not Moses on the Mount, one thing at a tl—"

A burp-like noise cut off the last word.

He said, "Call waiting. Hold on, that could be John Nguyen. I put in a call to talk about Bitt being a pedophile, let's see what he has to say about *this*."

He was off the line for several moments, came back talking fast.

"Not John, Petra. My stars and planets must be aligning weird, check this out."

My turn to listen.

I said, "The citizenry going that extra mile."

"Obviously, you wanna be there."

"Wouldn't miss it."

The woman's given name was Sarabeth Sarser. Her street names were: Sadie, Sammantha, Samanthalee, Bettisam, and, inexplicably, Beanie Baby.

She'd worked the street for fifteen of her thirty-one years, shuffling identities in order to confuse law enforcement as she traveled up and down the state and into Nevada and back. The past seven years, she'd concentrated her efforts in Hollywood, energy for the road fading due to poly-drug usage.

No more fooling anyone; she solicited with little guile, got arrested, paid her tickets, kept working.

She'd been picked up for the fortieth or so time by a cop named Harry Bucksteen. Bucksteen had irritated a superior, gotten pulled off a cushy paperwork job and transferred to the prostitution prevention program Petra had described. Instead of following the early intervention directive, he'd gone the conventional route: waiting for girls to complete transactions with clients, then stepping in and harassing both ends of the sex-trade supply-demand curve.

"Believe that?" said Sarabeth Sarser. "Lazy fat fuck totally broke the rules."

Petra said, "Lucky for you he's lazy. Now you have something to trade with."

"I was gonna call you anyway. It's the right thing to do," said Sarser. "Ma'am."

She had a well-formed, perfectly oval face marred by under-the-eyes meth smudges and vicious skin eruptions layers of makeup couldn't conceal. A black poly cocktail dress, skull earrings, plastic pearls, and white knee-high boots formed her ensemble of the evening. Long white-blond hair that probably looked okay in nighttime lighting was turned to straw by coffee shop glare.

The shop was a dingy place called Happy Losers, renamed last year by its latest owners because Joan and Bill's didn't have that ring. No change to the décor in decades; that and overpriced coffee explained the hipster-slackers nursing cracked mugs of Arabica while studying their phones. The coffee accounted for the rest of tonight's customers, as well: pushers, procurers, other streetwalkers, and the cops who played legal Ping-Pong with them.

A couple of uniforms on Code Seven in a corner booth recognized Sarser when we walked in and gave her a finger-wave.

She said, "Hey, boys," and wiggled her hips in a way that sent a shimmer up to her shoulders.

The cops laughed, saw Milo, returned to their sandwiches.

Petra picked a booth in the opposite corner. "Sit here, Bean." Tapping blue vinyl. When Sarser complied, she slid in next to her. Milo and I sat opposite.

Sarser said, "I feel so popular."

"You are," said Milo. "Thanks for helping us out."

"Of course, sir. I am kind of hungry."

Twenty minutes later, she pushed aside the few bites of cheeseburger she'd managed. Her eyes were pinballs. The black dress bagged and twisted as her torso shifted constantly.

She looked at the burger with the longing of an abandoned lover. Plenty of reach, no grasp. All those amphetamine nights killing appetite and sleep.

"Shit deal," she said, "but we're glad, no?"

"Shit deal about what?" said Milo.

"The guy got killed, sir."

"You know him?"

"No, sir, never even saw him." Sarser belched. "Oops."

"Never saw him before he got killed."

"Never saw him ever, sir. Just heard." Flicking a skull earring. "The gun-pops. Then I saw what I saw and knew I had to help you guys 'cause you guys have a job to do and I totally get that. Sir."

"You made the first call anonymously to our desk," said Petra. "Why not 911?"

"You know, ma'am."

"Know what?"

"Privacy?" said Sarser.

"Aha," said Petra.

"What's the diff, I told you now, ma'am."

"So you did, Beanie. As the lieutenant said, we all appreciate your stepping forward."

Sarser smiled and played with a piece of limp lettuce. Her nails were inch-long vinyls the color of arterial blood.

No one talked and that seemed to unsettle her. "You know, guys, I saved up."

"Saved what?" said Petra.

"What happened. In my head, it's still there. You have to save thoughts like money, my gram always told me."

"Did she," said Petra. "Where does Gram live?"

"Now she's in the cemetery, ma'am."

"Sorry to hear about that."

Sarser's pale, pimpled shoulders rose and fell. "It's okay, she was old."

Milo said, "She raise you?"

"Uh-uh, no way, Mom did. Then Mom went to prison then she died and I got fostered but I used to visit Gram. She had all her money 'cause she saved it."

Her face hardened. Remembering.

And during your visits, you decided to let her share involuntarily.

Milo said, "Okay, let's go over it again, Bean."

"I already told her—told you everything, ma'am, right?"

"Right," said Petra. "The lieutenant's the boss, go over it again."

"The boss," said Sarabeth Sarser. She shot Milo a ragged tweaker smile. "Can I have pie, sir?"

"Still hungry?" He pointed to the barely touched burger.

"Pie's different, sir. It's like a different thing."

"Gotcha, Bean. Soon as we're finished, pie it is. Go over it again."

"I was there and heard it and later I saw it." Another grin.

Milo said, "That's not pie, kid, that's crumbs."

Sarser laughed. "Okay. All right. Okay. I was there—"

"In room thirteen of the Sahara."

"Don't know the number."

"It was thirteen," said Petra.

"Really? That's a shit unlucky number," said Sarser. "Maybe that's why."

"Why what?"

"Something bad happened."

"In room fourteen."

"Well . . . it's like the whole thing was a bad deal."

Milo said, "You know the Sahara pretty well?"

Sarser took a moment to reply. "A little."

"We couldn't care less about your job, Bean."

"Job" made her sit up straighter. Validated. "Yeah, I'm there some-times."

"That night who was your client?"

"We were just talking, sir."

"Whatever. Who?"

"Talking, I swear, sir."

"That's fine, Bean. Tell us about your client."

"Talking," she said for a third time. "He was a little guy, I didn't understand him 'cause he was Spanish." Jagged-tooth meth grin. "Lit-tle dude. Cute. We was talking and we heard it. Little Dude got scared and hid in the bathroom."

She clapped her hands together. Feeble act, producing a faint, puffy sound; not much muscle left in her arms.

Milo said, "You heard the gunshots. Little Dude's hiding in the bathroom, where are you?"

"In the front room, ready to pee my panties. Little Dude comes out, gets dressed real fast." Giggling. "He's like getting his feet caught in his pants and his thing is waving. He opens the door and books, I shut it and get down on the floor."

She tucked in her head and covered it with both arms. A schoolkid during one of those pointless Cold War drop drills.

I said, "Must've been tough, waiting."

Her arms dropped and she looked at me. A ribbon of fear curled across her face, rippling sections of ashy skin. "I was scared, sir. Waiting for more."

"More gunshots."

"A lot of times there's more. Right?"

"Right," said Milo. "Then what happened, Bean?"

"Nothing happened, sir," said Sarser. "So I looked." Spreading the air with her hands, she created a two-inch space centered on her face.

I said, "Through the blinds."

"The what?"

"The window covering."

"Oh," she said. "I thought you were saying I'm being blind. For not seeing more."

I aped the spreading motion.

"Yes, sir. I did that a little and peeked."

"And saw . . ."

"A guy."

First time that had come up.

Milo looked at me, then Petra. No one spoke.

Sarabeth Sarser said, "That's it. Can I have pie?"

"A guy," said Milo.

"And a girl." Breezily, as if one went inevitably with the other.

"From room fourteen."

"Yeah."

"What'd they do, Sara?"

"Booked."

"They ran off together?"

A beat. "He musta pushed her, she like . . . tripped a little? But she didn't fall."

"Then what?"

"He put her into the back of the Rover and booked."

All new material.

Petra said, "Did she put up a fight?"

"Uh-uh, no. But like I said, she kind of . . . fell when she walked. But not down. Just like she was . . '. I dunno."

I said, "She stumbled."

"Yeah!"

Petra said, "Okay, this is the important part, Sara. What did these two people look like?"

"Don't know, ma'am. It was dark, I was scared shitless."

"Tall? Short?"

Head shake. "I didn't see nothing but shapes and they were moving fast."

"Black, white, Spanish?"

Head shake. "If they were purple I couldn't tell you, ma'am, I swear." To me: "Guess I *was* kind of blind."

Petra said, "Age?"

"Couldn't *see.*"

Milo said, "No idea at all about age or race?"

"Sorry, sir."

"What about clothing?"

"Sorry, sir, I wasn't P.R.'ing."

"P.R.'ing?"

"*Project-Runway*-ing," she said. "Like when you study the creations?" Frown. "I streamed a bunch of episodes then my iPad got ripped off."

Petra said, "Bean, in your first call to the station, you didn't mention any of this. And you didn't tell me when I talked to you a few hours ago."

"I was scared."

"But now you're telling us."

"I figured I should."

"Saving up for a rainy day," said Milo.

"It's not raining," said Sarser. "Not all year, I like that."

"Like what?"

"When there's no rain." Another giggle. "Less clothing, sir."

"See your point," said Milo. "So you were saving up the information for when you could use it."

"That's what I do, sir. I listen to Gram."

Petra said, "Let's go over it again."

Sarser pouted. "Really?"

"Really."

Puffing her cheeks while tearing lettuce into shreds, Sarser retold her story. Nothing new.

"After they drove away and didn't come back, I booked. Got rid of my panties, sir. Like I said, I was scared shitless."

She laughed. "Can I have *pecan* pie?"

We left her facing a mammoth slice of pecan pie, glazed nuts crystallized past optimal freshness, the wedge topped by a runny heap of vanilla ice cream. The enhancement, Milo's burst of generosity.

À la mode, Bean?

Told you, sir. I don't speak Spanish.

Pie with some ice cream?

That would be cool, sir.

Literally.

Huh?

35

O ut on the sidewalk, Petra said, "Sorry for bringing you out for that. She kept hinting around she had more but obviously she just played me to get her solicitation ticket wiped off."

Inside the coffee shop, a man walked up to Sarser. Ten years her senior, dark-complexioned, lazy eyelids, lizard face. He wore a black leather jacket, a flashy flowered shirt, diamond earrings in both lobes. Tattoos ran up his neck, flirting with his carotid.

"Look at this zombie-scum," said Petra. "How many priors would you say?"

Milo scratched his chin. "Twenty, minimum."

"I say thirty." She stared at the newcomer, squinting, tight-jawed. Hoping he'd notice her. He didn't. Kept talking into Sarser's left ear. Sarser's hands were flat on the table.

Petra said, "Pathetic. Next time I hear about her, she could be *my* client." She turned away. "Okay, guys, let's get some sleep. Wish it had made a difference."

Milo said, "Nothing to be sorry for, kid. We learned plenty."

"What?" she said.

"The woman with Chet wasn't the caller, making her likely collateral damage, maybe dumped along with the Range Rover, so let's keep our eyes out for the vehicle. Also nothing we just heard budges Bitt off the radar. The whole Bitt-and-Felice thing is nuts. Old boyfriend moves next door?"

Movement from inside the coffee shop caught our eyes. Iguana Man had looped one arm over Sarabeth Sarser's shoulder. Smiling slackly, ripe with entitlement.

His mouth got close enough to her left ear to insert his tongue. Maybe that's what he did. Maybe he just spoke. Either way, she squirmed.

His other arm moved, dangling over her meth-shrunk bosoms.

He began eating her pie.

Petra went in and said something to him. He bristled but slithered out of the booth and left the coffee shop. Making sure to avoid Milo and me.

Petra returned with her phone out, read a text and smiled. "Aww, Eric claims to miss me. I'm straight home, guys."

She walked away, alert, gracefully athletic. To outward appearances a good-looking woman far too stylish for this section of Hollyweird. One hand rested near the gun beneath her jacket. We watched her slender form melt into the darkness, then headed for our cars.

At the Seville, Milo said, "No more bullshit, tomorrow before Felice takes the kids to school, I'm calling her to see if she can convince Bitt to talk to me. She doesn't want to cooperate, I'll inform her there'll be police banging on his goddamn door day in day out, the press will find out, the entire Westside's gonna know she's been in a sneaky relationship with someone who draws obscene, violent cartoons."

"The kids will be impacted."

"Got something better?"

"Let me call and ask her."

"That would work because . . ."

"I began something this morning, maybe I can build on it."

"Building rapport through psychological sensitivity," he said.

"That would be the hope."

"Rather than the spontaneous invasion of the Visigoth-Mongol-Hun known as me."

I laughed. "Yes, Attila."

He ran his hand over his face. "Fine. You get one try. Also, thanks. From the depths of my insensitive heart."

CHAPTER

36

The following morning, Robin did her usual early rise, up at six, ready to work half an hour later. Usually, she's way ahead of me. This morning, I was with her for coffee, had walked the dog, showered, and dressed, was ready to call Felice Corvin at seven fifteen.

Before I got to my office phone, it rang. "Dr. Delaware, I've got a Ms. Corvin on the line."

I said, "How convenient."

"Pardon, Doctor?"

"Please put her on."

"Good morning, Felice."

"I know it's early but I wanted to catch you. I gave what you said a lot of thought, went over to Trevor and talked to him and he'll speak to you."

"The key is talking to the police."

"I meant 'you' as in plural. I'd prefer it was just you, but I'm realistic. But *could* you be there? To monitor?"

"I don't monitor, Felice."

"Whatever you do, then," she said.

"Sometimes I do nothing."

"Well, just the fact of your presence, then. Instead of a . . . I don't know, a regular police thing. Something . . . military."

I chose my words. "If I'm allowed to be there, I will be. But this is a double murder case and it will be a regular police thing."

Pause. "What I'm trying to get across is the issues are sensitive. They require a specialized approach."

Honest concern? An attempt to manipulate?

I said, "Of course. I'll pass that along to Lieutenant Sturgis."

"I guess that's all I can hope for," she said. "Would five p.m. today work out?"

"I'll let him know and someone will get back to you."

"Someone," she said. "By the book."

"I'm afraid oo."

"I guess I understand that, Doctor. People are dead."

People. Detached way to talk about a murdered spouse, even one you planned to divorce.

I phoned Milo.

He said, "Five today? Yeah, I can do that if Sean and Moe and a few others can."

"Strength in numbers," I said.

"Guy's a nut and he's been known to wave a firearm. She can say what she wants."

"She wants me there."

"For what, an encounter group? If once we're inside it goes smoothly, yeah, you can observe. Sounds like she's trying to run interference for him. Or interfere in order to control the situation."

"The thought occurred to me."

"Good. I'll call you if it firms up. Obviously, you're not gonna be Dr. Door-Buster."

"Anything else happening?"

"Not unless you count two false sightings of Chet's Range Rover and San Berdoo sheriffs not rushing over to the A-frame. I did get a call from Dave Brassing. He drove by last night, no Camaro or anything else."

"Let's hear it for the citizenry."

"Love-hate relationship," he said. "Nice when it's love."

The approach to Trevor Bitt's house began at four thirty, Milo's unmarked leading two black SUVs halfway up Evada Lane, the three vehicles parking in a row.

Early arrival because, "It's my timetable, not theirs."

To the uninitiated that might sound petty. On Planet Cop, anything you can control raises the odds you'll walk away breathing.

Sunny afternoon, nowhere to hide, but no obvious reaction to the convoy from any of the neighboring houses. Bart Tabatchnik's BMW wasn't in his driveway, the same for Edna San Felipe's Mercedes. The busybody factor diluted.

Milo removed two black tactical vests from his car trunk, strapped one on, gave the other to me and made sure I secured it properly. Soft armor but I felt like a turtle with a carapace. A vulnerable turtle, no way to retract head and limbs.

The same gear was worn by Sean Binchy, Moe Reed, and two burly sergeants Milo had enlisted as supplementary help. Tyrell Lincoln and Marlin Moroni had worked with him on a takedown last year. Someone had died, but not their faults. Both were veterans, attentive and unflappable. Both loved the overtime for the same reason: alimony.

We stood in back of the rear SUV and Milo began briefing. Pointing out Bitt's Tudor, the black truck parked in front. The adjoining driveway where Felice's Lexus had taken on dust.

Reed said, "She in her place or his?"

Milo said, "She's supposed to stay in hers per my chat with her this morning. The plan is I call her, she takes us over to Bitt, supposedly to smooth things out. But I don't trust either of them. He's her daughter's baby-daddy, lived next door for years without the husband knowing."

"Until maybe recently," said Binchy. "And then the husband dies."

"Exactly."

Moroni said, "Years, that's freakin' manipulative."

Lincoln said, "Lady can keep a secret that long, she'll never get a government job."

Chuckles all around. Undertone of tension.

Milo said, "Like I told you all before, Bitt's been known to flash a long gun and he's a possible 5150."

Citing the state regulation that enabled involuntary commitment. It's also LAPD radio code for a mentally ill suspect. "Unless Dr. Delaware sees different."

I said, "It pays to assume the worst."

"Mental with a gun," said Moroni, rolling massive shoulders.

Reed said, "A long gun and Braun's face was full of shot."

Milo said, "Once we know Bitt's under control, priority is to clear his house of weapons. I've got a limited search warrant for firearms and edged weapons, including power saws because Braun's hands were severed."

Reed said, "So we check any garage or work space."

Moroni said, "A 5150, the hands could be in a pickle jar."

"If the jar's in plain sight, we take that, too."

More laughter, masculine, growing edgier.

Tyrell Lincoln looked at me. "With craziness a factor, you're the SMART guy today, Doc?"

Not a compliment, a municipal anagram: System-Wide Mental Assessment Response Team.

Milo said, "Yeah, today we've got real smart instead of regular SMART."

He told them about Bitt's stonewalling for weeks, recounted the specifics of the cartoonist's gun-show with Maillot Bernard.

No more levity.

Marlin Moroni said, "He doesn't come to the door, we force entry?"

Milo said, "I wish we could but the warrant isn't a no-knock."

"Why not?"

"D.A. got involved."

Lincoln said, "The caution-cooties."

"He stonewalls," said Reed, "we all go home."

"Unfortunately."

Moroni said, "That's chickenshit. D.A. should be 5150'd."

"The thought occurred to me, Marlin. The issue is, this level of neighborhood, they're paranoid about something going real bad."

Reed said, "Murder suspect with a gun? You think?"

Milo said, "We deal with reality, guys. That's why I agreed to work with Felice Corvin, even though she twangs my antenna. She's doing the door-knock."

Moroni said, "Open up, honeybuns. Pu-leeeze."

Lincoln said, "Assuming we get in, incapacitate the psycho, then search."

Moroni said, "Discreetly, of course, Ty. This neighborhood, don't want to mess up the interior decorating." He glanced at the Tudor. "Cartooning can buy that?"

Milo said, "There's family money."

"Loony *and* rich? Just add water and you've got Entitlement Soup. I'm assuming Bitt gets cuffed."

"Soon as possible," said Milo.

"If we get the hell in."

"Think positive, Marlin. One concession I did get: If there's serious grounds to suspect something nasty, we can use the ram. I've got it in my car."

Lincoln said, "We've got ours, too. What constitutes nasty?"

"Suspect engages in obviously threatening behavior or a hostage situation."

Moroni said, "Or a nuclear bomb goes off."

Lincoln said, "Nope, a bomb, we need to clear it with the ACL-Yooo."

Milo said, "Assuming nothing happens God forbid, we're stuck with a frontal entry because access to the back of the property is blocked by a serious gate."

Lincoln said, "What about the rear neighbor?"

"High wall."

Moroni sighted Bitt's house again. "Okay if I take a look at the gate?"

Milo thought. "Make it quick."

Moroni sprinted up the block, tucked himself into the space where Chelsea Corvin smoked. Big, thick man in his late forties but he'd held on to some college football speed. He returned seconds later. "Someone boosts me, I'm over."

Lincoln held up a hand "You're not wearing golf cleats so I volunteer. Maybe I can do it just by throwing you."

"Big talk, Stiff Knees," said Moroni. "If there's a turn bolt on the inside, I might let you hobble in."

A blond woman in sky-blue yoga clothes emerged from a Greek Revival two houses up, arms folded across her chest, cellphone in one hand. As she lifted it, Milo said, "Sean, tell her to go inside and not call anyone. Tell her world peace depends on her."

Picking Binchy because he had the softest approach.

Binchy ran over and graced the woman with his Born Again smile. His vest and gun made the woman go stiff. He slouched and did his best to look un-cop. Same relaxed stance I'd seen in old photos of his ska-punk band: Fender bass held low over the groin as he provided bottom.

By the end of a brief chat, the woman was smiling and nodding and returning inside.

Binchy returned. "Nice lady, no prob."

Moroni said, "Hot little ass. You get her number? You don't want it, I'll take it."

Binchy blushed.

Reed said, "In terms of a bad outcome, what about Bitt's window views?"

Milo said, "Unfortunately, Moses, there's no way to totally avoid scrutiny. Once we're a property away, let's shift north, stay as close to structures as we can so the angle's restricted. When we get to Bitt's house, keep near the front. That way he'd need to angle any weapon over a sill and shoot straight down. And once we're in that entry alcove over the door, he can't get to us unless he blasts through the door with an AK."

Silence.

"I know it's not an optimal situation but it's what we have."

Moroni said, "We're doing daytime not nighttime because . . ."

"Too many variables after dark. At least this way we can see what's happening."

"Hmm . . . okay."

"Any other questions? Then, I'm calling her."

No answer at Felice Corvin's mobile or her landline.

Reed said, "So much for cooperation. Don't like the feel of this."

Milo said, "Plan B. We go anyway. Unless there are other suggestions."

Head shakes. No one cracking wise.

"One more thing," he said, fooling with the straps on his vest. "Try not to fall in the cactus."

Touching his weapon, he began walking, a general leading a mini-battalion of four armed men into the unknown.

One unarmed man standing back, feeling extraneous.

When we passed the yoga-blonde's house, a curtain ruffled. Other than that, quiet and still. Moroni and Lincoln positioned themselves at opposite corners of Bitt's house as Milo and Reed and Binchy crowded into the covered alcove, guns in hand.

I waited near the front porch of a Cape Cod Revival. Junk mail piled up near the door, no security consciousness.

Milo knocked on Bitt's door. It opened immediately. That threw him and he stepped back. Then, Glock in hand, he stepped in.

The young D's followed. Nothing for a moment, then Binchy came out and gave a thumbs up.

Lincoln and Moroni came forward from the flanks. Binchy said, "You, too, Doc."

On TV and in the movies, when the crisis fritters out, hot-dog cops express regret because they crave Rambo-action. Marlin Moroni's and Tyrell Lincoln's shoulders dropped as they sheathed their weapons. Both of their faces were slick with sweat and when I joined them the pulses in their thick, sturdy necks were still racing.

As I followed them in, Moroni said, "Amen, Jesus."

37

T revor Bitt sat on a tufted living room sofa, hands cuffed in front.

Milo stood over him, Reed behind. Binchy was off to the left, next to Felice Corvin. To the right stood Moroni and Lincoln.

Bitt appeared serene. Felice's face was tight with anger, arms rigid, hands rolled into fists.

The room was just beyond a vacant entry hall, a dim space with a vaulted ceiling crossed by beams of pseudo-antique timber.

Milo eye-cued the veteran cops and they headed for the stairs at the rear of the room.

Felice said, "Where are they going? Chelsea's up there."

Bitt said, "In the studio."

Milo said, "Where's that?"

"Right above here."

Milo said, "She's seventeen, guys. Be nice."

Moroni said, "Storm troopers are always nice."

He and Lincoln took the stairs two at a time. Seconds later, Moroni's voice from above: "Hi, there, my name is Marlin, no one's going to hurt you, we need to go downstairs so you can be with your mom . . . that's a good girl."

Chelsea, wearing a paint-specked artist's smock, appeared on the landing. In one hand was a sketch pad, in the other the kind of black artist's pencil Robin used. Moroni and Lincoln bracketed her descent. When she reached the bottom, she looked at Bitt. Saw the cuffs and stumbled and made a gagging noise.

"It's okay, honey," said her mother. "This will all be cleared up real soon." Looking to Milo for confirmation.

He said, "Everyone cooperates, that's the plan."

Chelsea screamed, "Daddy!" and went for Milo with the pencil.

He managed to feint away from her, right eye barely avoiding a sharpened point. Inertia pitched the girl forward. She landed on the floor, flat on her back, the pad and the pencil a few feet away.

Felice Corvin said, "Now look what you people have done."

Milo touched the outer rim of his eye socket. Moroni stood over Chelsea and extended a hand. Her head flipped side-to-side and she let out a manic "No!" Moroni edged closer to her but didn't push it.

All the other cops were looking at Milo.

He said, "Felice, you and Chelsea need to go over to your house."

Felice turned to Trevor.

"*Now*, Ms. Corvin. Or your daughter will be charged with attempted assault."

Felice said, "Why'd you come early? This could all have been prevented."

Milo said, "You could've answered your phone."

"I had it on vibrate, didn't hear."

Chelsea made a pathetic bird-like sound. A chick threatened by an owl. Bitt said, "Are you hurt, Tamara?"

The girl sniffled. Lunged for the pencil.

Marlin Moroni kicked it away, caught her by one wrist, captured the other and held her fast. She struggled for a moment, then went limp.

"Cuff her?" he said.

Felice Corvin said, "She's a child, don't be stupid!"

Milo, still massaging the rim of his eye socket, said, "Stupid is someone gets hurt. We're going to zip-tie her until we're sure she's calmed down. Anyone who doesn't cooperate will be restrained. Officer Lincoln, take them next door and stay with them."

Felice said, "Trevor—"

Bitt said, "I'm fine."

Chelsea said, "Daddy."

Bitt said, "Tamara, please listen to these guys."

A magical incantation: The girl broke into the kind of smile you see in dreaming infants. No resistance as Lincoln zip-tied her.

Felice said, "This is shameful." To me: "In your case, it's malpractice."

Moe Reed stepped in front of her. "Shameful would be your daughter blinding the lieutenant."

Felice gave a start. "That didn't . . . he's okay, right? Obviously."

Reed shot her a death-glare. Ditto from Moroni. Even Binchy was looking stern.

Chelsea said, "Let's go home, Mommy."

Lincoln propelled them out the door.

I turned to Bitt. "Why do you call her Tamara?"

"Tamara de Lempicka was a great artist."

"Building up her confidence."

The suggestion seemed to puzzle Bitt. "I want to encourage her."

Milo said, "Before we got here, what were you two doing?"

"Painting," said Bitt. "We've just gotten into acrylics."

He looked down at his tethered hands. Some of the nails were nearly covered by pigment. The rest of him was pallid. He was dressed much like the last time I'd seen him: green cashmere crewneck, brown polo, the same compulsively ironed khakis, brown deck shoes with white soles.

I said, "How's Chelsea taking to it?"

A beat. "She gets frustrated."

He sat lower, as if betrayed by a rubbery spine. The furniture all around us was dark, heavy, overstuffed. Castoffs inherited from a maiden aunt. The paintings on the wall were a whole different flavor. Abstractions, sparsely hung on white plaster walls pretending to be the hand-troweling of an English manor.

Nice stuff. I got up and checked the signatures. Judy Chicago, Billy Al Bengston, Larry Bell, Ed Ruscha. Members of the artistic brain trust who'd worked in L.A. during the sixties and seventies. Back when they were affordable, I couldn't afford.

Trevor Bitt had swiveled and watched as I inspected. When I returned, his eyes dropped back to his hands.

I said, "Before you moved here, did you live in L.A.?"

"Never."

"You just like L.A. artists."

Bitt smiled. "I've got a room of French fauvists in my bedroom, Hudson Valley landscape painters in the spare. Art's an easy way to see the world."

Milo's hand left his eye socket. He waved a piece of paper in front of Bitt. "This is a warrant to search for firearms and edged weapons on your premises. Would you like to read it?"

"No, thanks."

"If you tell us what you have at the outset, we can do it quicker."

"What I have isn't much," said Bitt.

Milo tapped a foot.

Bitt said, "Does edged include flatware and palette knives—that's a tool used to spread paint on a canvas."

"If it can hurt someone, it's included."

"I've got aluminum flatware, one butcher knife that's still sharp because I rarely use it, and three palette knives."

"Location."

"Kitchen, kitchen, studio."

"Firearms," said Milo.

"Arm singular," said Bitt. "A Holland and Holland rifle I inherited from my father. He shot grouse with it. Or quail, some kind of defenseless little bird. I never went along, it held no interest for me."

"But he left you the weapon."

"Maybe he figured I'd come around."

"Did you?"

"It's never been loaded."

"You're sure about that."

"I think I'd remember, Lieutenant."

"You've never brandished it in front of anyone?"

Bitt sat back and stared at his hands.

Milo repeated the question.

"That I have, Lieutenant. More than once."

"Under what circumstances?"

Bitt said, "Being an idiot. A long time ago."

"What's a long time?"

"Decades. I was a countercultural pretender and sometimes used it for dramatic effect. A prop. It's never been loaded."

"Why do that?"

Bitt raised his hands to form quotation marks, setting off jingles and rattles. "I wasn't a 'nice guy.' My art wasn't nice, either. I thought I was being clever and au courant but now it all seems stale."

I said, "Has your art changed?"

"To the extent that I make any," said Bitt.

"What do you paint, now?"

"Currently I'm tackling orchids and birds in the style of Martin Johnson Heade. He was an itinerant painter who sold door-to-door. I admire that flavor of enterprise."

Milo said, "Back in the day, you enjoyed scaring people with your rifle."

"When I was stoned or drunk or just being a jerk."

"We won't find any ammunition in your house."

"None."

"What about the garage?"

"There's nothing in the garage," said Bitt. "Literally."

Milo motioned to Reed, who headed for the rear of the house.

"Where's the rifle, Mr. Bitt?"

"In a burr-walnut case at the back of my bedroom closet."

"Anything else you want to tell us about before we search?"

"In the same closet, there's a samurai sword. Tourist junk. I re-ceived it as payment for an illustration back in . . . probably '67, '68? A concert poster, some band. When I tried to sell it I learned it was worthless."

Milo motioned to Moroni and Binchy. Up they went.

Trevor Bitt said, "I had nothing to do with the man who was killed at Felice's."

Braun had been killed elsewhere. Feigning ignorance or misdi-recting?

Milo said, "We're dealing with two dead men."

Bitt nodded. "Chet."

"What do you think of that?"

"People getting murdered? It's terrible."

"Maybe not for you," said Milo.

Bitt blinked. "I'm not following, Lieutenant."

"With Chet Corvin gone, you're free to be with Felice."

No emotion on the grayish face.

"Mr. Bitt?"

"I suppose I can understand you thinking that."

"It's not true?"

"There'd be no . . . Felice and I aren't involved romantically. Not since our relationship in San Francisco."

I said, "The one that led to Chelsea's conception."

For the first time Bitt's demeanor changed. Blinking half a dozen times, brow forming a V-crease as his lips folded inward. "Yes. But by the time I found out, we were over."

"When was that?"

"When Felice called me five years ago."

"And you decided to move next door."

"That took some pondering," said Bitt. "I moved the following year."

Milo said, "Living next to your ex-girlfriend-baby-mama and your secret daughter."

Bitt's shoulders rose and fell. "It came at a time when I was ready to make a change. I'd considered Venice. Italy, not California. My aunt owns a deteriorating villa on the Grand Canal."

"Felice's call changed your mind."

"After some deliberation."

I said, "Ready for fatherhood."

"I didn't aim that high," said Bitt. "I was hoping for some sort of relationship."

"Chelsea calls you 'Daddy.'"

"For the past two days."

"Before that?"

"She called me Trevor. I tried to be her friend. To inspire her art."

"But you hoped for more."

Bitt blinked. Footsteps from above vibrated the ceiling.

I said, "How quickly did the relationship develop?"

"Not quickly at all," said Bitt. "At first, I did nothing. Then I asked Felice if I might do something. She said absolutely not. She wasn't happy I was here, had done her best to ignore me and I kept to myself. Last year, she came over, said she'd changed her mind and I could do art with Chelsea if Chelsea agreed and I swore to be discreet."

"Just like that."

"Just like that, Doctor."

"Impulsive," I said. "Like calling to tell you about Chelsea."

"She can be that way. It's part of why I was attracted to her back in San Francisco. I have difficulty being spontaneous."

"Being discreet meant the man Chelsea thought was her father never knew."

"He and everyone else, including Chelsea," said Bitt.

"Any idea what changed Felice's mind?"

Bitt's fingers moved as if typing on an unseen keyboard. "She told me she told you. Her marriage had slid downhill."

"Why?"

"You'd have to ask Felice."

"She never explained."

"Just that," said Bitt. "I don't like talking about that kind of thing."

"Emotions."

"Negatives."

"Such as?"

Bitt sighed. "Infidelity."

"Felice learned Chet had been unfaithful."

"She'd discovered some credit card bills. I told her I didn't want to know so that's where it ended."

Milo said, "A little chat."

"That's it."

"Just talk?"

Bitt looked amused. "If you're asking about sex, I don't do sex anymore." He patted his chest. The cuffs clinked.

"Vow of chastity?"

"Heart problems. In more ways than one."

"Meaning?"

"I've never been an emotional man, have been called emotionally flat. Over the years, I've flattened out further."

Milo said, "You are a *stubborn* man. I've been trying to speak with you for weeks. Why'd you stonewall me?"

"I had nothing to tell you."

"That's your answer."

"All right," said Bitt. "I do tend to one emotion." To me: "Someone in your profession called it free-floating anxiety. Treatment would involve drugs so I've passed."

Milo said, "You don't do drugs."

"Not anymore, Lieutenant. The result is an undercurrent of dread. I live with it and it propels me inward."

"Doing the hermit thing."

"In San Francisco I used to get out and do social things for business. I never enjoyed them."

Another look at me: "It's not agoraphobia, any kind of phobia. I don't have panic attacks and when I need to leave the house, I can. I just don't prefer it, so I limit my excursions."

I said, "To what?"

"Shopping when I can't get something delivered. Brief walks to avoid blood clots per my doctor. Doctor visits. That's where I was the night Chet died."

Passive word choice.

I said, "Nighttime doctor visit?"

"Hospital visit," said Bitt. "St. John's, for tests. They put a belt on me that monitored my heartbeat. It needed to be done at night so they could observe my sleeping patterns to make sure my system doesn't go haywire when I'm unaware."

"You've had symptoms."

"I'd been waking up short of breath. I called my cardiologist, he scheduled the test."

Milo took out his pad. "Name?"

"Dr. Gerald Weinblatt," said Bitt. "Sometimes I see his partner, Dr. Prit Acharya. Neither of them was there, the procedure was done by a technician. An African American gentleman, I don't know his name."

I said, "When did you learn about Chet Corvin's murder?"

"Felice came over the following day and told me what had happened."

"What was her demeanor?"

"Her demeanor? She was upset. Used up half a box of Kleenex."

Sean Binchy came downstairs, gloved hands holding a bronze-fitted wooden case and a cheap-looking gray cardboard box fastened by an oversized rubber band. Placing both on the floor, he undid the latches on the case and lifted the lid carefully.

The rifle lay in fitted green velvet. Same beautifully figured walnut as the case, with tarnished, hand-engraved metal tooling.

"Hand-etched, Loot, looks like thirties or forties."

Bitt said, "Probably thirties or even the twenties. Father received it as a boy."

Milo said, "Mr. Bitt says he's never fired it."

Binchy lifted the weapon, sniffed the end of the barrel. Sneezed. Coughed and sneezed three more times. "It's full of dust and stuff, Loot." To Bitt: "This is a valuable rifle, sir. You don't believe in taking care of it?"

Bitt shook his head.

Binchy undid the rubber band. No velvet interior for this receptacle, just more cardboard. Inside was a dull-looking blade, pitted and corroded along the cutting edge, the handle wrapped in white twine that had browned unevenly.

Binchy said, "Looks like pot metal." He peered at the corrosion. "Don't see blood, but . . ."

Bitt said, "There is none."

Milo said, "Test it—take it to the lab, now."

Binchy left with both weapons.

Trevor Bitt said, "When you're finished testing the sword, throw it out. I forgot I had it, only held on to it to remind myself not to be so trusting."

Milo said, "You're generally a trusting guy."

"When I took hallucinogens, I was. Except for when I overdid and became paranoid."

"Paranoid and brandishing a rifle," said Milo.

"It's nothing I'm proud of, Lieutenant."

"No more illicit chemistry for you. Not even for your free-floating anxiety?"

"For that I use solitude."

"Stonewalling the cops was therapeutic."

"I wouldn't expect you to understand. I regret inconveniencing you."

Milo touched the spot Chelsea's pencil had missed. His eyes got tight and he rhino-jawed.

Sense memory leading to anger.

Bitt said, "I knew I couldn't help you."

Milo said, "Where were you the night the body was dumped in the Corvins' house?"

"Dumped?" said Bitt. "What do you mean?"

"Not a complicated word, Mr. Bitt."

"Someone put him there?"

"You didn't know that."

"I knew what Felice told me."

"Which was?"

"They came home and found a dead man in Chet's den. I assumed he'd been killed there."

"What else did she tell you?"

"That's it. As I said, we don't talk much."

"No relationship."

"Only as it concerns Chelsea," said Bitt. "Felice lets me spend time with Chelsea as long as she sees it being helpful to Chelsea."

I said, "You're on probation."

He looked at me. Blank face, frozen eyes. "I guess you could say that, Doctor."

Milo said, "Why'd you and Felice break up?"

"She initiated. My guess would be I was dislikable, she'd had enough."

"You didn't talk about that, either."

Head shake. "She stopped taking my calls. I didn't call for very long."

I said, "How'd you react when she told you about Chelsea?"

"Surprise," said Bitt. "And, I admit, some anxiety. I spent a long time fretting. What did it mean? Eventually, I began wondering if something positive might develop."

"Did you worry about Felice making demands?"

Bitt said, "She assured me she wasn't interested in money. Then she said she'd been wrong to draw me in, I should forget about it."

"You didn't."

Bitt's lips worked. What began as a frown ended as a smile. "As you've seen, I'm not always cooperative."

Moe Reed returned. "Nothing in the garage, L.T." A glance at Bitt. "Like he said, literally. No car, no tools, just dust. There is a toolbox under the kitchen sink, couple of Phillips, one wrench, a measuring tape. In terms of blades, he's got flatware for two, looks pretty flimsy, and one Henckels knife with no visible blood but I'll bag it."

"There won't be blood, I'm a vegetarian," said Bitt.

Milo said, "Do it. I told Sean to drive to the lab. If he's close enough, have him come back and add the knife."

"There's no blood," Bitt repeated. "I promise."

38

Moments after Reed's exit, Marlin Moroni came thundering down the stairs. "Can I talk in front of him?"

"Go," said Milo.

"Did a second sweep, zip." To Bitt: "That picture on the easel, you did it?"

"Work in progress."

"You're pretty good."

"I try."

Milo said, "Marlin, go next door and see how Tyrell's doing."

I said, "Just thought of something—the son, Brett, may also be there."

Moroni said, "Check it out," and made his exit.

Trevor Bitt said, "I imagine the boy's having a tough time."

Milo said, "Why's that?"

"Chet was his father."

"How'd Brett relate to you?"

"If we passed on the street, he'd sometimes make a face at me. I assumed Chet had told him things about me. Or maybe he's just that kind of kid."

I said, "You were seen having a confrontation with Chet Corvin."

"I was?" said Bitt.

"Up the block, shortly after the body dump."

Bitt squinted. "Oh, that. Someone saw it?"

"What happened?"

"It was nothing."

Milo said, "Tell us anyway."

"I'd bought Chelsea some chocolate candy. The second time, the first was for her birthday, Christmas. I told her to keep the box hidden for obvious reasons. She was careful the first time but forgot the second time and left it on her desk. Chet browbeat her and she told him I'd bought it. I was taking a walk and he came after me."

"Because . . ."

"He'd gotten the wrong impression."

"Meaning?"

"I need to spell it out?"

Milo said, "You do."

"He implied something inappropriate was going on. I assured him that wasn't so, I was merely helping Chelsea with her art, the chocolate was a reward for her applying herself. He told me that sounded like bullshit, she had no talent. I assured him it wasn't. He threatened me. If anything ever did happen, I'd be sorry. At that point, I said nothing. I thought he was going to hit me, my heart was taching—beating far too rapidly. Fortunately, he left and I tried to walk it off. We never spoke again and Felice told me my contact with Chelsea would be reduced to when Chet was out of town for more than a day or two. She said Chelsea cried."

Milo said, "Why'd you pick chocolate as a gift?"

"Because I like it," said Bitt. "This brand is especially high-quality, I got it at a boutique in West Hollywood. One of the things that got me out of the house. She finished every piece of the first box. That's why I got her a second box."

I said, "How often did your contact with Chelsea take place late at night?"

Bitt sighed. "That. We thought she understood but she began sneaking out, even when Chet was home. Sometimes she'd kick the side of my house, sometimes she'd just stand around."

I said, "How'd you respond when she kicked?"

"I tried to do nothing, Doctor. Sometimes I'd hear her crying softly and if that wasn't bad enough, I'd be worrying Chet would find her and everything would go to hell. Luckily that never happened but I was careful to avoid any sort of face-to-face with her when Chet was in town. To the point of not leaving in the morning until after Felice had taken the kids to school."

"You never let her in?"

"I did," said Bitt. "A few times. She wanted to do art but I said we didn't have time. So we'd sit and drink tea and then she'd return home."

Milo said, "I'm going to call that cardiologist right now. If you've lied to me, sir, now's the time to admit it."

"I haven't. Speak to the technician. Twenties, African American, strong features, especially the cheekbones. He'd be an excellent portraiture subject."

Milo took out his phone and called Moroni back.

"Everything okay?"

"Girl's still zip-tied but she's quiet, mother's cleaning up the kitchen, boy's upstairs, when I looked at him, he flipped me off."

"Kids," said Milo.

"Mine did that, you know what would happen."

Bitt hadn't followed the conversation. Eyes shut, he rested his neck on the top roll of the sofa. Within moments, his mandible had dropped and he was snoring openmouthed.

Moroni and Milo looked at each other, then me. Interrogation 101: The guilty ones were more likely to doze.

Milo pulled out his phone and walked to another room. He came back looking as if he'd drunk a punch bowl of spit. Stepping up to Bitt, he stomped his foot hard. Bitt roused. His eyes worked to focus.

"Your lucky day, Mr. Bitt, courtesy cardiac tech Antonio Jenkins."

He undid Bitt's cuffs. Bitt said, "We're finished?"

"Not quite," said Milo. "You're covered for the night of Chet Corvin's murder but that doesn't mean you weren't involved in it."

"I don't understand."

"You're a man of means, Mr. Bitt."

Bitt squinted. "You're saying I paid someone to kill Chet?"

"Did you?"

"Of course not. Why would I do that?"

"He scared you, he was mean to Chelsea, you wanted to help Felice be free of him."

"That's not how I deal with things," said Bitt.

"What's your thing?"

"Retreat," said Trevor Bitt. His fingers fluttered on his lap. "I am, at heart, a coward."

I said, "Dogs sometimes bite out of fear."

"I've never harmed anyone or anything physically in my life. That's why I refused to hunt with my father. That's why I got pounded on in prep school."

Milo said, "A vegetarian." Leaving his favorite carnivore wisecrack unspoken: *So was Hitler.* "Let's talk about the body left next door. Where were you that night?"

"Here."

"Doing what?"

"Drawing."

"New cartoon?"

"I don't cartoon anymore," said Bitt. "A sketch for a painting. A pair of parrots—follow-up to the berylline hummingbirds I'm work-ing on. What that other officer saw on the easel."

"Love to see it myself."

Bitt looked puzzled. "That will verify my whereabouts?"

"Nah, but I'm into art appreciation."

Bitt climbed unsteadily, gripping the banister, stopping every few steps to catch his breath. When we reached the landing, his chest heaved. If this wasn't theater, he was in no shape to transport a body and drag it across a house.

Milo said, "You okay, sir?"

"I'm fine." Bitt leaned on the banister. "The night of the first mur-der, I saw something. I thought it was unimportant. It probably is. A truck drove past my studio window."

He pointed to an open door. An easel faced the front of the house, soaking in friendly southern light.

Milo said, "What time?"

"Before the hubbub—maybe an hour before? Can't say for sure. The engine sound is what caught my attention. I was painting, looked outside and saw it. At first I thought I'd been robbed."

Milo said, "Robbed of what?"

"My truck, Lieutenant. It resembled mine."

"Dodge Ram."

"I'm not saying it was the same make, just a general resemblance. About the same size and a dark color, possibly black, like mine. I went downstairs, saw that my truck was still there, and forgot about it."

Milo looked at me. Both of us remembering Binchy's witness spotting a pickup leaving the neighborhood.

He said, "A murder next door but you figured it wasn't impor-tant."

"Would another apology do any good?" said Bitt, sounding dispirited.

"What time did this take place?"

"Don't wear a watch," said Bitt. "Don't pay attention to time. All I *can* tell you is well before the Corvins returned. I heard their engine, too, that SUV he drives rumbles. I saw them get out and go inside the house and went back to work. A while later, the light in my studio changed, the window was striped with color. Those bars atop your police cars are extremely color-saturated. Then those other lights on poles. People talking."

"You weren't curious enough to come out and check?"

"When I saw Chelsea leave the house—the others, as well—I assumed it was a burglary. The next day, Felice told me what had happened."

Milo said, "Does Chelsea have a pal who drives a dark truck the same size as yours?"

Bitt's head swung toward him. "You can't be serious."

"We consider everything."

"Chelsea's gentle."

Milo touched the side of his eye. Bitt winced.

"I don't know anything about Chelsea's friends. She's never talked about having any. But she had nothing to do with anything."

"You know that because . . ."

"I know my daughter."

"Would you be willing to release your financial records for inspection?"

The topic shift threw Bitt. Classic detective trick. When he stopped blinking he said, "What kind of inspection?"

"Unusual cash withdrawals."

"For what—really, Lieutenant?" said Bitt. "As if I'd know how to hire some kind of assassin?"

"A look at your records could clear up the issue."

"Be my guest, Lieutenant, but there are no records here, everything's handled by a trustee."

"Who's that?"

"A management firm in Palo Alto. Swarzsteen Associates, they've worked with us for generations. The executive for my account is Don Swarzsteen."

Milo said, "Spell that, please."

Bitt recited slowly.

"So how does it work?"

"I suppose I'll need a release. Get me a form and I'll sign it."

Milo said, "I meant how do you get your bills paid?"

"Swarzsteen pays them—credit card bills, utilities, taxes. For odds and ends, they send me a monthly allowance."

"How much?"

"Two thousand a month."

"Tight budget," said Milo.

"Enough for me," said Bitt. "At the end of the year, I send some of it back and Don reinvests it. That I *can* show you."

We followed Bitt as he opened the door to a bedroom set up with a Chinese wedding bed, a Victorian dresser, three paintings on the three walls, and little else. He rifled in a drawer and handed Milo a computer printout.

Year-end summary below the letterhead of the investment company, most of the activity co-managed by the Palo Alto office of Chase Private Client. Current balance in an "extraneous expenses account," $12,356.13, monthly deposits of $2,000.00 on the third of each month, slightly over half making a return trip.

Bitt said, "My needs are simple. I use it for food and art supplies."

I said, "Speaking of art," and headed for the studio.

Not one easel, a pair, the second positioned against a windowless section of the western wall, invisible from the doorway. The one facing the street propped a painting of two luminous, beautifully rendered emerald-breasted birds hovering in midair. The other displayed a canvas the same size filled with muddy blotches.

Bitt pulled a sketch pad out of a flat file and showed us a pencil sketch of two macaws. "What I was working on, that night."

I said, "Why don't you cartoon anymore?"

Bitt said, "I came to see it for what it was. Mean-spirited, seize on deformity and magnify. I had enough." He pointed to Chelsea's painting. "Interesting, no? Bringing order to chaos. To me, this paler section up here represents dawning clarity."

That sounded like art-speak b.s. I saw blotches.

Love knows no bounds.

Bitt took our silence as debate.

"It's conceptual," he insisted. "She's the only thing *I've* ever really conceived."

CHAPTER

39

We left Bitt in his studio and convened on the sidewalk. Afternoon was conceding to evening, trees zebra-striping sidewalks, a mustard glow limning rooftops.

Milo said, "Please tell me you don't agree."

"About what?"

"Bitt's clean."

I said, "Cardiac tech verified his alibi?"

"Belted and hooked up for eight hours, never left the sleep lab."

The door to Bitt's house opened and the artist stuck his head out. "I just got off the phone with Don Swarzsteen. No form necessary, call him at your convenience."

Milo said, "My new pal. Dammit."

"Your level of charm, you're surprised?"

Another door opened a few houses down. Another head, peering out briefly then withdrawing. Suburban whack-a-mole.

A brief phone chat with Donald Swarzsteen III left Milo shaking his head as he pocketed his cell. "Guy has that 'tude you get from people who live off the rich."

I said, "Thinks he's more than a babysitter."

"You must be a psychologist. Yeah, he's a stick-up-the-ass snoot. He also backs up Bitt's claim that there's no other money."

We entered the Corvin house. Marlin Moroni stood watch on the upstairs landing. He came down, looking bored.

"Girl's in her bedroom doing whack drawings. I figured it was okay, she gets ideas about her fucking pencil, I can handle it."

I said, "Whack as in?"

"Hope you don't want me to get medical, Doc. Whack as in tiny little squares over and over. But what do I know about art? She's also got headphones on. Attached to a—get this—CD player, Country Joe and the Fish, my older brother was into all that flower-power crap."

I said, "San Francisco, her father's era."

Moroni said, "You cleared him?"

"Disgustingly alibied," said Milo. "What about the boy and Mrs. C?"

"He's in his room, playing videogames, she's at the kitchen table pretending nothing happened. I got a look at her screen, something about curriculum."

"She works for the school district."

"Figures, she's got that mean-teacher vibe. Anything else you need?"

Milo said, "Nah, you can go. Thanks, Marlin."

"Thank *you* for the overtime," said Moroni. He checked a rubber-strapped diver's watch. "Shift's not officially over but I'm assuming we're not going to get all fractional."

Milo said, "I'll put it in as a full, enjoy life."

Moroni rolled his shoulders and put on mirrored shades. "This one chalks up as a good day. Had nothing to do in the first place and I'm walking away healthy."

Felice Corvin sat typing at the kitchen table. She saw us but kept working.

Milo said, "Let's talk about Chelsea."

Felice's fingers rested on the keys. Her eyes faced her screen. "Hasn't there been enough stress for one day?"

"Not as much as there could've been, ma'am, as in I don't need a white cane."

"That was unfortunate."

"Fortunate for me, ma'am."

"Of course. I'm *sorry. Chelsea's* sorry."

"She can atone by cooperating."

"She has nothing to offer, Lieutenant."

"I won't know that until I talk to her."

"I'm her mother, trust me."

Milo said nothing.

Felice shut her laptop. "She's a minor."

"She comes of age in a few days."

"Rules are rules." That sounded like something she was used to saying.

"I have no problem with rules," said Milo. "The penal code's got one about attempted assault on a police officer."

"Oh, please! She didn't even touch you."

"Not for lack of trying, Ms. Corvin. She can be arrested right now, for a serious felony. I'm assuming you'd rather I talk to her."

"This is extortion."

"No, ma'am. Extortion is a crime and I'm not a criminal. I'm laying out contingencies."

She didn't answer.

He said, "Have it your way." Reaching around under his jacket, he produced his cuffs.

Felice shot to her feet. "Please!"

Milo looked her in the eye. She made a fist but uncurled it quickly.

"You're wasting your time, but fine, let's go talk to her. You'll see she has nothing to say."

"Sorry, no."

She squinted. "No, what?"

"I talk to her, you stay here."

"You're not allowed, she's a minor."

"I'm allowed if you say so." His fingertip began a slow climb toward his eye.

"Stop that, I get the point."

Milo smiled. "Interesting choice of words."

Felice Corvin gritted her teeth. "You're being vindictive."

"I'm working two murder investigations."

"That Chelsea knows nothing about."

"I hope you're right."

She crossed her arms. "I don't see why I can't be with her."

"I want to talk to her when she's not being influenced."

"That's absolutely moronic."

"You're entitled to your opinion, ma'am. If you prefer, Chelsea can be taken in, booked, and put in a holding cell. You'll hire an expensive lawyer who'll get her bail and block access to her. But the process will continue and that means indictment and either a deal or trial."

"This is . . . Orwellian—how can you go along with this, Dr. Delaware? A so-called healthcare professional."

I said, "No one's out to harm Chelsea. We realize raising her has been a challenge."

"Oh, you have no idea."

"Now that she knows who her father is, new challenges will come up. The quicker she can be eliminated from the investigation, the better."

Her chest rose and fell. "You'll guarantee her emotional well-being?"

"No one can guarantee anything. I can assure you that she'll be treated with sensitivity."

"Then why can't I be there?"

"Because it's important that Chelsea be treated as an individual."

"Oh, sure, it's for her own *good.*"

"It might be," I said. "When's the last time she was taken seriously?"

Her cheeks reddened. "You have no right to say that, she's always—fine, do whatever useless thing you think you need to do. But I'm holding you responsible. Both of you. I'm also going with you to the stairs and staying there. If I hear anything the least bit inappropriate, I'm going to step in."

Milo said, "Fine with me."

He beckoned her toward the doorway with an arm flourish. She sat there. Waved dismissively. "Oh, forget it, I'll stay here, the onus is on you."

As we crossed the dining room, Milo whispered, "You disapprove of my methods?"

I said, "She did try to blind you."

He grinned. "Friend in need."

40

When we reached the stairs, he said, "How about you take this?"

"What do you want me to concentrate on?"

"Friends, social life, the Camaro, her love life—hell, anything she wants to say. Not that I'm hoping for much."

"I'm the court of last resort, huh?"

"That's why you get the big bucks."

Chelsea Corvin hunched at her desk, headphones mussing her hair. She'd filled a quarter of the sheet with precise rows of raisin-sized ovals. A tongue-tip protruded between her lips.

Milo stood back. I stepped in front of the girl, ensuring I was visible.

She shifted her grip on the pencil, holding it in a curled fist, like a toddler. I stood there. Her line broke and she switched back to an adult grip and kept working. Like mother . . .

Keeping my eye on the graphite point, I removed the headphones. No reaction. "Hi, Chelsea. I'd like to talk to you."

She shifted her hand, embarked on a new row of ovals. Stub-nailed, grubby fingers tightened around the pencil.

"Chelsea—"

"About what?"

"First of all, I want to let you know Trevor's fine."

"Dad."

"Dad's fine."

The pencil point hovered above the desk.

I pulled up a chair beside her. "Finding out he's your dad is a big change."

"Uh-uh."

"It isn't a big change?"

"No." She finished the row.

"Chelsea, is there anything you can tell us about the man left in your house?"

"The dead guy," she said. "Uh-uh."

"What about what happened to—what should I call Chet?"

Silence. New row.

"Should we call him Chet, Mr. Corvin—"

A smirk stretched her lips. "Used-to-Be-Dad."

"Used-to-Be-Dad it is."

She gave a start. Muttered under her breath.

I said, "Pardon?"

She half turned. Hot black eyes; cigarette holes on paper. "He never liked me."

"Never?"

"He liked Brett."

"Any idea who killed him?"

"Someone he got mad."

"Like who?"

She looked at me again. "Someone he got mad. That's probably why the dead guy was in *his* room."

"You think Used-to-Be-Dad was targeted."

"He got them mad."

"Them," I said.

"Anyone." Shrug. "What-ever."

"No idea who that might be?"

"He's not my *dad*," she said.

"I know. So who might've targeted him?"

"He's not my *dad*." Whining. "How can *I* know?"

Irritation, then indifference. But no tension, no tells. I waited out two more rows.

"Chelsea, do you know anyone who drives a Camaro?"

"Nup."

"A black Camaro?"

"Nup."

"None of your friends drives a black Camaro."

"I don't got friends." Matter-of-fact, no visible regret.

Milo's phone beeped a text. She looked back at him, said, "Sorry. For before."

"No prob, kid." He read the message and frowned.

I said, "No one you know drives a Camaro."

"Nuh."

"Dad drives a pickup."

"Uh-uh, a Range Rover."

"I meant Trevor."

She turned scarlet. Her hand faltered. "Yeah."

I said, "Do you know anyone who drives a truck like Dad's?"

"Him." Hooking a thumb to the left.

"Him?"

"Him," she said.

"Who's that, Chelsea?"

Another leftward jab.

"I don't get it, Chelsea."

"Him. In that house."

I said, "Mr. Weyland drives a truck like that? I saw him in a Taurus."

"He got a car and a truck."

"Mr. and Mrs. Weyland."

"Yeah."

"What color is it?"

"Gray."

"Dark or light?"

"Dark." Another row completed, she smoothed the paper with her hands. Judged herself and scowled.

"Anything else you want to tell me, Chelsea?"

Two deep breaths before she put her pencil down. She twisted clumsily in her chair and faced Milo. "Sorry. Really."

He said, "Forget it, kiddo, no big deal."

She mouthed, *Kiddo*. Smiled. Turned grave. "Sorry. *Really really.*"

"It's *really* no prob, Chelsea. Just be careful in the future."

"You won't put me in jail?"

"Not a chance."

"Mom said . . ." The girl shuddered.

"Mom told you I was gonna put you in jail?"

"If I don't shape up soon, I'm in for trouble." Tears pooled in her eyes. "I don't *do* that."

"Do what?"

"Hurt people."

Like father . . .

Her hands fluttered. Opening a desk drawer, she took out a sheet and held it out to him. Rows of diamonds.

"For you."

"Original art? Thanks, kiddo. Though I'm really not supposed to take gifts on the job."

"Uh . . . Mom could mail it to you?"

Milo said, "No need, Chelsea, this'll be fine."

She hung her head, placed her palms on her cheeks. Some of the flush had faded, leaving her skin with the mottle of raspberry swirl ice cream.

I said, "We're going to leave now. If you think of anything you want to tell us, Lieutenant Sturgis will give you his card."

Three immediate, staccato nods. Mechanical movements, as if an unseen puppeteer was manipulating her head.

Milo handed her the card. She studied it. "Rectangle. I'm gonna draw rectangles."

Milo looked relieved to step outside. The sun was gone, mustard rooftops deepened to smoky brown. Backyard chatter updrafted from somewhere. Someone was grilling meat.

I said, "Who texted you?"

"Sean took it upon himself to recheck Chelsea's social media. Still nothing."

I said, "With a secret boyfriend, she'd have reason to avoid social media. But when I brought up the Camaro she didn't blink and this isn't a glib girl."

Reaching into his pocket, he unfolded the page of diamonds. "Why does she do this?"

"No idea."

"Take a guess."

"Maybe striving for order? Or it's all she *can* do."

He took another look before refolding the paper and slipping it back into his pocket. "I've seen worse in galleries."

I said, "Put it in your investment portfolio, one day she might be famous."

"A truck," he said. "One of the Weylands, there goes another lead."

"Has to be Donna. When we were with Paul, the Taurus was in the driveway."

"Makes sense, they're splitsville. She packed her stuff in the bed and left."

"He told us she was visiting her mother, I can see him not wanting to get into his marital problems. But at the time, I got a clear sense she'd been away for a while, not a few hours."

He rubbed his face. "Where are you going with this?"

"Probably nowhere," I said. "But it might not hurt to take a closer look at the neighbors on the other side."

"What, Donna didn't take the truck, Paul did? Then he stashed it somewhere, swapped for the Taurus, and got back in time to play benevolent neighbor? Why?"

"Like I said, it's likely nothing. On the other hand, a pickup would be great for transporting a body, the return trip perfect for ditching a shotgun and a bloody tarp. If you knew the cops would be at your house, you'd want to be careful."

He rubbed his face. "Weyland's a homicidal maniac? You're giving me mental whiplash, amigo."

"We've been focusing on Bitt because everyone pointed us in his direction. Including Weyland."

"That's because everyone knows Bitt's weird."

"Sure. But step away from that and the same factors making Bitt a suspect could be applied to Weyland. He could know the Corvins didn't set their alarm, he'd be familiar with the layout of the Corvin house. In fact, he'd have an easier time than Bitt transporting a body to the Corvins because *his* property abuts their garden gate."

Both of us turned toward the pseudo-hacienda. Empty driveway, lights off.

Milo said, "Paul the mild-mannered blood-fiend?"

"Like I said, probably—"

"Nothing, yeah, yeah. What would be Weyland's motive and how does Braun figure in?"

"I've got no explanation for Braun," I said. "But the motive could be classic: jealousy. What if Donna left Paul because she was one of Chet Corvin's on-the-sides? On top of that, Chet was derisive toward Weyland. Even when Weyland had taken his, he lorded his finances over the guy—you rent, I own. Sexual jealousy plus long-simmering resentment? We could be talking a combustible mixture."

"Chet and Donna," he said. "If she's screwing Chet, you're right, she's only one of his honeys. That picture we found isn't the brunette he bought the necklace for and shacked up with in the Arrowhead love nest. Which *still* hasn't been processed by San Berdoo, some twit named Livingston seems to enjoy shining me on."

I said, "Hair color's easy to change and pounds can be taken off. Interviewing Donna could clear it up but in all this time we've never laid eyes on her. What if she was scared of Paul and was hiding out at the Arrowhead house, moving to hotels with Chet for security? Maybe the two of them decided to make the break and run off together, beginning with a bon-voyage at the Sahara kicked up with wine, lingerie, and dirty movies? What if Weyland stalked Donna to the motel, got in with a ruse, executed Chet, and abducted her at gunpoint."

"In Chet's Rover? Weyland's already got two vehicles that he supposedly shuffles like cards. Why add a third?"

"If he used his own wheels and someone copied the plates, he'd be toast. There could also be symbolic value to using the Rover: *I'm retrieving what's mine and taking your fancy wheels.*"

"So where's the Rover now?"

"If he stashed the truck or the Taurus a few minutes away, he could've driven over and swapped it. My guess would be a dark side street, so he could transfer his captive without being spotted. If he left the Rover unlocked with the keys in the ignition, how long would it last in East Hollywood?"

"On its way to El Salvador." Jamming his hands in his pockets, he walked away from me, paced thirty steps, walked past me and did another twenty.

He returned and looked up and down the block. "Oh, man, the way your gray cells pop."

I said, "Chet and Donna isn't that far-fetched. Take away online hookups and how do affairs begin? At work or between friends and neighbors. Not that I've got evidence but—"

"Neither do I after twenty-two days but who's counting. Shit."

He beelined to the Weyland house where he stopped in the driveway and glanced at the Corvins' garden gate. I caught up as he continued to the Weylands' front courtyard.

No mail piled up at the door. The view through the front windows was unfettered and unremarkable. The same bland space the Corvins had used for sanctuary while a corpse moldered next door.

Milo said, "Hopefully ol' Paul's doing his school district thing and I can pay him a visit soon. Meanwhile, let's learn more about him and his missing missus."

We sat in the unmarked, where he scanned the recovered-vehicle list. Still nothing on Chet Corvin's Range Rover. Pass-coding onto DMV revealed no registrations under Paul Weyland's name but Donna Weyland was the owner of a four-year-old silver Taurus and a three-year-old gray Ford Ranger pickup.

Milo copied down the VINs and the tags, moved on to the criminal databases.

Both Weylands appeared to be solid citizens.

I said, "Okay, so it's an air sandwich. Though I do find it interesting that the cars are in her name. Maybe he has credit problems. If she controls the money, there's another layer of resentment."

He tapped the steering wheel. "You know I take what you come up with seriously but there's a problem with the stash-the-evidence theory. Weyland couldn't go too far because he had to be back in time to play Mr. Helpful with the Corvins. Making it to PCH and back might be possible but finding a rural dump spot in Malibu would be a serious drive, no way."

I thought about that. "Are there any storage units nearby? In the best of all worlds, one with ample tenant parking and CCTV."

He said, "I'll have Sean check but first I need to keep Petra in the loop."

He tried her numbers, got no answer. The same for Raul Biro. Both Hollywood D's were sent a long text, catching them up, and asking them to reexamine video footage for evidence of either Weyland vehicle on the night of Chet Corvin's murder.

No return texts. "Can't begrudge them private lives," he said, sounding as if he might one day believe that.

Sean Binchy was still at the station, a man without any apparent circadian rhythms and cheerful as always. Milo asked him to look for storage units near the Corvin house.

"Got it, Loot."

"Also, put BOLOs out on the Weylands' vehicles, here's the info."

Binchy copied. "Something come up on them?"

"Not yet, Sean, but maybe it's not a beautiful day in the neighborhood."

"All that nice real estate, go know, Loot, huh? Glad you called, I was just about to try you. The desk left me a message slip for you. Someone named Henry Prieto, want me to follow up?"

"No, I'll handle it. Thanks, Sean."

"Hey, I love my job!"

"Prieto residence."

"Lieutenant Sturgis, sir. Got a message—"

"Three hours ago you got it," said Prieto. "Right after I saw that black Camaro driving up and down my street in a suspicious manner. It made two circuits, parked in front of her place—Maria Braun's. Driver proceeded to exit, continued toward her front door, observed me observing him, and ran off like a scared bunny. Male Caucasian, nineteen to early twenties, five-eleven, thin build, one forty to fifty, stringy blond hippie hair to his shoulders, acne pimples on his face. Too far away to ascertain eye color. I wrote down the plate. Tags are *not* current. Blue, could be '14, '09, '04, et cetera depending on how far back you want to go."

"You're a gem, Sergeant."

"Doing my job. Got a pencil?"

Back to DMV with the Camaro's plates. As expected, no match to currently registered vehicles but fees had been paid in 2009. Milo took the time to put out this BOLO, listing the car as stolen, before sending another text to Petra adding another CCTV target.

Onward to the Camaro's last owner of record: Edda Mae Halversen, the 1200 block of Laguna Street, Santa Barbara, California.

I said, "Hal Braun went up to Santa Barbara and came back fired up about something."

Milo looked up Edda Halversen. Ninety-one years old, five-four, one sixty, white and blue, corrective lenses required. No license for five years.

I said, "She can't drive anymore so her grandson—or great-grandson—gets the car but lets the reg lapse. Or he's just someone who bought it from her and she can give you a name."

"Let's find out," he said. "If she's still breathing."

If a current landline was evidence of life, Edda Halversen was inhaling and exhaling. The number was unlisted and took a while to get, Milo finally getting help from a Santa Barbara detective he'd worked with before named Braxton, who scoped utility records.

Milo thanked her and made the call. No pickup, no voicemail. He logged back to NCIC.

"Ninety-one," he said. "This'll be a waste of time unless she's Ma Barker . . . yup, pure as milk. Okay, let's try the Camaro kid. Maybe he's a Halversen, too, and naughty to boot."

Several men with that surname had run afoul of the criminal justice system but none came close to matching the skinny blond youth Henry Prieto had seen.

I said, "Whoever he is, he is linked to Braun and Arrowhead. Meaning he might know about Chet and Donna."

"Arrowhead," he said. "Let's see if I can make someone guilty enough to get off his ass."

His notepad gave up the number of San Bernardino detective Roger Livingston. Off shift but Milo pulled rank with the desk making no mention he was L.A., not local, and got a personal cell number.

Livingston picked up, sounding confused by Milo's name.

Milo began to explain. "Oh, yeah, that," Livingston said, sounding as if he was sitting on a monumental hemorrhoid. "You needed to call me at home?"

"I'm working two homicides. Some kind of schedule would help."

"Yeah, well, don't count your chickens, we're short-staffed, get shootings on a regular basis, not like Beverly Hills."

"I'm West L.A."

"Whatever," said Livingston. "It's serious, here. Like yesterday. We picked up a 187 in need of *boo-koo* tech attention. Torched vehicle, victim in the driver's seat with a bullet hole in his head, we're still trying to I.D. him."

Milo said, "Where'd it happen?"

"Coming down from Arrowhead into the city," said Livingston. "Gully off 18. Tight curves in the road, we get go-overs all the time but this wasn't no accident. Gasoline used as an accelerant, plates removed, VIN number filed off. Obviously a drug-gang thing. Some of those weekenders are scumbags."

"By any chance are we talking about a Taurus or a Ford Ranger?"

"Nah, a lot more painful," said Livingston. "Hot wheels gone to waste. One of those Range Rovers."

Milo clamped his hand atop his head and worked to keep his

voice even. "A Rover could be related to my cases. Put money on it, in fact."

Long silence from Livingston. Other voices drifted into the background. Kids.

Livingston said, "Hold on," and moved somewhere quieter. "What the *hell*?"

"One of my vics—the owner of the house I asked you to process—drove a Range Rover. The guy who shot him took it, along with a female hostage."

"A female," said Livingston. "Well our vic's a man. Despite being barbecued, you could see a few beard hairs. Long ones. And a leather hat that looks like grilled steak. Now I got to go take care of my kids—"

"Guess what, Roger. I might be able to I.D. your vic."

"What?"

"The *caretaker* at the house I asked you to process had a beard and wore a leather hat. Name's David Brassing."

"You're shitting me," said Livingston.

"Where in the head was the wound?"

"Temple."

"Which side?"

A beat. "Left. I think."

"So the killer either fired from outside the car or your vic was in the passenger seat while it was parked, shooter got out and lit up and staged the push-over."

"Anything's always possible," said Livingston.

"David Brassing," said Milo. "If you want I can call his house, find out if he's been missing. Then again, it's your case, Roger."

"Shit," said Livingston. "Hold on, I need to write all this down."

He went offline for a minute. "Okay, got a pen. Let's have everyone's names."

Milo read off the list: Chet Corvin; Paul Weyland; Donna Weyland; David Brassing. "Got all that, Roger?"

"Yeah . . . shit, *my* loo's gonna love this. Not."

"Who's that?"

"Lieutenant Ahearn."

"Gimme his number."

"Wouldn't do that if I were you," said Livingston. "He don't like being called unless it's an emergency."

"Three related homicides in two jurisdictions," said Milo. "That's kind of emergent, Roger."

Two beats. "Okay, here it is but don't blame *me*."

Despite Livingston's warning, Detective Lieutenant Alan Ahearn took the call calmly and graciously. No kids in the background, just jazz. Something syncopated, a Latin beat.

He and Milo agreed on a first-name basis. Milo's posture loosened, someone he could communicate with. He gave Ahearn a summary, repeated Livingston's assessment of a drug hit.

Ahearn said, "Roger said that, huh? Caretaker at the house . . . can you hold for a sec, see if we've got anything on him?"

"Sure."

Ahearn was gone briefly. When he returned, no more music. "Brassing has a record with us but small-time and not recent, I doubt this was a big drug thing. More important, his wife filed a missing on him when he didn't come home two days ago, which fits the initial pathology on the Rover. What's your theory, he went over to check out the house, got unlucky and surprised someone?"

"Exactly, Al," said Milo. "How far is the dump site from the house?"

"Not terribly close," said Ahearn. "Three, four miles."

"But walkable if you're in shape."

"Your guy Weyland a fitness type?"

"Don't know."

"You like him for Brassing because . . ."

"I've got zero evidence, Al, but his truck was seen driving away from the scene of my first murder, his wife could've been fooling with my second victim and she hasn't been seen in a while. It's possible she was hiding out in the A-frame when she wasn't meeting up with Corvin in those hotels. We're wondering if Weyland found out but waited to make his move until she shacked up with Corvin in Hollywood. Probably because a hit at a motel with direct door access to each room was a helluva lot easier than prowling the halls at some Hilton or making noise up in Arrowhead."

Ahearn said, "He offs the competition, takes his lady back. But why would he return here and off Brassing?"

Milo said, "Good question. All I've got are questions."

"Know about that, Milo."

I held up a finger.

"Hold on for a sec, Al." Milo listened to me and returned to Ahearn. "If sexual jealousy's the main motive, returning to the A-frame could be symbolic, Al. He wants to have his way with her in the same place she cheated on him."

"Symbolic . . . who was that?"

"Consulting psychologist."

"You got one of those? Man, we've been trying to get funding for two years, all we have are counselors for when officers get PTSD. I'd ask you if it's worth it but he's sitting right there."

Milo smiled. "It's worth it."

"Good to know," said Ahearn. "Okay, what about the kid in the Camaro?"

"Still a total blank, Al, but he's linked to my first victim and Brassing saw him in your neck of the woods."

"And now Brassing's dead. Maybe the kid's the bad guy."

"He's involved somehow," said Milo. "The plan before I heard about Brassing was to head up tomorrow to Santa Barbara, talk to the woman who last registered the car."

"No reason to change that, we'll take care of here," said Ahearn. "Let me know what you learn and I'll do the same. First thing tomorrow, one of my D's will talk to Brassing's wife and find out who his dentist is. If he didn't take care of his teeth, we'll go the DNA route but there's about a month turnaround. I'll also schedule drive-bys of the A-frame and have my guys looking out for both of Weyland's cars and the Camaro. And the place *will* get processed."

"Appreciate it but be careful," said Milo. "For all we know, Weyland's holed up there with her. The way the street's laid out, it's hard to conceal approach."

"Know it well, used to patrol there," said Ahearn. "Yeah, good advice. Okay, good talking to you and sorry for the delay."

"No need to apologize," said Milo. "Livingston says you're swamped."

"Roger," said Ahearn. "*He's* always swamped. Don't ask."

We got out of the unmarked and walked to the Seville.

"Poor Brassing," he said. "First I nearly shoot him, then someone does. What's your take on the Camaro kid, now? Aiding and abetting Weyland or a baby-faced contract killer?"

I shook my head.

He said, "That's also my level of insight. You up for a nice coastal drive tomorrow?"

Before I could answer, his cell played Debussy. He looked at the screen, clicked on. "What's up, Sean?"

"A whole bunch of storage places in Santa Monica and West L.A., Loot, but only one in the Palisades and it's small. Off Sunset, north of that village shopping area. Google says it's fifteen minutes from the Corvins in moderate traffic."

"On a Sunday night a hop and a jump. Go over and talk to them."

"Can't, right now, it's one of those DIY setups at night. Let yourself in with a card key, no staff. I can do a drive-by, see if they have cameras and let you know. Or wait until tomorrow when someone'll be there."

"Go home and get some rest, kid."

"I'm not tired, Loot."

"Let's keep it that way."

CHAPTER

43

L.A. to Santa Barbara can be a gorgeous ninety-mile cruise along the Pacific or a gray-air freeway slog for two-thirds of the distance finally graced by glimpses of water on the northern outskirts of Ventura. The last time Milo and I had made the trip was all business, the worst kind.

He picked me up at nine thirty, said, "I lied about scenic," sped north on the Glen, crossed Mulholland, and dipped into the Valley before picking up the freeway at Van Nuys and Riverside.

Chrome soup until we got past Canoga Park and the traffic demons stopped snarling. At eleven forty-five, we were exiting at the odd, left-hand Cabrillo exit, turning right on State Street, and GPS'ing toward the top end of the shopping district.

Edda Halversen's street was a western offshoot filled mostly with small prewar houses, some cute, others tatty, plus a few unseemly, obese, newer additions.

The district had begun as solid working-class, housing the people who serviced the mansions of Montecito. Now, except for retirees who'd managed to hold on due to Proposition 13 tax relief, out of reach of anyone with a blue collar.

The house we were looking for was a mint-green wood-sided bungalow. A full-length porch trimmed with lattice and millwork was painted white. Birds-of-paradise and yucca filled a skinny, trench-like bed of dirt paralleling the front. A brown Kia in the driveway bore a *Waikiki, It's A Kik!* bumper sticker. The tags were current, the rear seat covered by a knitted afghan.

A metal ramp was propped atop a four-step, concrete stairway. Not enough room on either side to use the steps. Milo and I made the climb.

A screen door framed with the same white gimcrack was unlocked. The solid door behind it was paneled and equipped with a brass knocker shaped like a sperm whale.

Milo said, "Thar she blows," lifted and lowered.

A pretty young Filipina in pink sweats opened the door. A sheet of black hair hung past her waist. Milo's badge furrowed her forehead.

He said, "Nothing's wrong. We're here to talk to Ms. Halversen?"

"I don't think so," she said. But she stepped aside.

The front room was as tiny and dim as EmJay Braun's. The air was filled with rose-based perfume and crowded by tables and stands hosting porcelain, ruby glass, and miniature teacups on miniature lace doilies. An upright oak piano sat along the right-hand wall. Sheet music on the rack. *Porgy and Bess.*

Unlike the Braun house, no wide swaths set aside for handicapped access, but space at the rear provided room for a white-haired woman in a wheelchair. She was covered to the waist by a pink quilt, legs propped on rests. A jade-colored sateen robe was buttoned to the neck. Baby-blue polish on her nails. The snowy hair was earlobe-length, combed, waved, clasped on one side with a Bakelite barrette.

She smiled at us.

Milo smiled back and showed her his card. Her eyes were an interesting mix of brown with blue rims. No change in focus as they stared straight ahead.

The young woman said, "She can't hear or talk, sirs."

I said, "Stroke?"

"Yes, sir."

"Recently?"

"This one, a year ago, sir."

I said, "Not the first."

"The first was two years ago, sir. She needed a walker but was okay."

"You've been with her all that time, Miss . . . ?"

"Vivian. Yes, sir."

Milo backed away, frowning.

Vivian's black eyes shot to him, then me. Curious but too frightened or discreet to pursue it.

Edda Halversen began waving her left hand. The smile had never left her face.

Vivian said, "She does that."

Milo said, "Maybe you can help us, Vivian. It's not really Ms. Halversen we're interested in. It's a young man who drives a black Camaro that used to be hers."

"Cory."

"You know him."

"Yes, sir."

"Is that spelled C-O-R-Y or with an *e*?"

"Don't know, sir."

"Last name?"

Weak smile. "Sorry, sir."

"How do you know Cory?"

"He's a friend of ma'am."

"A friend."

"From working for her, sir."

"What kind of work?"

"Yardwork, sir. Cleanup. He also visited, sir."

"Back when ma'am could still talk."

"Also after, sir."

"When's the last time he was here?"

Vivian's index finger stroked cupid lips. "Maybe six months, sir? I don't know, really, sir."

"Was he here to work or to visit?"

"Both, sir."

"Any idea why he stopped coming by?"

"Joining the army, sir."

"A half year ago."

"Maybe a little more, sir. Or less. I'm sorry, sir, I don't know."

I said, "You're doing great. So Cory came to tell Edda he was joining the army."

"Yes, sir. She did that, sir." Pointing to the still-waving arm.

Milo said, "Does she understand anything?"

"Food," said Vivian. "She eats three times a day, also snacks. Her blood pressure is good, sir."

Edda Halversen's arm lowered. The smile endured.

I said, "Vivian, how was Cory paid for his work?"

"Cash, sir."

"Who handles Ms. Halversen's finances—paying her bills."

"The bank, sir. They pay me, too."

"Which bank?"

"First Coastal."

"Are they around here?"

"Fourteen hundred State Street, sir."

Milo wrote it down.

I said, "How did Cory come to drive Edda's car?"

"It was her son's car," said Vivian. "Stuart. He died, sir."

"Sorry to hear that. When?"

"Before I knew ma'am, sir."

"Any idea how Stuart died?"

"She told me cancer, sir."

Milo said, "The car was Stuart's and Edda sold it to Cory."

"No, sir, she gave it to him. He was so happy." She smiled, as if to demonstrate.

"When?"

"After the first stroke, sir."

"So a couple of years ago."

"Yes, sir."

"She gave him the car because . . ."

"She didn't drive anymore, sir."

"Still, that's a nice gift."

"Cory helped her."

"Nice boy."

"Very nice, sir."

I said, "Does he live around here?"

The question seemed to genuinely perplex her. "He rode a bicycle, sir."

"Before he got the car?"

"Yes, sir."

"You have no idea where he lives."

"I'm sorry, sir."

"Anything else you can tell us about him?"

Another finger tap, this time covering both lips. "He was always nice." Her wristwatch beeped. "Time for peach yogurt. Okay, sirs?"

"Of course," said Milo.

She left and returned with a carton and a spoon.

I said, "Is there anything else you can tell us about Cory?"

"He plays that." Pointing to the piano. "Very good, sir."

I walked over and pointed to the sheet music. "Did he play this piece?"

"Oh, yes, sir. Very good. Stuart played trumpet, ma'am said."

"Professionally?"

"No, sir. Ma'am said he was a rooter man."

"A plumber?"

"A rooter man, sir. The drains. Ma'am's husband, too, sir."

"Rooter men—any pictures of Cory, here?"

"No, sir." She gave a start. "Oh, sorry, yes, sir." She looked at the yogurt.

I said, "I'll feed her."

Her stare was skeptical.

"I promise to do a good job. Could you please get that photo?"

I spooned peach-flavored crème between Edda Halversen's lips. She licked them between each swallow. By the third time, her hand was clutching my wrist. Cold, thin, fingers digging in. Strong grip.

Vivian returned with a small color shot. Edda Halversen looking exactly as she did now, in her wheelchair, behind her a wall of shrubbery. Between her and the vegetation stood a young man in a black T-shirt. He'd smiled for the camera but the downward cast of his eyes—focusing on the diminished woman before him—clouded the effort.

Skinny, long-haired, zits. Two years ago, I'd have taken him for seventeen. So maybe closer to nineteen than early twenties. But otherwise, Henry Prieto's description couldn't be improved upon.

I handed the photo to Milo.

"Who took the picture, Vivian?"

"My friend Helen. She's at night, sir."

"Just the two of you taking care of ma'am."

"Two weekends a month Vera comes."

"Who visits ma'am?"

Head shake. "No one, sir."

"No friends or relatives?"

"Stuart was her only child," she said, pouting. She took the yogurt from me and I unpeeled Edda Halversen's talon from my wrist.

Vivian said, "Very sad." Flash of white teeth, sway of long hair. "But we try to be happy. Right, ma'am?"

◆

Outside, Milo reexamined the photo. "Cory no-name. She never asked why we were curious about him."

"Probably intimidated by authority," I said.

"Or," he said, "she's covering something."

"Or," I said, "he really is a nice kid and she can't imagine him being in trouble."

"Spare me nice."

A text jingled. Petra returning his of last night. She was home with a rotten cold, Raul would recheck the CCTV for the other cars.

He lowered the phone to his pocket. Before it got there, it began playing Saint-Saëns. Some site had cached French romantic music for the working detective?

Sean Binchy said, "Just went over to the storage facility, Loot. They specialize in fancy antiques and art and neither Weyland rents a unit, sorry. What I'm *really* sorry about is the captain's shifting me to some cold armed-robbery assaults. Five unsolved up and down Pico."

"Go for it, kid."

"Boring, Loot. Captain says this is the wave of the future, low crime rate, time to open up the worm cans."

"Gotta have a sit-down with the bad guys, Sean. Tell 'em to get their felonious asses in gear."

We did door-knocks at Edda Halversen's neighbors. Most weren't home; a few recalled seeing the blond boy in the photo mowing the lawn but no one knew his name or where he lived.

As we headed back to the unmarked, Milo said, "Not that nice of a kid. Long hair says he's not in the army, so he lied to Edda."

I said, "Or he tried to enlist and got rejected. Or got in and was discharged."

"You're everyone's defense attorney today? I woke up at three in the morning thinking about Weyland being my bad guy all of a sudden. I can't get it to settle as a solo deal, Alex. We're looking at a helluva game of musical cars. The night of Braun's murder, he uses his truck to ditch evidence and trades for the Taurus, which he stashed in parts unknown. The night of *Chet's* murder, he stashes whatever he's driven to Hollywood, walks to the Sahara, pops Chet, abducts Donna or whoever the woman is, and drives away in Chet's wheels. That's not enough, he drives to Arrowhead in the Rover, gets surprised by Brassing and pops him, does the torch deal and walks back to the A-frame. There's no garage there, so what's he driving now?"

I said, "Two drivers could explain it."

"Two drivers would sure as hell make it more feasible," he said. "And who better for an accomplice than someone who's been seen skulking around both victims' houses? Who, on top of that, lies about military service, thinks registering a car is a suggestion, and rabbits when he sees Prieto watching him. That sound like innocence to you?"

I said, "He does play piano."

He laughed. "There you go, artistic license. Seriously, am I missing something?"

"You're making sense. And if Cory is a criminal, it could work in your favor."

"How so?"

"Un-solid citizens are often known to the authorities."

Detective Sheila Braxton was in her car. She said, "Need another phone number?"

"That was helpful, thanks, but no, I need info on a possible suspect I got via the number. Kid named Cory, nineteen to early twenties, skinny, blond, drives a black Camaro with '09 tags. You ever run into him?"

She said, "I suppose the age and physicals could fit if Cory's short for Cormac."

"All I know is Cory."

"Hard to see the Cory I'm thinking of as a murder suspect."

"Nice kid, huh?"

"Nice enough, but it's kind of complicated," said Braxton. "I'm on my way to lunch. You have time?"

"You bet. Where?"

"I was planning on Burger King."

"Upgrade, Sheila. On me."

"Well, that's nice of you, Milo, but not necessary."

"Life's about more than necessity, Sheila. Name a place with table-cloths."

"Hmm. You into seafood?"

"Like a shark."

Braxton laughed. "Cabrillo just north of Stearn's Wharf. New place they say is good. Moby Richard."

"Cute," said Milo. "They call me Fishmeal."

"Pardon?"

"See you in ten."

The *Moby Richard* sign featured a weirdly slim whale—a cetacean personal trainer.

Checked blue oilskin tablecloths, black-and-white period photos on gray walls, raw bar to one side, open-grill kitchen to the left. New place but three-quarters full.

Milo said, "There she is," and headed for a typical cop's table: rear corner, clear view of the action.

Sheila Braxton was in her fifties, tall, pretty, with a wry smile and a mop of iron-colored curls. She wore a deep-green crewneck, black slacks, and olive flats, tiny diamond studs in her ears.

Milo made the introductions.

She said, "Psychologist. Crazy world, I'm sure you're always busy."

A waiter in a man-bun and a waxed mustache came over and read off a long list of catch-of-the-day specials in a French accent. Sheila Braxton looked amused as she ordered scampi and a side salad. I went for grilled salmon.

Milo said, "Surf and turf."

Man-Bun said, "Pard*on*?"

"Right here." Jabbing the menu. "Filet steak and Pacific lobster. Medium rare on the steak."

"Combination two, very good."

"Take your word for it."

"Pard*on*?"

"Merci."

Man-Bun pranced five steps and returned. "Drinks, please?"

Iced teas all around. The waiter's second departure was durable. Braxton grinned. "You always liked that, Milo. Throwing people off balance."

"Call me Lieutenant Sumo."

"Lieutenant? Congrats. And you're still working cases?"

"It's complicated, Sheila."

Braxton looked at me.

I said, "He threw the right people off balance."

She was laughing as Man-Bun brought the tea in jam jars. Took a sip and put hers down. "I was a little guarded on the phone because I see the individual in question as vulnerable. No, I haven't turned into a social worker. The case wasn't even mine, it was Bob Mannings's, I was the secondary."

Milo said, "Big Bob. He finally retire?"

"He died before he could." To me: "My mentor, Doctor. Used to be LAPD, moved here and worked violent crimes."

"Good man," said Milo.

Braxton said, "The best. He took me under his wing when the female thing was a lot different."

Man-Bun brought bread. No one touched it.

Braxton said, "Anyway, I'll lay it out: Bob caught the case and it got away from him. What we all hate: likely homicide but no body, a darn good idea who the bad guy was but no way to put it together. It stuck in Bob's throat, kept him on the job longer than was good for him."

"Mission unaccomplished," said Milo. He nudged me. "What's

that technical term, something with a *Z*, Freud's mark of Zorro, whatever?"

I said, "Zeigarnik effect."

Braxton's eyebrows rose.

I said, "Tension for unfinished business."

She said, "I'll have to remember that for parties." Her tone said she wouldn't. "So here's the deal: Seven years ago a teacher named Jacqueline Mearsheim disappeared. Married for the third time, one kid from the first, a twelve-year-old boy. She was widowed the first time, divorced the second. Husband Two was also a teacher who'd moved overseas—some oil country in the Mideast, he got looked into, totally out of the picture. Mearsheim was Hub Three, also worked for the school district, some kind of administrative job. He and Jackie met on the job, got hitched pretty quickly. A year later, he reported her missing. Three days *after* she failed to show up for school. His story was he wanted to give her space, she'd been depressed, had taken a couple of days to sort herself out. Conveniently, the son was also away during that time, class trip to Sacramento."

A busboy brought the food.

Milo said, "Three days after. Yeah, I can see Bob twitching."

"Plus Mearsheim gave him a bad feeling from the get-go. Too theatrical, crying, going all Mr. Sensitive but no real tears, it seemed rehearsed. Add that to the obvious: He's the spouse and the last person to see her alive. *Plus* no one else ever saw Jackie as being depressed. The final factor was the boy. Cormac Thurber, yes, he was called Cory."

Out came Milo's pad. "With an *e* or no?"

"C-O-R-Y. He ended up telling Bob his mom had confided she was going to leave Mearsheim because he had no human feelings for her."

I said, "He ended up?"

"Quiet kid, hard to get anything out of him, Doctor."

"That was his wording—'no human feelings'?"

"It was," said Braxton. "I remember thinking it was pretty sophisticated for a twelve-year-old. And something his mother might actually say. Bottom line, everyone—even Mearsheim—agreed Jackie would never walk out on Cory."

I said, "Mearsheim's theory was a stranger-danger thing?"

"Exactly, Doctor. Snatched by the convenient shadowy villain."

"Was her car ever found?"

"Nope. And no charges on her card or ATM withdrawals. A super-meticulous shadowy bad guy, right? Bob's gut said that was bull."

Milo said, "Before we go on any further," and showed her the photo from Edda Halversen's house.

She took a while examining it. "I knew him when he was prepubescent but if I had to bet, I'd say yes."

She cut off a nibble of scampi as if eating was expected of her. Milo began sawing into his steak. No reticence, there.

I took my phone out, logged onto a pay-per-view yearbook photo site, and pulled up Santa Barbara High. Keywording *cormac thurber* brought up nothing.

Braxton said, "What are you scanning?"

I showed her. She said, "It's possible he didn't go to a regular high school. After Jackie's disappearance, he ended up in the foster care system and when Bob ran into him a couple of years later, he was studying music and going to some alternative program. It was a comfort to Bob, at least the kid had something going for him."

I returned to the Internet. *Alpha Alternative School, Goleta.* For working actors, athletes, musicians, or anyone benefiting from an individualized curriculum.

A hundred or so students. In lieu of yearbooks, faces had been collected each graduating year and cached for public use.

The face I was looking for had appeared two years ago. I showed it to both of them.

Milo said, "Our boy."

Braxton said, "No doubt, then."

"The foster system, Sheila? Stepdad bailed?"

"That's what I meant by part of the story. Six weeks after Jackie disappeared, Mearsheim was gone along with every penny Jackie had put away. Including insurance money from her first husband's death. Supposedly she'd signed everything over to him and left Cory with nothing. Bob found out later that Mearsheim had inquired about cashing out a hundred-grand term life insurance policy he'd taken out on her a few months before. But with no body, no payout. He was too smart for his own good."

Milo said, "Paul Mearsheim," unclasped his attaché case, and brought out the DMV shot of the man we knew as Paul Weyland.

Braxton took her time. "He had a beard back then but yup, it's him. He's *your* suspect? Amazing."

"He goes by Paul Weyland and he works for the L.A. school district."

"The system working for our kids," said Braxton. "Unbelievable. So what's he done now?"

Milo summarized. "Unfortunately, Sheila, we've also got nothing solid."

"Multiple murder," said Braxton. "This is really ugly. So what's your interest in Cory?"

"His car was seen near the houses of both victims."

"You figured him for an accomplice? Uh-uh, Milo, I can't see it, there was no relationship between him and Mearsheim. Just the opposite, the bastard abandoned him."

I said, "He could be seeking out Mearsheim to find out what happened to his mother."

"If so, dangerous pursuit," said Braxton.

I stood. "Be back in a sec."

I found a quiet corner in the adjoining parking lot and pulled out my phone.

Mary Josefina "EmJay" Braun answered on the fifth ring. "Oh, hi. You solve it?"

"Working on it. How're you doing?"

"In pain, as usual," she said. "Pretty bad a few days ago. It would help if I could clear up Hal's disability but the government's being a butt."

"Hope it works out."

"It sure better."

"Can I ask you something?"

"What?"

"Did a young man in a black Camaro ever drop by your house?"

"Once," she said.

"When?"

"Right after Hal got . . . a few days after you guys were here. He brought me some food. Said he was a friend of Hal's, Hal had tried to help him out, he wanted to help me back. I didn't eat it, greasy burger, I don't like grease, also he made me nervous."

"How?"

"Twitchy. I had him leave it outside, once he left, I threw it out."

"Skinny, long blond hair?"

"Yeah."

"Did he say how Hal helped him?"

"I didn't give him time to say anything, sir. It was Hal on one of his missions. Why, you think he killed Hal? I saved my life by keeping him out?"

"Not at all," I said.

"Whatever," she said. "I *was* smart not to let him in."

"If he returns, please let us know."

"If he returns, I'll call 911," said EmJay Braun. "I don't like strangers."

Mary Ellen Braun answered after one ring. "Oh, hi. You solved it?"

"Still working on it."

"Oh." Deflated. "What's up?"

"Did Hal ever talk about helping someone in Santa Barbara?"

"No, I can't say he did. Did someone from Santa Barbara kill him?"

"We're trying to get a handle on his activities. Did he ever mention helping teenagers or one boy in specific?"

"He liked kids, I could see that," she said. "Not in a *sick* way, I hope you're not going *there.*"

I said, "Not at all. Mary Jo told us Hal went on what he called quests. We're wondering if one of them might've put him in danger."

"In Santa Barbara? I can see him hiking there, it's so pretty up there, you never think of it as dangerous. Then again, Hal was such a nice *man* and look what happened to him."

I returned to the restaurant. Milo and Braxton looked up from their food.

I told them about Cory Thurber bringing a burger to Mary Jo.

"That nails it," said Braxton. "He didn't do anything bad." Not much confidence in her voice. She studied me.

I said, "I'm thinking Cory and Braun ran into each other up here, nothing planned, maybe just two people sitting on the beach or the pier. Cory opened up about his mom, Braun was a good listener and offered to help."

Milo said, "Help how?"

"Either locate Mearsheim or, if Cory already had tried that, find Mearsheim and demand to know what happened to Jackie."

Braxton said, "That would be crazy."

I said, "Braun fancied himself a knight errant."

"He'd do that for a stranger?"

I told her about the McDonald's incident, the tree, the snake. Braun going off for days at a time.

She said, "Living dangerously. He confronts Mearsheim, it's lamb to slaughter. But why would Mearsheim leave his body in your second vic's house? If we're right about Jackie, his thing was to conceal the corpse."

I said, "With Jackie he knew he'd be the prime suspect. With Braun, there'd be no obvious connection so no need to conceal. Who'd suspect the kind neighbor who opened his doors? We didn't."

Milo said, "He's right, Sheila. Guy came across as total Beta Male. If he knew his wife was fooling with Chet, there'd be no shortage of motive for using Braun's body as an eff-you."

"You think he disappeared Donna, just like Jackie?"

"Weyland said she was visiting her mom, I'm gonna try to find out."

I said, "Any idea what Cory's been up to for the last seven years?"

She wiped her hands on her napkin and stood. "My turn to take a break outside."

She was gone for fourteen minutes. During that time, Milo tried to reach Donna Weyland at the school district but was waylaid by sadistic voicemail instructions devoted to keeping callers away.

I picked at my salmon and, while on hold, he consoled himself with half a dozen Grassy Bay oysters on the half shell and an equal quantity of Kumiais from Mexico.

Braxton returned, shaking her head. "No hint where Cory is. My contact at social services says he was a chronic problem for his foster families. Five families, he kept running away. He also messed up in school, refused to study. Alpha provides home-study plans and a couple of the fosters are good folks who really tried."

I said, "Any drug history?"

"Not as far as she knows, Doctor. But that doesn't mean much, does it?"

Milo said, "Smart enough to avoid the system or lucky."

I said, "Or he stayed clean."

Braxton said, "You're an optimist?"

Milo said, "All these years, he refuses to see the light."

"It would sure be nice to be that way."

I said, "Maybe piano helped. Something positive he could build on."

"Hmm," said Braxton. "Apparently, he does have talent, my contact said one of the fosters had a piano and each time she visited Cory was playing and sounding really good. I hope you're right, Doctor. He's sure had a rough road."

"When he showed up at Braun's house, it was to bring food to Braun's wife and to tell her Braun had helped him. But there was no indication he knew Braun had been murdered. In fact, I think he might've really gone there to find out where Braun was but never got the chance."

"Then why Arrowhead?" said Milo.

"What if Braun had traced Donna and Chet there and he wanted to warn Donna about her husband?"

Sheila Braxton said, "Oh, geez. If Mearsheim ever found out, that would be nuclear explosive."

Milo said, "We need to find this kid."

We parted ways with Braxton, cruised Cabrillo south, and parked illegally on the beach side as Milo ran searches on Paul Mearsheim.

"Clean. Big deal, he stinks of con man, who knows what his real identity is."

I said, "He's used 'Paul,' maybe because that's his actual given name. 'Mearsheim' morphing to 'Weyland' could be identity theft of some random dead person. Or he assumed Donna's name."

"Why would he do that?"

"Playing the Beta to the hilt, letting her think she was in charge. The cars were in her name because he pled poverty, meanwhile he's got Jackie's money hidden from her."

"Another wife disappeared."

"Maybe this one can be found," I said. "Brassing's murder could've resulted from his discovering something buried in that forest behind the A-frame."

"I told him to stay away." He thumped the steering wheel with the heel of his fist. "The place *has* to be processed—let's see if Ahearn's a man of his word."

We got onto the freeway where he immediately ignored speed limits. Just before Carpenteria, with the road sun-brightened and nearly empty, he pulled out his cell then lowered it as something to the right caught his eye.

A CHP Dodge Challenger was parked just beyond a road curve on the western shoulder, blue ocean gleaming through the passenger windows, tan-uniform at the wheel, aiming a radar gun.

Geography providing a nifty little speed trap. Maybe Milo could've skated, maybe not. Professional courtesy between the highway patrol and city cops is unpredictable.

He slowed precipitously. The Challenger's beefy tires rotating toward the highway said it was ready to pounce. Milo altered that plan by turning off onto the right shoulder and coming to a stop three car lengths ahead of the cruiser. By the time he rolled down his window, the trooper was out of his car, one hand on his holster.

A quick flash of Milo's I.D. and a few pacifying words about heading to a new crime scene and *not* wanting to drive distracted turned the trooper contemplative.

Milo consulted his phone. "Oh, man, this is serious. Multiple victims."

The Chippie, young, beefy, sunburn-ruddy, said, "Good thinking your getting off the highway, Lieutenant, the law's for everyone." Looking crushed, he swaggered back to his black-and-white and sat there as Milo punched in Ahearn's numbers.

Ahearn didn't answer his cell or his desk phone. A desk officer said the lieutenant was out but wouldn't give details.

Milo said, "Any word on a forensic analysis at—?"

"No idea. I'll give him the message."

As we got back on the highway, Ruddy pretended to ignore us.

◆

At Oxnard, Milo looked around and speed-dialed. Nothing to report from Binchy, Petra, or Biro.

He handed me the phone. "Look up the school district I called before, punch it, and hand it over. Please."

He weathered bureaucracy through Camarillo and well into Thousand Oaks. Hopping like a frog in a lily pond, transferred from one bureaucrat to another. Near Lindero Canyon, I spotted another CHP stalk and said so.

He passed me the phone and I pretended to be him with three L.A. Unified functionaries.

Finally, a woman named Estrelle said, "Neither person is currently employed by the district."

"Did they quit or were they terminated?"

"I can't give out that information."

"Could you make a theoretical guess?"

"I'm not sure I know what you—"

"It's important to find them. They could be homicide victims."

Estrelle said, "Really?"

"Really."

"Well . . . is this being taped?"

"No."

"All right," said Estrelle. "All I can tell you is voluntary leaves of absence have been known to take place."

"How long ago? Theoretically."

"Well . . . could be a month. Around."

"Thank you."

"Victims," said Estrelle. "That's bad."

I handed the phone back to Milo.

He said, "You should be me more often, amigo. Though you *would* need to up your caloric intake. A month. So they both left around the same time."

I said, "Maybe Donna gave notice first because she was hiding from Mearsheim and prepping to run away with Corvin. Mearsheim found out and quit to go looking for her, finally nabbed her at the Sahara. Then he took her back to Arrowhead to finish her off. Returning to the scene of her crime to mete out justice, but maybe not swift justice. Brassing's death says Mearsheim was up there recently. One good reason would be to have his way with Donna."

"You think he tortured her?"

"Someone who could blow a man's face off, sever his hands, and take the time to stage the body in a neighbor's house is capable of anything."

He had me speed-dial Ahearn, still no luck.

"Just like TV," he said. "Solved by the fourth commercial."

I said, "By adorable things using whiz-bang DNA."

He was quiet for the next few exits. Then: "That goddamn place *has* to be processed."

46

No news by ten the following morning.

I had a custody evaluation scheduled, initial session with an eight-year-old girl named Amelia buffeted by her parents' guerrilla warfare.

She arrived with her father, a grim screenwriter with a history of depression. That, alone, wouldn't prejudice his case; his ex, a former model, had been in and out of rehab.

Amelia held his hand but pulled it loose when she saw me. Chubby, ginger-haired kid with gray, war-orphan eyes. Tear streaks down her cheeks had dried to salty granulation.

Her father said, "You need to know: She didn't want to come."

I bent and smiled, made sure to talk normally, not with that saccharine *I'm-so-sensitive* shrink-voice amateurs use. "Hi, Amelia. I'm the kind of doctor who doesn't give shots. We won't do anything you don't want."

Her mouth twisted.

Grim said, "I just got her a dog and she wanted to bring it. I told her it was against your rules."

"What kind of dog do you have, Amelia?"

Grim said, "Maltese mix," as if letting out a state secret.

"What's your dog's name, Amelia?"

Whispered reply. I bent lower to catch it as Grim said, "Snowy."

"You can bring Snowy next time, Amelia."

Grim said, "Speaking of which, how many next times are we talking about?"

"Amelia, do you like all kinds of dogs or just Snowy?"

"All kinds."

"Any allergies to other dogs?" I asked Grim.

"Not that I know so far. She's into Snowy, not dogs in general."

I said, "Hold on for one sec, Amelia," left, and returned with Blanche trotting at my side.

Gray eyes expanded like a water lily encountering sunlight.

Amelia said, "Wow."

Her father said, "Hmh. Do I wait here or out in the car?"

An hour later, a perked-up, affectionately licked Amelia was hugging Blanche near the front door as Grim tapped a sandal. "Gotta go, Meel. Meeting at Warner Brothers."

He reached for her hand. She touched his fingers briefly, dropped her hand to her flanks.

I said, "Next week, same time. With or without Snowy."

Grim said, "Hope this doesn't drag on."

Amelia smiled at Blanche, then stooped and kissed her. Her father waited for a while as child and dog communed.

Just as I finished charting the session, my private line rang.

Milo said, "Ahearn finally called."

"The A-frame got processed."

A beat. "In the process of being processed."

"Great."

"Not so simple. Not—how's your schedule?"

"Just got free."

"I'll drive, you can look out for radar guns."

He picked me up four minutes later. Meaning he'd called while driving over, confident of my answer.

I got in the unmarked, had barely closed the door as he sped off.

I said, "A few minutes earlier, I was in session."

"You some kind of a doctor?" He told me why we were driving to Arrowhead. We spent some of the ride talking, most of it in silence.

We reached the A-frame by one fifteen p.m., asked for Ahearn, and were directed to the house's rear deck.

The San Bernardino lieutenant was midfifties, stocky and barrel-chested, with a shaved freckled head and a bristly white mustache. He wore a white shirt, gray slacks, a blue tie, and black lace up military boots.

The body lying faceup in the grass wore a navy shirt, jeans, a tan tie, and brown walking shoes. Male, around the same age as Ahearn, tall and long-limbed, with a heavy-jawed face blued by stubble.

He'd been shot once in the left side of his chest and once in the right cheek. Sidearm still holstered. Taken by surprise.

No problem identifying this victim or estimating time of death. Sheriff's detective Roger Livingston had been sent by Ahearn at nine o'clock this morning and ordered to stand guard pending the ten a.m. arrival of the crime scene techs. He'd logged his arrival at nine eighteen, had recorded nothing further. At ten forty-four a two-person team from the San Bernardino lab showed up, delayed by a street-clogging truck collision on the north side of the city.

Livingston had checked out a squad car from the motor pool and parked it at a careless slant in front of the house, forcing the techs to walk around the black-and-white in order to reach the front door. They rang the front doorbell and when that brought no response, circled around back.

Techs are unarmed. The panic these two felt was understandable. Fleeing to their van, they drove a quarter mile and called in. Now they were inside, working their phones manically, waiting for the coroner's investigator to release the body so they could move from Livingston to the house.

In San Bernardino, the sheriff is the coroner and C.I.'s are uniformed deputies. On duty this morning was Deputy Sandra Kolatch, forty or so, square-faced and stunned. She'd been held up by a gang shooting, had entered the scene just before Milo and me.

She went through Livingston's pockets. "No phone."

Ahearn said, "Got it in my car, Sandy. It was on the ground out back so I bagged it."

Breach of procedure. Kolatch nodded, took notes, and shut her eyes. When they opened, she looked defeated. It's different when making an I.D. isn't necessary.

The basics accomplished, she stood, said, "Sir," to Ahearn, and left. As if part of a meticulously choreographed revue, two morgue attendants techs appeared with the collapsible morgue gurney—a contraption I've seen so many times but always find jarringly efficient.

They worked fast, slipping Livingston into a body bag, zipping and loading.

Ahearn watched, eyes dry and bloodshot. His mustache did a poor job of concealing a lip tremor.

Milo said, "So sorry, Al."

"He must've walked right into it." Ahearn clenched both fists. "I sent him 'cause I figured it was a piece of cake." Grinding his jaws. "I figured it was something he could *handle*."

Milo said, "This was an ambush, no way to know."

Ahearn said, "Watching an empty house? What could be more Mickey Mouse?"

He headed out of the yard, toward the driveway. The three of us stood by as the gurney made contact with the butt-edge of the van's rear compartment and snapped flat with a cruel *snick*. Body straps were checked, rear doors slammed shut, the van was gone.

Ahearn said, "I had problems with Roger. Not my sharpest blade in the drawer. An empty house and he was armed for God's sake."

Moisture had collected in the corners of his eyes, turning the bloodshot vessels maroon.

Milo said, "No way to know, Al."

"Try telling that to his widow. Like she could ever admit he was an idiot—oh, screw it, I'm not going to blame him, could've happened to anyone."

We said nothing.

Ahearn said, "It was so Mickey Mouse, I almost sent a rookie. Could've been Ramona." He eyed a dark-haired deputy standing on the deck. Easy pass as a high school junior. "She has no idea how lucky she is—sorry we didn't process when you first asked, Milo. That was Roger, too, sometimes he got like that. I'm not going to make excuses but it gets insane down in the city. Don't know about your situation but the gangs here are multi-racial, you have no idea who you're dealing with."

A click rose from his throat. "You think your suspect— Mearsheim—did this?"

Milo said, "If we're guessing right, he's got no problem killing people."

"So that's how many?" said Ahearn.

"My two male victims, Brassing, your guy, probably his first wife, maybe his second—or she's his third or fourth, who knows?"

"A psycho. Shit. Someone was keeping house here recently. I did a walk-through, there's coffee, cereal, milk, lunch meat. Not a *lot* of grub, nothing that looks the long haul, and beds are made. Don't worry, I bootied and gloved, didn't touch a thing. If there was visible blood, it's been cleaned up. I think I did smell some bleach near the kitchen. How was the traffic coming in?"

Sudden injection of trivia as a pathetic distraction.

Milo said, "Not bad. When we were here, there was none of that, whoever did it came back recently."

Ahearn said, "I was planning to have a sit-down with Roger tomorrow. Suggest he think about something else, maybe detective wasn't his thing. I was going to go easy but also firm, our kids go to the same school—you really think you've got a Manson on your hands? I mean the other alternative is what, a random psycho squatter? Sometimes we get that in the rurals—cabins and lean-tos and hunters' blinds that aren't used much, you're a homeless, why not? Here, in the nice neighborhoods, what we get is burglaries. But from what I saw, no sign of break-in and no obvious toss."

The crime scene techs left their van and came toward us, carrying equipment cases. "Okay to continue, sir?"

Ahearn said, "I might've smelled bleach near the kitchen. But do the yard, too."

I said, "Any sign more than one person was here?"

"I didn't observe on that level, Doctor, just did an in-and-out looking for obvious. Why?"

"Looks like Mearsheim abducted his wife. Bringing her back here made sense if he wanted to humiliate her."

"Humiliate her how?"

"Same place she stayed with Corvin."

Milo said, "Like I told you, they also shacked up in hotels but harder to hostage in the Hilton."

Ahearn said, "Humiliate—you're thinking ultra-nasty happened here. *Shit.*"

He showed us the spot that had been found. Shallow depression beginning to fill as the grass perked up.

Ahearn said, "Cadaver dogs are good but we both know they're not perfect. They don't find anything, I should probably still dig."

"I would."

"Unbelievable," said Ahearn. "From bad to worse."

Milo said, "There could be evidence back there in the neighbor's property."

Ahearn's eyes shifted to the forest. "That's a rich guy. Request to disrupt a fancy property? Can't wait."

I said, "Did anything interesting come up on Livingston's phone?"

"He called his wife when he got here. Knowing Roger, he probably fell asleep in the car, decided to take a stretch out back, and got surprised."

"Way he blocked the door with his cruiser, the bad guy mighta felt he was being hunted."

"Makes sense." He sucked in breath. "Roger was a regular guy. You can't be regular and do what we do, right?"

Milo said, "Ain't that the truth."

I said, "No streetlights, must get pretty dark at night."

Ahearn said, "With no stars or moon it's a total blackout. You're figuring your boy's been coming and going at night?"

"Maybe when Brassing surprised him. Any idea what time of day that happened?"

"Still waiting on the pathology, Doctor, but you've got a point. For sure Brassing was shoved off that cliff in the dark. That section of 18 isn't always traveled heavily but there's always some day traffic, you couldn't count on not being seen."

Milo said, "A fire would be more visible at night but no one reported any."

Ahearn knitted his fingers and cracked his knuckles. "If it was timed right—two, three a.m., put the car in neutral, soon as it starts rolling, toss the match, it could've been mostly shielded from view. And the arson guy says the fire was brief, not successful if evidence destruction was the goal. Most of the scorch marks were in the rear section of the Rover and that's where they found the accelerant splashes. The body was damaged but not burned up so it weakened as it moved forward. I'd still bet on a night thing."

He unfolded his hands, stretched a few fingers, and produced more pops. "Something's bound to come up."

Milo said, "You're an optimist."

"I'm a realist. Or as my college son says, a surrealist. Whatever that means. Kid wears black, is writing one of those plays where they dance around like who-knows-what."

He laughed. "Kid used to like football."

One of the techs emerged. "We smell bleach, Lieutenant, but so far no visible blood or bloody swabs. But there's a lot of area and with all the glass and no drapes it's too bright for Luminol."

"You'll do it after dark."

"Someone will, sir. The next shift."

"Don't want any communication issues," said Ahearn.

"There shouldn't be any, sir."

The tech returned inside.

Ahearn faced us. "It's all about communication, right? That's always what goes south. So what else should we talk about?"

Milo said, "Who does what."

"One of ours goes down, it's ours. We'll handle everything in our jurisdiction."

"Fair enough, Al."

"No one will screw up." He walked us to the unmarked, specified his plan. Nervous, like a kid delivering an oral report.

The house and yard would be processed "to the nth," including the use of infrared sensors and cadaver dogs. The neighbor to the rear would be contacted and if an informal request to process the forest wasn't granted, a request for a warrant would be submitted to "the best judge I can find."

Ahearn would also make sure all the hotels where Chet Corvin had stayed would be re-contacted about sightings of the Weylands.

I said, "Expanding to some of the nearby motels might be a good idea."

Ahearn's glance at Milo said, *This one's full of ideas.*

Like the true friend / ace detective he is, Milo said, "He means the whole synchrony thing. Mearsheim did Corvin in a cheap motel, maybe he stalked him at others but the situation wasn't right."

Ahearn said, "Cheapie dump . . . we've got our share of those. I'll try. Anything else?"

Milo said, "Be on the lookout for Cory Thurber, the kid in the Camaro."

"You see him as a suspect or a potential victim?"

"At this point, victim makes more sense. But Mearsheim's likely to have an accomplice, so who the hell knows?"

I said, "With Donna out of the picture, the accomplice could be the new woman in Mearsheim's life."

Ahearn said, "He trades them in, huh?"

Milo said, "More like sends them to the wrecking yard."

47

Milo fidgeted as he raced toward Arrowhead Village. "Not sure what that accomplished."

I said, "At least the house will finally get worked."

Three miles passed before he spoke again. "Seven years between Jackie and Donna."

"Good chance of someone else," I said. "When did he marry Donna?"

"Good question. Call Moe, see if he can find out."

I phoned Reed, got voicemail, left a message.

"Try Sean."

Same result.

Milo said, "It's like everything's turned swampy and just walking's a hassle—try Petra."

The third time wasn't a charm.

Without waiting for further instruction, I phoned Raul Biro.

He said, "You're on the Loo's phone, Doc."

"He's into safe driving."

"Driving from where?"

I told him.

He said, "A cop? Oh, shit. And you think it's the same guy who did the handyman—Weyland."

"Best guess, so far. His real name's Mearsheim. Maybe."

"Whatever his name is, I might have something. When do you plan to be back?"

"Couple of hours."

"That'll work," said Biro. "Got someone you'll want to meet, listen to this."

Fueled by the news, Milo sped well past the limit, making adventurous lane changes, and when we reached the jam near the four-level downtown interchange used the shoulder to press his way onto the 101.

Ignoring honks and dirty looks, he said, "Goddamn pretzel and they don't even give you salt."

Squealing exit followed by more creative driving on side streets.

When we pulled up in front of the Hollywood station on Wilcox, Biro was waiting. *GQ*'d as always in a light-blue suit, white shirt, Windsor-knotted paisley tie. But the look in his eyes was anything but composed. He remote-opened the staff lot and sped ahead of us as Milo sandwiched between two other sedans.

"Thanks for sticking with it, Raul."

"Petra's idea," said Biro.

"How's she feeling?"

"Sick as a dog—more like a flu than a cold." Biro looked at his watch. "You made it unbelievably fast."

"Luck," said Milo.

Biro said, "I'll bet." His right foot moved up and down as he scanned the street. "A little late. He doesn't show up, I know where to find him."

A minute later, a white taxicab trimmed in blue and red approached from the south. *Prestige Cabs* above a medallion impressive enough for a minor European functionary.

Biro pointed the cab to the staff lot, remoted it in. By the time the cab had parked, we were at the driver's door. A short, wide man in a gray cardigan got out. Sixties, sparse white crew cut topping a face that looked as if it had spent years in the ring, a physique designed for trudges across the steppes.

Biro said, "Hello, Mr. Grinshteyn. Thanks for coming."

"Boris," said the driver.

Milo extended his hand. "Lieutenant Sturgis. Thanks for taking the time, sir."

Boris Grinshteyn hesitated before shaking, as if concerned about digit theft. His fingers were cocktail franks. "The please say come, I come."

Bassoon voice, Russian inflection. I flashed back to a record favored by my "educated" aunt Edith. *Peter and the Wolf.*

Biro said, "We really appreciate it, sir. You brought what we need?"

"Yah, Lieutenant."

"He's the lieutenant, I'm just a lowly detective."

Grinshteyn's face compressed, taking on the look of a cabbage left too long in the fridge.

Milo said, "He's being modest. He's a commissar."

"Hoh," said Grinshteyn. "Commissars we don't need."

He key-opened his trunk, took a while finding what he was looking for among piles of laundry and Cyrillic-lettered magazines.

Finally, he handed Milo several loose sheets of paper, dog-eared and stained by what looked like tea.

Logs, written in a shaky, Old World hand.

"A week of driving I brought you," he said. "Company made me photocopy before I give you."

Biro said, "Is there more than one pickup for the same client?"

"No, no, one."

"You brought all of this because . . ."

Grinshteyn gave a sour look. "With please, you do more than they ask."

Milo flipped pages. "Okay, *here* we go."

Pointing to the bottom of one sheet. Nine p.m. call, the night of Chet Corvin's murder.

The client: Mr. Korabin. The destination, Whitely Avenue, just south of Franklin.

Walking distance from the Sahara.

Milo said, "Mr. Corvin."

"Yah, Lieutenant," said Grinshteyn.

Milo showed the driver Chet Corvin's photo.

"Nyo."

Out came Paul Weyland's DMV.

"Yah."

"You're sure."

"He didn't tip me," said Grinshteyn. "Bastards you remember."

Milo's attention returned to the log. Eyes widening as they found the pickup address, Marquette Place, Pacific Palisades.

Biro already had his cellphone out, preset to a map app. He fiddled, showed us the screen. Two red dots, Marquette and Evada Lane. Short drive between the two, ten minutes tops under the cover of night.

Milo said, "House or apartment?"

Biro and Grinshteyn answered in unison: "House." Grinshteyn added: "Dump. Pacific Palisades? I expect nice." Three derisive snorts.

I said, "The Palisades isn't your usual route?"

"I do Brentwood, sometimes Beverly Hills. There also, you get dumps." He threw up pudgy hands, the image of world-weary disillusion.

"That night you were in the Palisades because—"

"A guy was sick," said Grinshteyn. "They call me, I say hokay."

Milo said, "How did Mr. Corvin pay you?"

"Cash. Paper and stupid coins." Another snort.

I said, "Cheapskate."

"Bastard."

"What else do you remember about him?"

"Nothing," said Grinshteyn.

"Any conversation between the two of you?"

"I say good evening, he tell me where to take him. I say hokay, he say nothing. After that, *I* say nothing." Three more snorts. "Bastard."

Raul hurried to the station and returned with an LAPD mug, the blue, gold-trimmed kind given out to citizens who raise money for feel-good police projects.

Grinshteyn tensed up. "Nyo, I don't take things."

"It's okay, sir."

"It could be okay but not for me," said the driver. "I want only what is mine. Not more."

The Hollywood station was a jumpier place than West L.A., the detective room filled with phoning, reading, writing investigators, multiple-line desk phones blinking, human voices vying with electronic noise. A couple of Palo Alto zombie types inspected computers, others seemed lost in thought.

Milo, Biro, and I convened in an empty interview room, sitting around the kind of table pushed to the corner to prevent suspects from feeling secure.

Milo said, "Another address answers a *helluva* lot of questions, Raul. Like a place to stash vehicles."

I said, "Or worse."

"Or worse. And if Mearsheim's there, you may have cracked the whole thing wide open. *Commissar.*"

"Don't those guys wear fur hats?" said Biro. "Don't want hat-head—it's no big deal, had no idea Grinshteyn could actually make a positive I.D."

I said, "How'd you find him?"

"There was nothing on the cameras so I tried taxi companies and Uber like you said, Milo. I started with taxis because Uber gets all pissy and want tons of paper."

"He'd be less likely to use Uber," I said. "Not wanting to be on record using the app."

"That, too," said Biro. "Anyway, Grinshteyn was the third driver I spoke to, I got lucky."

Milo said, "You're selling yourself short, Czar, but fine, let's concentrate on business. First obvious step: Check out the address. Even if the bastard's not there, there could be some serious evidence, so the goal is to actually get inside. I'm gonna bypass John Nguyen and his lawyerly bullshit, someone told me about a new judge, Sonia Martinez. Her brother was a cop in Oakland, got shot."

"Heard that," said Raul, "but haven't used her yet."

Milo said, "If I can pry Sean or Moe away from kiddie stuff like robberies, I'll get a drive-by done now, just a quickie to get the lay of the land. This is not a stupid criminal so if he is there, we can't afford to show ourselves and have him rabbit."

Binchy was out, Reed just back from "dinner." He said, "Sure."

"Look for the Taurus, the Ford truck, and the Camaro."

"No Ferraris or Bentleys? Shucks."

Milo said, "Next time we'll pick a dot-com bad guy." He hung up.

Biro said, "The serious drive-by is way after dark."

"You bet, Emperor. He makes night moves, so do we."

Knock on the door. A Hollywood uniform said, "Detective Biro? You've got a call from the lab on a case."

Raul said, "Which one?"

"Benitez."

"Thanks." Biro stood and buttoned his jacket. "Shooting on Argyle we got the day after Corvin. Nothing exotic, prescription drugs, this might even be the shooter wanting to turn himself in."

"Love when they see the light," said Milo. "Thanks again."

"What time tonight do you figure?"

"You're always an asset, Raul, but don't want to take you away from the wife and kids."

"They're in Colorado visiting her family for two weeks," said Biro. "First few days I tried to eat healthy and live right. Now it's microwave crap and ESPN reruns. Take pity and call me."

"Always happy to do a favor."

Biro walked to the door. "You're joking but I'm going out of my mind."

Milo drove out of the Hollywood lot. Slowly, no risk-taking. His mind elsewhere.

I said, "Raul's wife being away reminded me of something. Mearsheim's story about Donna visiting her mom. Her family are likely worried by now, would want to help."

"When we looked her up, we found nothing on social media."

"A controlling husband could explain that. Maybe birth records? Or back to the school district to see if she listed anyone other than Paul as an emergency contact?"

"Good ideas, both of which will take time," he said. "I'll do it if nothing pans out at the house on Marquette."

I said, "Be good to know who owns it. Same for the house on Evada, which, as Chet pointed out, is a rental."

"Dick-waving with Mearsheim. Did you happen to notice how Mearsheim reacted?"

"Don't recall that he did."

"Guy came across so mild. Sitting there and playing everyone."

"Part of the thrill," I said.

"Well, let's de-thrill him. Yeah, I'll look for the deeds on both houses before tonight."

His phone played four notes of Ravel's "Bolero." The caller I.D. made him sit up straighter. "Hey, Al, what's up?"

Ahearn said, "Giving you a progress report. We sure can't see any signs of excavation in the backyard. Between us and these walls, I did a little trespass over to the neighbor's trees and nothing there, either. My cadaver dog lady is away for a couple of days, I tried someone else but no dice. So she'll be doing the sniff when she gets back. I've asked for an infrared thing, should probably have that in the morning. In terms of the interior, we're waiting for darkness to do the luminol. So far, no obvious crime scene."

Each bit of bad news lowered Milo's bulk, like a dirigible steadily drained. "Thanks for calling—"

"Hold on, saving the best for last," said Ahearn. "We pulled up a usable print in the master bath. Corner of a shelf in the medicine cabinet, nice clear thumb and forefinger and Lordy-be, AFIS knows who put it there."

"Please tell me it's someone with a record," said Milo.

"Nothing violent and let's face it, we have no idea how long the print's been there, for all we know she was a housecleaner. But so far, we can't locate her, which makes my nose itch. In a perfect world, she's what your doctor guessed— the new girlfriend. You want the basics on her?"

"I want everything on her. I'm driving, how about texting or emailing?"

"High-tech transfer of data," said Ahearn. "My college kid thinks I'm a dinosaur. The other five do, also. Sure, coming your way."

Milo handed me his cellphone. The info arrived just as we reached La Brea and headed south.

Trisha Stacy Bowker, forty-three, had a record beginning at age nineteen and stretching sixteen years. Convictions in Massachusetts, Vermont, New Hampshire, and Missouri for petty theft, grand theft, larceny, embezzlement, illegal appropriation of property, and fraud. She'd gone years at a time without being arrested, pled out most of the time in return for probation or minimal jail time.

Bowker's last bust—identity theft in St. Louis—had earned her a year of probation. No violations for eight months had terminated her supervision after six months.

I re-read the record. "She's been free and off the radar since a year before Jackie Mearsheim disappeared. Maybe she's kept her nose clean because she hooked up with a smarter criminal."

"Jackie's dead, Donna's dead, Bowker seduces Corvin but has been playing house with Mearsheim for years?"

I said, "Why not? Couple of cons working lonely hearts. They hit on a winning plan and milk it."

"Fall for Paul, lose your money and your life. What does this princess look like?"

The mugshot photo Ahearn had sent was tiny and indistinct even under enlargement. Caucasian face topped by a thick dark mop of hair. Twenty-seven at the time.

A red light at La Brea and Beverly gave Milo a chance to examine the image.

"Damn this is small." He put on reading glasses, squinted. "Looks like . . . five-five, hundred and twenty-eight. Brunette with a normal build. Could be."

"If Bowker is Mearsheim's girl, there was no abduction at the Sahara. All we really have on that is Sarabeth Sarser's description. But she was scared and meth-addled, so maybe what she really saw was two people hurrying off together."

"Or," he said, "she saw things clearly and Mearsheim decided to upgrade his hardware."

"Bowker's gone, too?" I said.

"Guy like that, women are expendable, why not?"

He drummed the steering wheel with both thumbs. Sitting tall, now, green eyes ignited. "Got a lot to do. Starting with checking out ol' Trisha on a normal-sized screen. Then I start playing keyboard Sherlock."

48

A larger image of Trisha Bowker brought no new wisdom. Her face fluctuated between barely pretty and plain, depending on her mood at arrest. Some shots showed her as various versions of blond. Flat, dark eyes. No identifying scars or tattoos.

Jane Average. That could be an advantage.

Al Ahearn's failure to find any recent data on Bowker didn't stop Milo from trying. No success.

He printed what Ahearn had sent him, included it in the murder book, went to get septic coffee from the big detective room. He returned, cell in one hand, coffee in the other, squeezed back into his chair, drinking and saying, "Why do I subject myself to swill? Reed's not answering. I hope he kept it simple on the drive-by."

Four sips later, Reed was knocking on the doorway jamb, shirt seams strained by musculature, ruddy and towheaded, your basic Viking raider.

"Phone ran out of juice, L.T., sorry. The house is small, oldish, in an area that's mostly apartment buildings. For the Palisades, I'd have to say a dump. None of the vehicles we're looking for were visible but there is an attached double garage. You wanted it simple so I only went back and forth twice, can't tell you if anyone's inside but there was no mail pile. So what's the plan?"

"Don't have one yet," said Milo. "Other than I'm aiming for tonight."

"I'll stick around."

"With lunch at four, take along snacks, Moses. We don't want you fading."

Reed smiled and flexed thigh-sized biceps. "No prob with nutrition, L.T. Been altering my workout, heavier weights, fewer reps, a little creatine. Also, I watch everything that goes into my mouth."

"What was lunch?"

"Four cans of Muscle Milk."

"I don't even want to know what that is."

"It actually tastes pretty good. Chocolate."

"Would it matter if it didn't?"

"Nope. I'll be at my desk, let me know."

Too late to call the school board for info on Donna Weyland. Milo tapped into county property tax records, found nothing, which fit her being a renter.

With no info on her origins, impossible to look for family.

He said, "All else fails, dig up what you have. Seven years ago, Jackie gets disappeared by Mearsheim in Santa Barbara, maybe he was already with Trisha Bowker, maybe not. Either way, with Jackie taken care of, Mearsheim looks for another victim, possibly finds one or more before he latches onto Donna. So what's Bowker's role in all this?"

I said, "Could be anything from confidante to full partner. If they're working as a team, she could've been used as a lure. Two women just happen to meet, become friendly, one lets on she's single and lonely, the other says, 'I know a good guy.'"

"With a nice job in the school district, like Jackie. Two districts hired him, can you believe that?"

"Maybe he did his job acceptably. Some sort of technical work with minimal supervision. It does show he's bright. Anyway, whether or not there were male victims prior to Chet, Bowker was used to seduce him. He would've seemed the perfect target: Mearsheim had come to despise him for the way Chet treated him and he understood Chet's overconfidence the way we did: vulnerability."

He shook his head. "Idiot's unable to imagine any woman who says she loves him doesn't mean it. Bowker's on him like a tracking device."

"Passion, dinner, and jewelry. Maybe they had bigger plans but Chet balked. So they killed him."

He let out a sour laugh. "Wages of sin 101. Okay, on to real estate."

The rented house on Evada Lane was deeded to a limited liability corporation registered as Scribble Properties. A bit of digging revealed that to be three people, two living in Seattle, one in Austin, Texas.

Bernard Leviton, Gray Winograd, Susan Minelli. Three separate social network pages but one story: a trio of TV writers, alumni of a long-running late-night show, had pooled resources by renting out their L.A. homes to leverage several Section Eight apartment buildings downtown. That in place, they moved to states with no local income tax.

Evada Lane had been Susan Minelli's residence so Milo began with her.

Voicemail; same for Bernard Leviton in Seattle. The converted Texan, Gray Winograd, wasn't home but his wife was.

"This is Meryl. The po-lice?" Bored voice, syllables elongated as if to prolong conversation.

Milo said, "This is about the property on Evada Lane."

Meryl Winograd said, "That place? Something happened? What?"

"We're doing a routine investigation."

"That sounds like movie dialogue. What did you say your name was?"

Milo repeated his credentials.

"Hold on . . . I just looked you up and you seem to be the real deal. What's your actual police phone number so I can make sure?"

Milo told her.

She said, "You sound mellow, guess I'll believe you. So what do you want to know about that place?"

"The tenants—"

"No idea about any of Gray and his pals' little endeavors. It all goes through the managers they hired."

"Who are the managers?"

"Some company named Aswan, Aslan, something like that," said Meryl Winograd. "They're no great shakes."

"You've had problems—"

"Apparently they're a humongous outfit and Gray and his pals are teensy french fries. I keep telling Gray being a landlord is a job not a hobby."

"You said, 'That place,' as if there'd been specific problems at Evada."

"You're reading too much into that, I don't know details and I don't care," said Meryl Winograd. "The whole real estate thing isn't my thing, they thought they'd be tycoons, meanwhile I'm in Texas. It's kind of cute, here, good food and music, but my allergies and oh God the humidity."

"So you're not aware of any—"

"If there was a serious problem, Gray would be bitching about it and he's not. So how's the weather in L.A.?"

"Nice."

"Figures."

◆

A call to Aslan Property Management brought up layers of manically paced, mostly incomprehensible button-push instructions. Multi-city company specializing in shopping centers and huge residential complexes.

Milo held the phone at arm's length as the robotic voice on the other end continued to natter. The 0 for Operator option brought up another automaton.

He clicked off. I said, "The castle moat for when tenants complain."

"Gimme some hot oil and a catapult."

The rented house on Marquette Place belonged officially to no one.

Once the home of Herbert McClain, deceased at age ninety-one, it had entered into probate six months ago because McClain had died intestate.

The court-appointed trustee was an attorney named Mitchell Light with an office near the downtown court building. Maybe one of those Hill Street hangers-on who dole out holiday gift baskets to judges and wait for assignments.

That guess was kicked up to probable when Milo found Light's garish website featuring an improbably black-haired man in a bad suit whose cap-filled smile screamed *trying too hard.*

Light's dual specialties were "easing the grief burden of survivors as they enter the world of probate court" and "speedily solving the problems of accident victims wronged by insurance companies."

Milo said, "Slip, fall, die, he's got you covered. Here goes more nothing."

To his shock, one of three garishly green "24 hour numbers" on Light's site banner was picked up on the second ring.

"This is Mitch," said a radio-announcer baritone. "What problem can I solve for you, my friend?"

Milo told him.

Mitchell Light, now subdued, said, "Police? I have no specific recollection of that property."

"You're the trustee, Mr. Light."

"I'm currently shepherding numerous estates through probate. The courts are overwhelmed, everything crawls."

"But you get your commission along the way."

"Do *you* work for free?" said Mitchell Light. "No need to be implicative, Lieutenant. I'll do my best to get you any information I have. *If* such information proves ultimately available and obtainable."

"Thank you. When could you do that, sir?"

"In as timely a manner as circumstances provide. *Assuming* no legal roadblocks or other encumbrances materialize."

"Could you give me an estimate, Mr. Light?"

"I'm in Cabo, right now, plan to be back in three days. The process will begin shortly after. Assuming no unforeseen circumstances."

"Could a member of your staff check—"

"My staff is with me, Lieutenant."

Female giggle in the background.

Milo said, "There's nothing you can tell me? Herbert McClain, died at ninety-one—"

"Good for him," said Light. "If he'd written a will, we wouldn't be having this conversation." Clink of glasses, more giggling.

Milo said, "How about the tenants? Can you recall anything about them?"

Silence.

"Mr. Light?"

"What tenants?"

"The place is currently occupied by—"

"That's unacceptable," said Mitchell Light. "I do *not* allow tenancy in my properties. Avoiding complications."

My properties. If probate went on long enough, his invoice would probably buy him the deed.

Milo said, "What type of complications?"

"Some *alleged* heir shows up and carps about the rent or the management? I keep *all* my properties vacant, Lieutenant."

"Someone's living in that one."

"Then *you* need to investigate and *you* need to mete out appropriate fines, penalties, whichever consequences are called for. When I return in four days, get back in touch with me. I'll *certainly* be initiating eviction procedures."

"Do I have your permission to enter the residence?"

"Well, I'd think so, Lieutenant."

"Could you put that in writing?"

"I told you, I'm on corporate retreat."

"How about by email?"

Long exhalation. Followed by a female murmur.

Mitchell Light said, "I will attempt that. But don't count on it, the Internet's sloppy, here."

"Thank you, sir."

"Preserving the rule of law," said Mitchell Light, "is my passion."

I said, "Squatting made easy. Check probate records, find out who's not paying attention, and move in."

Milo's desk phone jangled.

"This is Susan Minelli," said a crisp, confident voice. "The police are asking about my old house? Why?"

Milo said, "The tenants are people of interest in a case, Ms. Minelli. What can you tell us about them?"

"Some sort of financial thing?" said Minelli.

"Can't get into details, ma'am."

"You just did," she said. "Okay, a money thing. Shit. Why am I not shocked?"

"You've had money issues with them in the past?"

"They've always been late with the rent and haven't paid a dime for the past five months. I only found out because we just got the quarterly from the management firm and there's a big hole on that one. I demanded Aslan—the managers—deal with it. They said eviction is the only option. They're being sloths. My partners and I had already discussed hiring someone else, now for sure, as soon as the contract's up."

"What a hassle, ma'am."

"Real estate," said Minelli. "If I only knew then. So you can't tell me what's going on?"

"Not right now," said Milo. "When that changes, I'll be sure to let you know. Meanwhile, don't try to make contact with the Weylands."

"That's their name?" said Susan Minelli. "Aslan just gives them a number."

"Either way, ma'am, please keep your distance from them."

"They're dangerous?"

"At this point, they're best left alone."

"Great, I'm renting my gorgeous Pali house to criminals. What? Drugs? Terrific. They'll probably take the carpets and the drapes and God knows what else."

"We'll do our best to look out for you, ma'am."

"Ma'am. That's nice—like in *Dragnet.* Do you wear a skinny black tie?"

"On bad days."

Susan Minelli laughed. "You sound like an okay guy. So how's the weather in L.A.?"

"Nice."

"Sure, why not?"

Milo put the phone down with delicacy and pulled off as much of a leg stretch as the closet allowed.

I said, "They're squatting in both places."

"The con's life."

"That kind of transience, they could be figuring to move on."

"God forbid." He scanned his email. "Nothing from Mr. Light of the Universe. You heard him grant me verbal authority to enter."

"I did indeed."

"Two squats, gotta keep my eye on both. But I'm getting the hell *inside* Marquette."

Judge Sonia Martinez was on vacation.

"Fishing in Alaska, hopefully a bear won't eat her," said Milo.

He called Biro for another name, Biro had nothing to offer. Several more calls finally pulled up Galen Friedman, a recent appointee with higher political aspirations and a rep as "a cop groupie, his daughter just started the academy."

Friedman listened to fifteen seconds of Milo's spiel and said, "You've obviously done your homework. Bring the application to my house and you're all set."

"Thank you, Your Honor. Where are you?"

Friedman gave him an address on June Street in Hancock Park.

"Terrific, Your Honor. Meantime, may I assume verbal—"

"Is sufficient?" said Friedman. "You may, go catch some criminals, Lieutenant Sturgis. And don't forget the little ones in December."

"Which little ones?"

"Ill children are my fervent cause, Lieutenant. I chair an appeal for Orthopedic Hospital at year's end. It defines worthy."

"I'm on board, sir."

"You bet you are, Lieutenant."

After completing the warrant application, Milo said, "Just to keep things smooth," and phoned Deputy D.A. John Nguyen.

Nguyen said, "You're still after the loco cartoonist?"

"No, he's off the radar."

"What, then? Something's changed?"

"A lot's changed, John."

When Milo finished, Nguyen said, "You've built up the grounds. I could've gotten you in with any judge."

"Didn't wanna bug you, John."

"Sure, that was it," said Nguyen. "Friedman hit on you for one of his charities?"

"Sick kids."

"See you at his party," said Nguyen. "You'll get to see his house. Freakin' castle. But shit hors d'oeuvres."

Milo got a uniform named Shari Bostwick to deliver the paperwork to Friedman.

She said, "Hancock Park, ooh," and left.

I said, "No desire to see the castle?"

"Not tonight." He stood, shook himself off like a wet dog, and tossed his jacket over his shoulder. "My real estate dreams are more modest. Let's see which troops I can convene."

Moroni was on a motorcycle trip to South Dakota, Lincoln visiting relatives in Birmingham, Alabama.

Leaving Reed and Binchy and anyone else Milo could muster.

Everyone he talked to had reasons and excuses. The most he could get out of a harried sergeant was patrol cars driving by Evada Lane "maybe two, three times" per shift.

Milo said, "Appreciate it, but don't bother."

He phoned Raul Biro again. "What you said before, bored? Still that way?"

"Ready to shed my skin."

"Okay, got something for you but it's not gonna actually be stimulating."

Biro said, "Better than the alternative."

Milo told him to keep an eye on the Evada house. "Be there when the sun sets."

Another email check ended with a smile. "Miracle of miracles, Mr. Light of Day actually came through—permission to enter the Marquette house by any means necessary. Okay, you go home and relax, Moe and Sean and I will handle it."

"Smaller team than with Bitt."

"Given what happened last year, maybe it's better keeping it light and tight."

I'd been there when a raid on another house had led to a murderer being shot to death by an overeager rookie. Ruled justified but the process had dragged on and the shooter had left law enforcement.

I said, "What time, tonight?"

He looked at me.

I said, "All this foreplay and no climax?"

"Listen to you, Dr. Salty. It's the vest again and you'll stand even farther back."

"I'm getting used to the look and I don't mind solitude."

"Fine, but first help me scheme."

50

By nine p.m. Milo and I were sitting in his unmarked, four properties north of the house on Marquette. The street was lit intermittently but the moon was well nourished and we had a decent view.

As Reed had described, the block was mostly apartment buildings. The exceptions were an acre of land, fenced, weed-choked, waiting for development, and the plain, little box Herbert McClain had lived in for six decades before dying without a will.

You see throwbacks like that in L.A.—people holding on, undeterred by real estate values as they seek the comfort of the familiar. Upkeep often suffers, and the house where Paul Mearsheim squatted looked unloved. The front yard was flat dirt and thistly stuff, the shingle roof checkered by bare spots. An old TV aerial perched on the peak. Drapes covered windows whose frames sagged and splintered.

All that was missing was a dented, dusty sedan with original blue plates.

In another city, the attached double garage might be deemed

overbuilt for the puny structure. In L.A., built around the car, it made sense.

Lights dimmed by heavy curtains illuminated the right side of the house but so far, no signs of habitation. Same situation at Evada Lane, per Biro's half-hour call-ins.

Milo said, "If they've rabbited, I'm cooked."

I thought that had a culinary ring to it but didn't comment. Situations like this, the less said, the better.

Per usual, I had no role other than "observer." Last year, that had expanded to witness. Subpoenaed on the police shooting, I'd spent unbilled time answering pre-cooked questions.

Time passed. An itch developed over my left nipple. When it didn't go away, I unbuttoned my shirt, managed to get a finger under the vest, and scratched.

Milo said, "They put something in the fabric. Next time be careful what you ask for."

I rebuttoned my shirt. "I'm content."

"Foreplay." He laughed. Phoned Moe Reed, parked down the block, south of the squat. Binchy was up a ways, on the opposite side of the street. Both young detectives were in civvies: brown shirt and jeans for Binchy, black sweats, sneakers, and a knit cap for Reed, his weight lifter's chest swelled ridiculously by the vest.

Milo had told him, "Lose the hat, you look like the McBurglar."

Reed said, "And I was going for Secret Agent." Now, he said, "Nothing, L.T."

Same message from Binchy.

The plan that had culminated with the suspect shooting had been a major production, featuring a day of serial surveillance by several vehicles and Reed impersonating a parcel driver. Tonight would be Milo knocking politely on the front door and, if spoken to, identifying himself truthfully.

Keeping his voice light and unthreatening, calling Mearsheim

"Mr. Weyland," and explaining that he had a few questions to ask about Trevor Bitt.

That might throw Mearsheim off but chances were the door-knock would be immediately threatening. If Mearsheim tried to escape through the back, Reed and Binchy would be there, waiting. If things went really south and he barricaded himself in, everything would change.

If that happened and Trisha Bowker was in there with Mearsheim, hopefully she wouldn't end up a hostage. Or, worse, a co-combatant.

High risk but the rationale for doing it this way—and I'd supplied part of it—was criminal predictability.

Psychopaths are, at the core, boring creatures of habit. What we knew about Paul Mearsheim suggested he was a high-functioning psychopath, a lifelong con, and a murderer who'd never been arrested because he operated with finesse. His performance the night of the Braun murder had been Oscar-quality.

My best guess was that, certain he could talk his way out of anything, he'd avoid impulsive violence and opt for cool, calm, and outwardly harmless.

But that was only a guess.

At nine thirty-two, headlights appeared from the south, reaching Binchy first. He called: "Not sure but I think so."

Cars had been coming and going on Marquette at a thin pace. This car turned up the driveway of the McClain house and parked in front of the right-hand garage.

Silver Taurus. Milo pulled out the night-binoculars he'd cadged from a detective assigned to protecting dignitaries.

The Taurus's driver's door opened. A smallish man got out and walked to the front door.

Easy gait, no backward glances as he unlocked and stepped in.

I said, "Like he owns the place."

Milo called Binchy and Reed. "It's him. Leave your vehicles in place and proceed on foot. You know the rest."

Within moments, both detectives had snuck around to the back of the house.

No movement from inside the house. Milo waited fifteen minutes, checking his watch every five.

"Okay," he said. "It's ten ten, in Asia double numbers are good luck."

He got out of the car, smoothed his jacket over his holster, and proceeded toward the house.

I found a spot we'd agreed on: shadowy niche of a neighboring apartment building, mostly blocked by a huge rubber tree.

He'd wanted me to stay in the car; I'd negotiated. The tree clinched it: overgrown, a vegetative umbrella.

I watched as he reached the house's front door. Knocked. Waited a few seconds and knocked again. His big form tightened up as a crack of light appeared between door and jamb.

Talking to someone. Tensing up.

He pulled the door open. Gun out as he rushed in.

Seconds later Binchy and Reed were out front, following him inside.

Guns but no gunfire. I took that as everything going smoothly, waited a few moments, and made my way over.

Paul Mearsheim, newly bearded, his head shaved clean, lay on his back, one arm folded beneath his body.

His mouth was agape, his eyes dull. A black hilt plus an inch of butcher knife blade protruded from his chest.

His throat had been slashed, flesh separating in a wet, ruby grin.

Milo and Binchy and Reed stood around the body. They'd holstered their weapons, and looked stunned. The woman between the young detectives shook and wept and clutched her sides with bloody hands. Each of them maintained a hold on her arm.

Forties, average build, short blond hair, a pleasant face.

Donna Weyland had lost weight since posing with her school district co-workers. She wore blue jeans, a white top, pink running shoes. Everything splotched and speckled with red.

Blood acned the wall behind Mearsheim's body. Folds in his shirt-front created opportunities for the blood pooling.

Crimson arterial blood. Some of it, commandeered by gravity, trickled over his narrow chest and spread on the floor, purpling old, gray carpeting.

Fresh kill.

Donna Weyland's hands clenched. She began to hyperventilate.

Milo said, "Breathe slowly."

She shut her eyes and sucked in air. Began forcing words out between gasps. "He . . . said . . . he . . . was . . . kill me . . . I . . ."

Pointing to a shotgun lying six or so feet from Mearsheim's right hand. "He . . . I . . . had . . . to . . ."

Bringing a knife to a gunfight had worked. Somehow.

My brain became a fast-shutter camera.

Sobs racking her body.

But no tears.

Walking around the four of them, I peered at Mearsheim's corpse.

No way to get a look at the hand pinned under his body but the one I could see bore no defense wounds.

The throat slash had smooth borders.

No hesitation marks. A massive wound that screamed murderous confidence.

Lopsided, beginning with an upward swoop that began at the left side of Mearsheim's skinny gullet and climbed to just under his right ear.

Right-handed slasher.

Coming from behind.

No sign of a struggle.

The shotgun. Too far to have been dropped by a mortally wounded man.

Placed there.

Donna Weyland was looking at me. Everyone was.

The house had gone silent.

For a split second, her face changed, theatrical terror given way to cold analysis.

A face I'd seen before. Cold-eyed, flat, barely suppressed hostility.

Portrait on a collection of mugshots.

I said, "Hi, Trisha."

Her shoulders jerked as she resisted reflexively. That elicited Reed and Binchy's reflexes: gripping her harder.

Milo took his cuffs out.

Like a virus taking hold, cop suspicion had set in and everyone knew it.

Four sets of eyes settled on Donna Weyland a.k.a. Trisha Bowker.

She was inert for a moment, shuffling through a mental Rolodex for the right facial expression.

First came a pout, bizarrely girlish. Even as it settled, she knew it wouldn't work and switched the channel to a pathetic mewl.

Milo cuffed her. She sagged as if trying to slip the restraints. Reed and Binchy held her fast.

Milo turned his back on her and assessed Mearsheim's body.

He spieled the Miranda warning, not even trying to sound interested.

With nowhere to go, but it's either fight or flight. Donna/Trisha was in no position to fight.

"It . . . was . . . I'm . . . so . . . sorry . . . please."

That didn't work. She spat in Milo's face.

◆

Once it's over, some criminals check out mentally. Trisha/Donna cursed and kicked and screamed as Reed and Binchy removed her.

Milo allowed himself some rapid breathing.

When he stopped, new sounds asserted themselves through the thin walls of the cheesy little house.

Low-pitched barks. Muffled but insistent.

What might've passed as an asthmatic dog protesting.

Then the noise began to sound human. Binchy came back, saying, "Moe took her in."

Milo and I were already moving toward the sound. Front of the house, the south side.

The garage.

The space was accessible through an empty service porch that reeked of bug killer and sported small heaps of dead roaches. No bolt on the interior door: a turn lever that Milo's gloved hand flipped.

Dim garage.

One bare bulb screwed to a socket in the rafters.

Parked side by side, a black Ford pickup and a black Camaro.

A chair was positioned between the vehicles. Moth-eaten love seat from another era.

The figure in the chair bucked and screamed through a duct-taped mouth. Body and limbs were pinioned to the chair by more tape.

The eyes above the gag were flickers of terror.

Male captive, barely able to see through swollen lids, unsure, now, if life had gotten better or worse.

Pipe-stem arms. Stringy hair, blond, matted, greasy. His gray T-shirt was blood-caked. Brown stains on his jeans coexisted with more blood—amoebic blotches of red. A crusted yellow circle marked the concrete near his bare feet where urine had settled and dried. The garage stank of gasoline and cleaning fluid and more insect poison and shit.

Several feet in front of the chair, near the rear bumper of the Camaro, lay a bloody ball-peen hammer.

The captive's right hand was a mangled blob.

Milo rushed toward him. "Police, it's okay, it's okay." He began removing the tape-gag as the boy in the chair convulsed.

Binchy's eyes had shifted to a corner of the garage. He pointed. "Oh, Lord."

A band saw, just beyond the nose of the pickup.

As Cory Thurber's parched, swollen lips were liberated, he made a gagging sound and drooled and struggled to speak. As Milo began freeing his arms, he managed a whimper that began feebly and continued to lose power.

Barely audible: "Heheh-hehehllllp me!"

Milo said, "It's okay, son, you're safe, just hold on."

CHAPTER

51

Once you know what to look for, collecting evidence is a whole new game.

Within ten hours of Trisha Bowker's arrest, the earliest link between her and Paul Mearsheim was found. The couple had gotten together nine years ago, when Mearsheim had worked as a computer consultant for a school district in Massachusetts and Bowker had served as a teacher's aide. Shared amorality had been the relational glue.

Both had used sanitized bios to obtain the public-sector positions, a pattern repeated as they traveled westward, Mearsheim's résumé leaving out several dismissals by financial firms due to "irregularities," Bowker's criminal record omitted.

Helping that along was the adoption of a new joint identity: the pseudo-married duo of Paul and Donna Weyland. Bowker, with solid talents as an identity thief, had usurped the personae of a couple who'd perished in a 1958 New Jersey house fire. Claiming matrimony had been a cinch; no one ever bothered to check marriage licenses.

For years, the Weylands had combined gainful employment at various public and private schools with illicitly obtained government handouts and on-the-side schemes, mostly slip-and-fall insurance fraud.

From everything Milo could tell, their first homicide had been Jacqueline, Cory's mother, a widow enticed into what she thought was legal marriage with Paul as he continued to spend fun time with Bowker.

No murders between Jackie and the brutalities of the current case surfaced, but he was still looking.

The search for biological evidence was complete within forty-eight hours, bloodstains and shreds of flesh in the teeth of the band-saw blade at the Marquette garage matched to Hargis Braun's DNA. Shotgun cartridges found in a kitchen cabinet were consistent with fragments embedded in the ruins of Braun's face. The garage floor had been washed with ammonia and insecticide but luminol glowed heavily in one corner of concrete and several feet of the tar-paper walls above. Techs had also discovered blood specks in the bed of the pickup truck and two errant hairs matching Braun's in the hallway of the still-being-processed Evada house.

Also in the Marquette home were a pair of crotchless leopard-print women's panties, several wigs including a brunette hairpiece whose strands matched those taken from the A-frame by Milo, and a silver-filigree necklace set with amethysts.

The necklace was confirmed as the one sold to Chet Corvin by Bijan Ahmani, owner of Snowbird Jewelers in Arrowhead Village. Ahmani also picked Donna/Trisha's brunette-wigged photo from a six-pack lineup, as did Briana Muldrew, assistant manager of the San Bernardino Hampton Inn.

Presented with what Milo chose to share of all that, Trisha Bowker, the DNA-confirmed wearer of the bracelet and the wig, was "enthusiastic" about talking to him, per her public defender, a tired-looking fifty-year-old named Hollick Wilde. Initially surprised by my presence in the County Jail interview room, Wilde recovered and said, "Great! This is at the core a psychological situation. The more insight, the better."

Bowker read a prepared statement. As she recited, Hollick Wilde smiled with self-satisfaction. That and stilted legalese made clear who'd put it together.

Simple theme: Paul Mearsheim, bad. Trisha, scared and intimidated, an often-unwilling confederate.

She described how Mearsheim had shotgunned and mutilated Braun in the Marquette garage, wrapped the body in thick plastic sheeting, bound it with duct tape, then transported it back to Evada Lane in the pickup. There, shielded by darkness and the quiet of the cul-de-sac, he'd "transferred the object" to the Corvin house.

Milo said, "Why there?"

Trisha Bowker seemed pleased by the question. "Exactly! Because he hated Chet. Chet was always making fun of him."

"Where are the hands, Trish?"

"I don't know. He took them somewhere."

"Where?"

Glance at Wilde.

The PD said, "Honestly. She has absolutely no idea."

"Okay, let's move on. Trish, you and Paul go way back."

Brief, whispered conversation between Wilde and Bowker.

She said, "A bit."

Milo said, "How long's a bit?"

"A while, I'm not sure."

"Nine years is what we've learned."

Hesitation. Trying to figure out where this was going. Another glance at Wilde. He nodded.

She said, "That sounds about right."

Wilde said, "Milo, all that time points out the severity of Trish's situation. She suffers from Stockholm syndrome." To me: "You know better than I, it's a chronic disease which when untreated, persists."

Milo said, "Nine years ago. You and Paul were an item when Paul met Jackie."

Silence from Bowker.

Wilde said, "We'd love to help, but is this relevant?"

Milo said, "Fair enough." Back to Bowker: "In terms of your relationship, would you say Paul was in charge?"

"Always," said Bowker. "Control was his total thing. His primary drive. His obsession." To me: "He had an obsessive, narcissistic personality disorder. He was like a movie director. Domineering and dominative. Like those wigs he made me wear. Everything was a production."

Milo said, "Wanting you to go brunette."

"Wanting what he wanted *when* he wanted."

"You went brunette when you hung out with Chet Corvin in Arrowhead."

"It's what *he* wanted."

"Chet or Paul?"

"Um . . . both, I guess."

"And here I was thinking blondes had more fun—so Chet liked the wigs, too."

"Another control freak," she said. "He put me in negligees. I had to do all sorts of things."

"Role-playing."

Pout. Eyelid flutter. "Everyone molds me like I'm clay."

Milo checked his notes. "When Paul brought the body back to Evada Lane, how did he know he had enough time to position it before the Corvins returned?"

Bowker's reply was too quick, a well-trained dog responding to a hand signal.

"He knew because he saw them leaving and talked to Chet. Chet was bragging. As usual."

"Bragging about what?"

"About how they were driving all the way to Restaurant Row even though no one but him wanted to."

"Another controlling guy."

"I sometimes don't make the best choices," said Trisha Bowker.

Wilde cleared his throat.

Bowker said, "I'm no expert, that's for sure."

"On men," said Milo.

"On life." She pouted, strained for tears, produced a droplet and gave up. "I don't *know* how it got so messed *up*."

Milo nodded, spent more time with his notes. "Okay . . . if the Corvins had stayed closer to home, what was the plan?"

Bowker's eyes left-shifted. Her body echoed the same route as she turned to her lawyer.

Wilde said, "If you know, sure."

Bowker said, "I don't. The plan was Paul's."

"Did Paul have a contingency plan for what to do with the body?"

Wilde said, "She already answered that."

Bowker said, "I really *don't* know."

"Got it," said Milo, "but could you take a guess? Seeing as you knew Paul better than probably anyone."

"Hmm," said Trisha Bowker. "He could just wait."

"For?"

"Another time."

"To bring the body to the Corvins."

"Yup."

"Putting the body in Chet's den was important to Paul."

"Chet *demeaned* him all the *time*. Paul decided to get him. He watched him. All of them."

Sudden passion in her voice. Shared anger.

She realized she'd overstepped and drew her head back. "Look, I can't tell you anything factual, just that Paul was a monster. He hated Chet but basically he hated everyone, he's a hateful, hateful person, always . . . planning." To Wilde: "Can I tell them about the alarm?"

"Please do."

"Here's an example of how premeditative he was, sir. He learned their alarm code by watching her punch the keypad and memorizing. He's got a great memory. A long memory, he gets vengeful."

"Her, being . . ."

"Felice. He was always playing up to her. Being Mr. Softie. Different from Chet, that was the key. He even stole a key from their kitchen."

The beginnings of a smirk. Slyly collaborative.

Again, Trisha Bowker caught herself and turned theatrically grave. "It wasn't even necessary. They didn't even put the alarm on. Paul told me. He bragged about the whole thing."

"The Corvins made Paul's job easier."

"Sure did." She shifted in her chair. Working hard not to gloat.

Milo shuffled papers. Without looking up, he said, "Another thing that made Paul's job easier was your wrapping up the body and helping him load it into the truck."

Wilde's mouth opened.

Bowker said, "No, no way, sir. I never did any of those things."

"What *did* you do when Paul was wrapping and loading?"

"Nothing, I was just in the house."

"Which house?"

"The little one."

"On Marquette."

Her face had lost color. "He made me stay. I was terrified, went to the bedroom and waited until he was done. It was horrible. I was paralyzed by anxiety."

"Stockholm syndrome."

"It's mental torture," she said. "I've had a severely chronic case for a long, long time. Even before I met Paul, men were abusing me."

Hollick Wilde looked at me again. "Some people think of it as a particularly severe variant of PTSD."

Milo said, "How long have you been afflicted, Trisha?"

"Since I was a girl," she said. "I was abused. A lot more since Paul."

"Paul scared you."

"He scared me out of my mind."

"Because of what he did to Jackie?"

Trisha Bowker blinked and folded her lips inward.

Hollick Wilde said, "Let's stay away from that, Milo."

"Can I ask if there were other victims besides Jackie?"

Bowker's eye shift was the answer. The search would continue.

Wilde said, "Sorry, please no. I'd rather we stick to the case at hand."

"Fair enough," said Milo. He shuffled papers. "All these rules, you may need to guide me as I proceed."

"Happy to."

Trisha Bowker's posture relaxed. Everyone getting along so well.

Milo had her go over the details again. She produced a nearly word-for-word version of her first account.

"Got the picture," he said. "Hmmm . . . here's something relevant to the case at hand, Mr. Wilde."

Smiling at the lawyer. Wilde said, "Relevant's always good."

Stupidest thing I've heard from the lips of a defense attorney. He gave Bowker a go-ahead nod.

Milo said, "Trish, if I told you we found Mr. Braun's hands buried in the backyard of the Marquette house, under an oleander bush, what would you say?"

Multiple blinks. Rightward roll of her body, a sailor accommodating a big wave.

"Trish?"

"I'd say that's good. I'd say I'm glad, now, you see what Paul's capable of."

"Scary guy."

"Terrifying."

"Stockholm syndrome . . . okay, now if I told you, Trish, that the skin on top of the hands we found buried in the Marquette backyard had your DNA on it, what would you say?"

She half rose, sank back down. "That's impossible."

"I'm afraid it's more than possible, Trish, it's actual. The pathologist found your DNA in little half-moon indentations on the top of the hand. Most likely from nails being dug in."

"No way," she said. "Paul must've put them there."

"He took the time to put your hand on top of Mr. Braun's hand and dug you in?"

"No, no, no, I never. He figured out a way . . ." Her head shook hard enough to inflict whiplash.

Wilde said, "I think we should—"

Bowker shot out of her chair. "He *made* me! He would've *killed* me!"

"Those nail marks, Trisha, tells me you were angry."

"No! Terrified. He would've cut me up, too!"

Milo said, "Speaking of cutting, we also found your fingerprints on the band saw in the garage."

"That's 'cause he made me use it!"

"To cut off Hargis Braun's hands—"

"It wasn't—he was already dead—"

Hollick Wilde said, "Sorry, guys, interview terminated."

Trisha Bowker pretended to cry.

Wilde said, "Hang in."

"How can I? They *don't understand.*"

"We'll get them to see the light," said Wilde. But his face was dark.

By nightfall, Wilde had come up with an offer: In return for revealing where Jacqueline Mearsheim's body was buried, Bowker would plead to accessory to manslaughter after the fact and a three-year sentence.

John Nguyen laughed.

The following morning, Wilde proposed accessory to second-degree murder before the fact and a ten-year sentence.

John Nguyen proposed twenty-five to life. Wilde tried fifteen.

Nguyen said, "I can go with fifteen to twenty-five but in the end it'll be up to the judge."

Wilde said, "Okay."

To Milo Nguyen confided, "I'll get Friedman. She'll get life."

52

E ven with Trisha Bowker's hand-drawn map, it took a while. After two days of searching, Jacqueline Mearsheim's partial skeleton was found under four feet of rich agricultural soil in the Santa Ynez Mountains above Santa Barbara. Private land, the failed vineyard of a music industry honcho who'd long given up on Pinot Noir. Getting his permission had involved calling the Cayman Islands.

Per Bowker's self-cleansing account, she and Mearsheim had visited a nearby winery during a weekend when Jackie languished in bed with the flu. Spotting the abandoned estate, Paul had made a mental note and returned months later at night with her body in the trunk of his car. Entering the estate by snipping barbed wire, then digging unmolested near a windbreak of blue-gum eucalyptus.

Unable to get Bowker to talk about additional victims, Milo called Sheila Braxton and gave her the basics.

She said, "Time to look at all the missings around here. How's he doing?"

"Well as can be expected."

"Give him my best, maybe I'll come by to see him."

Milo and I updated Cory Thurber, still hospitalized at Cedars-Sinai four days after his rescue. Rick Silverman had been off duty the night Cory was ambulanced to the E.R. but Milo's call brought him in. He tended to the boy's immediate health issues and called in a hand surgeon to see what could be done for Cory's mangled fingers.

Milo said, "He's a piano player."

The surgeon said, "Fuck," and walked away.

This morning, Cory was able to talk through cracked lips, his hand a bandaged mitt.

Milo introduced me.

"Someone thinks I'm crazy?"

Milo explained. Cory said, "Okay," but he avoided looking at me.

"So," said Milo. "Anything you feel like telling us?"

"What I told you yesterday," said Cory. "She's the one who did it."

Milo said, "She hit you with the hammer."

"She laughed while she was doing it," said the boy. Amazed; as if reciting a weird factoid. "He taped me up and held me down but she hit me. She was laughing. He was a pussy. That's why she killed him."

"Because he was . . ."

"A total pussy," said Cory Thurber. "She gave him the shotgun, told him to shoot me. He said, 'Not again.' She started yelling at him."

His eyes shut. "After she hit me like two times, three, I passed out. When I woke I was . . ." Staring at the mitt.

When brown irises reappeared, I said, "What was she yelling about?"

"He *had* to shoot me. He was saying if it was so easy, she should do it, the last time made him sick. They must've gone into another room because the yelling got softer but it kept on. Then she said, 'Where the fuck do you think you're going?' Then there was this noise."

"What kind of noise?"

"Something hitting the floor," said Cory. "Like a person. Then it got quiet and she came in all covered with blood. I thought she was going to come in and shoot me but she didn't have no gun. She kept saying, 'Fuck.' Then the door knocked and she left and she was talking to someone else."

"That was us, Cory."

"Good." The boy's eyelids fought gravity, lost.

He stayed asleep.

53

Two days later, I sat by Cory's bed in the surgical unit, polishing a custody report on my iPad as I waited for him to emerge from anesthesia.

The first of many operations had ended an hour ago. Results were "as well as can be expected," per the surgeon. She was donating her services. So was Rick. The hospital was working with Medi-Cal to recoup whatever it could.

By three fifteen, Cory's eyes had cleared. A few minutes later, he focused on me and managed a nod. I'd been in and out of the room, yesterday, pouring water and soda for him, avoiding anything remotely therapeutic. It's what I taught my interns and fellows when I worked oncology: Patients whose diagnosis isn't psychiatric hate anything shrinky, so don't make matters worse and just be a nice person.

By day's end Cory had relaxed.

Now he gave a goofy smile, licked parched lips. I went over and held a cup of water to his barely open mouth.

He croaked, cleared his throat. Moments later: "Thanks, Doc."

His eyes closed and opened. "You're here . . . a lot. Have a lot of time?"

"For you, I do."

"Because I'm screwed up?"

"Because you've been through hell and I want to help."

"That's why you did the GoFundMe?"

"That was Lieutenant Sturgis's idea."

"It came in super-fast," he said. "After that big donation in the beginning."

Part of this year's tax deductions. I said, "People see it as a worthy cause, Cory."

"Hmm . . . all the time, since my mom disappeared, only a few people have been cool with me. Like Miss Edda, without her . . ." Trying to raise his hand, he failed and winced.

I said, "More water?"

"Um . . . don't want to be bratty, Doc, but I'd kind of like 7UP?"

"What a demanding guy," I said, reaching for the can.

He smiled.

Half a cup of soda later, he was talking.

"I always knew he did it. I thought from the way the police were that they knew but they never admitted it. Probably figured I was a stupid kid, I shouldn't know. But I knew. I wanted to go up and *tell* I knew but I was scared shitless. He left anyway. That made me happy even though I didn't know what was going to happen to me by myself. You know what happened, right, Doc?"

"You got put in fosters."

"A lot of 'em . . . that was okay. I told myself to stop thinking about it. About Mom. I stopped for a while. Then, I couldn't. Especially when I was older, working, the thoughts just kept coming back, like songs would do that, like opening up a window in my brain. I got angry. Went looking and found where he was."

"How'd you do that, Cory?"

"It wasn't so hard, Doc. He used to work for the school district doing computer stuff so I called, said I was his son, just got out of the army, was away for a long time in Iraq, needed to find him. I lied about that because it was part true, I tried to join the army, even the Coast Guard, but there was something with my spine, a fused bone. So I used that and they looked him up and said he'd transferred to the school district in L.A. I called *them* and told them the same thing."

Pushing lank, pale hair off a pimpled forehead. "I added another lie. I'd been shot in Iraq. They gave me the address."

"On Evada Lane."

"Yeah. The other one I found by following him."

A glance at his damaged hand. "Maybe that's why it happened, huh? Lie about a bad thing that doesn't happen and you get one that does happen?"

I said, "I could get all moralistic with you, Cory, but I seriously doubt that."

"You don't believe in karma?"

"Not literally."

"How *do* you believe in it?"

"Sometimes the things we do bring direct consequences, sometimes stuff just happens."

"And people get away with it."

"I'm afraid they do, Cory."

He looked at his empty cup. I poured soda and helped him drink. When he finished he let out a puff of air, then a burp. "'Scuse me . . . it actually doesn't hurt that bad. Probably the dope they put me on." A beat. "I never did real dope, just some weed. Like when I was playing at The Carpenter, there was all kinds of pills and shit around. I never did that, didn't want to screw up my playing."

"The other musicians offered."

"How'd you know?"

"I used to play in a band, went through the same thing."

"When?"

"When I was about your age."

"Before you were a doctor."

"Way before, to make money to pay for college."

"Piano?"

"Guitar."

"Huh. So you never fooled with dope, either."

"A little weed."

He grinned. "That's acceptable."

I said, "So you got the address on Evada and began watching him."

"I got it but I chickenshitted out of going up to him. It was this real nice neighborhood. A lot nicer than where we ever lived. That seemed so totally *wrong,* he was a rich guy and Mom was . . ."

He looked away. "I got kind of a hollow feeling, drove back to Santa Barbara feeling like a total loser. For a long time I thought about . . . doing a bad thing. I always chickenshitted out. Smoked weed, not going to lie to you, also beer. Trying not to feel, you know?"

"Sure."

"But I still felt, Doc. Shitty and like a loser and tired. At night, I played at The Carpenter and other bars. During the day I had nothing to do so I hung out on the beach, slept in the Camaro—is it okay? The Camaro?"

"Safe and sound," I said. After being gone over with an LAPD technical comb. "You mind if it gets a wash and wax?"

Big smile. "Sure. The tags—"

"Taken care of."

"Wow," he said.

"So you hung at the beach."

"Always liked the beach. 'Specially when there wasn't a lot of people around. Sometimes down in Carpenteria or Oxnard, sometimes back in the city near Stearn's Wharf. Mom used to take me there, we'd go up to the pier, have fried shrimp, look at the sea lions."

Brown eyes filmed.

I said, "Stearn's is where you met Hal."

"Yeah. He was also hanging out. Sitting on a blanket, I was sitting on sand. I thought he was a pervert because when I looked at him, he smiled. But he didn't do anything pervy, just looked at the water and drank Diet Coke except if he'd catch me looking, then he'd smile. I still thought he was weird. Then he got up and came over, limping, and said, 'You okay, son?'"

Cory grimaced. "The way he said it. Like he meant it. Like . . . he could tell I was a messed-up loser. Like he . . . I didn't want to tell him anything but I don't know why, I ended up telling him."

"About your mom."

"About her. About *him,* an evil fucker living in Pacific Palisades. He sat down next to me on the sand, listened and didn't say nothing. When I was finished, he said, 'I'm no superhero, kid, but if you're scared to face him alone, I can go with you.' I should've decided he's definitely a perv. But I didn't. Something about the way he—I know I could've been totally ripped off but I guess I wasn't. So I guess I was right."

"Hal was sincere."

"But I told him no, thanks. He said, 'Just putting it out there.' Then I got a little mad and said why would you do that, you don't know me? He said, 'Yeah, it's pretty stupid and weird but I've had my problems, I know what problems are, kid.' Then he pointed to his leg, said he'd messed it up a long time ago, couldn't work a real job, was always trying to find usefulness in his life. Or something like that."

"He wanted his life to be meaningful."

"*That's* the word he used! *Meaningful,* everyone needed to be *meaningful.* I told him my meaningful was finding Mom and having the fucking devil punished. I told him I'd given up, now it was just piano that filled in . . . the spaces in my brain. He said, 'At least you're good at one thing, most people aren't.' I'm thinking how does he know, he never heard me? But why argue, someone says something nice?"

He choked back a sob. "He was a great guy. I'm *so* sorry for what happened to him."

"Not your fault."

"I let him do it."

"Talking to Paul was his decision, Cory."

"That's all it was supposed to be! Talking. What he called 'appealing to his humanity.' I said I don't think he has any, he said everyone has *some*. So I gave him the address. He was supposed to call me after he went but he didn't. I figured he changed his mind and never went. I got mad at *him*. For being another bullshitter. I knew where he lived because he gave me his address, told me I could crash there if I needed. I went there to talk to him. A bunch of times but chickenshitted out. The last time I really was going to knock on his door but there was this old guy giving me the evil eye so I got out of there. Thinking the Camaro, the tags, if the cops came, I'd lose my home."

He threw up his undamaged hand, stared at the other, as if it had let him down.

"It was messed up, Doc, I was angry with everyone. Then I decided, take care of your own business, dude. When I had enough gas, I went back to Pacific Palisades, late at night, so no one would see me. Did it a bunch of times, I'd park blocks away and walk and look at his house. I never saw much. That was the bad part of at night. Nothing can happen. Except, then . . ."

"You did see something."

"Nothing important, this girl, from next door. She'd come out and look at the other house—on the other side. Sometimes she'd smoke, sometimes she'd just stand there, I thought she was weird."

I said, "Eventually, you discovered the Marquette house. And the cabin in Arrowhead."

"Both of them were kind of connected. One night, I was watching and finally, she came out. Not the girl. His new wife. Her." Grimacing.

"She came out late at night, got into the truck, and left, so I followed. I thought maybe I'd tell her about him, mess him up at least a little. I don't really know what I was thinking, Doc. I'd already spent so much time watching and nothing happened, I felt like a loser . . . she drove to the other place. The place where she . . ."

He shuddered. Limp hair swayed. "It was weird. She drove into the garage but came right out and waited. This was like two in the morning. Soon after, the Range Rover showed up. I recognized it because it was from next door—where the weird girl came out of. But she wasn't driving, a guy was. I'd seen him, too, coming home in a black Uber or some kind of limo. The guy who lived there, big, he looked like a coach."

"Chet Corvin."

"Didn't know his name, just that he was next door. She got into the Rover and they left. I figured maybe I'd tell him. *Your wife's doing the guy from right next door and you don't have a clue, you're a total loser.* Turns out, he did have a clue, huh, Doc?"

"You followed them all the way to Arrowhead?"

"Barely made it, barely had gas money but I'd done a few extra gigs at The Carpenter, also a pizza place in Goleta, rich college kids, no one tipping but I had at least some dough. When I hit San Bernardino, I needed to fill up but I was lucky, so did they. I pulled into the same station they did, they never noticed me."

Smiling. "I'm like that. Invisible."

"I'm not so sure about that, Cory."

"No? Hang out with me and you'll see, I just kind of fade out—" Blushing. "I'm not being weird, Doc."

"I know that. So you drove to Arrowhead."

"All the way up to that pointy house. I turned my lights off for the last part of it, pretty hairy driving in the dark except for I could see their taillights. They went into the house, his hand was on her ass, her hand was on his pants, in front, over his dick, it was pretty obvious this was their fuck pad. I'm thinking, *Asshole, I'm going to take pictures, want to see the look on your face when I tell you you're a loser.* Then all of a sudden, he shows *up.*"

"Paul."

"I don't even use his name, he's Mr. Evil . . . yeah, him, in his Taurus, he drives right past me, I was off the side of the road, it was dark, under some trees, I nearly shit. What if he was there from the beginning and saw me get gas? But I guess he didn't because he just cruised up the road and sat there looking."

"At the house."

"For a long time, Doc. Then he drove away. I was freaked out, it was unreal. I called Hal but he didn't answer. I was sure he was blowing me off. I had no *idea.*"

"No reason for you to."

"You think so?"

"I know so, Cory."

"F'you say so . . . I got outta there, drove back to Santa Barbara, couldn't stop thinking about it. Figured my best shot *was* talking to her. Telling her what a dick she was married to. What he did to Mom, she was in danger."

His laughter began as a light, not unpleasant sound, ended up acid running down a pane of glass. "That sure worked out well . . . I'm tired, Doc. I'm like, there's nothing inside me, I'm *real* tired."

CHAPTER

54

I pushed the call button and a cute nurse around Cory's age came in and squirted something into his I.V. He was already out but the juice slowed his breathing.

She watched him for a second, touched his arm.

"He's so brave, Doctor. A real hero."

I went down to the hospital cafeteria. Milo was at a corner table eating a sandwich filled with some kind of meat and drinking a sweating glass of iced tea.

"How's he doing?"

"Pretty well, considering."

"Can you talk about it? He waive confidentiality?"

"He waived yesterday." I recapped.

He said, "Braun thought he could just walk up to Mearsheim and tell him to do the right thing? What the hell was that, a death wish?"

"Hard to say."

"Is it really, Alex? C'mon, it's like those do-gooders who pack up and go to the Congo or Syria or wherever hell currently is and get their heads chopped off. I'm not saying their intentions are bad, but still."

I said nothing.

He said, "Fine, be profoundly nonjudgmental." He drank tea. Put the glass down. "I am not blaming the victim, but still, it's a death wish, right? Maybe even a type of suicide."

I got up, poured coffee from the doctor's urn, and returned.

Milo said, "You look offended."

"God forbid," I said. "Just thinking."

"About . . . ?"

"You probably won't like my answer."

"*What*, Alex?"

"People vary. There are all types of stories."

"Fine," he said. "We won't malign the dead. At least not the noble dead, like our man, Braun." Under his breath: "Virtuous idiot."

My cell chirped. I read the window, clicked in.

Felicia Corvin said, "Lieutenant Sturgis filled me in. I'm so glad it's over."

"He's right here. We're at the hospital."

"With that poor boy."

"Yes."

"Please give him my best, Dr. Delaware. I contributed to his fund, he's been through so much—if you were a girl, I'd say give him a kiss for me."

"I'll pass along the message."

"Good . . ."

Silence.

"What's up, Felice?"

"This might be awkward but I'm calling about *my* boy. Bretty's started having problems. I knew it would happen, he's been too un-emotional about . . . Chet . . . losing his dad. He was the one who really loved Chet. Chet cared about him . . . as much as he could anyone . . . anyway, Brett's having problems."

"Hold on," I said. "I'll go somewhere private."

"Not necessary, Dr. Delaware. Lieutenant Sturgis already knows more about my family than anyone, right?"

I walked away, anyway. "What kind of problems?"

"Like I told you, he cried a bit at first but then stopped. Now it's all the time. Sobbing. He thinks he's hiding it from me but I hear it. Loud sobs. When he's alone. After he's gone to bed. In the morning, he's been looking ghostly, has no appetite. His schoolwork was never great but it's gone totally to pot, he won't even pretend. And sports, his favorite thing? Forget that, no interest—he's getting gaunt, Doctor. He doesn't even torment Chelsea anymore. She's being nicer to him but that's not it, he ignores her. Ignores me. It's like he's become this sad, old, diminished man."

She sniffled. Said, "Sorry," and began sobbing. When she spoke again her voice was a burning pile of twigs.

"So anyway, Dr. Delaware, that's the story with my Bretty. Would there be any way for you to see him? I've had so much bad luck with therapists and you know the situation. I know I wasn't gracious when Chet tried to get you—"

"Let's set up an appointment."

"Oh. Great." Sighing. "When?"

"Sooner's better than later," I said.

"Thank you, Doctor. I can't tell you what it means to me. Is there any chance even today?"

I checked my calendar. "I can make it at six."

"We'll be there. Thank you, thank you."

I notated the appointment. Returned to Milo.

He said, "People to do, places to meet?"

"You know me, Big Guy. Popular."

"Bet you actually were in high school. What, a custody case?"

I said, "Another story."